LINDSAY BUROKERS

Dark Currents

AN EMPEROR'S EDGE FANTASY ADVENTURE

ACKNOWLEDGEMENTS

Before you jump into the next adventure, please allow me to thank Becca Andre and Kendra Highley for reviewing early versions of this. More thanks go to Shelley Holloway for editing services and to Glendon Haddix for the cover art. Lastly, thank you, good reader, for trying the first novel and coming back for more. This book would not have been written if not for you.

CHAPTER 1

THE CLANGING OF THE ALARM BELL REVERBER-
ated through the aqueduct tunnels. Marl "Books" Mugdildor
squished along the slippery ledge as quickly as the footing
allowed. It was a long, twisty walk to Pumping Station Five's Intake
Duct Number Nine.

"How about you speed it up, Booksie?" his comrade asked. "It'd
be nice to figure out what's blocking up the tunnel *before* piles of city
workers come down to check on the alarm and realize wanted men are
hiding out in their pumping house."

Books glared over his shoulder. Of course Maldynado had no trouble
with the treacherous footing. He was younger, stronger, more agile,
and—according to the women—the most gorgeous human being in the
city. Not that the latter offered an advantage in navigating aqueducts,
but it added to Books's overall annoyance with the man.

"Do you want to go ahead?" Books asked.

"Gladly." Maldynado planted a hand on Books's shoulder and
mashed him against the wall to pass.

Books dropped his kerosene lantern and nearly lost an important
appendage when Maldynado's sword hilt grazed him. "Blundering troglodyte," he muttered.

"Save your endearments for later. There's work to do."

Books rolled his eyes toward the arched ceiling but picked up his
lantern and followed. He increased his pace to keep up. More than
once his foot slipped off the ledge and splashed into the water flowing
through the channel. It could be worse: they could be hiding out in a
sewage pumping station.

Maldynado slowed down when the water rose over the ledge and
lapped at their boots. "I didn't know this would involve getting wet."

"When the waterway is blocked, the water rises. Surely even warrior caste louts such as yourself have heard of dams."

Maldynado lifted a soggy leather boot and grimaced as droplets dribbled from the tassels. "Yes, but these were made by Svunn and Hilderk. They cost a fortune, and we're making...rather less than a fortune."

Books rolled his eyes. "Just keep moving."

They slogged through ever deepening water, and Books shivered as icy currents tugged at his calves. Somewhere nearby, machinery clanked and ground. They had worked their way through the maze of tunnels and now walked close to the pumping station's exterior wall. Books hefted his lantern, figuring they should be able to see the blockage soon.

There.

Steel glinted, reflecting the lantern flame. A grate across the channel marked an entrance to the pumping house. Something dark and shadowy pressed against the rusty bars, partially blocking the water flow.

Books leaned out for a better look. His heel slipped off the ledge, his butt slammed into the slick brick, and he bounced into the channel with a startled squawk. His lantern flew free. Cold water engulfed him, flooding his mouth and nostrils. He flailed for the surface.

Despite the blockage ahead, a strong current tugged him down the tunnel. Books maneuvered his head above water, but the only light was behind him. Maldynado, still standing on the walkway, soon faded from view, and darkness smothered Books.

He groped with his feet, trying to find the bottom. The water was too deep. He reached for the ledge, but the slick surface evaded his scrabbling fingers.

He bumped against something. Not the grate, but... cloth? A rigid protrusion jabbed into his ribs. He tried to swim away, but it tangled in his clothing.

Or something was deliberately grabbing him.

Heart thundering, he kicked, desperate to break the hold. His foot caught in something else. He flailed uselessly until his knuckles rapped against metal. The grate. If he could grab it, he could use it to pull his way to the side of the tunnel. But when he reached for it, his hand brushed against seaweed. No, not seaweed. Hair. He gripped something smooth. A forehead and a nose and...

"Gah!" Books shrieked. He was tangled up with human bodies. "Get them off, get them off!"

He tried again to push away, but he grew more entwined in the mess. There were bodies underwater too.

Finally, a hand grabbed him by the collar and dragged him free. Maldynado. Books latched onto his arm like a starving tick clinging to a dog's tail.

With Maldynado's help, Books found the ledge with his feet and braced himself against the brick wall. More than five feet of water covered the walkway, and it offered little respite. Water streamed past his chest, still tugging at him.

Panting, Books maneuvered behind Maldynado before turning to look at what their one remaining lantern revealed.

At least three bloated bodies were caught in the grate. With a shaking hand, Books rubbed water off his face. It took him a moment to realize a new sound had joined the clanging alarm bell. Maldynado's deep laughs echoed off the walls with riotous enthusiasm.

"Oh, be quiet," Books muttered.

"That was priceless." Maldynado wiped tears from his eyes. He imitated Books's screams and burst out laughing all over again.

Though cold water surrounded Books, the heat flushing his cheeks kept him warm. "Are you done yet? We need to move these bodies so that ancestors-cursed bell will stop."

Maldynado wiped his eyes again. "Oh, my. Even if the pay is lacking, I must say I love my job."

They dragged the corpses back to a dry alcove. With the obstruction clear, the alarm cut off, and Books allowed himself to relax an iota. He removed his shirt to wring it dry. Rivulets of cold water dripped from his shoulder-length hair and ran down his back.

"Did you know," Maldynado said, "you are possibly the hairiest Turgonian man I've ever seen?"

Books sighed, wondering how much torment he would have to endure before the day ended. "Let's examine the bodies, see what they're doing down here."

"I'm not even sure why you wear a shirt. I've seen sweaters with less fuzz."

"Why are you looking anyway?" Books wrestled the sodden shirt back on and pushed past him. "I thought you preferred ladies."

"Oh, I do. And you've thoughtfully reminded me why."

Books made a point of turning his back to Maldynado as he studied the corpses. They had recovered three men and one woman. All the bodies had the bronze skin and dark hair of Turgonian citizens. Fortunately, the icy water had preserved them somewhat, and they did not stink yet. The men wore shredded gray utility uniforms, torn open where deep, garish wounds scored their chests and limbs. Someone had slashed the lady's throat. She wore a businesswoman's long black skirt and jacket, both torn and stained from the trip through the channels. All appeared to have been killed before they hit the water. Unless there was something clawed and inhuman lurking in the capital city's aqueducts. Books grimaced at that thought.

"Where do you figure they came from?" Maldynado picked a clump of something green off his shirt.

Books paced around the corpses, in part to think, in part to generate warmth. His sodden clothing clung to him, damp and cold. "The aqueduct access points are locked, and only city workers have keys," he said. "Either someone got a hold of one of those keys and dumped the bodies, or they've been in here since the source."

"The source? The lake?"

"Municipal water doesn't come from the lake," Books said. "Dolt."

"How would I know?"

"We've been living in, and stoking the fires for, a pumping house for a month and you never looked at any of the diagrams on the wall?"

"Unlike you, I don't intentionally bore myself with tedious information," Maldynado said. "I prefer action—a fencing match or wrestling bout, for instance."

"You may get both if whatever mauled these men is roaming—or swimming—around these tunnels."

That dimmed Maldynado's ever present smile.

"Our sewer waste goes into the lake," Books said. "The drinking water comes from Lake Karmast Dam in the mountains and is carried to municipal pumping stations and reservoirs via underground aqueducts. That protects it from outsiders thinking of poisoning it or otherwise

interfering. The empire has made a lot of enemies during its centuries of conquering and plundering."

"Thanks for the history lesson, professor. What're we going to do with the bodies?"

"Why don't you search them for clues?"

"Me?" Maldynado asked. "You've already been close and intimate with them."

Books wiped his hands on his trousers, wincing at the memory. "I assumed a scion of the warrior caste would not be squeamish."

"Warriors stick swords in people's bodies; they don't grope them after the fact."

"Let's just search the pockets."

A few minutes later, Maldynado and Books pooled their findings. A few coins, a metal ring with a fob and two keys, and a waterlogged envelope from the woman's buttoned jacket pocket that snared Books's curiosity.

He managed to open it and retrieve the paper inside without tearing it. The writing was in pencil and still legible. Legible but unhelpful. Two strings of numbers, one sprinkled with letters. The other had a decimal and might represent a monetary amount. A large amount, if so.

"Huh," came a surprised grunt from Maldynado. He rubbed the flat circular fob on the key ring, and an oval in the middle glowed red. Even after he released it, the soft light continued. He touched it, then withdrew his finger quickly, as if he had brushed against something hot. "Magic? That's not something you expect to see in the empire. Especially not in this subterranean portion of it." He lifted his gaze toward the variegated mold decorating the ceiling.

"That came out of one of the men's pockets, didn't it?"

"Bald and Stubby, yeah."

"Nice of you to create such respectful names for the corpses," Books murmured, returning his attention to the paper.

"This thing looks handy." Maldynado prodded the fob, causing it to glow red again. "You could see the keyhole to your flat late at night. I bet this is hot enough to light a candle wick too." He squinted. "There's writing on the back side. Ergot's Chance. There's an address."

Books glanced up. "That could be useful. Keep that."

"Oh, I am. This is a good find. Sorry yours isn't as fun."

"Different people, different definitions of fun." Books tapped the numbers. "I wonder if this is some kind of secret message. Some cipher created by a cryptographer?"

"Or the work of a three year old using Father's pencil. What're we going to do about all this?"

"Consider ourselves fortunate."

Maldynado's jaw slackened. "How so?"

"Amaranthe's birthday is next week and, with our limited funds, I didn't think I'd be able to find her a gift."

"So, you're getting her... dead bodies?"

"Perfect, don't you think?" Books smiled.

"Most women like jewelry and flowers."

"Do you honestly believe she would prefer jewelry over a mystery to solve?"

Maldynado jiggled the key fob thoughtfully, then nodded toward the bodies. "Can we say one is from me?"

* * * * *

Amaranthe Lokdon sharpened the last pencil. She placed it in a holder on the desk and knelt to compare its height with the seven others in the cup. A hair too high still. She removed it, twisted it through the sharpener a couple more times, and checked the height again.

"Better," she murmured.

A steam whistle pierced the air. In the factory outside the office, the fleet of sewing machines stopped. A hundred women and children grabbed brooms and dustpans, hastily cleaning their areas so they could go home.

"Finally," Amaranthe said. "Maybe Ms. Klume will deign to meet with us now."

"Likely," Sicarius said, laconic as usual.

Clad in fitted black clothing that bristled daggers and throwing knives, he stood in the shadows against the wall, his gaze covering the door and the window. Neither his angular face nor his dark eyes gave any hint of impatience, but then they rarely hinted of anything.

"Good." Amaranthe stood. Her thighs, still rubbery after the morning's training session, twanged in protest. "There's nothing left to tidy."

Thanks to her restless fingers, the trash bin now housed scraps of material, windowsill dust, and pencil shavings, all of which had plagued the office when she entered. The papers and files that had scattered the desk were stacked in a tidy pile, edges aligned with the corner.

"There's an alphabetical misfile on the bookshelf," Sicarius said.

Amaranthe gave him a startled look, more surprised he had said something than that he had noticed. His expression never changed, but she thought she spotted a faint glimmer of humor in his eyes. She crossed the office, short sword swaying on her hip, and moved *Marketing to the Imperial Mind* to its proper place.

A shadow fell across the threshold, and Ms. Klume walked in. She wore a cream blouse, the top buttons unfastened, and a short plaid skirt that did not seem practical given the early spring weather. Vivid ruby paint adorned her lips, and clashing rings gleamed on every finger. The woman's gaze slid past Amaranthe, as if she were a particularly bland piece of furniture, and landed on Sicarius.

"Ms. Klume. I'm Amaranthe and this is—"

"Sicarius." Klume's gaze roved from his black boots to his short blond hair, taking in everything in between. "You're just what I expected."

"We're here because you have work to propose," Amaranthe said, not sure whether she was more annoyed because the woman was ignoring her or because she appeared to be three seconds away from inviting Sicarius back to her flat. Maybe less.

"Is it true you single-handedly killed a platoon of soldiers?" Klume asked him. "And walked past Lord Satrap Dargon's fleet of household security to assassinate him? And killed the empire's most notorious bounty hunter with the throw of a knife?"

Sicarius stared at her in stony silence. If the woman's interest affected him in any way, he kept it hidden behind an unreadable mask. For once, Amaranthe appreciated his standoffishness. She took a deep breath, telling herself it did not matter whether Klume spoke with her or Sicarius, and gave him a single nod.

"Your offer," Sicarius told Klume.

The woman blinked, smiled, and glided to her workspace. "Business first, yes, of course." Confusion flashed across her face as she noticed the tidy desk, but she recovered and located a fat file. "This is all the

information I have on a Kendorian woman named Telnola. She's the new owner of Farth Textiles. She's an old wart who strode in the day Emperor Sespian enacted those tax incentives for foreign businesses and investors." She mimicked spitting in the waste bin. Not a fan of the policy, apparently. "She bought out Farth, promptly tripled profits, and cut *my* business—the business of a loyal Turgonian citizen—in half. She hasn't been to a proper school, and I'm certain this unprecedented success has to do with some magical aid. If she *is* using magic, it's completely illegal here, and the punishment is death. If she isn't..." Klume shrugged. "Either way, her success displeases me. I want her dead. I'm paying five thousand ranmyas for the job. An extremely fair price for a night's work."

Amaranthe sighed. She had feared the offer might be something like this.

Sicarius met Amaranthe's eyes, and she sensed the question there, even if his expression did not change. Yes, he would have no problem taking the job, but that was *not* the image she wanted to establish for her team.

"I'm sorry you lost time contacting us," Amaranthe said, "but we don't do assassinations, Ms. Klume."

The woman considered Amaranthe for the first time, though she pointed at Sicarius. "That's not what his reputation says."

"He's changed." Sort of. "He's working for me now." Amaranthe checked Sicarius for a response; though he had said as much, she still felt presumptuous and uncertain making such claims.

He merely stood, arms folded across his chest and back to the wall.

"I see." Klume's eyes narrowed as she glanced back and forth between them. She settled on Amaranthe. "You're the agent and must see to your cut. Six thousand then."

"You misunderstand me, ma'am," Amaranthe said. "We're not assassins or simple mercenaries. We only take on work that helps the city or the Turgonian people. We call ourselves The Emperor's Edge because we aim to win Emperor Sespian's approval." And pardon. And a place in the history books.

"Your negotiation tactics are shrewd, but I don't believe you. You're fugitives with bounties on your heads. *His* bounty—" Klume pointed

at Sicarius, "—is signed by the emperor himself." She lifted her chin. "Seven thousand."

"What you say is true, but my bounty is a misunderstanding, and Sicarius has... uhm... decided to work toward exoneration."

"Eight thousand."

Amaranthe closed her eyes. Trying to explain was a waste of time. "I think we're done here." She headed for the door.

"Wait," Sicarius said. "Leave us," he told Klume.

Though no warmth softened his words, Klume smiled triumphantly and gave Amaranthe a we'll-see-who's-in-charge look as she strode out.

Amaranthe pushed the door shut and faced Sicarius. "No."

"We need the money," he said. "Books's job in the pumping house isn't enough to outfit six. To create the force you wish, we need better gear, practice swords, armor, firearms, and a steam carriage so we don't have to use the trolleys and risk running into bounty hunters and enforcers."

"I'm aware of that, but we aren't assassinating people, especially not for the crime of being good at business."

"If she's using the Science, she's violating imperial law."

"What Kendorian would be dumb enough to use magic in a city where it's not only forbidden, but where people are so superstitious they'll turn you over to the enforcers just for talking about it?" Amaranthe shook her head. "No assassinations."

"You don't need to come," Sicarius said.

"We'll get money another way."

"Sespian need never know."

"No." Amaranthe slashed her hand through the air. "You can't work to earn the emperor's favor in the open while sneaking about in the dark, committing vile crimes. Why do you think he hates you?"

It was the wrong thing to say, and she regretted the last sentence as soon as it came out. Sicarius's expression never changed, but those dark eyes grew flinty. He stalked past her and opened the door.

"I'm sorry," Amaranthe said. "I didn't mean to—"

Ms. Klume, who stood outside the door, raised her eyebrows as Sicarius strode by. Amusement curved her ruby lips when Amaranthe burst out, hand stretched after him.

She lowered her arm and stopped. If she wanted outsiders to believe she led the group, chasing after Sicarius like a spurned lover would not help. Coolly and calmly, she faced Ms. Klume.

"Thank you, but we won't be accepting your offer."

Though she doubted she fooled anyone, Amaranthe clasped her hands behind her back and strolled through the factory, chin lifted. Since the number of workers had dwindled, she wondered if anyone would stop her if she chucked a wrench into one of the steam looms. Alas, that would probably not create the image she wanted for her team either. Disgruntled by the whole encounter, she yanked her parka off the hook by the door and strode outside.

Rain pelted the sidewalk. Streams ran down the concrete street toward storm drains. Gray clouds promised an early dusk, and gas lamps already burned at intervals. She did not see Sicarius, only workers with their collars turned up. They hustled toward trolley stops or pedaled bicycles vigorously to reach dry destinations.

She tugged her parka on and pulled the hood over her head, trying not to see the dismal weather as a portent for the future. She had only been the leader of her group of outlaws for a couple of months, so she supposed it was natural for everyone to assume Sicarius, with his years as an assassin, was in charge of their outfit. He had agreed to work for her because she had proven she was a creative—technically, crazy was the word the men used—schemer who could surprise victory even from powerful opponents. And the team had worked well together in the past weeks, doing more than a few good deeds. The problem was nobody important *knew* about them. It was time to change that. It was time to find high profile work that would attract attention. Maybe the woman Klume hated was worth investigation, if not assassination. Maybe there *was* something suspicious about such rapid success.

A sharp report sounded behind her.

Something whizzed past her ear. Stone cracked and sheered off the corner of the building beside her. Amaranthe darted toward a nearby alley, glancing down the street as she ran.

Not ten paces back, a figure pointed a smoking pistol her direction. Though a cowl obscured the owner's face, she glimpsed a brand on the hand gripping the weapon. In the fading light, she might not have

recognized the symbol, but she had seen it often as an enforcer: a skull and an X. The Buccaneers gang.

"Idiot!" Amaranthe shouted at the man. "The mark is up ahead. Didn't you listen to anything Coxen said?"

She sprinted into the alley, hoping her invocation of the Buccaneers' leader would befuddle the man momentarily. She pounded up narrow stairs between two towering factories. A question floated back, too muffled to hear clearly. Amaranthe turned into another alley paralleling the main street. The last corner fell behind her, and she raced down a cobblestone slope slick from the rain. Only when she neared the main thoroughfare again did she slow, softening her footfalls.

She peeked around the corner. The pistol shot had cleared the streets of everyone except the cloaked man. His back was to her. He finished reloading the pistol, drew a short sword, and crept toward the first alley she had turned up.

He called out, but the rain drowned his words.

Silently, Amaranthe slid a dagger and her own sword out. She slipped after him. The man reached the alley and stuck his head around the corner. He drew back and peered about. Knowing a single glance back would reveal her approach, Amaranthe turned her stealthy advance into a run.

The man must have sensed it. He turned, cowl spilling around his shoulders. Amaranthe sprinted the last few yards.

He raised his pistol. Without slowing, she hurled the knife.

Though it was not balanced for throwing, the hilt clipped his hand, knocking the pistol from his grip. It clattered to the sidewalk, firing when the hammer struck. The man cursed and jumped, probably afraid the wayward ball would hit him. It gave Amaranthe time to close the remaining distance.

Rushed, he threw a wild first strike. She parried and startled him by darting past him instead of launching a jab of her own. A kick to the back of his knee stole his balance. She grabbed his flailing arm, wrenched it behind him, and twisted his hand against the wrist. His sword clattered to the sidewalk beside the pistol. She pressed the point of her blade against his kidney.

She said, "Tell Coxen—"

A throwing knife spun out of nowhere and lodged in the man's neck. Startled, Amaranthe jerked back, releasing him. The thug died before his body crumpled to the ground.

Sicarius glided out of the shadows across the street.

"Why did you..." she started, but he pumped his arm and threw a second knife.

In the dim light, Amaranthe could not follow its path. A pained grunt came from the roof above her. A heartbeat later, a man smashed onto the sidewalk, the throwing knife lodged in his eye. A repeating crossbow flew into the street, and the impact sent a bolt flying. It skidded into a curb beneath a gas lamp, revealing a green smudge of poison on the tip.

Amaranthe rested her hand on the damp stone of the building for support. Maybe it was time to get more serious about looking for a disguise to wear in public. The fact that she had the most common eye, skin, and hair color in the empire had served her well so far, but apparently no more.

"Mercy has no place out here." Sicarius retrieved his knives. "If you're lenient with bounty hunters, they'll try again, and they'll speak to others of your leniency, which will encourage every pauper to take a chance."

"I can't argue with your logic, but it's not in my nature to stick knives in people's backs." Amaranthe grimaced at the broken body of the man from the roof. "Or eyes."

"Adapt." After cleaning and sheathing his knives, Sicarius searched the bodies of the dead men, removing their valuables, before coming to stand beside her. "Are you injured?"

She straightened. "No. Of course not. That was all part of my plan. I was acting as bait to lure bounty hunters to attack, so you could sneak over and kill them and take their ill-gotten thug earnings, *thus*—" she lifted a finger, "—alleviating our money problems." That sounded plausible, didn't it? He might even believe it. If he had the intelligence of a sloth.

The flat look Sicarius gave her suggested that sloth would have to be drunk to be fooled by her extemporizing. He handed her a few crumpled bills, not enough money to buy a meal much less gear. "Bait doesn't survive long."

"Well, if you hadn't left in a huff, I wouldn't have been bait. You know I need a keeper to watch over me while I'm dreaming up fanciful schemes." She smiled to let him know she was not truly accusing him of anything; she had been the idiot, and she knew it.

"I don't huff," Sicarius said, though his tone softened.

"Ever?" She nodded toward the street, and they strode away from the dead men. In the city, only soldiers were permitted by law to carry firearms, so enforcers would doubtlessly show up to investigate the shots soon. "Must be disappointing for the ladies."

Apparently the comment did not deserve a response, for he only said, "What's the new scheme?"

Business first with him. Always.

"I want to investigate Ms. Klume's adversary before returning to the pumping house," Amaranthe said. "Just in case something interesting is going on there. Waiting for the right people to hire us isn't going to get us where we want; we need to go out and find..." She groped for the right word. A mission? A project? A job?

"Trouble?" Sicarius suggested.

"An endeavor that will help the city and prove to the emperor that we're undeserving of the bounties on our heads *and* we're invaluable resources to his regime."

"Trouble," Sicarius said.

She grinned sheepishly. "Well, probably. Yes."

CHAPTER 2

T HE KENDORIAN BUSINESSWOMAN'S OFFICE boasted neatly filed papers and meticulously organized bookshelves. A hint of lye soap hung in the air. The potted plant perched on the windowsill sported no dangling dead leaves.

Within seconds of walking in, Amaranthe was glad she had refused the assassination gig. One probably should not form opinions about people based on the cleanliness of their workspace, but she promptly liked this Telnola more than Ms. Klume.

Of course, that did not keep her from rifling through filing cabinets and desk drawers. Working by lamplight, she spent thirty minutes investigating, or, as Maldynado often called it, snooping.

Engrossed in logbooks, she almost missed the door opening. She reached for her sword, but it was only Sicarius. Coal dust smeared his hands and darkened his blond hair.

Guilt nudged Amaranthe to say, "Sorry to send you to investigate the machinery. I figured you'd be more likely to sense magical doodads than me."

"Artifacts," Sicarius said.

"What?"

"The Turgonian language lacks words to define the various contraptions crafted by practitioners specializing in Making, but artifact is the word most frequently used to describe imbued devices, especially those small in nature. Construct, such as the soul construct we battled, has similar connotations, though tends to refer to ambulatory creations."

Amaranthe nodded, absorbing the information, though his monotone delivery tempted her to tease him. "Are either constructs or artifacts sentient enough to be offended by being called doodads?"

"Rarely," Sicarius said without blinking.

She sighed. The man was impossible to tease.

Amaranthe closed the file she had been perusing and returned it to its proper place in a cabinet. "Did you find anything magically suspicious in the factory or about the furnace?"

"No."

"Me either." She waved to encompass the office. "From what I've learned, Telnola is visionary, efficient, and willing to take risks. She established a small fortune by buying faltering mother-daughter sewing shops and turning them profitable by introducing mass production through sewing machines and mechanized looms. Everything about her background suggests she's the type of person who would hustle to accept an opportunity to start a business in the empire where steam-powered facilities are the norm instead of an anomaly. There's no unexplainable efficiency in the logbooks. If she's beating Klume, I'm guessing it's because she's good, not because she's magically assisted."

Sicarius listened. Fortunately, or unfortunately perhaps, he was not the sort to tease her for going on and on. He simply said, "Agreed," and added, "though I haven't checked the loading docks and bay yet."

"We can go out that way," Amaranthe said, "but I suspect Telnola is innocent of any crimes. She's hired more than a hundred workers in the last month, and she's excelling here. In short, she's exactly the type of entrepreneur Sespian hoped to attract with his tax incentives. Which means the trouble we hoped to find here isn't likely to manifest itself. At the very least, you can feel good for choosing not to assassinate her."

"I did not make that choice."

No, and even knowing what she had just told him, he would probably still accept the assignment if motivated enough. "Then *I* can feel good for choosing for you."

She smiled. He did not.

"Loading bay. Right." Amaranthe grabbed her lantern and headed for the door.

Night pressed against the windows overlooking the factory's main floor. Her lamp illuminated the first couple of sewing machines in rows that stretched throughout the cavernous room. Before they had gone more than a few steps, the scrape of a key fumbling for a lock whispered through the silent building. The front door.

Sicarius disappeared into the shadows below a fifteen-foot-high loft that housed more rows of sewing machines. Amaranthe cut off her lantern.

The front door swung open. Two figures stepped inside, each holding lanterns of their own. One man, one woman, both with blond hair, advanced down the central aisle. They lacked the furtive mien of robbers, and the pale hair suggested they might be Kendorians. They chattered in what was presumably their native tongue.

Using the wall as a guide, Amaranthe eased beneath the loft. She assumed Sicarius, who had explored more than she had, was heading toward the loading bay and a back way out.

Amaranthe bumped into someone. She expected Sicarius, but a knife rasped free of a sheath. She jumped back. Shadows hid details, but the dark figure loomed too tall and wide to be Sicarius.

An uncertain pause from the person gave her time to switch her lantern to her left hand and slide her sword free.

"Rovich?" the figure—a man—asked, voice dull and stunned, as if he knew she was not who he thought but could not imagine who else she might be.

"No," Amaranthe whispered, "but if you tell me who you are and what you're doing here, I'll tell you who I am." She glanced over her shoulder, fearing the scuffles and whispers would alert the couple, but they had reached the office, and a conversation flowed from within, the words sounding casual and unconcerned.

"Uh," the man said. "No, you tell me who you are, or I'll—" He sucked in a startled breath.

The shadows cloaked movement behind the man, but his reaction suggested someone had come up behind him with a weapon. Sicarius.

Amaranthe followed as he pushed his prisoner past a large, sliding door and into the colder air of a loading bay. On the far side, beyond aisles of barrels, crates, and bolts of fabric, a roll-up door was open to the night.

The toe of Amaranthe's boot nudged something, and she halted.

"Close the door," Sicarius said before she could investigate.

Assuming he meant the order for her, she groped for the handle. She eased the door shut, trying not to make noise.

"What were you doing in here?" Clothing rustled—Sicarius jostling his prisoner.

Amaranthe knelt to relight the lantern.

"Eat street," the thug said. "I ain't telling you nothing."

Her light stirred to life, revealing the thug with Sicarius standing behind him, a knife to his throat. The heavyset man wore ill-fitting, mismatched clothing and bracelets that might have been working wrist shackles once.

Another bounty hunter? If so, an inept one.

The lantern also illuminated the cut throat of a second man, the body Amaranthe had bumped against. The man Sicarius restrained paled when he spotted the body.

"What were you doing in here?" Sicarius asked again, his voice colder than the room.

"You might want to answer." Amaranthe decided revealing names might move them to the information-sharing portion of the interrogation without the application of imperial torture techniques. "If Sicarius has to ask twice, it's a sure sign maiming and pain are imminent."

The man's eyes bulged. "Sicarius?" he whispered.

"Is whatever you're doing worth dying for?" Amaranthe asked.

A puddle formed between the thug's boots, and she figured that was a good sign he would talk—and that she should step back—but he whispered, "No, but I can't...can't say anything."

Sicarius's blade bit into flesh, and blood trickled down the man's neck, staining the collar of his shirt.

"Please, I can't." A tear slid down the thug's cheek, out of place on such a hardened face.

"Why?" Amaranthe asked. "What were you doing that's so important to keep secret?"

"They just wanted us to—" He gasped in pain, back arching.

At first, Amaranthe thought Sicarius had done something, but the man's eyes rolled back in his head, and quakes wracked his large body. A seizure?

"Let him go," Amaranthe said.

Blood oozed from the thug's nostrils. As soon as Sicarius stepped back, the man collapsed. A final spasm wrenched his body, then he lay still.

"Uhm." Amaranthe stared. "That's unexpected."

Sicarius opened the man's mouth and probed about with a finger.

"Think he poisoned himself?" she asked. "Or are you searching for gold teeth to help with our financial problems?"

"No residue or capsule in his mouth that I can detect, and I didn't notice him swallow anything."

With his knife at the man's throat, Sicarius probably would have felt that.

She nibbled on a fingernail. "Any thoughts on what might be responsible? He's too young to spontaneously seize up and die. Think someone...didn't want him sharing secrets? And somehow rigged it so he'd die if he did? Is that even possible?" She had never come across the like during her enforcer career, but she had never dealt with magic in those days either. Until a few months ago, she had not known it existed.

"Possible, yes." Sicarius rotated the dead man's head and leaned closer. "There's fresh scar tissue and something under his skin, a nodule or shot from a blunderbuss perhaps."

"Does the other man have it?"

He gave her a sharp look, then examined the second body. Amaranthe slid the door open a crack to check the factory. Light and voices still spilled from the office.

"Not in exactly the same place," Sicarius said, "but yes."

His black dagger appeared in his hand, the metal so dark it seemed to swallow the lamplight. He sliced into one of the men's necks, and Amaranthe looked away. She ought not be squeamish about such things by now, but the idea of cutting open a corpse to investigate inside unsettled her.

"Huh," Sicarius said.

"What'd you find?" She drew closer, despite her stomach's protests.

"I didn't." He was probing around inside the wound. Blood dripped from his fingers and onto the floor. "Whatever I felt disappeared."

"Maybe you...imagined it?"

He gave her a flat look.

Right, he was about as imaginative as a stump.

Amaranthe waved toward the loading bay. "Shall we see if we can find evidence of tampering?"

Sicarius searched the bodies first, then slipped into an aisle formed by crates on one side and bolts of textiles piled head-high on the other. She supposed that meant yes.

Footsteps sounded in the factory. Cursing under her breath, Amaranthe cut off the lantern again. She felt her way down the aisle after Sicarius.

The heavy door slid open.

Light pushed back the shadows near the entrance. Amaranthe lunged around a crate at the end of the aisle, though she left her head out far enough to peer around the corner. The blond couple walked inside, lanterns held aloft. Alarmed chatter broke out when they spotted the bodies.

Amaranthe wished she could understand their words, though she had no trouble reading the surprise in their tones.

Sicarius touched her shoulder and murmured, "They stopped by to check something on the way to dinner. They don't recognize the men, and they're—"

The couple ran out the door, and darkness swallowed the bay.

"Leaving?" Amaranthe guessed.

"Going to get the enforcers," Sicarius said.

"Emperor's warts. We won't have much time to investigate now."

She relit her lantern and jogged down the aisles, eyeing crates, sewing machine parts, and more fabric than she had ever seen in one place. Nothing appeared unusual or out of place. As minutes skipped past, she clenched her fist, sure they were going to be denied clues to some heinous plot.

Steam brakes squealed outside—an enforcer vehicle pulling up, Amaranthe wagered.

Sicarius appeared out of the shadows. "We must go."

"Did you find anything?"

"No."

"Nothing they might have left? Nothing special they might have come to steal?"

"No." Sicarius gripped her shoulder and rotated her toward the end of the aisle. "Go."

Vehicle doors slammed, and voices drifted in through the open loading dock entrance. Amaranthe cut off the lantern and reluctantly let

Sicarius push her toward the sliding door. They could return tomorrow night and investigate more thoroughly.

Footsteps sounded outside the roll-up door, and she picked up her pace. Flickering lamplight came from behind as enforcers crowded the loading docks.

She and Sicarius slipped past the bodies and into the factory. He halted. Another pair of enforcers had entered through the front door. Their lantern light gleamed against the brass sewing machines on that end of the building.

"Not good," Amaranthe whispered. "If we're seen here, it'll incriminate us. Further."

She knew she was stating the obvious, but Sicarius moved without comment. They crouched low, easing along the wall until they reached a corner near the entrance. She had hoped the enforcers would go down the center aisle to meet with their comrades in the loading bay, but they remained up front. One leaned against the frame of the door, and she grimaced. They must believe criminals were still on the premises, and they had set up a perimeter to watch the exits. She thumped her fist on her thigh. They—*she*—had dawdled too long.

Perhaps they could escape through a window, but the enforcers would spot them if they opened one at floor level. If they could reach the higher ones....

"Loft," Sicarius murmured, following her gaze.

Amaranthe eyed the ladder leading to the second level of sewing machines. No more than a few meters from the door, it rose well within the enforcers' sight. But Sicarius did not head that direction. She followed as he weaved through the workstations and stopped at a support post halfway down the center aisle.

Before she could question him, Sicarius shimmied up the post as if it were a rope. He lunged sideways, caught the edge of the floor above, and pulled himself through the open railing.

Not sure she was agile enough to duplicate the feat without making noise—or falling to the floor a few times—she eyed the enforcers. She had worked this part of town when she was a patroller, and these men had familiar faces. She thought she knew the name of the older fellow, but that meant little. Last she heard, she was more hated by enforcers than by anyone else, both for the role she had played in getting her

old partner killed and for allying with Sicarius to—according to the newspapers—kidnap the emperor. As far as she knew, nobody knew the truth, that she and Sicarius had saved Sespian.

The enforcers turned to speak to someone outside. Figuring that was the best chance she would get, Amaranthe gripped the worn post and hopped up, digging into the support with the inside edges of her boots. Squeezing and pushing with her legs, she clawed her way toward the ceiling.

The hilt of her short sword clunked against the post. Wincing at the noise, she checked the enforcers. One frowned her direction. She froze.

The ease with which she saw them made her feel vulnerable, perched halfway up the post. She reminded herself their light should dull their night vision, and she ought be cloaked by darkness.

The enforcer walked her direction, his lantern in hand. He drew his sword as he advanced. He might not see her, but he had heard her.

Amaranthe was about to drop down and dart into the shadows when a soft clank sounded across the building, in a corner near the front door. The enforcer's head whipped about.

Trusting the distraction came from Sicarius, Amaranthe hustled the rest of the way up the post. At the top, the smooth floorboards offered nothing to grab, and the edge of the loft hung five feet away. Figuring her legs were stronger than her arms, she maneuvered herself as best she could to push off. After a final glance toward the enforcer, who was now investigating the corner where the noise had sounded, she lunged, making a horizontal leap.

One hand caught the lip, and one didn't. Her knuckles smashed against the floorboards, and for a moment she hung by one set of fingers, her legs dangling free.

Amaranthe forced calm and pulled herself up enough to grab the lip with her loose hand. With both arms anchored, she rocked her legs from side to side to create momentum. She swung them up, catching the lip with the inside of her foot. From there, she was able to scramble though the railing.

"Good," came Sicarius's voice, soft and nearby.

She gaped into the darkness. "If you were right there, why didn't you give me a hand?" she whispered.

"Training."

If not for the enforcers below, she would have let out a long groan. Sicarius pulled her to her feet and gave her no time to complain further. Stepping carefully, toe first, she followed him across the floorboards without a sound.

Sicarius stopped below a window not visible from ground level. He eased it open, checked the alley below, then led the way outside.

Cool, damp air breezed past Amaranthe's cheek. The brick exterior might have proved as hard, or harder, to scale than the post, but another window adorned the wall above the first, providing ledges and sills for handholds. Soon they reached the flat roof. From there, they found adjacent buildings lower than the factory and close enough to reach by jumping the alleys. When they dropped to the ground a half a block away, Amaranthe leaned against the wall to catch her breath and appreciate their escape.

Not one for idle chatter, or chatter at all, Sicarius waited in silence.

"Interesting evening," she said, hoping to draw him out. "When you said 'good,' did you mean *I* looked good, as in all those workouts are improving my skills, or it was good that I didn't fall?"

"Yes."

She snorted. "Thanks."

When he did not speak again, she headed for the street. Sicarius walked beside her.

"I guess we better check on the others," she said. "It's always possible they've found some trouble of their own."

He said nothing.

"You're an awful conversationalist," Amaranthe said. "How is it possible I prefer spending time with you?"

"Most people don't *want* to talk to assassins."

"I'm a unique individual."

"Yes," he said, deadpan.

"I'm never quite sure if you're complimenting me...or not."

His eyes glinted as they passed a streetlamp. "Good."

CHAPTER 3

WHEN BOOKS AND MALDYNADO RETURNED TO the rumbling, clanking, hissing belly of the pump house, Books searched for Amaranthe with a bounce in his step. He strode into the warm boiler room, which had been claimed as the recreation/training/dining room for the group.

A knife whistled through the air, almost giving him a second shave for the day.

He jerked back as the sleek steel thudded into a scarred log propped upright in the corner. The knife, hilt quivering, joined others. Several more littered the concrete floor.

Books glowered at the thrower.

"You should knock." Seventeen-year-old Akstyr was the age Books's son would have been if he were alive, but there were no similarities. Dressed in oversized shirt and trousers, Akstyr wore a perpetual sneer and would have looked like he made a living mugging old ladies even without the spiked black hair and arrow-shaped gang brand on his hand. "Bad to walk up on a man handling his weapons."

"There's no door." Books smothered the urge to tack on "young man," instead tapping the brick archway for emphasis.

"Then you should at least look before popping in. We're having a lesson."

Basilard, the putative instructor raised an apologetic hand toward Books. The ex-pit-fighter, with a briar patch of scars crisscrossing his pale face and shaven head, appeared as thug-like as Akstyr. Yet the mute man rarely caused trouble, so Books was inclined more favorably toward him than Akstyr or—

Maldynado bumped into Books as he passed into the room, a half-devoured pastry dangling from his lips. "You tell them about the bodies

yet?" he asked, the food churning in his mouth on display like concrete in a mixer.

"Bodies?" Akstyr hurled another knife into the log.

"Not yet." Books crossed the room to check the boiler, figuring it would be safer over there than near the practice area. He peered into the furnace and was mildly surprised someone had shoveled more coal in recently. "Is Amaranthe here?"

"Nah." Akstyr collected his knives. "She and Sicarius are out, asking about a job."

"I'd prefer to wait so we only have to tell the story once."

"Not me." Maldynado grinned and launched into gory descriptions of the bodies, speculations about an evil man-eating tunnel beast, and—his favorite part—how Books had fallen into the water, gotten tangled up, and screamed like a girl being mauled by a bear. He acted out the last part, which put Akstyr on the floor in guffaws. Even the saturnine Basilard smiled with appreciation for the flamboyant storytelling.

Books turned his back to them and checked the gauges on the boiler. He fiddled with the pressure regulators and pretended he could not hear Akstyr and Maldynado's continuing mirth.

Basilard joined him, held out a throwing knife with one hand, and twitched a sign with the other: *Practice?*

Though Books was not as apt at reading Basilard's hand codes as Amaranthe—who seemed to know what others were thinking whether they used words or not—he had seen that sign often enough to know it.

"I appreciate your willingness to instruct," Books said, "but the four hours of training Sicarius inflicts on us every morning are sufficient for me."

At five-and-a-half-feet tall, Basilard stood a foot shorter than Books, but he had the sturdy stoutness of a brandy still. Books poked at the coals in the furnace, so he could pretend he did not see the man's stern frown.

You practice more, Basilard signed, which Books took to mean he needed more work than the others. No great illumination there.

"If the fate of the group ever rests on me being able to hurl a knife into a person at twenty paces, I suspect we'll be doomed, extra practice notwithstanding. I'm not even sure I could—" Books didn't finish his thought aloud—that he did not know if he could kill anyone. Thus far,

the job had not required it, not from him. Amaranthe had never implied he need do more than defend himself. Still, Akstyr and Maldynado had fallen silent, and Books sensed them listening, waiting for more laughter fodder.

Basilard merely stood, knife held out, gaze unrelenting.

"Fine." Books took it and went to the chalk mark on the floor, the one spot from which he could usually make the throw.

Maldynado and Akstyr leaned against the wall. An audience. How delightful.

Books faced the log, lifted the knife above his shoulder, held his left arm out to sight along, and threw. The blade spun three times and landed point first in the log. It quivered a foot below the black heart some artistically challenged soul had painted in grease, but he was tickled whenever the knife did not bounce off or miss altogether.

Basilard pointed to the floor three feet farther back, and Books groaned.

Maldynado chuckled. "No bounty hunter is going to let you line up at precisely ten paces for the throw."

"Unlike you, I don't have a bounty on my head." Books shuffled back and accepted another knife. "I'm here because..." He wanted to be? That wasn't exactly it. Because Amaranthe had come to him, seeking a research assistant, and he had been tired of drinking himself into oblivion every day, dwelling on the past, and relying on his landlady's charity to survive. If he had known he was signing up for hours of running, calisthenics, and weapons training every day, he would have kept the bottle. Maybe. A year had passed since his son died, and more seasons than that since his wife left. He had grown weary of mourning and feeling sorry for himself, but he had no other family. Two decades had disappeared since the Western Sea Conflict, where his father and older brothers, marines all, had fallen in naval battles. Not that they had been much of a family, even when they were alive. It depressed him to realize he was probably only here, with these men, because he did not want to be alone.

Basilard bumped his arm: *Throw*.

"Right," Books murmured.

He lined up and threw again, but he judged the revolutions poorly, and the knife bounced off the log.

Not for the first time, Basilard demonstrated the no-spin method he and Sicarius used. They could stand anywhere and hit their targets; Sicarius did not even need to be standing. More than once, Books had seen the man hit moving targets while jumping off roofs, rappelling down cliffs, and other athletic feats Books could barely manage by themselves.

"Relax, Books." Maldynado snickered as the sixth or seventh knife clattered to the floor. "I've never seen anybody look so uncomfortable doing—well, everything. How can you have been born in the empire and not have more familiarity with weapons? Didn't you go to the mandatory training classes when you were a prim little student reading encyclopedias?" He pointed toward the knives. "Your arm needs to do a whip action. You've got to be relaxed to make that."

"Pardon me if the idea of hurling four inches of steel into someone's chest doesn't *relax* me."

"That's a log, not a person," Akstyr said.

"Though we can see how it'd be confusing," Maldynado said. "Here's a tip that helps me tell the difference: people scream a lot more when they get hit."

There were times Books wished he had the gumption to walk over and punch Maldynado in the mouth. Actually, it wasn't so much a lack of gumption as the knowledge that he would be the one who would end up with his face smashed into the floor.

Basilard waved for Maldynado and Akstyr to give up audience status and practice as well. Unfortunately, that did not silence their tormenting.

When Amaranthe walked in an hour later, Books dropped the knives and greeted her with wide arms and a hearty, "Amaranthe!" that probably sounded desperate. Fortunately, the boys tended to be more civilized when she was around. Despite her gray military fatigues, combat boots, short sword, and dark brown hair swept into a no-nonsense bun, she always struck him as the kind of girl he would have wanted for a daughter rather than some knife-hurling mercenary.

She observed the knives and gave him a sympathetic smile. "Who's supposed to be on watch?"

"Oops," Maldynado said. "Forgot on account of the alarm bell and bodies." He jogged out, path wide to avoid Sicarius, who was gliding through the door.

"Bodies?" Amaranthe arched her eyebrows.

"Remember, one is from me," Maldynado called back.

Books explained the situation. Amaranthe's eyebrows remained perked throughout, and he could imagine ideas stirring in her mind. Sicarius stayed silent throughout the story. He stood near the door, back to the wall, arms crossed over his chest. If anything interested him, one would never know. Just having him watching always made Books nervous. He finished the story and handed Amaranthe the key fob and the damp note.

"Bodies in our own backyard," Amaranthe said. "This may supersede the other mystery we were delving into."

"Anything interesting?" Books asked.

"Complaints about magic usage."

"Magic?" Akstyr bounced to her side, the model of an attentive school boy—except for the baggy sleeves pushed up to his elbows, displaying a few other brands from his gang days.

"Sicarius can fill you in," Amaranthe said. "He knows more about doodads, er, artifacts than I."

Akstyr shrank back, appearing less than enthused at the idea of a private chat with the assassin. Sicarius's expression did not change, but Books had the impression of a cranky wolf lizard known for eating its young.

Amaranthe examined the key fob, not batting an eye at the glowing feature. "Ergot's Chance. What is that? A gambling house?"

"That's a new place." Akstyr flipped a knife into the log. "Run by a foreigner. Real popular for some reason."

"How do you know about it?" Books asked. "Given our current fiscal situation, it's unwise to spend time blowing money on gambling."

"It's my money." Akstyr sneered. "I'll do what I want with it. Anyway, I was planning to win, not blow anything. Place is rigged though."

"A rigged gambling house," Books said. "Imagine that."

"Rigged by a practitioner, I mean," Akstyr said. "I should've been able to win with the new tricks I learned in that book."

He was studying magic from an ancient Nurian tome, a project that frequently involved pestering Books for translations. If the youth

learned anything that way, Books would be shocked, but he had no interest in arguing.

"They were using their own non-imperial tricks." Akstyr threw another knife, clipping the log this time. "That one isn't weighted right."

"We'll check it out tomorrow night." Amaranthe tossed the fob to Akstyr, then considered the numbers on the damp note.

"Why don't I research that while you take the others to the gambling house?" Books could use a break from his belligerent-minded brethren. A long break.

"Sounds good," Amaranthe said. "I like a man who volunteers to do research."

He straightened, pleased at the thought of proving himself useful.

"I've run into trouble at the real estate library before though," she said. "Why don't you take Maldynado? Even if there aren't any assassins lurking on the upper tiers—" she tossed a significant look at Sicarius, "—Maldynado can distract the clerk if you need to sneak out with documents."

Books had his mouth open to complain that Maldynado was the *last* person he wanted to spend more time with when his brain circled back to the first thing she said. "Real estate library?"

"Isn't that where you were planning to research? That's a lot number, isn't it?"

Books scrutinized the note, but he knew little about real estate, so he had no idea. His shoulders slumped. He read and wrote six languages, had taught world history for a decade, and could find anything in a library in under a minute. *He* was supposed to be the expert on research. If he wasn't that, what was he in this group? "Well, there were a number of possibilities that came to mind, but that's certainly on my list of items to check."

Amaranthe smiled, brown eyes knowing, but all she said was, "If that *does* match up with a lot on record, see if the other number represents a recent appraisal."

"Right." He tried not to feel disappointed that his scrap of paper was not something more interesting. Like that cipher he'd mused about. He would have enjoyed a cryptographic challenge, but real estate? Enh. Worse, he had to take Maldynado.

"That'll get you out of tomorrow's fun." Amaranthe winked at Books.

"What fun?" Akstyr asked suspiciously.

"The rest of us can dig out the as-built drawings for the aqueducts and figure out where those bodies came from."

"Looking at pictures all day?" Akstyr grimaced.

"Oh, I'm sure there'll be some field work." Amaranthe's eyes twinkled. "Got any magic tricks for waterproofing boots?"

"Uhm, maybe?"

Without comment, Sicarius left the room. Unless the team was planning a mission, or he was leading training, he never spent time with the men. It would not surprise Books if he randomly killed everybody in their sleep some night.

Basilard and Akstyr returned to knife throwing. Books fiddled with the sheet of paper, though his thoughts were elsewhere, particularly on how he could sneak out in the morning, leaving Maldynado behind.

"You doing all right?" Amaranthe asked him.

"I'm fine."

She nodded for him to follow her to a quiet area of the room, near the warmth of the furnace. "You look glum."

"That's my normal expression."

"I've noticed. With those perennially dour faces, you and Basilard could start a convincing crematory business."

Books shrugged. "I've just been wondering if...perhaps this was a mistake. I'm not sure how I...enhance the group. Research skills, I thought, but you've proven adept in that area yourself."

"Only in matters where I have previous experience. I studied business—including real estate—in school before my father died and I had to drop out. Please don't undercrestimate what you have to offer."

"It's not only that. I've little in common with a band of mercenaries, so I don't fit here, not like I did at the University. But, of course, I can't go back there."

"Having a record as someone who cavorts with outlaws isn't usually a draw for employers," Amaranthe agreed.

Books prodded the corner of the coal bin with his boot. "Maybe I should leave the capital, find a small town where nobody knows me. Start over."

"Sounds lonely."

"Or peaceful. I'm grateful to you for the role you played in helping me get past my grief." And out of the bottle. "I'm just not sure this is a life I'm suited for long-term."

"I'd certainly miss you if you left, but you don't owe me anything, and I can't make you stay. Well, with Sicarius's help I probably could." Amaranthe smiled.

He returned the gesture warily.

"No, I'm joking." She patted his arm. "Think on it for a while, please. You may feel that you don't have much in common with the others, but don't mistake not fitting in with not having a place. We care about you."

Books snorted. "You, I believe do. The others, less so."

"Maldynado would be bored if he didn't have you to trade insults with."

"I see. And Sicarius?"

"Ah, he believes you're progressing with your training."

"And that's equivalent to caring about me?" Books asked.

"Most people he ignores. Or kills."

"True."

"Think about it," she said. "No leaving while we have a mystery to solve though. I expect we'll find some excitement tomorrow, one way or another."

Noting the gleam in her eyes, he said, "Why does that worry me and excite you?"

"You're saner than I am?"

"That must be it."

CHAPTER 4

WATER PATTERED ONTO THE MILDEW-SLICK walkway, and Amaranthe struggled to keep her map dry. The maze of pipes, tunnels, and holding tanks was tough enough to decipher without soggy stains. Occasionally a trolley or steam vehicle rumbled by on an overhead street, but for the most part only the sound of running water stole the silence.

Akstyr and Basilard followed her while Sicarius scouted ahead. What he expected to find in the darkness without a lantern, she could not guess, but he seemed to prefer the shadows.

"Huh," she muttered, pausing to peer about. "This should be a four-way intersection, not a three-way one." Unless they were lost. She frowned at the map and pictured the tunnels they had traversed. She had taken note of each turn they made, so she did not see how they could have gone astray.

Amaranthe glanced over her shoulder. If they *were* lost, she did not want to admit it. She had a notion leaders were supposed to be unflappable and infallible, or, at the least, have good senses of direction.

The two men behind her were not paying attention.

"Truth, Basilard?" Akstyr asked. "You can't tell me anything about how your people work the mental sciences?"

Basilard shook his head.

"But you're not from the empire," Akstyr said. "I thought all Kendorians knew something about *rakinyaw*." Akstyr puffed his chest as he said the foreign term, no doubt proud he knew a Kendorian word.

Basilard signed a response, hands and fingers moving in a series of curt gestures.

"What?" Akstyr asked.

"Basilard is Mangdorian, not Kendorian," Amaranthe said. "And he doesn't know that word you just used."

Basilard inclined his head her direction.

"Huh?" Akstyr asked. "Oh. Well, whatever. Only the empire is so backward that it..."

Amaranthe returned her attention to the map. Even if those two were talking about something else, they would eventually notice they were standing still. Unfortunately, the channel she wanted to take was the one not there. Only a flat brick wall waited in that direction. Maybe if they turned left, they could loop back around and—

Basilard tugged at her shirt. Akstyr had a hand on the wall, his face toward the ceiling, and his eyes distant and thoughtful.

"Find something, Akstyr?" she asked after a minute passed without him moving.

He blinked, then pointed down the channel to the right. "No, wait." He pointed left. "Er." He shrugged and lifted his arms.

"Something odd with the intersection?" Amaranthe asked. Maybe there was a reason they were lost.

"I don't know. It's just...strange."

Sicarius appeared at Amaranthe's shoulder. Startled, she took a step, and her heel slid on a slimy patch. A quick arm flail kept her from toppling into the channel or falling against him, but it was anything but graceful. She attempted to turn the movement into a casual lean against the wall. Basilard's eyebrows lifted, but Akstyr was still puzzling out the channels and did not seem to notice her lack of suaveness.

"So, Sicarius." Something moist fuzzed the wall beneath Amaranthe's hand. She gave up the pretense, slipped a kerchief out of her pocket, and wiped off the mildewy residue. "Find anything interesting?"

"No."

"Find anything boring?" She smiled.

Sicarius favored her with his usual humorless face.

"I wanna check something," Akstyr said.

He backed up for a running start and leaped across the channel to the other side, the side where a flat, bland wall stood instead of the fourth passage the map said should be there. The ledge was only a foot wide, and his momentum smashed him into the bricks, but he managed to keep from bouncing back into the water.

"Something over there?" Amaranthe asked.

"The wall is solid." Akstyr massaged his hand where it had mashed against the brick.

"You don't sense anything odd about that spot, do you?"

"The wall?" Akstyr asked. "No."

Sicarius was watching her, probably wondering at her string of questions. She showed him the map, which he studied briefly.

"An error," he said.

She had feared he would simply say she had led them the wrong direction and was glad he thought it a problem with the map.

"Akstyr thinks this intersection is odd," Amaranthe said. "Do you sense anything?" He had far more experience with the Science than she did and likely more than Akstyr as well.

Sicarius considered the passages. "No."

"Really? Is it possible his nose for magic is better than yours?"

She meant it as a simple question, not an insult, but his expression grew chilly.

"In their eagerness to practice their craft, neophytes learning the mental sciences often sense things that are not there."

Akstyr scowled at him. "You think I'm imagining things?"

Sicarius turned the chilly gaze on him. Akstyr's chin lifted mulishly, but he looked away first. A resentful curl remained on his lips.

"Basilard, why don't you and Akstyr explore that direction?" Amaranthe pointed to the right. "Our goal is still to find the source of those bodies, so check manholes and access points along the way, but if Akstyr senses anything more, feel free to veer off to investigate."

"A waste of time," Sicarius said.

Amaranthe gave him a nudge toward the channel on the left. "Sicarius and I will explore this direction." She dug out a pocket watch. "Unless you find something worth exploring, meet back at the pumping house in two hours, and we'll investigate the gambling joint."

Basilard nodded and led the way down the indicated tunnel. Akstyr, hands stuffed in his pockets, slouched after him.

As Amaranthe and Sicarius headed the opposite direction, she clamped down on her tongue to keep from bringing up his lack of tact and the problems inherent in offending people. It would sound like nagging, and she did not want to alert him to her hunch that Akstyr did not seem the sort to forgive insults. Suggesting he might be a threat one day would only get him a knife in his back. Besides, she hoped, amongst comrades who cared, Akstyr would grow into a better man.

Water spilled out of a massive pipe in the far wall. Amaranthe eyed it as they passed, still suspicious of that side of the channel. Maybe the old waterway had been bricked in and the flow diverted to this exit point. If so, why would the map not have been updated?

She thought of investigating it, but the channel had widened around the pipe, creating a pool too great even for Sicarius to jump.

They continued onward until they reached a ninety-degree turn. Amaranthe halted on the corner.

"This is supposed to be a T-section," she said.

The waterway was narrower here, and Sicarius hopped the six-foot channel as if it were a puddle. He probed the wall on the far side. "If it ever was, it's not apparent. The bricks and mortar are aged."

"Odd and odder." Amaranthe took out the map and marked the missing passage. "If we had the construction blueprints, I could understand if there were differences in what was actually dug out down here and the original plans, but this is the as-built drawing from the pumping house for this section of the city aqueducts. It should have been completed after the construction and updated anytime there was an expansion or alteration."

"The pumping house has mediocre security," Sicarius said. "Perhaps only dummy drawings are kept there."

"To what ends? If something breaks, city workers need accurate maps to fix the problem."

"There's no machinery that would need repairs out here."

"Just miles and miles of brick passages, huh?"

Though Sicarius had inspected the wall, Amaranthe felt the need to look herself. She pocketed the paper, considered the mildew-fuzzed bricks on the ledge, and found a spot that appeared slightly less treacherous than the others.

She lunged across the channel. Her foot skidded on the narrow ledge. Sicarius surprised her by catching her elbow and keeping her from thudding into the wall.

"Thank you." Amaranthe arched an eyebrow. "Though I'm not sure why I deserve the gentlemanly treatment here, after you let me scrape the skin off my belly button climbing into that loft last night."

He released her elbow. "I didn't want you to drop the lantern."

"Ah, so I merely appeared less competent and more in need of assistance today." Amaranthe set the lantern down and ran her fingers along the damp bricks.

"There is nothing here," Sicarius said.

She continued probing. Maybe Akstyr's mulishness was contagious. Or maybe she just relished the idea of finding something when he had searched and discovered nothing. She took her sword out and tapped on the wall with the hilt, thinking she might hear hollow clanks that suggested a secret space behind. Alas, none of her banging sounded unnatural, and running her hands along the wall revealed nothing but slimy and slimier bricks.

"Let's go back to that pipe," she said.

He followed her along the ledge, but she had the feeling he thought they were wasting time. Or perhaps, he simply did not think roaming aqueducts a suitable task for his skills.

"If trailing along with me is boring you," she said, "you could go check on Books and Maldynado in the real estate office."

He did not speak at first, and she thought he might be considering it, but then he said, "My presence unnerves Books."

"Your presence unnerves everyone." Amaranthe grinned over her shoulder to soften the comment.

"Not you," Sicarius said.

"No, but I'm told my sanity is questionable."

She wriggled her eyebrows at him. Someday she was going to get him to smile, maybe even laugh. The one and only time she'd seen him truly break his facade, it had been in anger. At her. It seemed fate should offer her the other side of the coin once.

"Huh," was the only response she got.

The outlet pipe came into view. More than eight feet in diameter, it rose well over her head. This side trip was a whim, and Amaranthe did not expect to find anything, but she lifted the lantern to inspect the pipe's rim by the light.

Splashing water flung droplets onto her clothing when she edged closer, and she was about to abandon the search, but Sicarius reached above her head. He plucked something from a gouge in the metal.

"What is it?" Amaranthe asked.

He held a soggy chunk of hair up to her light. Human hair.

Amaranthe probably should have been horrified, but excitement thrummed through her. The dark brown hair could have belonged to half the people in Stumps, but she said, "Think that came off one of the bodies the boys found?"

"Impossible to tell."

"Well, I have a hunch it did. I bet those bodies flowed into the aqueducts through this pipe." She ticked the cold metal. "I'd really like to know what's on the other end." She leaned out, but so much water flowed from the pipe that no air pocket lay at the top. Even if there was air, one could never swim into the current that way, not that she'd be foolish enough to try. Probably.

Sicarius gripped her by the collar and pulled her back a few steps.

"I was just looking," Amaranthe said.

He grunted.

"Really. Did I look like I needed assistance again?"

"You looked like you were considering...trouble."

She grinned. "I wouldn't go for a swim without consulting you first. But, given your past history working for Hollowcrest and skulking around dark places, I wonder if you have any insight into these tunnels."

"Skulking?"

"Yes, is that not what assassins call it?"

"We call it working."

"All right," Amaranthe said. "While you were *working*, did you ever have reason to travel through our aqueducts?"

"No."

"Can you venture a guess as to what these cartographical errors could be about?"

"Security," Sicarius said.

"Security? Like a false map designed to throw off enemy infiltrators who might sneak into the capital to sabotage the water supply?"

"You could ask Books who was emperor when the aqueducts were built. We've had some paranoid rulers."

"True. 'Paranoia is awareness' was one of Emperor Vakar's sayings, wasn't it? One that's been oft-quoted throughout imperial history."

"Yes."

"So, if the map is intentionally inaccurate, what would it be hiding? It's not as if it's a mystery where our drinking water comes from." She waved in the direction of the Tork. "Though I suppose it'd be hard for a saboteur to poison a river. Maybe attacking a reservoir down here would..."

An expectant cant to Sicarius's face made her pause. It was as if he was waiting for her to figure something out. She closed her eyes and pictured the topography of the city above her, the direction of the water flow, the location of the pumping houses.

"Our drinking water *does* come from the Tork, doesn't it?" Amaranthe asked.

"So your drawing says."

"Right, and my drawing is lying about things." She pulled out a knife and scraped a rough map into the mildew on the wall, noting the river, the streets around the pumping house, and then the passages they had explored that morning. "That wall that's blocked off and shouldn't be...it runs parallel to this side of the river, doesn't it? And we've got a gap of—what do you think?—fifty, one-hundred meters in between? What if that pipe makes a turn somewhere in the space in between? What if the water is actually siphoned from elsewhere? An underground source. Or even another river up in the mountains. And the aqueducts were purposely built like a labyrinth to hide that fact?"

Sicarius was listening, but, as always, remained hard to read.

"Am I being too fanciful—too paranoid—or do you agree with the possibility?"

"The paranoia of past rulers is a well documented fact."

"I can't tell if you're agreeing with me or simply acknowledging that there's a remote possibility my fancy-filled mind has latched onto the truth," Amaranthe said.

"You have a lot of hunches. Sometimes they are correct."

"Well, if this one *is* right, this water and those bodies could have come from anywhere." Amaranthe rubbed her face. "They might have been dumped in a river hundreds of miles away. We could be on a purple

lumpbat chase. Although...perhaps not. The gambling house is local, and one of those dead fellows had that key fob, so..."

Sicarius was studying the darkness beyond the lantern's influence, and he did not seem to be listening. Amaranthe cocked an ear, wondering what had caught his attention, but she could hear only the gush of water flowing from the pipe.

"What is it?" she whispered.

A minute head shake. "Perhaps nothing. Perhaps what Akstyr felt."

"He wasn't imaging things? Are you going to apologize to him if it turns out he was right?" She knew fully well he would not—if she found out he had ever said "sorry" in his life, she would fall over in surprise—but her playful side, or perhaps it was her unwise side, wanted to tease a response from him.

"No," Sicarius said.

Well, it was a response. Sort of.

"All right," Amaranthe said. "Let's get out of here before something more sinister than you shows up."

His eyebrow twitched, but he said nothing. It would take a lot of work to get that smile out of him.

CHAPTER 5

THE FILES WERE A MESS. WHILE THE CITY LOT RE-
cords were somewhat orderly and searchable, whoever had
come up with the system for cataloguing rural properties
ought to be publicly castrated. Rather than using a grid system, the lots
were delineated by their proximity to landmarks: some by nearest town,
some by ancient battle sites, some by prominent terrain features, and
one by the fact that an appraiser's uncle had fallen off a cliff and died
on the property.

Despite the disorder, Books found himself enjoying the challenge
of the research. Here, amongst books, ledgers, parchments, and dusty
shelves, he felt at home. He dug a fistful of pencils from his satchel
and lost track of time as he scribbled notes. A part of him wanted to
devise a new system entirely, but he doubted the front-desk clerk would
appreciate it.

Whistling pierced his concentration, and he scowled, recognizing
the tune—a bawdy ditty about an army officer's sister—and the whistler.

Maldynado ambled out of a narrow book-stuffed aisle, plopped a
brown bag on the desk, and straddled a seat.

Books curled his lip and moved the bag to an out-of-the-way corner.
It left a greasy splotch on a centuries-old parchment. He sighed and
bent lower over the paper he was studying. Maybe ignoring Maldynado
would encourage him to go away.

Maldynado dug a handful of walnuts out of his grocery bag, cracked
one open with his teeth, and proceeded to nosh loudly. "Find anything
luminous yet, Booksie?"

Books bent his head lower, deepening his can't-you-see-that-I'm-
ignoring-you pose. "No."

"Want a walnut?"

"No."

"We can't eat too many. Basilard is going to use them to prepare a fancy breakfast for Amaranthe's birthday tomorrow."

"Her birthday isn't until next week."

"She'll expect something then, but not tomorrow. It'll be a surprise."

Books snorted. Maldynado had not even known Amaranthe's birthday was coming until Books said something.

"Isn't it Sicarius's turn to cook tomorrow?" Books asked.

"Oh, no, we are *not* going to let that happen for a birthday breakfast. And preferably not ever. I can still taste that llama lung and bone marrow surprise he made. The surprise being if it took you more than five minutes to vomit after eating it."

"I'm sure it was very healthy." Though Books would not show it, he shuddered inwardly at the memory of the dish too.

"Healthy maybe, edible no. And don't pretend you didn't avoid it. All you ate were those raw unflavored parsnips." Maldynado lifted a hand. "Anyway, we need something good tomorrow. After we serve up a fine breakfast for Amaranthe, it'll be time to let her know about the date I lined up for her."

Books lifted his head for the first time. "Date? What date?"

"A man I know. He's smart and witty, and his father owns *The Gazette*. Good warrior-caste family. Cute fellow too. If I were a woman, and I couldn't have me, I'd want him."

Books rubbed his forehead. "When did she say she wanted you to find her a date?"

"She didn't." Maldynado tipped his chair back, balancing it on the rear legs. "She's too focused. But we know what's best for her."

"You and...Basilard?" Books cringed. Why did he have a feeling Amaranthe would not appreciate this meddling? "Did you warn her you were going to... What exactly *are* you going to do?"

"Just set things up for a little romance. She's a girl. She needs that sort of thing."

"I imagine she could find her own romance if she sought it."

"Of course she seeks it. *All* girls seek it. Plus, if she had it, she might spend a little less time waking us two hours before dawn for Sicarius's training sessions and more time blanket wrestling."

"I see. Your interest in her love life stems from your own laziness."

"Not entirely." Maldynado gripped the table for balance and rocked farther back. "She's a good girl. She should be happy. She spends too much time with Sicarius. How can you be happy with that dour puss in tow? And why's he always lurking around her, anyway? If you ask me, the whole arrangement is a little—"

A shadow moved behind Maldynado. Sicarius. Surprise jolted Maldynado, and he lost his grip on the table. His chair pitched backward. Sicarius could have caught him, but merely stepped aside to avoid him as he flailed to the ground. Maldynado's boot struck the table, and walnuts flew, pelting bookcases with resounding cracks.

Maldynado lurched to his feet. "Sicarius! I was just, uhm, how long were you..." He turned to Books and whispered, "How long was he there?"

A smirk wanted to find its way to Books's lips, but the coldness of Sicarius's face stole his mirth. Best not to get involved. Or show interest.

Maldynado wilted under Sicarius's stare. He stepped back to put space between himself and Sicarius, but landed on a walnut. His heel flew out from under him, and he almost ended up on the floor again. He caught the edge of a bookcase and recovered.

"Hard to believe you're our second best swordsman," Books said.

Maldynado cleared his throat, picked up the walnut, and offered it to Sicarius. "Hungry?"

Sicarius's expression did not change. If he blinked, Books did not notice it.

"Er." Maldynado pocketed the nut. "I'll just keep it."

"Akstyr and Amaranthe have gone ahead to the gambling house," Sicarius told him. "Basilard is on his way to replace you as Books's guard dog."

Books might have protested that he did not need a "guard dog," but he was relieved to have Maldynado replaced. He wondered if Amaranthe had known he would need a break from him by now. He also wondered if she knew he had gone shopping in the middle of his shift.

"Where am I going?" Maldynado asked.

"Amaranthe wants you to acquire a disguise for her, then meet us at the gambling house. She trusts you can get a good price."

"Does she trust it'll be in good taste?" Books asked.

Though Sicarius never emoted, he could ooze disapproval with the force of a cannon. Books cleared his throat and fiddled with his pencil.

"She wants me to buy clothes?" Maldynado beamed. "I do believe I know a couple merchants who'd be willing to stay open late for me."

He grabbed the grocery bag and trotted down the aisle, no doubt eager to leave Sicarius's presence. Unfortunately, that left Books alone with the man. He waited for Sicarius to ask a question or demand an update. Long moments ticked past, and Books felt like he was being judged for being a part of Maldynado's dating conversation. He was tempted to defend himself—after all, he hadn't said anything derogatory—but feared it would make him sound guilty.

"What have you discovered?" Sicarius asked.

It took Books a moment to realize Sicarius meant the real estate research. He wrenched his mind back to the work on the table. "A mess."

Sicarius folded his arms across his chest.

"I believe I'm in the right area." Books waved at the scattered texts and papers. "But I'm still looking for a match. It's definitely a rural property, probably in the mountains, I can tell you that."

Nearby, boots clacked on the tile floor. A few visitors had come into the vast real estate library that day, but none had made their way back to his remote corner. The clacking boots drew closer, however, and he turned his head toward the noise.

A woman stepped out of the aisle and started at seeing him. She recovered quickly and smiled. Though a few creases framed her lips, and threads of gray wound through her wavy black hair, the smile was pleasant.

Books checked on Sicarius, afraid he would scare her away with his glare. He was gone.

"Hello," the woman said.

He stood and gave her a bow. "Help you, ma'am?"

She frowned slightly, and he wondered if he'd guessed incorrectly on the title. "My lady" would be appropriate for a warrior caste woman, but she did not wear the expensive—and often obnoxious—trappings of that class. With simple blouse and trousers to match her calf-high boots, the woman seemed someone who preferred the simple to the ostentatious. She was handsome, too, he couldn't help but notice.

"My father sent me to research some of the family's property."

Ah, so she *was* warrior caste. Books winced at his social flub and searched for a way to correct it. "You seem...mature to be doing errands for your parents, my lady."

She titled her head. "Did you just call me old?"

He winced again. Maybe he should have kept his lips shut. "No, er, not intentionally. I was just noting that...uhm...research, you say?"

"Indeed, so. I need to find the map for the area." She eased past his table and started rifling through oversized scrolls, some frayed from time's passing.

Books tried to concentrate on his own work, though he wished he could say something that would engage her in a conversation and make her forget his bumbling tongue.

A few moments later, she turned and eyed the papers before him. "Do you have the map for Irator's Tooth Valley?"

"Ah." He shuffled through scrolls. "Yes."

She slipped into the seat next to him. "Mind if I take a look?"

"Not at all," he mumbled, noticing she wore a pleasant perfume that smelled of spring wildflowers. The part of his mind able to think of other things wondered if it was coincidence that had her researching in the same part of the library as he was, or...not.

"Here we are." She spread the map and traced the boundaries of a miles-wide swath of land stretching through a valley that lay in the midst of one of the passes across the mountains. The northern one, which lay near Mangdorian territory.

While she pulled a small notepad out, Books leaned closer to the map. His gut lurched. The lot number he had been hunting all over for was written in the center of a chunk of land adjacent to the property holding her interest. The plat map did not show contour lines, but from its proximity to the river and the limestone makeup of those mountains, he guessed it a rocky hillside.

"Do you know who owns that lot?" he asked before he could think better of it.

As soon as she turned narrowed eyes his way, he knew he should have said nothing. "Why do you ask?"

"I'm, ah, looking at properties I might be able to afford for retirement. A little cabin in the mountains sounds nice, don't you think?" He hoped that tale did not sound as woefully fabricated to her as it did to

him. Maybe adding flattery would improve it. "And a spot with a pretty neighbor would be nice."

"I live in the city and am only able to visit my parents a couple of times a year. Also, you're a little young to be thinking of retirement, aren't you?"

He sat taller. "You think I look young?"

"Yes, that's the sort of complimentary thing you're supposed to say when talking to someone with gray in his—or *her*—hair." She appeared more amused than offended. Good.

"Sorry, I've been told I don't have the smoothest tongue. My name is...Marl. Well, Books these days. Yes, call me Books."

"Vonsha," she said.

He wanted to chat and find out more about this unlikely coincidence, but he feared he would give her more information than he received himself. Maybe he should simply find out where she lived and have Amaranthe visit. Of course, even that might prove difficult if he couldn't unearth some charm.

He steeled himself with a deep breath. He had to try.

"Would you like to have hot cider later?" he blurted, then winced. That was hardly charming.

A rustle came from an aisle behind Books. He glanced back but did not spot anybody. Night had fallen outside the library's windows, and the deep shadows between the lights on the outer wall could have hidden...much. Only the lamp on the desk illuminated the area around Books and Vonsha. For a moment, he thought it might be Sicarius, but Sicarius did not rustle.

"Something wrong?" Vonsha asked.

"Thought I heard something."

"It's a public library," she said, though she glanced down the back aisle too. "Other people could be here this late."

"Could be."

Though he figured regular patrons would walk normally, with their footsteps thudding on the tile floor, not sneak about without making an appearance. He wondered if Sicarius remained in the building, monitoring, or if he had left, knowing Basilard would arrive soon.

Books slipped his hand beneath his jacket and touched the hilt of his dagger for reassurance.

"...back here?" someone whispered.

"...the light."

Vonsha's eyes widened. Books held a finger to his lips and pushed his chair back silently. He folded the Irator's Tooth Valley map and another of the surrounding mountains, then slipped both into his satchel. Vonsha opened her mouth, as if she might object, but a scuffle in a nearby aisle stopped her.

Books backed away from the table, crooking his finger for her to follow. After a brief hesitation, she eased out of her chair. The back of it bumped against a bookshelf.

"You hear something?" one of the voices whispered.

"This way."

Hesitation gone, Vonsha rushed to join Books in the shadows. He drew her back into an aisle in the opposite direction from the voices and found a spot where they could peer over the tops of books between shelves and glimpse the table.

A man with a scruffy beard and scruffier clothing shambled into view. Bulges beneath his coat at waist-level may have represented weapons. He eyed the table, glanced around, then shuffled back the way he had come.

"Homeless?" Vonsha whispered.

"What would a homeless man hope to find in the real estate library?" Books whispered back.

"Maybe he's looking for retirement property in the mountains."

The shadows hid her face, but Books had no trouble deciphering the teasing in regards to his weak cover story.

"I sense you're a sharp lady," he said.

"I teach young people. When it comes to lies, I've developed a knack for shifting through people's slag piles to find the nuggets of ore."

"You teach?" Delight at finding a kindred soul infused his tone, and he had to force himself to lower his voice. After all, they were being stalked by someone. "I taught history for more than fifteen years at Bartok," he whispered. "Do you—"

A clatter stilled his tongue. An unmarked tin can had landed on the table. It rolled toward the edge, a lit fuse sticking out of one end.

"Back, back!" Books grabbed Vonsha and pulled her down the aisle.

An explosion roared. Wood shattered, and shelves toppled into aisles, hurling their contents. Something sharp struck Books's temple, and heavy tomes pelted him from all sides. The book cases framing his aisle wobbled and tilted inward, cracking together. He ducked. They met over his head, forming an A. Certain one would collapse, burying Vonsha and him beneath it, Books hustled faster. Still pulling her, he lunged out of the aisle and planted a hand on the brick wall at the end.

She slumped into his arms.

"Vonsha?" he asked.

Blood saturated the front of her shirt and dripped from a shard of wood embedded in her neck. Closer to her collarbone than her throat, it did not appear to have hit the jugular, but he hesitated to pull it out, fearing that would make the injury worse.

Light—no, flames—grew behind them. Fire.

The light revealed movement, someone stepping out of an aisle farther down the wall. The figure, a young man in ill-fitting clothing, lifted a crossbow and aimed for Books's chest.

"Sicarius!" Books blurted. "Would you take care of this bloke?"

The crossbowman spun to look behind him. Too bad Sicarius was not truly there.

Unable to move quickly or draw his knife without dropping Vonsha, Books shuffled toward the aisle they had exited, hoping his ruse would buy them time. The shelves chose that second to collapse, barring the route.

Even with wood crackling nearby, Books heard the twang of the crossbow bolt firing. He ducked his head, and turned his shoulder. The bolt flew high.

Books set Vonsha down, prepared to attack the archer, but he halted. The rumpled man dropped the weapon. Eyes wide, face frozen in a rictus of pain, he went down.

Sicarius stood above him, his black dagger dripping blood. Books gaped, surprised his summons had worked. A hint of annoyance hardened Sicarius's dark eyes, and Books imagined him thinking, *I can't leave for five minutes without you getting into trouble....*

"There are others," Sicarius said. "Get out."

"Out is good." Books reached for Vonsha, intending to sling her over his shoulder.

"Leave her."

"No."

Books lifted Vonsha without waiting to argue. He turned his back on Sicarius and followed the outer wall, figuring the aisles were too dangerous. Numerous sets of shelves had toppled, and flames burned in several rows as well as on the ceiling, which was charred from the explosion. Heat rolled from the growing fire, warming Books's cheeks and forehead.

Behind him, someone screamed. It ended abruptly.

With the corner closest to the front door in sight, Books broke into a jog. He rounded it and almost crashed into the homeless man—and the pistol in his grip.

Hands busy holding Vonsha, Books jumped to the side and lashed out with a kick. His shoulder rammed the wall, but his boot found its target. The pistol flew from the man's grip. Books shoved him into the wall and ran past. He only wanted to get out of the building with Vonsha, not start a fight. Besides, Sicarius could handle that more proficiently.

No one else blocked his route on the way to the front door, but a steam horn pierced the air in the street outside. Someone must have heard the explosion and reported it.

He paused at the threshold, juggling Vonsha so he could free a hand to open the door. He peered outside. Two steam wagons painted with enforcer red and silver chugged to a stop in front of the building.

Books wavered. As far as he knew, he had no bounty on his head, but the enforcers might know he worked with questionable types by now. He glanced over his shoulder, expecting Sicarius to be behind him. Someone was there, yes, but it was not Sicarius.

A spiked club whistled toward his eyes. Books ducked, but not quickly enough. The club glanced off the top of his head, and pain erupted in his skull.

He stumbled back, losing his grip on Vonsha. She hit the ground and moaned.

Books's attacker, another man who looked as if he had come off the streets, swiped at him again. Dodging, Books reached for his dagger. Blood dripped in his eyes, and numbness made pulling the weapon out harder than it should have been.

Shouts came from outside along with footsteps pounding up stairs. Books cursed and ducked another wild swing. The man had the finesse of a steamroller, but it was all he needed. Dizziness gripped Books, and his limbs were not moving quickly enough. He swiped blood out of his eyes and almost cut himself with his own knife.

"Not thinking," he muttered. "Not—"

The man hefted the club overhead, and Books stumbled back, not sure he could evade the blow this time.

The door flew open. Books's attacker froze, then whirled, charging them.

"Enforcers! Halt!"

A crossbow twanged.

Someone grabbed Books's arm from behind. He tried to spin and pull away. It was Sicarius.

"Stairs," he barked.

"But Vonsha—" Books slurred.

"They have her." Sicarius yanked on Books's arm, dragging him forward.

He stumbled up the stairs after Sicarius, and they escaped through a window. He slipped, trying to climb down, and landed hard on his back. Sicarius yanked him to his feet. Blackness flirted with Books's consciousness, and the rest of the retreat faded to a blur.

CHAPTER 6

AMARANTHE LEANED AGAINST THE SIDE OF A headless statue, one of thousands in the capital that gave it the dubious nickname of "Stumps." She wore the hood of her parka pulled low over her eyes while she watched the busy street.

Though evening had fallen hours earlier, people clogged the sidewalks. Numerous drunk men meandered onto the cobblestones where they provided ambulatory obstacles for bicyclists and the occasional steam carriage. Gambling houses, sport venues, and drinking and eating houses packed the neighborhood. Many of the male passersby wore the lush, vibrant clothing—and gold-gilded swords—of the warrior caste, but just as many had the miens of off-duty soldiers. More than one black-clad figure wearing weapons strode past, and Amaranthe did a few double glances, thinking one might be Sicarius. But, despite his disinterest in disguises, he had a knack for invisibility, and he would likely find her first.

Disguises were on her mind as the sea of people moved about her, any one of whom would turn her in, either for the reward, or simply because she was a wanted felon. She touched the hilt of her short sword, reassured by its presence. She wondered what Maldynado would find for her to wear. She probably should have gone shopping with him, though more than once he had pointed out he had an easier time getting bargains from the predominantly female merchants in the city if they thought him unattached.

A familiar man ambled past, hand on the ruby-crusted pommel of one of his own swords, obviously selected to offset crimson embroidery on his black vest. Maldynado. He had no shopping bags tucked under his arms. So much for her disguise.

Figuring he would not spot her with the hood, Amaranthe lifted a hand and stepped away from the statue.

"We have a problem," came a voice from behind.

Amaranthe jumped before recognition caught up to reflexes. Sicarius.

"Your ability to find me despite the fact I'm hiding incognito in the shadows?" she asked.

He drew her into an alcove behind an overflowing bicycle rack. Maldynado stopped on the street corner to chat with a group of ladies. He must have come with Sicarius.

"What's going on?" Amaranthe asked.

Perhaps as a concession to the number of weapons dangling on nearby hips, Sicarius, too, wore a jacket with a hood. Black, of course. "The area where Books was researching was attacked," he said. "There was a woman with him. He may or may not have been the target, but someone sent six men to do the job. I took care of them while he fumbled through rescuing the unconscious woman."

"Is he all right?" she asked, more concerned by that than whether Books had pulled his own weight in a fight.

"He's injured but not mortally so. I found Basilard, and he assisted Books back to the pumping house."

She wrestled with the temptation to forgo the gambling house visit and check on Books. Sicarius's idea of "injured but not mortally so" could involve missing limbs and eyes. But if he had Basilard to watch over him, Books ought to survive without her for a few hours. It was not as if she had vast medical expertise.

"Thanks for making sure he got back. Shall we head into Ergot's Chance?" Amaranthe pointed to a dead-end street across the way. "Akstyr went in ahead to scout for magic. Or so he said. He might be putting all his pocket change on the lucky Wolf Star Tile."

She took a step, but Sicarius caught her arm.

"There's more," he said. "The woman Books was with, she's from the warrior caste, someone who used to do work for Hollowcrest during the Western Sea Conflict."

"Oh? What use did Hollowcrest have for a woman? Er, assuming it wasn't for the usual male-female after-sunset activities." From what Amaranthe remembered of Hollowcrest, he had not respected women overmuch, especially not those with any sort of ambition.

"Her name is Vonsha Spearcrest," Sicarius said. "She taught cryptography at the University, and Hollowcrest brought her in to build unbreakable keys during the war."

"Didn't some brilliant Kyattese linguist break all our keys?"

"Yes. Spearcrest disappeared shortly after that."

"You're certain it's the same woman? It's been nearly twenty years." Amaranthe had been a toddler during that war, and since most of the fighting had been at sea, over a thousand miles away, she remembered little of the details. Sicarius probably would have been in his teens, but he had been trained from birth, so she would not be surprised if he had already been killing people for Hollowcrest by then.

"I'm certain. She was injured in the explosion, but the enforcers took her for treatment."

"I wonder if Books was the target or if she was." Amaranthe tapped her leg. "You didn't hear their conversation?"

"I stayed out of sight, so she wouldn't recognize me."

"She knows you? Er, knew you?"

"Not well, but I was there at a couple of their meetings."

"You're older now." Amaranthe smiled, wondering if she could draw any indignation out of him. "Grayer."

"I don't have any gray."

He said it in his monotone, and she could not tell if it was an indignant denial or a simple statement of fact. In truth, he appeared no older than thirty, and it was only that Sespian was close to twenty that told her otherwise, though Sicarius still must have been very young when Sespian was conceived. *That* was a story she wanted to wheedle out of him someday.

"Ah, forgive me. I guess it's your perennial stodginess that leaves me with the impression you're old." There, that *had* to get a response out of him.

He studied her, as if she were some exotic specimen of fish he'd pulled up from the lake depths and he was deciding whether to keep her or throw her back. "I'm not old," he finally said.

"But no argument on stodgy, eh?"

"Akstyr is waiting, is he not?"

Amaranthe grinned and patted his arm. She shouldn't have fun teasing him, but considering his reputation, she found it encouraging that he let her. Of course, if she were a more mature person she would tell him she cared for him instead of poking fun, but the latter seemed...safer.

"Yes, he is." She lifted her hand and gestured toward the dead-end street.

When they drew even with Maldynado, Sicarius grabbed him and propelled him alongside.

"Hullo, boss," Maldynado said. "Didn't see you under that jacket. It's bulky. You almost look like a boy."

"That's one method of disguise, I suppose," Amaranthe said. "Though I thought you'd have a costume for me."

"Oh, I bought one." He smiled. "It's having a few custom alterations done, but I can pick it up later."

She would have to hope nobody who memorized wanted posters was gambling tonight.

Drum beats and guitar strums floated from a cider house on the corner where a female singer extolled the virtues of battle engaged in the spring. Several gambling houses and entertainment venues lined the wide avenue, all with fresh, new brick or stone facades. People crowded the sidewalks, though they all seemed to be jostling toward the building at the end of the street. Indeed, the venues on either side were sparsely populated. Outside an eating house, a red-haired woman's shouts alternated between announcing the meal specials and advising a worker scraping graffiti off the wall.

A freckled man on the opposite side of the street tried to foist samples of a dark liquid on passersby. Two soldiers spat at his feet and shoved him aside.

"Filthy foreign slug," one snarled.

It seemed Amaranthe's team had turned down a street overtaken by aspiring entrepreneurs from beyond the borders. And only one of the businesses was doing well.

"That's the place." Maldynado nudged a couple of smaller men aside and pointed at the brick wall stretched across the end of the street. Gold-gilded doors stood open, and people flowed in and out of the building. A pulsing sign read Ergot's Chance. Two giant glowing orbs perched upon spinning poles.

"That's blatant," Amaranthe said. "You'd think a place daring to use magic in a city where it's forbidden would be more subtle. Especially

since the sentiment around here is anti-foreigner, and most of these businesses seem to be struggling."

"It's possible the effects are mundanely created," Sicarius said.

She stepped around a puddle and drew her men to the side. "Sicarius and I will try to find the manager or owner and see what these key fobs are about. Maldynado, link up with Akstyr if you see him. I'd like you to go around to the tilers and table masters and ask questions. See if anyone recognizes the fellow who had the fob in his pocket."

"You want me to describe a bloke I've only seen after he's been horribly mauled and dead in frigid water for days?" Maldynado's head swiveled to track a pretty lady strolling past.

Amaranthe turned his face back toward her with a finger on his chin. "Do your best, please."

"Books is the one who should be doing the describing. He spent more time developing a personal relationship with those corpses." Maldynado snickered, then surprised her by turning glum. "Too bad he nearly got himself blown up."

"I'm sure he'll be fine," Amaranthe said, though she wanted to check on Books as soon as they finished here. She gripped Maldynado's arm, then nodded to Sicarius. "Ready?"

They went first, leaving Maldynado to follow a few minutes later.

Inside, people meandered through a vast, high-ceilinged room and gathered in clumps around gaming tables. A hundred chandeliers and sconces burned. Steam whistled from coal-powered contraptions that offered moving puzzles and mechanized games of chance. The stuffy heat emanating from the people, lights, and machines reminded Amaranthe of a muggy summer day before a storm.

She let Sicarius lead since he had that knack for getting people to move out of his way without doing anything. Amaranthe, on the other hand, received elbows in the ribs or suggestive jostles from drunken men. Maybe she should try wearing all black and glaring more often.

A familiar key fob dangled from someone's belt. Several patrons had them. So, not a special token, but items produced in quantities and given out, perhaps as prizes. But why, in this superstitious core of the empire, would someone risk creating dozens, or hundreds, of magical trinkets with the establishment's name on them? Amaranthe was surprised the glowing orbs outside had not resulted in someone torching the building.

Sicarius surprised her by pausing to watch a complicated version of the shell game. Three table masters sat cross-legged on cushions, sliding containers around with tokens hiding beneath. One had to watch six blurring hands at the same time and point to all the correct spots to win.

"Want to play?" she asked. They had more important things to do, but it did seem like something made for him to win. Perhaps the earnings could pay for some supplies.

"Not challenging," he said and moved on.

"Cocky, aren't we?"

"Self-aware."

"Cockily self-aware?"

He gave her a cool look. She smiled sweetly.

Before they reached the back of the room, a commotion drew a crowd that blocked the way.

"I'm not a cheater!" a familiar voice cried.

Amaranthe groaned. Akstyr.

The meaty sound of a fist striking flesh followed.

"I didn't—ommph!"

She hustled forward even as the crowd parted. Two bouncers appeared, dragging Akstyr between them. Blood streamed from his split lip and spattered his shirt. Amaranthe stepped forward, lifting a hand, intending to rescue him from the manhandling. But when he spotted her, he widened his eyes and gave a minute head shake.

"Let go of me, you mother-forsaken street eaters!" Akstyr roared and flung his arms wide.

He escaped his escort and stumbled forward, crashing into Amaranthe and Sicarius, seemingly by accident. The bouncers were not thrown for long. One lunged, wrapping an arm around his waist. Akstyr pressed something into Amaranthe's hand before the thug tore him away. The bouncer threw Akstyr over his shoulder and stomped toward the front door.

Patrons moved out of the way. Amaranthe closed her fist, hiding whatever Akstyr had given her. Cool and metallic, it felt like a key.

Sicarius continued onward without comment. Amaranthe kept herself from looking back to check on Akstyr. He obviously thought they should pretend not to know each other, and that she should investigate... whatever the key led to.

The crowd thinned in the back where two bouncers framed the entrance to a hallway. Amaranthe hustled to slip in front of Sicarius. No doubt he could get past them with force, but she wanted to try honey first.

"Good evening, gentlemen," she said, feeling short as she craned her neck back to look each man in the eye. They even towered over Sicarius, though his six feet did not make him tall by imperial standards.

"Employees only," came the response.

"Yes, I guessed that from your forbidding presence here." She smiled. "How would we make arrangements to see the boss?"

"Come during the day, and look important."

"Do I not look important?" Amaranthe asked Sicarius.

"Moderately," he said without taking his gaze from the bouncers.

"I'll have to work on increasing my importance aura." She considered the men again. "What'd that young fellow who was just dragged out of here do?"

"Lady, we're not here to chat with you."

"No, but it's got to be more interesting than standing here like mute statues."

One grunted in what may have been agreement. The other frowned at Sicarius. Gears whirred behind his eyes, and his face screwed up in concentration. Trying to place Sicarius's face, Amaranthe guessed.

"He cheated, that's what they said," she said. "Is that common?"

"People try it all the time," the more amenable bouncer said.

"Do you have to inform your employer when it happens?"

"Our employer trusts us to handle such situations ourselves."

"Yes, I suppose your boss is only interested in fiscal issues that aren't so easily resolved," Amaranthe said, an idea percolating through her mind.

Sicarius was watching her, probably wondering if this chat had a purpose.

"Yes, and we're not paid to talk to girls," the surlier of the two bouncers said.

"Unfortunately," the other muttered.

"Of course," Amaranthe said. "I understand. Thank you for speaking to me."

As she moved away, the quieter man leaned close to his comrade, whispering something and pointing at Sicarius. Apparently the hooded jacket was not enough of a disguise.

"Looks like you might get some practice defending your head tonight," Amaranthe told him, veering toward the shell-game table.

"They are not the first here to recognize me," Sicarius said. "What now? It would be a simple matter to force our way past those men."

"There are a lot of bouncers on the floor. If those two were knocked out, it wouldn't go unnoticed for long. I'd like to have a nice conversation with the owner, and given what happened to the fellow we tried to question at that factory, I'd prefer not to do it at knife point."

He gave her a sharp look. "You think that incident is tied in with this place?"

"I don't know." She pointed at a key fob dangling from a man's pocket watch chain. "But there's suddenly a lot of magic use popping up in the city."

"More foreigners."

"More foreigners who should all be smart enough not to use magic in a city where it's forbidden." Amaranthe waved a hand. "We'll talk to the owner about it."

"How?"

"I have a hunch we'll be invited in to chat soon."

"You have a plan. Should it concern me?"

"Only if your cockiness is unfounded."

They approached the table.

Sicarius stopped her with a hand on her arm. "You want me to play?"

"I want you to play and win. A lot."

Seconds ticked past before he released her arm. "Very well, but it'll take concentration. I'll need you to watch my back."

Sicarius had never asked that of her before. Though he watched *her* back all the time, he had never needed the favor returned, and she did not miss the admission of trust in the request. It meant he was willing to put himself at risk for one of her crazy schemes. The bouncers knew he was here, and who knew who else might have noted his passing and started scheming to collect the bounty?

Amaranthe nodded once. "I understand."

Sicarius stepped up to the table, cutting in front of a man who had been in line.

"I'm next." The fellow puffed out his chest and curled a lip.

Sicarius responded with silence and an icy stare. The man stared back, but was the first to lower his eyes.

He licked his lips and backed from the table. "Never mind. I'm still sorting my money."

Sicarius placed a coin on the table. "Begin."

The three table masters smiled and nodded to each other.

Amaranthe leaned her back against the edge. As much as she wanted to watch Sicarius play, she meant to take her task seriously. Still, she could not help but glance at the action from time to time.

The shell men were spaced far enough apart that one could not observe each directly. Sicarius studied the middle table master and presumably watched the other two with his peripheral vision. As soon as the shuffling ended, he promptly pointed to each of the shells holding the tokens. The first time, the table masters shrugged and congratulated him. As he continued to win, the congratulatory comments grew less frequent. He never said a word, simply pointing to the correct shells. His one coin turned into a stack, and then several stacks of coins and ranmya bills, both of which he kept tidy and even.

A buzz grew amongst the onlookers. More people drifted over, blocking Amaranthe's view of the surrounding area. She wished she were taller. With so many bodies pressing close, it would be hard to pick out onlookers with malignant intent.

Maldynado ambled by with a woman on his arm. He asked the lady if she might be inclined to fetch a couple of drinks, then strolled close enough to speak to Amaranthe.

"How come I'm working and he's playing games?" Maldynado tilted his chin toward Sicarius, who remained focused on the table.

"Is that what you were doing with that woman?" Amaranthe asked, continuing to watch the crowd. "Working?"

"Of course. She's my cover. It'd be unnatural for such a fine looking fellow as myself to be here without a woman."

"Uh huh. Find anyone who recognizes that man yet?"

"Nope, but those fobs are everywhere," he said.

"I noticed. Keep asking about the man, please."

Maldynado shrugged and ambled off to accept a drink from his lady. They disappeared into the crowd.

A gorgeous woman in a low-cut dress slithered up to Sicarius's other side. "You're doing well, aren't you?" she purred, leaning against him.

"Oh, please," Amaranthe muttered.

Sicarius, eyes focused on the game, did not acknowledge the woman. Amaranthe wondered if she worked for the house. A pretty lady to distract male customers earning too much money?

"How would you like to take your winnings and go off to have some fun?" The woman started to reach an arm around Sicarius's waist, not daunted by the number of weapons sheathed there.

Without looking at her, he caught her wrist. "Leave."

In the next breath, he pointed at the appropriate shells. The table masters revealed his correct choices and shared sighs with each other.

Sicarius pushed the woman away. She was smart enough to go.

Someone two rows back grunted and tipped forward, as if bumped hard from behind.

Amaranthe smacked Sicarius's arm. "Might be—"

A pair of swordsmen shoved people aside and launched themselves at Sicarius's back. Amaranthe had no time to draw a weapon. She threw herself into a roll at the men's legs, hoping to distract them long enough for Sicarius to take action.

A boot slammed into her ribs. One of the men toppled, landing on her. She grunted and managed to jab her elbow into his jaw as she squirmed away. He dropped his sword, and, ignoring her, jumped to his feet and lunged toward Sicarius...in time to receive a dagger in the chest.

The other man was already dead on the floor, a throwing knife protruding from his eye.

The crowd fell silent, staring at Sicarius.

Hand pressed to her side, Amaranthe climbed to her feet. Sicarius raised his eyebrows slightly. She nodded. Her ribs would hurt tomorrow, but she would be fine.

He collected his weapons and cleaned them with unhurried precision. A couple of his coin stacks had toppled. He fixed them, straightened the bills, and told the table masters, "Begin."

Bouncers came to collect the bodies. A new buzz started up in the crowd, though the people continuing to watch Sicarius play stood farther back. Good. More space made it easier to see attackers coming up.

One of the table masters flagged a bouncer down and whispered something in his ear. Also good. That ought to be the message to the boss. In the meantime, Sicarius's stacks continued to grow.

"Why have you been assassinating people all your life," Amaranthe whispered, "when you can earn this kind of money in a single night?"

Sicarius pointed out another series of winners. "Gambling houses exist to profit; they quickly get rid of people who win too much. But your plan implies you already know that."

Amaranthe smiled and put her back to the table again, wincing as she bumped her ribs. She hoped the blood staining the rug would deter further bounty hunters.

"Next time just warn me," Sicarius added. "I can handle two men without you emulating a footstool."

Heat flushed her cheeks. It had been a thoughtless move. She had martial arts and swordsmanship training; she ought not end up in a tangled jumble on the floor.

She groped for a face-saving comment. "So, I should wait until there are six men before trying to help you?"

She must have sounded stung, because he looked away from the game to meet her eyes. She thought he might say something apologetic, or at least conciliatory, but a table master called for bets—others were cashing in on his success now too—and he returned his attention to play. Amaranthe went back to standing watch.

Soon more bouncers showed up, the two from the hallway and two new ones. The one who had been most talkative gave her a why-am-I-not-surprised-this-is-about-you head shake.

"Will you come with us, sir?" he asked Sicarius, his tone far more placating than earlier.

Sicarius removed his winnings from the table. He lacked space for it all and handed half to Amaranthe. She ogled the stack of ranmyas before stuffing them into pockets and her shirt. If the house let them walk out the door with it all, she could think of a lot of gear and supplies she could purchase for the team. Sicarius might even get his steam carriage.

The bouncers led them into the rear hallway, and Amaranthe forced her thoughts back to the present. The owner would be scheming to keep Sicarius from escaping with his earnings.

The hall spawned several other halls, and they turned and turned again. Closed doors lined the walls, all with locks. She fingered the key in her pocket. Maybe she should have taken the time to go outside and talk with Akstyr.

A shirtless young man walked out of the door at the end of the hallway, his hair tousled and bite marks on his neck. He ducked his head as he passed the bouncers and hastened through a doorway.

"Guess we know why the owner is too busy to talk to folks without an appointment," Amaranthe muttered.

The talkative bouncer grunted in what might have been agreement. He knocked at the door.

"Send him in," a woman said.

Him. Guess that meant Amaranthe was going to be reduced to furniture in the conversation again.

A pair of bouncers strode in ahead of Sicarius and Amaranthe, and the two others crowded after. The office inside was spacious, but not that spacious. Elbows bumped her, and someone trod on her foot. The scent of musk oil thickened the air.

Responding to some gesture Amaranthe could not see, the four bouncers lined up against the wall, two on either side of the door. Sicarius stood so he could watch them and the woman behind the desk without putting his back to anyone. Amaranthe stepped onto a rug in the center of the office.

The woman sat in a chair, posture perfect, graying hair in a bun, and not a wrinkle marring her khaki dress. She had plucked her eyebrows out and drawn precise thin lines in their place. She was...not what Amaranthe expected, and she glanced about, wondering if someone else— someone younger—might be in the room. Maybe her assumptions about what the shirtless man had been doing in here were incorrect.

The woman smiled, and, despite her prim appearance, it did have a predatory edge. Her gaze settled on Sicarius. Her green eyes and the paleness of her skin suggested she was not a native Turgonian, but no hint of an accent clung to her words when she spoke.

"Imagine my surprise," she said, "at having the empire's most wanted assassin stroll into my humble establishment tonight." She surveyed Amaranthe, though no recognition sparked in those eyes, and she focused on Sicarius again. "I wouldn't think you'd frequent such busy venues."

"We came specifically to talk to you," Amaranthe said. "Ms...?"

"Ellaya," the woman said.

"Makes Sunshine?" Sicarius asked.

Amaranthe crinkled her brow at his response.

The woman smiled, showing teeth this time. "Yes, that is the name my mother gave me. How rare to find someone here who understands Mangdorian. But then...I shouldn't be surprised. They must have taught you some before they sent you to my country."

Amaranthe watched Sicarius for a reaction, though she should have known he would give nothing away. Did he know what the woman was talking about?

"You didn't expect me to know about that, did you?" Ellaya asked, though she must have been guessing, since Sicarius's face never changed. "The canaries have been chirping in this dreary coal mine of a city. It seems you were the one to wrong my people years ago, and now you're here, attempting to alleviate my coffers of hard-won coin."

"We simply wished to gain a meeting with you," Amaranthe said, putting aside the mystery of Sicarius's past in Mangdoria in favor of the current mission. "It seemed a more expedient way than others."

"Then you're willing to leave the coin you've won?"

Amaranthe hesitated. They could use that money. Ellaya had been polite thus far—she must respect Sicarius's reputation enough not to make careless threats—but that might not hold out if she realized they meant to leave with the money.

"I don't suppose you'd like to discuss the purpose of this?" Amaranthe dangled the key fob and thumbed it so it glowed.

"No. Do you intend to walk out with the coin, or not?"

"I won it abiding by the rules of the game," Sicarius said.

The bouncers shifted and eyed each other uneasily.

"Perhaps we could reach an arrangement," Amaranthe said. "We could use that money, but you're reluctant to let a winner walk out with so much. That's understandable. You need something equally valuable

in exchange. Perhaps Sicarius could spend the evening going over the games with you, suggesting improvements so even people with his sharp eyes would have difficulty winning often."

And while Sicarius was wandering around, advising Ellaya and the bouncers, perhaps nobody would pay attention to Amaranthe, and she could explore the premises.

Ellaya tilted her head, considering Sicarius. "Did you cheat or did you actually win all those games?"

"There was no need to cheat," he said.

"Hm."

Amaranthe nodded. *Hm* was promising. "Surely, the best way to improve your games to a level where you can ensure the house always comes out on top would be to employ someone who can beat them."

"Possibly."

"And," Amaranthe went on, "as you can guess from his reputation, Sicarius is a master of entering establishments undetected. Perhaps if you're willing to let him walk out with his winnings, he could survey your security and advise you on improvements."

Sicarius's gaze settled on Amaranthe. Yes, she was volunteering him for a lot of stuff, especially considering he had won the money without violating any rules, but she figured he knew her well enough to guess her motives.

"Interesting." Ellaya pushed her chair away from the desk, stood, clasped her hands behind her back, and strolled to a bookcase. She picked up a feather duster and ran it over a spotless shelf. Moments ticked past before she turned to face them again. "Interesting, but I don't want a one-time consultation. Advisement on the games would be helpful, but I could use you for ongoing security, protection, and...other tasks." Her eyes bored into Sicarius. "I want you full time."

"Uhm." Amaranthe raised a finger. "That's not the offer."

"How much is she paying you?" Ellaya pointed her nose in Amaranthe's direction and sniffed haughtily. "I can double it."

Amaranthe dismissed her initial objection and lowered her finger. Playing along should not hurt.

"Perhaps..." She scuffed the carpet with her boot and pretended to mull. "Perhaps you should consider the offer."

Sicarius turned an unfriendly stare Amaranthe's direction, letting her know he did not care to play along. Dead ancestors knew he was not, for all his skills, a good actor. She had found that out before, but if he could buy her even a half hour, the ploy could prove beneficial. She ignored his glare and focused on Ellaya.

The woman arched her eyebrows. "You'd let him go so easily?"

"I haven't been able to afford to pay him much, and Sicarius is too good to be working with our scruffy group anyway." She did nothing so obvious as tap the pocket where the key rested, but she hoped he gathered that she wanted him to keep Ellaya busy so she could snoop.

"Make your offer," Sicarius told Ellaya.

"Happy to." The woman opened a file and withdrew a pen and paper. "Let's go over the expected duties first." She flicked a dismissive hand toward Amaranthe. "You're no longer needed, child."

Amaranthe walked out. The bouncers stayed inside, no doubt viewing Sicarius as the prime threat to their boss. Perfect.

She slipped the key out of her pocket. Simple and bronze, it appeared little different from hundreds of others. The same logo that marked the key fobs was etched in one side. She rubbed it and it glowed softly. Ah.

Amaranthe padded down the hall. She eased a couple of doors open and found dark offices inside. Others were locked, but her key did not fit the holes. She wound deeper into the maze of hallways.

She tried a door near an intersection, pushing it open as retching sounds came from inside. She halted. A bouncer hunched over a washout, clutching his stomach. Fortunately, his heaving kept him from noticing her. She shut the door again and mulled as she continued forward. Checking every room might not be feasible, and her luck probably wouldn't hold—sooner or later she would run into someone and her spying hour would be up.

A clank came from behind her—a trap door in the floor being thrown open.

Amaranthe jumped around the corner and slipped through an open door opposite the retching bouncer. The cluttered shelves of a storage room rose around her. She left the door cracked and peeped out.

"That deposit ought to even things out," a woman's voice said.

A man laughed. "Don't worry. Mrs. Ell will get that blond bub's money back."

The pair turned into Amaranthe's hallway and strode past.

"True, he went in the back not out the front. Probably already dead."

"Or in her bed."

The two shared laughter.

The conversation continued, but distance muffled the words. When the hallway grew silent, Amaranthe headed straight for the trap door. The pattern of the tiles hid the cracks, but knowing where to look made it discernible. She found a slight gap, enough to wedge her knife into, and pulled the door open.

A ladder stretched down into blackness.

She tapped one of the gas lamps on the hallway walls, but they were permanent fixtures. Aware of time passing, she ran back to the storage closet and dug around until she found kerosene and lanterns. A few moments later, she slipped down the ladder, pulling the door shut over her head.

A short hall stretched both directions at the bottom. Identical steel vault doors waited at each end. Amaranthe eyed the key in her hand, doubting it would open either. The existence of two doors piqued her interest, though, and she went to investigate. One would doubtlessly hold funds. What about the other?

The doors had wheels instead of knobs. She tried one on the chance the employees had left it open, but it did not budge. To her surprise, a sliver in the center looked like a keyhole.

Her key went in, and a pulse of red light flashed. Amaranthe nearly dropped the lantern in surprise. Despite the red glow, the key did not turn. She tried the wheel, but it did not move.

"Huh," she muttered.

Amaranthe jogged to the other vault door. Her key slid into an identical hole. This time a pale blue light flashed. Red, fail, blue, pass? She applied pressure, and the key turned in the lock.

In the stillness of the subterranean hall, she felt her heart thumping against her ribs.

The wheel turned.

She hesitated before trying to open the door. If magic controlled the locking system, might not some otherworldly trap wait inside as well? Or was it presumed that someone with a key had a right to go in? Akstyr would not have handed it to her if he thought she would get herself killed. Probably.

Amaranthe pulled on the wheel. She had to bend her legs and lean away from the six-inch-wide door to get it to open, but it moved silently on oiled hinges. Soft clanks came from within.

Inside lay an eight-foot-by-eight-foot vault dominated by a contraption that reminded her vaguely of a steam loom with spinning belts and a large flywheel. No visible furnace or boiler powered the machinery, but a fist-sized red orb was bolted to the top where it glowed softly. A small pedestal up front held a round indention the size of one of the key fobs. Maybe this machine made them. That defied what little she knew about magic though. Only a trained Maker ought to be able to craft imbued objects.

She dug out the fob and snugged it into the indention. The orb pulsed.

"Adner Farr. Government employee, Waterton Dam." It was Ellaya's voice, her tone utterly bored. "Salary five-thousand ranmyas a year. Saved funds, meager. Return compulsion stored."

Amaranthe had never heard of Waterton Dam. She waited for more, but the recitation was complete.

"Maybe that's information stored in the key fob," she guessed. "Maybe they're individualized for each person, a quick way to look up how much money people can spend here." Footsteps sounded overhead, someone walking down the hallway. "And maybe I should stop talking to myself and get out of here," she finished.

A draft whispered against her cheek. The flame in her lantern wavered. She spun as the massive door thumped shut.

She cursed and lunged for it. Too late. It did not move.

CHAPTER 7

BACK AT THE PUMPING HOUSE, BOOKS SAT IN THE communal sleeping area while he surveyed the maps from the real estate library. His head throbbed, his body ached, and fresh scabs threatened to reopen every time he moved. He drank from a jug of apple juice, wishing for apple brandy instead. Amaranthe must have said something to the others, for nobody ever offered him alcohol or left any out.

He stole a couple of pillows from Maldynado's sleeping area, the only one in the tiny room that had such luxuries. Maldynado had procured a straw bed, sheets, and furs for himself. Perhaps Books should have done the same. Even without injuries, he was getting too old to sleep on the floor. More than once, Amaranthe had offered him the closet-sized caretaker's room, which had actual furnishings: a washout, a hammock, and a clothes trunk. She probably would not mind sleeping on the floor, but he would feel like an ungentlemanly lout if he accepted the trade.

Besides, Sicarius had oozed disapproval at the idea, something about leaders not sharing quarters with the lowly peons they led. He, of course, slept elsewhere. Books did not know where, nor did he care.

Before they parted ways, he had made the mistake of thanking Sicarius for helping him in the library. Sicarius's version of "you're welcome" had been a lecture on inattentiveness and the foolishness of divulging information to strangers. It was not as if Books had told Vonsha any great secrets. He had been too busy blurting inanities.

Would he ever see her again? If Vonsha was a warrior caste woman, the enforcers would have taken her home and brought in a doctor. He should have found out where she lived so he could check up. Maybe he could go under the guise of sharing the maps with her.

The maps he was supposed to be studying. He grabbed paper and a pencil to make notes, but Basilard walked in before Books made much progress. He carried skewers of meat, and the scent of rosemary wafted in with him.

Basilard frowned at the candles, the map, and the fact Books was not lying down.

"Couldn't sleep," Books said. "Are you sharing that?"

Basilard handed him the skewers, which bulged with grilled lamb, onion, and carrots. Books's mouth watered before he sank his teeth in. Basilard sat cross-legged on the other side of the maps.

"Thank you." Books wiped juices from his chin and wondered if he should say more.

Though Basilard did not make him as uncomfortable as Sicarius, he had not spent much time with the man and did not fancy he shared any interests with a former pit fighter. Still, the fact that he could cook made Books wonder what depths might lie beneath his silent facade.

Basilard pointed at Irator's Tooth Valley on the map and flicked a few hand signs: *Headwater city?*

"Uhm. What?"

Water, Basilard signed, then pointed at the city and raised his eyebrows.

"Does that water feed the city? Is that what you're asking?"

Basilard nodded.

"Ah, you need more verbs in your language."

A wistful expression crossed Basilard's face. *Hunting signs.*

"The language is only for hunting?"

Yes. Basilard mimicked parting reeds, peering at prey, and lifting a finger to his lips.

"A hand code developed for use on the hunt when silence is required," Books said, "but nothing more. I see. You could always add to it, and we'd learn. The Kyatt Islands have a sign language like that; it's used by deaf people."

Basilard cocked his head as Books spoke, then tapped a thoughtful finger to his lips.

"To answer your original question, no, the city gets its water from the Tork River, which originates..." Books stopped.

Basilard was shaking his head. He grabbed a pencil and scribbled for a few minutes. Books read the note and learned the details of Amaranthe's suspicions about the aqueduct.

"That's...interesting." Books tapped the map. "But this river flows past fifty miles north of the city. It empties into the Maiden Lake, the first in the Chain Lakes of which we are a part." He waved in the general direction of their body of water.

Basilard traced the river with a finger, as if to double-check. He signed, *Supply city*, then shrugged.

"It could supply the city if the infrastructure was there?"

Basilard nodded. He touched his chest and pointed to the valley in the mountains.

"You've been there?"

A nod.

"And seen the river?"

Yes. Basilard stretched his arms wide.

"And it's large. Where are you from, Basilard?" Books should have asked long before. He had always found the scars off-putting and never bothered to converse with the man outside of work.

Basilard pointed into the mountains north of the pass.

"Mangdoria?"

Yes.

"Really. An offshoot of the Kendorians. When my people conquered their way inland hundreds of years ago, the natives who weren't assimilated, went east and north while the Kendorians went south, right? And it wasn't race that determined the distinction, but religion. Your people believe in one god, a benevolent deity that says pacifism is preferable to war." Books eyed the scars crisscrossing Basilard's shaven head.

Basilard looked away. Sadness, or maybe guilt, lurked in his blue eyes.

Best to shift back to the problem. "But you decided to come here at one point, and you passed through the mountains and saw this river."

Snared, Basilard signed.

"You were? By slavers?"

Yes.

"Ah, but you're free now. Why not go home?"

Basilard hesitated, then shook his head.

"Nothing to return to? No family?"

Another head shake. He lifted his hands, hesitated, then tapped his chest and signed. *Female.*

"You have a wife?"

No. Dead. Small female.

"*Daughter?*" Books stared. When Basilard nodded, Books went on: "Why? Why wouldn't you go back? How old is she?"

Basilard closed his eyes for a moment, and Books wondered how long he had been a slave. Had there been owners before Larocka? So much for the practice being outlawed in the empire.

Ten, Basilard signed. *Yes, ten now.*

"Don't you want to see her again?" Thoughts of Enis flooded Books's mind. What he wouldn't give to see his son again.... To live those fatal moments over and this time save Enis. How could Basilard *not* return to a daughter?

See her, yes, Basilard sighed. *Her see me…no.*

"Why?"

Basilard pointed to the sky, then to his scars, then shook his head sadly.

Books puzzled over his meaning. Basilard scrawled on the page: *God requires peace.*

Understanding dawned, and Books frowned, thinking of what the man must be going through. "Your people are pacifists, but you've killed."

Basilard's chin drooped to his chest.

"A lot." Books raked his fingers through his hair, thinking of what he knew of the Mangdorian religion. Hell. They believed in an eternal hell for those who committed acts of violence. He wondered if Amaranthe knew Basilard's story. He remembered how she had swayed Basilard to let them go from the cell in Larocka's basement by seeming to read his persona and voicing his guilt. Had she guessed at some of Basilard's torment even then? "You had to kill to survive, didn't you? You had little choice."

The pencil wrote: *Always a choice.*

"Death isn't much of a choice." Books grabbed the jug and took a deep swig, again missing the days of drinks stronger than apple juice. "You know, you could convert to the Turgonian 'religion.'"

Basilard's eyebrow twitched. *Atheism?*

"Absolutely. There's no heaven, but there's no hell either. It's all about what you do in this life. Of course, a lot of folks still believe ancestor spirits float among us and are available for consultation. I've noticed these spirits tend to give the advice the living want to hear. Either way, it sounds better than having one's soul condemned for eternity."

Heathen, Basilard wrote.

Books chuckled and handed him the jug. "We've been called much worse by those we conquered. And traded with. And talked to. Are you sure you don't want to return to your homeland?"

After a deep swig of his own, Basilard wrote, *Perhaps someday. When we've...mattered. Better empire. No illegal slavery.*

Books smiled. So Amaranthe had convinced him to become a crusader too.

Books showed Basilard the plat map, thinking he might prefer a distraction. "This is the lot that was on that sheet of paper that came from the dead woman's body. It overlooks this river. Do you remember this land, by chance?"

Basilard lifted his eyes in thought. *Trees, rocks, hills, snow.*

"You just described the entire mountain range."

Maybe goat.

"So, nothing distinctive there." Books let his finger stray across the enormous plots of land. Though the topography map showed much of the area was steep and inaccessible, ore and lumber could mean a lot of wealth. Vonsha had not struck him as someone swathed in riches though. "You said trees. Was there a lot of timber up there?"

Basilard made a circle with his fingers.

"Small trees? New growth?"

A nod.

"So, it's already been logged. That's not surprising, since there's a river and road running through the valley."

Basilard pointed at the maps, at Books, and shrugged.

"You're wondering if there's a purpose to my rambling? Well, I'm trying to figure out what's interesting about this land. Someone hired that appraiser we found in the aqueduct, then slit her throat after she delivered her information. Presumably there's something to hide up there. Though—" Books fished out the original scrap of paper, "—while

this seems like a lot of money to me, it's not enough to imply there's anything valuable on the land."

Dead men? Gashes?

"Yes, I'm curious about the dead workers too. I have a feeling we're going to end up taking a trip soon."

Basilard yawned and pointed to his own sleeping area.

"I guess that's enough research for tonight." Books blew out the candles and lay down with a groan. He wondered if the others had found anything interesting in the gambling house.

* * * * *

For the seventh time, Amaranthe tried the door. For the seventh time, it did not move. She pried at the hinges, probed the ceiling, and peered into every corner of the unimaginative vault, but no escape options presented themselves. By now, it felt as if days had passed, though it had probably only been an hour.

She nibbled on a thumbnail and tried to tell herself she had no reason to worry. "Herself" did not listen, choosing instead to contemplate the worst.

Since this was not the money vault, no one would come in at the end of the night to deposit earnings. For all she knew, this contraption was only checked once a week. She had no food or water, and the air was probably limited. Worse, she had to pee.

She put her back to the door and studied the machine again. The chest-high contraption took up most of the space in the cramped vault. It clanked and whirred, oblivious to her presence. Maybe if she broke it, someone would sense a problem and come check on it. That would open the door, but it would also get her captured. Most likely by someone irritated she had busted the machine.

Still…

What other options did she have?

She pulled out her short sword and utility knife and debated whether finesse or brute force would be best for the task. Too bad she did not have a pistol. Or maybe not. She eyed the hard walls and pictured a pistol ball ricocheting everywhere.

Sword in hand, she stalked around the machine, searching for weaknesses. The glowing orb caught her eye. If it powered the machine, destroying it should halt everything. Of course, the orb might throw off some magical surge of energy that would electrocute her faster than a lightning bolt...

"Why do I get myself into these situations?" she muttered.

After taking a deep breath, she gripped the sword in both hands, raised her arms above her head, and slammed the tip into the orb.

Amaranthe expected it to shatter like glass or repel her blade like metal. Instead the sword sank in slowly, as if through dense mud, and the orb deflated, collapsing in on itself. The magical light faded, leaving her lantern as the only illumination. Machinery whined and ground to a halt. Silence filled the vault.

Until the alarm went off.

The sound, something between an alley cat's yowl and a baby's scream, reverberated from the walls and hammered Amaranthe's eardrums. Footsteps pounded through the hallway overhead.

She sucked in her belly to slide past the machine, crouched behind it, and cut off the lantern. Scrapes sounded on the other side of the door. Amaranthe gripped her sword, though she hoped to hide and slip out during the confusion.

The door swung open. Keeping her head low, she peered around the corner of the machine. Light from the hallway silhouetted two figures and threw their shadows across the floor. Maybe she would get lucky and one would be Sicarius.

"Someone's in here." It was Ellaya's voice.

So much for hiding.

"Get the others!"

Amaranthe sprang. She landed on top of the machine and leaped between Ellaya and a bouncer holding a pistol. Amaranthe shouldered the woman into the door, even as she slashed at the man. Her intention was not to do major damage, but the bouncer lifted an arm in a hasty block, and her blade sliced through clothing and flesh. He roared and dropped the pistol.

Amaranthe grabbed it and ran past them. The bouncer lunged for her but clipped Ellaya, and his fingers only brushed Amaranthe's shirt. She jammed her sword into its sheath and sprang up the ladder.

She had to stop at the top to fiddle with the trapdoor latch. A hand clasped her ankle. The bouncer. She leveled the pistol at him, pointing it between his eyes. He released her.

Amaranthe threw the trapdoor open. She sprinted down the hallways and darted between the two bouncers guarding the entrance to the back rooms. One let out a startled yell and reached for her, but he was too slow.

In the crowded gambling room, Amaranthe's size was an advantage. She ducked and dodged, crawling under a table at one point, while the larger men struggled through the patrons.

"Crazy woman with a pistol!" someone shouted.

"Where?" a bouncer called.

"Get her!"

"There. She's running for the—oomph!"

Amaranthe wondered if that was Maldynado, doing his bit to help. Or had he left long ago? And where *was* Sicarius?

She ducked arms stretching to grab her. One caught her hood and nearly tore her jacket off. She tugged away, seams ripping. Only in the empire would people attack someone with a pistol instead of throwing themselves to the floor.

The path cleared as Amaranthe neared the entrance, and she thought she might escape without shooting anyone. The double doors stood open, the night street stretching beyond, but two bouncers blocked the exit. With bare muscled arms that blacksmiths would have envied, the men appeared strong enough to rip someone's head off with their hands—and stupid enough not to move at the sight of a firearm.

A wise woman would have stopped and tried to find another way out. Amaranthe sprinted toward them, pistol raised. They saw the weapon and crouched, but did not move from the doorway.

One slipped a hand into his belt. Steel glinted. A throwing star spun toward Amaranthe.

She ducked but kept running. Movement blurred at the corner of her eye. Someone barreled toward her from the side, diving for her legs. She leaped over the flying bouncer. He missed his grab and skidded into the crowd.

Another ten feet, and she would crash into the men blocking the door. The one with the throwing stars reached for a second.

Amaranthe fired the pistol, aiming at the wall behind his head. Her ball grazed his ear, but he only roared. She threw the pistol at his face. While he batted it away, she angled to his side, choosing to go around him instead of between the two. He grabbed for her, but she shifted her weight to the outside foot and launched a sidekick into his knee.

His leg crumpled, and he stumbled against his comrade.

Amaranthe raced out the door. Mist thickened the air, and the street traffic had thinned. That meant fewer people to hide her escape, so she did not slow down. Sweat plastered her clothes to her body, and strands of hair that had torn free from her bun whipped in her eyes.

Halfway to the main street, a twang sounded behind her. A crossbow quarrel skipped off the concrete at her feet.

She urged her legs to greater speed. Her breath rasped her in ears. A few more paces, and she would reach the intersection where she could duck around the corner and—she hoped—disappear.

"Down," a familiar voice ordered from ahead.

Amaranthe threw herself into a roll. Another crossbow quarrel zipped over her and clanged off a streetlamp.

She came up running and lunged around the corner. She almost crashed into Sicarius. He sidestepped to avoid her and hurled something with a burning fuse. It spun down the alley and clattered onto the concrete.

Amaranthe kept running and did not see the result. A moment later, coughs and curses came from the dead-end street.

Sicarius fell in beside her and they ran several blocks, turning a few times before slowing.

"Smoke bomb?" Amaranthe sucked in a few deep gulps of air, but her breathing returned to normal quickly. She was glad for all the training they did, or she would likely be on the ground wheezing after that long sprint.

"An acrid one, yes." Sicarius gave her a sidelong look. "I'd almost gone back to the hideout. What were you doing in there so long?"

"Snooping. Getting trapped. Getting found. Running. Evading. It was quite the full evening."

"I see."

"Have you heard of Waterton Dam?"

"No."

"I'll ask Books. I'm not sure if Ellaya is involved with those murdered people or not. All I know for sure is that she's storing people's personal information in those fobs, and there was something about a 'return compulsion.' Any idea about that? A magical way to coerce people to come back to the same gambling house and spend money again and again?"

"Possibly."

"Also, I may have done some physical damage to a magical device, which might leave Ellaya rather peeved at me."

"Might?"

"All right, it's a high probability."

"That the device is damaged? Or that Ellaya is peeved at you?"

"Yes." She smirked at him.

Footfalls slapped the concrete behind them. A boy dressed in rags scurried up to them.

"Ma'am." Though he could not have been older than eight, he thumped his fist to his chest in a soldier's salute and lifted his chin. "I have a very important message for you."

"Oh?" she replied.

The seriousness with which he took his delivery task was somewhat diminished by the fact that his "message" was scribbled on the back of an apple taffy wrapper.

Nobody recognized the dead bloke, despite my pinpoint description. Akstyr got beat up. Taking him to The Pirates' Plunder for a night of relaxation. Will meet at the hideout at daybreak. Or nine. Or noonish.
~M

"The Pirates' Plunder is a brothel, isn't it?" Amaranthe asked Sicarius.

"Yes."

"Relaxation. Right."

The boy cleared his throat. "The mister who told me to deliver this said you'd give me a tip."

"That mister is a pretty generous fellow," Amaranthe said, though she fished in her pocket for a coin, "and I'd be shocked if he hadn't already given you that tip."

The boy shifted his weight and studied the street. "Well, I did have to wait longer than he said I would…."

"Ah, of course. Your patience is admirable." Amaranthe tossed the coin to the boy.

He jogged away.

"Shall we check on Books?" Amaranthe asked. She wanted to have a powwow with Books *and* Sicarius, to see if they could figure out if all these events were connected. Basilard would be there, too, and he might offer some insight on Ellaya, since they were both Mangdorian. That reminded her....

"I don't suppose you'd like to tell me what that woman was talking about when she brought up Mangdoria?"

"No," Sicarius said.

Amaranthe clawed through her memories, trying to think of Mangdorian atrocities Sicarius might have caused, but it was such a minor nation—small scattered tribes rather than anything with a central government—that it rarely made it into the imperial newspapers. "Can you at least tell me if it's something that'll cause a...problem if Basilard finds out about it?" she asked.

He did not answer.

"Aren't we to the point in our relationship where you feel you can tell me some of your secrets?"

"That didn't go well last time," he said, voice hard.

Amaranthe frowned. He was right about that. She ought not to pry. Yet, if Sicarius had done something to irk Mangdorians in general, and Basilard learned of it, she could end up with a rift in her group. Or worse.

Sicarius handed her a folded piece of paper. "I found this in the woman's desk drawer."

"You snooped? Excellent, excellent." She veered toward a gas lamp. "I thought you might find such tasks beneath you."

"The acquisition of information is a job I've performed frequently."

"When you say it like that, it almost sounds noble."

Sicarius remained in the shadows while Amaranthe held the page to the light. Though the hour had grown late, pedestrians were still walking in pairs and groups. Most were boisterous with drink, but she had best not spend too long with her face limned by lamplight.

"We thank you for putting us in contact with the Maker," she read. "Please accept our protection, free of charge, for the next year. After that time, additional coverage may be purchased at the rate of ten percent of your net profits."

Amaranthe lowered the page and joined Sicarius in the shadows.

"You read it?" she asked.

"Yes."

"Who could provide that kind of protection? Forge?"

"Many organizations could, gangs included." Sicarius started walking.

Amaranthe caught his arm. "If it *is* Forge, this could mean they have an inventor who can make magic things, right? That's what a Maker does, isn't it? Create devices like the one I may have possibly—probably—damaged. What do you think?"

"That I'm tired of standing in an alley." He pulled his arm away and strode forward, not bothering to see if she followed.

Surprised by his abrupt dismissal, Amaranthe ran to catch up. "Any reason you're being stiffer and snippier than usual tonight?"

"Next time you need someone to distract a woman while you snoop, Maldynado would be a better bet," Sicarius said.

Ah, so that's what he was sour about. Ellaya might appear mature and prim, but it seemed Amaranthe's first impression had been right, and she had a healthy...appetite. Sicarius had no trouble rebuffing people—obviously—but he had probably had to humor the old woman to buy time for Amaranthe to explore. Well, there were worse things in the world. He would get over it.

"Sorry, but Maldynado couldn't have won the shell game over and over," Amaranthe said. "Besides, I'm not sure he would have stirred that woman's imagination."

"He's far prettier than I."

"Oh, he's gorgeous. But attainable. Your aloofness and your reputation make you seem unattainable." She laughed to herself, not sure why she'd used the word "seem." "Some women like a challenge."

She wriggled her eyebrows, hoping for...she did not know what exactly. For him to ask if she was one of those women? Or perhaps to state he *wasn't* unattainable?

Sicarius kept walking.

CHAPTER 8

A S DAWN TURNED THE ALLEYS FROM BLACK TO
dark gray, Amaranthe jogged the last few blocks of the
miles-long route. Usually Sicarius picked their path, and the
rest of the men ran with them, but he had not shown up that morning.
Books was recovering from his wounds, and Basilard had complained
of a stomach bug. Not surprisingly, Maldynado and Akstyr had yet to
return from The Pirates' Plunder.

Amaranthe made sure nobody was following her, then trotted
through another alley, up a concrete staircase, and into a door she'd left
unlocked. She slipped past the pipes and control valves of the above-
ground portion of the pumping station, not expecting anyone inside this
early.

The sound of voices made her halt.

"...nothing wrong with the controls, my lord. I assure you, we've a
man who works here day in and day out. I'd have heard if there was a
problem."

Amaranthe recognized the voice; it was the supervisor who had
hired Books. He oversaw the utilities building for the industrial area
and rarely visited the pumping house.

"Something's going on," a second man said. "You figure out if there
are rusted pipes or malfunctioning machines, or I'll send a private company in with the expense taken out of your salary."

Footsteps thudded on concrete—the men heading for the door
through which Amaranthe had entered.

She squeezed between a fat pipe and the wall, hoping the shadows
hid her. Little light came in through the windows yet.

"I know how to do my job, my lord," the supervisor said. "If something strange is going on, it has nothing to do with my machinery."

The men passed within a few feet of her. Amaranthe held her breath. The supervisor carried a lantern, but it did not illuminate the face of the other man. He was well-dressed in slacks and a frock coat, as one would expect from the warrior caste. The lord who oversaw the public works?

The door opened, then clanged shut. Amaranthe waited, not sure if both had left, but no more footsteps sounded. She was tempted to follow them outside to see if she could hear more of the conversation, but dawn's light would make staying close difficult on the open streets.

She eased out of hiding and slipped through the control room to the access shaft in the back of the pumping house.

She wondered what had come up to bring the public works supervisor here. The corpses? After considering several options, she had finagled her team into taking the bodies of the appraiser and the workers to another part of the aqueducts. She had sent a note to Enforcer Headquarters in hopes they could be identified and their families informed. But this sounded like something unrelated to the deaths.

When Amaranthe reached the lower level where she and the men stayed, the sound of someone retching waylaid her thoughts. Basilard?

Frowning, she wound through passages toward the source. Maldynado hunkered over the washout, sides heaving, face pale.

"Are you...uhm?" Amaranthe stopped herself from saying "all right," since clearly he was not.

Maldynado issued a final heave and sank back against the wall. "Just regretting the night's activities."

"You're back earlier than I expected."

"I was too miserable to stay." He dragged a sleeve across his mouth and rubbed his face. "I didn't think I was imbibing that deeply. I even drank a bunch of water, figuring Sicarius might come yank us out of bed before dawn for some of his horrible exercises. I—" He lifted a hand, cheeks bulging out, and returned to his previous activity.

Amaranthe backed away. "Let me know if you need anything."

Strange, she had seen Maldynado hung over, but not sick like this. If Basilard also felt poorly, and he had not been drinking, some bug must be about.

Amaranthe stopped to grab a jug of apple juice, then headed past the boiler room, through the following door, and into a cramped space she called, for lack of an official-sounding name, the big pipe place. Most of the chamber lay underground, but shafts of light angled through windows high on one wall. Sicarius's latest sleeping spot lay in an elevated, dark corner atop a round cap that appeared as uncomfortable as a blanket on the concrete floor. Of course, he could see people coming from the perch. And he, unlike she, apparently had the unconscious wherewithal not to roll off in the middle of the night and crash to the floor.

"Sicarius?" she asked.

When no answer came from the depths, she clambered across the fat pipe leading to his spot, an act that would have been easier if she left the jug behind, but if he *was* there and also sick, he might like a drink. She struggled to imagine him ill. If he had ever so much as sneezed in front of her, she could not remember it. Of course, he might be out, skulking around the city for his own reasons. He did that from time to time, but he always showed up for morning training.

"Sicarius, are you there, or am I crawling up here for no reason?" Her knee cracked against a wheel for regulating water flow, and she grimaced. "For no reason except to bruise myself, that is."

Amaranthe hopped off the pipe and onto wooden scaffolding left against the wall after some project. From there she could climb to Sicarius's niche.

"I'm here." His voice gave little away—as usual.

"Are you sick too?" This close, she could make out his supine form on the wide pipe cap. "I promise I won't run out and tell your enemies you're an easy mark right now if you admit you have the flu," she said.

Wood cracked at Amaranthe's feet. The hilt of his black knife quivered, the tip a centimeter from her big toe. His way of saying he was not an easy mark, sick or not. She hoped there was not more of a message behind the flung weapon than that, but it sent an uneasy chill down her spine. A reminder that, though he seemed to tolerate more from her than most, she might be unwise to presume he found her teasing amusing.

Out of a sense of stubbornness, or maybe some delusion it would impress him, Amaranthe opted for bravado rather than outward unease—or an apology. She tugged the blade free and held it up. "You dropped this."

His soft exhalation might have been a snort.

The strange black metal of the knife seemed to swallow the wan light coming through the window above. He had never explained where

he had acquired it or what it was made from. She shuffled over and laid it next to him.

"Do you want some apple juice?" She hefted the jug.

"No."

"You're probably not that practiced at being sick, but the doctors say you're supposed to drink liquids."

"Bring water then. That's too sweet."

"You say that about everything that tastes good," Amaranthe said. "Maybe the reason you're sick is that you don't eat anything except fish, meat, and vegetables, and all you ever drink is water. You—" She halted as a new thought ricocheted through her head. "Water. Is that it?"

Sicarius issued an inquisitive grunt.

"When did you start feeling sick?" she asked.

"Last night."

He *had* been snippier than usual the night before, and maybe not just because of Ellaya's interests.

"You drink a lot of water," Amaranthe said. "Where'd you drink yesterday? The city fountains?"

"Yes, and the tap here."

"Maldynado's sick, too, and he said he drank a lot of water. I feel fine." She closed her eyes, thinking about what she had consumed the previous day. "I had water yesterday morning, but switched to a pitcher of tea in the afternoon—tea I made the day before." Was it possible the public works lord had come because of a complaint about water? Were other people in the city ill? Maybe it had been the water itself Akstyr had sensed down in the tunnels. Some kind of magical poison? "I have to talk to the others."

Amaranthe started to turn away, eager to check her hypothesis, but she paused, remembering Sicarius probably felt miserable. She touched his shoulder.

"Can I get you anything? Milk? Tea?"

"I require nothing," Sicarius said.

Of course not. He had probably never accepted help from anyone in his life. "You know," Amaranthe said, "you've saved my life countless times. I owe you a lot, and I certainly wouldn't mind taking care of you while you're sick."

"Go solve your mystery." Sicarius rolled onto his side, turning his back to her.

Amaranthe sighed and left to talk to the others.

* * * * *

Books finished his glass of milk and bent over a three-day-old copy of *The Gazette*. More newspapers, those from underground presses as well as government-approved ones, scattered the desk. He scribbled notes onto a piece of paper, cursing when his pencil pierced the page, thanks to a knot hole beneath.

The wood plank balanced on crates made a poor desk, and the lack of windows left him grumbling about the lamp's weak illumination, but at least he had the boiler room to himself while the other men moaned and bellyached in the sleeping area. Though not Sicarius, of course. He would never deign to wallow in communal misery.

Amaranthe walked in, a fresh newspaper tucked under her arm. "How's it going?"

"How's it going? Last night, I was nearly blown up, then I was attacked by a loon with a club, and then I almost smacked into a pile of enforcers, and finally I twisted my ankle following Sicarius out a window. Today I have a monstrous headache, not to mention scabs in places that should never be exposed to violent acts. Also, at some point, I tripped and stubbed my toe against the end of my boot. The nail is turning purple. I think it may fall off."

She pointed at the desk. "I meant the research."

"Oh." His cheeks warmed. "The research is fine. I'm your researcher extraordinaire. You know that. Why else would you have given me this pile of work?"

Someone else would have made a snide comment, pointing out he was the only other person in the group who hadn't been drinking water and wasn't sick, but she simply patted his shoulder and said, "Because you can handle it."

He shuffled through his notes. "I haven't found anything about the water in these papers, or remote lots in the mountains, but there are a lot of incidents of vandalism and violence toward the foreigners who have set up shop here in the last few months." He paused at the sound

of rustling papers. Amaranthe was tidying the desk, though she watched him as she did it, maybe not aware of her busy hands. "These problems aren't all that surprising," Books went on, "but they do seem to be escalating. More incidents in the last couple of weeks than in the previous months combined."

"Interesting." Amaranthe finished straightening the papers, swept pencil shavings into her hand, and carried them to the furnace for disposal. "The question is, does this tie in with the water problems, or are we looking at two mysteries?"

"You don't look daunted by the possibility."

"More problems, more work. We need to focus on the water issue though. It's more of an...opportunity. More of a chance for us to get noticed if we solve the problem." She laid the morning's newspaper on the newly tidied desk.

The front page headline of *The Gazette* screamed: THOUSANDS ILL; EPIDEMIC COMES TO CITY.

"Ah, I see." Books skimmed the article. "No mention of the water."

"My guess could be incorrect, or maybe they hadn't figured out the connection when the paper was put together."

"Or they may know and not want people to burst into hysterics," Books said. "As much as this city enjoys its juice, brandy, and wine, it wouldn't take long to run out of water alternatives and for people to start hoarding. Theft and fights would break out. It could be utter chaos."

"The soldiers in Fort Urgot would impose martial law before complete pandemonium broke out, but, yes, this represents a massive problem." She bounced on her toes and smiled.

"Good birthday present, eh?"

"Well, I don't wish people to be sick, especially our own men."

"But..."

"But, yes, this is a gift. Maybe. If we're able to make use of it."

"You have something in mind?" Books asked. "A journey into the mountains to investigate the source?"

"That *would* be a good idea, but we're not sure where that source is yet. I think another trip is in order first." She nodded at him. "And you're the perfect person to go on it."

"A mission for just the two of us?" The incident at Mitsy's Maze— where he had proven completely ineffectual in a crisis—still haunted him. Though their daily training had improved his fitness and combat skills over the last couple of months, he worried how he would react in another desperate situation.

"More like an errand," Amaranthe reassured him. "I want to seek out your new lady friend and have a chat."

"Lady friend?" he asked casually, though a tingle of anticipation fluttered through his belly at the thought of Vonsha.

"Aren't you wondering how she's doing after the explosion? And why there was an explosion to start with? Was she the target? Were you the target? Would anyone who was researching that spot in the mountains have been targeted? Is it all tied in with this new illness? That lot is on a river, maybe a river that feeds into the city's water supply. I want to know what she knows."

"She didn't tell me where she lives."

Amaranthe pointed at the paper stacks. "I thought you were a researcher extraordinaire."

He rubbed his lips. "That *is* true...."

"You find out. I'll check the men and see what my new disguise looks like—Maldynado picked it up before heading to The Pirates' Plunder last night."

"This should be good," Books murmured as she walked out.

* * * * *

A breeze blew a rumpled food wrapper across the empty street. Sidewalks that should have been busy with workers running about on lunch break were sparsely populated. More than one business had its windows shuttered or a CLOSED sign hanging on the door. Books could not believe how quickly this "epidemic" had manifested.

With few trolleys running, he and Amaranthe had to bike to the upscale urban neighborhood at the base of Mokath Ridge, a task she found difficult in her "disguise." At least, he assumed that was what the frequent invocations to dead ancestors signified. The curses may have been for the disguise itself.

A flamboyant white-brimmed hat with a dangling tail of mink fur perched atop her braided hair. Her low-cut blouse revealed...a lot more than he was used to seeing from her. The short skirt hugged her thighs like a sausage casing, giving her legs little freedom for pedaling. The short hem caught when they parked the bikes and got off.

"Don't say it," she said when Books opened his mouth.

"As you wish."

"I assure you, I already discussed the inappropriateness with Maldynado, and I pointed out my thought had been to cover up more of my body rather than less, to which he said, 'Yes, but nobody will be looking at your face in that.'"

"Possibly true."

"I am grudgingly trying it until I have time to shop for something more my style. I did make a modification." She untied a sash, revealing a hidden belt with a sideways knife sheath. "A spot for my sword would be better, but so few women carry them that it's a suspicious accoutrement."

"Yes." He fought to keep a smile off his lips. "I, too, believe Maldynado would say it clashes with that outfit."

"Wouldn't want that." She jammed the bicycle into a rack with more force than the task required. "At least you're armed." She nodded to his short sword.

Lucky him. "The address is a couple of blocks down the street."

Books led the way down an old but well-kept cobblestone lane. Tall, narrow row houses rose three stories high on either side. One or two steam carriages were parked in the street, but most houses had bicycles secured out front. An upscale neighborhood, but not as drenched-in-ostentatiousness as the ones further up the hill where people looked down upon the city from their vast estates.

"Nice area." Amaranthe waved at early spring flowers peeping from window planters and hanging baskets.

"Nothing I could have afforded as a professor." Books and his wife had rented a small house near campus. The empire did not pay its educators well unless one happened to be a retired officer teaching at a military academy.

"Maybe she'll let you move in with her."

"Premature to speculate on such things. Though...I wonder if, ah... The directory only listed her name under the address."

"Hoping there's no lover, eh?"

"No," Books said. "Well. Maybe."

Amaranthe smiled. It was a gentle, warm smile, not an amused one, and he sensed she actually cared and would root for him to find happiness, even if it meant leaving the group.

She paused on a corner and laid a hand on his arm. "I am concerned though—did Sicarius tell you about their past?"

"*Their* past?" Books stumbled and caught himself on the pole of a gas lantern. "They weren't—I mean, he doesn't even..." Dear ancestors, he did not want to think about Sicarius sleeping with a woman at all, much less one he had an interest in.

"No, no, I didn't mean to imply..." Amaranthe lifted a hand in apology, though amusement quirked her lips. "She used to work for Hollowcrest at the Imperial Barracks, part of the intelligence department. She's a cryptography expert, or she was, and she made ciphers for the empire during the Western Sea Conflict."

"Oh, that's actually... Well, naturally, I loathed Hollowcrest, but working for the Imperial Intelligence Network isn't necessarily ignoble. Indeed, if she's that smart, I am...further intrigued."

Amaranthe's smile broadened. "I love that you'd be interested in a woman because of her brain."

"Yes, well, you haven't seen her. She has other fine...attributes as well."

She chuckled. "Of course."

They circled a clunky statue towering in the center of the wide intersection. The bare-chested Darkor the Deathbringer held a sword aloft while a shoulder-high wolf stood beside him, water squirting from its maw. The address on one of the corners behind the statue matched the one Books had written down.

A snake wriggled a dance in his belly. Time to see her again. Would she be mad he had left her to the enforcers' care the night before? Would she blame him for the explosion?

Stairs rose from the sidewalk to the front door. Amaranthe spread her hand, indicating he could go first.

Books paused at the front door, more worries churning through his head. He stared at the knocker, noting the handsome vine and leaf pattern comprising the heavy brass ring.

Amaranthe cleared her throat. "Knocking is usually Step One in these situations."

"Yes, I've heard that." Books drew back his shoulders and thumped the ring three times. As they waited, a new worry reared its head. He eyed Amaranthe—and her revealing attire. "If she's here, can we say you're my..." He groped for a relation that would suggest absolutely no sexual connotations.

"Daughter?" Amaranthe suggested.

"Dear ancestors, no. She'll think I'm ancient. Er, my age, anyway. And what would she think of my parenting influence if she saw you in that outfit?"

"Did you just, in the same breath, call me old *and* promiscuous?"

"Uhm."

Fortunately, her eyes twinkled as she waved at the door. "I imagine she would have answered by now if she were home."

Amaranthe headed down the stairs.

Books knocked again. "We're leaving? After riding all the way up here? I thought you'd want to snoop around even if she wasn't here." He tried the knob, but it was locked.

"Naturally, but invited guests enter through the front door for all to see. Snoopers enter through the alley."

"Ah."

Books followed her around back, where a fence contained garden beds with a few green sprouts thrusting through the loamy soil. He and Amaranthe let themselves through a gate and followed a stepping-stone path to a sturdy door. It too was locked.

"Keep watch." Amaranthe delved under her sash and withdrew a small case of fine tools.

"I didn't know enforcers were taught to pick locks." Books put his back to the wall, so he could watch the side street and the alley.

"They're not." She slid two slender tools with crooked ends out of the case. "That particular deficiency in my education has proven inconvenient at times, so I asked Sicarius to teach me."

"Are you sure you should spend so much time with him? He's a dubious influence."

Metal scraped as Amaranthe worked the lock. "You gave up the chance to play the role of my father today."

"But not your friend, I hope. You do realize how much easier it'd be to clear your name if he wasn't on your team, right? I know you like

to see people as better than they are, but you must be aware of at least a portion of the heinous acts he's perpetrated in his career. Even if you're not, I'll wager the emperor is."

A click sounded, and Amaranthe pushed the door open. She did not respond to his comments. She *was* spending too much time with Sicarius.

Books stepped into a hallway after her. He hoped Vonsha was not simply recovering in bed and choosing to ignore the door. But the air held a chill, as if no one had been there that day to feed the stove.

He and Amaranthe padded through the hall and explored rooms. Sparse furnishings adorned the home, all of a lower quality than one expected from the warrior caste. Common woods with few ornaments comprised the chairs and tables. He did nod with approval at a well-appointed library that overflowed into other rooms. Even the hallway had bookshelves. By the front door, a stack of tomes leaned precariously on a boot bench.

Amaranthe's fingers strayed toward the haphazard pile.

Books cleared his throat. "It's probably unwise to clean the house you're illegally trespassing in, assuming you don't want the person to know you were there."

"I've heard that." Amaranthe clasped her hands behind her back. "Though, if people invaded my home, I'd view the intrusion with less animosity if they dusted while they were there."

The house was not dirty by Books's reckoning, but he did have the impression of someone who devoted more time to her internal world than the external one. He brushed a finger across an easel as he passed, admiring the beginnings of a landscape of the Emperor's Preserve.

Amaranthe detoured into an office and checked a filing cabinet.

"Should we be prying into her personal life?" Books leaned against the doorjamb, frowning disapproval. "I suspect her of being a victim, not a criminal."

"I'm not prying." She flipped through files, reading the labels. "I'm snooping, an activity we discussed outside and of which I thought you approved."

"It's true I'm curious about her, but..."

"As for the rest, don't you find it suspicious she was there, checking lot lines, at the same time we were investigating the adjacent parcel?"

"I doubt it's coincidental, but I don't find it *suspicious*," he said. "Perhaps her family is being vexed by the same people who killed the appraiser."

"Hm." Amaranthe flipped through a dusty file she had pulled from the back. "Vonsha earned a lot of accolades in school and received her professorship at a young age. As Sicarius said, she was recruited by Imperial Intelligence to work on encryption keys during the war. Ah, this is interesting."

"What?" His disapproval forgotten, Books joined her and peered over her shoulder.

"She was the first woman *and* the first civilian invited into the intelligence office at the Imperial Barracks, and she was quite the star. Lots of praise from Emperor Raumesys. Less from Hollowcrest. He probably couldn't acknowledge that a woman might be useful. But then things changed when that Kyattese cryptanalyst started cracking her ciphers. She was under increasing pressure and her position was terminated after a final failure led to the Nurians gaining the upper hand. Looks like a permanent demerit was added to her record, and she wasn't able to return to the University."

"Permanent demerit?" Books asked. "It's not her fault an enemy nation fielded an equally capable cryptographer. The Kyattese are known for academic achievements."

Amaranthe flipped through more files from the past twenty years. "Since then, she's made a living as a math tutor." Her gaze lifted to take in the room. "Hard to imagine that job paying for this house."

"If she's warrior caste, she may have inherited it."

"True."

"I, for one, find her recovery from her falling out admirable. The emperor's disapproval must have come with a huge stigma, social as well as professional. She's an intelligent and fascinating woman."

Amaranthe smiled. "You're not falling in love after one evening with her, are you?"

"No." He sniffed. "But, if I were, I'm sure there are worse people I could fall for."

Amaranthe looked away, face unreadable. "Yes."

A rattle came from the front of the house. The doorknob.

"Vonsha!" Books whispered. "We can't let her find us trespassing."

He jumped into the hallway while Amaranthe remained calm, replacing the files. The front door was still closed, but a shadow moved beyond a curtained window. Maybe there was time to flee out the back.

He raced down the hallway, toward the rear exit.

"Books, wait," Amaranthe whispered after him.

He was already at the door. He flung it open and started through.

Amaranthe caught him by the shirt tail and yanked him back.

A crossbow quarrel thudded into the doorframe, passing so close it buzzed his eyebrow. He lurched backward, scrambling for the safety of the hallway.

Amaranthe shut the door and threw the bolt. "Vonsha would have the key."

"Good point." Books touched his eyebrow. His finger came away blood-free, but he still snorted in disgust. He kept waiting for Sicarius's training to turn him into someone whose brain functioned during tense situations.

"I'll check the roof and windows." Amaranthe slid the dagger out of her hidden sheath and grimaced. "See if you can find me a decent weapon, please."

"What kind of weapon am I going to find in a woman's home? It'd be odd to see a sword—most ladies aren't fighters."

"Are you calling me odd, Books?" She jogged for the stairs.

"Eccentric, perhaps."

"Just check, please," Amaranthe called over her shoulder.

Books peeped through the small window in the back door. A shadowy figure lurked between two houses on the other side of the alley. He pulled the curtain across the window.

Hoping they had time, he trotted around the bottom floor, checking rooms. Nothing so obvious as a sword or musket perched on a wall. He headed into the kitchen and grabbed the fireplace poker leaning against the wood stove.

His wrist brushed the cast iron. It held a hint of warmth.

Books tapped the stove thoughtfully, an idea germinating. He peeked into the firebox, prodded the ashes with the poker, and unearthed a few orange coals. He tossed dried moss and kindling inside, then turned his attention to ingredient hunting. A canister on the counter held sugar. No problem there. As for the other ingredient....

He lifted a trap door in the back of the kitchen. A narrow stair led to a low-ceilinged root cellar with a packed-earth floor. Jars of pickled vegetables lined shelves, while bins of apples, potatoes, cabbage, and onions sat in the back. A few strings of salami hung from the ceiling. Books nodded. If Vonsha had cured the meat herself, she would have—there: a box on a shelf read "saltpeter."

"Perfect."

He grabbed it, returned to the kitchen, and selected a pan in a pot rack hanging from a thick wooden ceiling beam. He poured in sugar and saltpeter and placed it on the cooktop. Amaranthe came in to find him stirring his concoction.

"I'm fairly certain I said look for weapons, not make lunch," she said.

Books handed her the fireplace poker.

"This is my weapon?" She arched her eyebrows. "Or are we skewering meat for kabobs?"

"It's all I could find. Do you want my sword?" He plopped spoonfuls of the gooey brownish mixture onto pieces of paper. He grabbed a few matchsticks out of a box behind the stove.

"No, you keep it. We're not getting out without a fight. There's one watching the alley, one at the front door, and one on the roof."

"Are they here for Vonsha? Or is it possible they recognized you through your disguise and are after your bounty?"

"I don't know. They weren't wearing uniforms denoting the goals of the dastardly organization they're working for." Amaranthe sniffed the hardening blobs on the paper. "Are you going to enlighten me?"

"Combustible smoke-creating devices."

"Smoke bombs?" She grinned. "You can make those?"

"Very simple, so long as you keep stirring the mixture to keep it from getting black and, er, self-igniting."

Her grin widened. "How long do your eyebrows take to grow back when that happens?"

Only she could be amused when there were snipers poised to shoot them if they opened a door.

"A couple of months." As they talked, he tore the paper and folded pieces around the incendiary gobs, creating small packets. He twisted the ends to form rudimentary fuses.

"You could start your own business. Do you know how much Sicarius pays for those?"

"His are probably fancier."

Glass shattered in a nearby room.

"Work time." Amaranthe set the poker aside to draw her knife.

"Do you want a couple?" Books held up a packet and a matchstick.

"You handle that." She eyed the kitchen speculatively.

"There's a root cellar if you want to hide down there."

"Too confining."

Boots sounded in the hallway.

Amaranthe gripped her knife in her teeth, hiked the skirt to her waist, and hopped onto a counter. She climbed up the hanging pot rack and wedged herself between two ceiling beams, poised to drop down on anyone who came through the door. She nodded readiness to Books.

He drew his sword, leaned it against the wall, then knelt behind the stove. He scraped a match along a brick, and its stink filled the air. The kitchen would soon smell of more than sulfur.

Books lit a packet and slid it across the tile floor. White smoke wafted from it.

The footsteps paused outside the kitchen door. He lit another packet and placed this one so its smoke would billow before the stove, hiding him.

The door opened. A man stood in the hall, features obscured by smoke, but Books glimpsed the cold brass detailing of a flintlock pistol.

"What the— In here!"

Leading with his pistol, the man lunged inside. Another set of footsteps pounded toward the kitchen, and a second figure soon loomed in the doorway.

Smoke hid Amaranthe's face—she had to be getting the worst of the stench up there, and she could not even wipe her eyes. He assumed she wanted him to take on the first man while she dropped down when the second entered. The second had paused, though, and he squinted as he searched the kitchen.

Books dug a cracked piece of mortar out from between two floor tiles and tossed it toward the wall opposite the intruders. It clinked against the window. Both men aimed their pistols that way, and the second stepped into the kitchen.

With all the smoke, Books would not have seen Amaranthe drop if he had not been watching. She landed on the second man. He grunted with surprise and went down beneath her.

Books grabbed his sword, adjusted his grip, and lunged for the first man, who was spinning about to check his comrade. Smoke hid Books's approach. He slammed the flat of the blade against the back of his target's head.

The man staggered but was not considerate enough to collapse in an unconscious heap. Trusting Amaranthe to handle the other, Books focused on his chosen foe. He sidestepped an attack and drove his heel into the side of the man's knee. This time, the fellow dropped, pistol clacking as it skidded across the tiles.

Books pressed the tip of his sword into the man's neck. "Don't move."

Two steps away, Amaranthe knelt, her knee in her opponent's back. She had fished twine from a drawer and was unraveling it to make bonds.

Smoke tickled Books's nose. He fought back a sneeze. "Who do you think—"

Movement stirred the smoke near the door.

"Look out!" he blurted.

Amaranthe was already moving. She leaped from the floor and lunged at the newcomer's knees. He proved agile and leaped over her, but she anticipated it. Instead of crashing into the hall, she spun, and her knife came to rest on the man's throat as he landed.

Books's man made use of the distraction. He rolled away from the sword and toward his lost pistol. Books jumped after him, but the man's hand clasped the weapon. He spun onto his back and pointed it at Books.

Books hurled his sword at the man and dropped to the floor. The pistol fired. He cringed, expecting a ball to rip into him, but glass shattered behind him instead.

A scuffle sounded at the door. Books scrambled up, intending to go after the pistol-wielder again, but he was dead. Amaranthe's knife protruded from his neck. She had saved Books's life, but that meant she had no weapon to hold on the man in the doorway.

Books scrambled about and found his sword. Amaranthe and the other man had disappeared from view. A thud sounded in the hallway. Books sprinted out of the kitchen, grabbing the jamb as he skidded

around the corner. He almost crashed into Amaranthe. The last man sprawled before the door, unmoving.

The fading smoke could not hide the blood trickling from Amaranthe's temple. She appeared otherwise unhurt, though grimness stamped her face. Books could guess at the reason. She was no more a natural killer than he, and they might not have had to kill at all if he had kept his attention focused on his prisoner.

He turned, realizing he had taken his eyes off another foe. Fortunately the remaining living man, the one Amaranthe had downed when she dropped from the ceiling, was unconscious. She tossed a purloined dagger on the floor beside him. Grim and irritated, Books decided.

"Sorry," he said, feeling guilty afresh. "I'm not very effective in these types of situations." Another reason this life was not for him. After this current escapade was over, he would find a new line of work.

"You're improving," Amaranthe said. "Let's check their pockets and see if we can figure out what they were after. Me, Vonsha, or something in her house?"

Books patted down the unconscious man, telling himself it was not cowardly to leave the dead blokes for Amaranthe. After all, she had to retrieve her knife. He found a folded paper in a back pocket.

"None of those things," he said, apprehension burrowing into his gut as he examined the ink sketch on the page.

"What'd you find?"

Books rotated the paper so she could see. His likeness marked the front, along with a caption: MARL MUGDILDOR WANTED DEAD OR ALIVE: 5,000 RANMYAS.

"That's...unfortunate," Amaranthe said. "I thought Sicarius and I were the only ones with bounties. And Maldynado, I suppose, if you can count his two-hundred-and-fifty ranmya one as a legitimate incentive. He'll be envious of you now."

She smiled, trying to cheer him, he sensed. It did not work. All he could think about was that he had waited too long. He had stayed with Amaranthe out of a sense of honor and obligation, but someone had noticed him in the company of outlaws, and now he was one. No walking away and finding a new job after all. Not unless he left the empire completely, and, even then, he would have to worry his whole life, watching his back for globetrotting bounty hunters.

"I'm sorry," Amaranthe said softly. "I know you were thinking of leaving. This will make things difficult if you choose that route."

"Yes," was all he said as he stared at the page.

CHAPTER 9

"**S**ICARIUS?" AMARANTHE CALLED FROM THE doorway of the pipe room.

He did not answer. She had sent Books off to purchase supplies while making a stop of her own on the way back, and she had not seen any of the men yet. She held a book under one arm for Akstyr, but she wanted to confer with Sicarius first, preferably in private. Books's interest in Vonsha concerned her, or, more accurately, Vonsha concerned her.

"Sicarius?" she called again, squinting into the gloomy corner where she had seen him last.

The only sounds in the pumping house came from the endless kerthunks of the machinery. Her mind conjured unpleasant thoughts. What if the water did more than make people sick? What if drinking it proved deadly? What if her men—her *friends*—were...

Down the narrow hall, a door slammed open. Maldynado, wet and naked, staggered out, a cloud of steam wafting out with him.

"What are you doing?" Amaranthe forced her gaze upward, toward his face, and fought against the blush encroaching upon her cheeks.

Maldynado pushed damp curls off his forehead and squinted at her. "Oh. Hullo." He yelled a warning through the open door: "Boss lady's back home in case you want to cover your dangle-sticks."

Apparently, he could not be bothered to take his own advice. He shuffled down the hall toward her, using the wall for support. She would have guessed him drunk, but supposed he was still sick. That kept her from lecturing him on the inappropriateness of nudity in the pumping house. Even if he did not worry about propriety in front of a woman, there were all sorts of machines with moving parts that could catch unprotected...protrusions.

"The outfit looks good." Maldynado smirked. "I'd flirt and charm, but I'm not feeling well enough for that."

"You seem to be doing better," she said, not wanting to fuel any comments about her attire. "You're standing...without vomiting."

Books climbed down the ladder with canvas market bags hanging from his shoulders. He landed in the hallway behind Amaranthe and groaned when he spotted Maldynado. "Why are you wet? And naked? Buffoon."

"A little better," Maldynado said, answering Amaranthe and ignoring Books. "We turned the boiler room into a steam bath. Sicarius and Basilard said the Mangdorians sit in steam huts to purify their contaminated blood and sweat out sickness, and some of them live to over a hundred. So we figured we could turn that big old furnace into a steam generator."

"Did you move my work—all those notes and newspapers—out first?" Books asked.

Maldynado touched a finger to a chin in need of a razor. "Perhaps... not."

"You thoughtless nude oaf. Why didn't you go to the public baths?"

"Because we're sick. And that would have involved walking. Far. And I'm a wanted man, you know. I can't be too careful what with the bounty on my head."

Amaranthe could not resist: "Books is wanted, too, now. His bounty is for five thousand ranmyas."

Maldynado staggered, pressing a hand against the wall for support. "What? How is yours more than mine? You're not even a threat to anyone. Now, me, I'm threatening."

"Especially to any paperwork left out," Books groused.

Amaranthe maneuvered past Maldynado, careful not to bump anything, and left them to squabble. She wanted to talk to Sicarius, preferably not with Books in the room.

Basilard and Akstyr shuffled out as she was about to enter. Thankfully, they wore towels about their waists. Amaranthe stopped, holding the book out for Akstyr, and his eyes locked on it.

"On Healing," he breathed.

"Is that what it says?" she asked. "I just figured it was a book on magic because the fellow I was talking to was very nervous about having it in his office."

Akstyr stretched out a hand. "For me?"

"Of course." Amaranthe handed the book to him. "Thank you, by the way, for taking a chance on getting that key for us in the gambling house."

Eyes fixed on the book, he did not answer. He almost dropped it in his haste to throw back the cover and examine the first page. He *did* drop his towel and shuffled off down the hallway without noticing.

"Women," Amaranthe muttered, ducking into the boiler room. "I should have put together a team of women."

Heat and steam wrapped around her, obscuring visibility. No lanterns burned, though embers glowed red behind open furnace slats. Water-drenched rocks spat and hissed.

Amaranthe assumed Sicarius would be dressed—or *un*dressed—to a similar degree as the others, so she kept her gaze downward. Well, maybe she peeked out of the corners of her eyes once or twice, but shadows cloaked the room, and she did not see him.

She swept Books's soggy papers and notes into a stack and met him at the door with them. She did not have to ask him to give her a moment alone with Sicarius, for he accepted them with an aggrieved expression and rushed down the hallway, waving the papers to dry them.

"Sicarius?" Amaranthe closed the door. "Are you better?"

"What fellow?" Sicarius's raspy voice came from a dark corner.

"Huh?"

"What fellow did you get that book from?"

"Roskar Rockjaw," Amaranthe said. "I've been getting to know some of the other mercenaries and underworld sorts in town. Ally shopping, as my marketing instructor called it. Anyway, I stopped in to see if he'd heard anything about the city water. He hadn't, and I ended up telling him what we knew since he was sick himself. He *did* verify that Ergot's Chance is under protection, but he didn't know whose. As for the book, I noticed it on Rockjaw's desk. He said one of his thieves had filched it on accident, and he didn't want anything to do with the vile thing. I volunteered to dispose of it. I even made him believe I was doing him a favor."

"Rockjaw is a murderer and a thief," Sicarius said, an edge to his tone.

"Yes. I don't imagine he's quite what Ms. Morkshire had in mind when she spoke of acquiring business allies, but this is the social set I find myself operating within these days."

"He's dangerous. You shouldn't have gone to see him alone."

"Funny, that's the advice people give me in regard to you."

He snorted. "You shouldn't see me alone either."

"Nobody's ever accused me of being wise."

Amaranthe sat on the crate next to the desk, annoyed that she had to cross her legs artfully to avoid displaying...areas she preferred to keep off-display. At least the darkness ought to hide the details of the skimpy outfit. She spent the next ten minutes telling Sicarius about the events at Vonsha's house.

"While we could wander around the city," she said, "digging for clues and questioning people for the next few days, I'm thinking we might get to the bottom of things more quickly by taking a trip into the mountains to see what's going on with that parcel. Do you mind if we use your winnings to purchase provisions? If Maldynado can recover enough to charm the heart of a matronly businesswoman, we might be able to afford a vehicle of some sort."

"Acceptable," Sicarius said.

"Good. There's something else I want to discuss with you. It's Vonsha. Books seems smitten. Do you remember anything more about her? That she spent time working for Hollowcrest and Raumesys isn't much of an endorsement."

"Really," Sicarius said dryly.

"Really." Amaranthe smiled. "Was she a good, honorable person, working for the welfare of the empire? Or was she someone involved in their underhanded plots?"

"You're asking me to act as a character judge?"

"Maybe?"

"We never spoke. She did her work professionally. That's all I know. Do you suspect her of playing a role in the water plot?"

"That's what I'm trying to decide. It's hard when I've never talked to the woman."

"No chance to wheedle information out of her yet?"

"Precisely. You know how I love to chitchat with folks."

"Yes."

"That must be why we get along so fabulously," Amaranthe said. "You being the less talkative sort and me being happy to fill in the awkward silences with...awkward un-silences."

Sicarius said nothing.

"Yes, just like that. See? We make a good team."

Amaranthe decided not to pester him further and headed for the door. When she opened it, letting light from the hallway in, Sicarius stopped her with a question:

"What are you wearing?"

More than the room's heat warmed her cheeks. She should have changed before looking for him. "Uhh, it's the disguise Maldynado got me. It's...not exactly what I had in mind. As I've recently discovered, it's not terribly practical for fighting, and, er, it was probably a mistake to send him clothes shopping, however good he is at obtaining bargains."

Though she felt ridiculous in the outfit, and a touch vulnerable, a part of her wished he would say she looked good in it.

"Yes," Sicarius said. "If you want the respect of the men, you should dress like a professional, not one of their conquests from the brothels. Also, costumes create a sense of security that encourages inattention. Better to remain vigilant."

Great. Not only did he *not* think she looked good, he'd compared her to a whore. Maybe it wasn't too late to put together that all-women team after all.

* * * * *

Rain thumped against the oilskin hood of Amaranthe's jacket and pooled on the footboards beneath the driver's bench. She sat next to Maldynado, who steered the newly acquired steam lorry, while Books, Basilard, and Sicarius rode in the large cargo bed in the back. Akstyr hunkered beneath a poncho behind the boiler with his nose inches from the pages of his new book.

Amaranthe's position offered her a cushioned seat instead of cold metal, though in return for this luxury, she had stoking duty for the furnace. Coal dust stained her hands and her gray army fatigues. She had torn her "costume" off as soon as she left the steam room the day before.

The lorry rumbled along a well-kept concrete road, with the tall buildings of the city fading into the distance behind them and sprawling homesteads and farmlands ahead. Tracks ran alongside, though few locomotives headed east into the mountains. Most imports came from the gulf, to the south, and the west coast with its populous port cities. Rika-vedk, the easternmost satrapy, had been the last chunk of land added to the empire, more out of Emperor Dausrak's ancestrally appointed vision that Turgonia should stretch from sea to sea than out of any value in the vast steppes on the other side of the mountains. Amaranthe imagined the spirits of dead rulers hanging around in the Valley of the Emperors, arguing over who had acquired the most land. Less lurid than comparing lengths of certain body parts, she supposed.

"All that money," Maldynado grumbled, wiping raindrops off the brim of a broad peacock-feathered hat.

"Pardon?" Amaranthe asked.

"All that money you two won, and you made me buy a used-to-within-an-inch-of-collapsing lorry with an open cab. An *open* cab in the rainy season."

"We may need money later on. I thought it best to reserve some of our funds." She was mulling over a ploy to feign interest in purchasing the mysterious mountain lot as a cover story to justify some poking about.

"I was *this* close." Maldynado held up two fingers a hair's breadth apart. "Almost had that dour old lizard ready to sell us a shiny green Dondar lorry for half its value. She was a beauty. Fast too."

"Perhaps if you'd spent less money on water—" Amaranthe eyed the crates in the cab with their gear, "—we would have had more for vehicular purchases."

"That's bottled safe water. It won't make us sick. You'll thank me later if all the rivers up here are poisoned."

"Safe water? What pretty young entrepreneur told you that?"

"A couple of girls selling them out of a cart. The water was bottled at an artesian spring at the base of the mountains."

"It's probably from the lake," Amaranthe said. "The city water hasn't been suspect long enough for someone to go up to the mountains and bottle anything from springs."

Books stuck his head into the cab. "Unless said person had previous knowledge of the impending calamity. I saw the cart. There was a line around the block to buy the water at five ranmyas a bottle."

Maldynado sniffed. "I didn't pay that much *or* stand in line."

"Nonetheless, it looked like a profitable business," Books said. "Maybe we should have questioned them. Perhaps they're behind the attack on the water. Make the city supply unsafe, then make a fortune selling imported water."

"Poisoning the source just to cash in on bottled water is extreme," Amaranthe said, "especially considering there will be hordes of competitors flooding the market within a day or two."

"Maybe our entrepreneurs didn't think their plan through well."

"It's probably someone taking advantage of the situation," Amaranthe said. "One of my instructors used to say, 'In every crisis lies opportunity.'"

"Yes, politicians have that motto too." Books clambered over the low wall dividing the bed from the cab and squeezed onto the bench beside Amaranthe. "Perhaps, when we're up there investigating that lot..." He glanced at Maldynado and lowered his voice. "Perhaps we should visit Vonsha's family estate. Since their property is across the river from the other one, they might prove a font of information."

"Oh, please," Maldynado said. "You just want to question her family about her interests so you can smooth-talk your way into *her* font."

Books coughed and cleared his throat.

Amaranthe lifted a hand to rest on his shoulder and noticed a plume of smoke smudging the road to the rear. The undulations of the terrain hid whatever vehicle was making it, but she shifted uneasily, wondering if someone might be after them. Aside from the usual possibility of bounty hunters, there was the doubtlessly irked Ellaya and her mysterious protectors.

"I don't think," Books said, "that people who resort to spending their evenings at The Pirates' Plunder should mock me for my interest in a woman."

"Nothing wrong with The Pirates' Plunder," Maldynado said. "Fine ladies there."

In the bed of the lorry, Sicarius stood, his head turned toward the smoke cloud behind them.

"In even finer costumes." Akstyr grinned. "I liked the woman with the eye patch."

"Oh, yes," Maldynado said. "Though I'm not sure if it's appropriate to call it an eye patch when it's actually covering—"

"Enforcer vehicle," Sicarius announced.

Maldynado cursed.

"Easy," Amaranthe said. "It might be a coincidence."

"What do you want me to do?" Maldynado asked. "Turn off the road?"

Amaranthe eyed the food, water, footlocker, and other gear piled between the men. Flintlock rifles and pistols lay beside her repeating crossbow and everyone's swords, but many people preferred firearms for hunting and laws forbidding their use were supposedly lenient outside the city.

"No," she said. "Just keep the tarp over our supplies. Akstyr, hide that book." His tome on magic was the most incriminating thing they had. "We're just a group of hunters, heading into the mountains to take down some..."

"Scrawny elk that are still all ribs after a long hard winter?" Maldynado raised his eyebrows.

She blushed. "Early spring isn't hunting season, you say?"

"Haven't been out of the city much, have you?" Maldynado's eyes twinkled.

Amaranthe imagined him plotting some trick to play on her, the wilderness neophyte. "I *have* been to the mountains before."

"Did you ever get out of the lorry?"

"It was a locomotive, and, yes, I stayed overnight in a cabin. A friend and I were visiting our fathers' work camp."

The twinkle failed to leave Maldynado's eyes.

"We'll say we're going to make a bid on some property," she said. "Which is sort of possibly a truth."

"Decision's made?" Sicarius called over the pumping pistons of the engine. "They're closing on us quickly."

"My grandmother on a bicycle could close on us quickly," Maldynado said. "This slag heap was probably the first model ever made."

"Yes," Amaranthe told Sicarius. "You might want to cover your blond hair though. We wouldn't want them distracted from their errand by your bounty."

The armored lorry drew closer. Black plumes spewed from a smokestack painted silver to complement the red sheen of the body. Enforcer colors.

"What if we *are* their errand?" Books asked.

"Let's hope we're not and they go right by," Amaranthe said.

"And if they don't?" Books asked. "This isn't enforcer jurisdiction, is it? If something out here was wrong, they'd call in the army, wouldn't they?"

"Depends on the incident. There are rural enforcer units."

The vehicle loomed behind them. A bronze plaque on the front of the lorry read: Ag. District #3. Maldynado steered their own vehicle to the side, leaving enough room for the other to pass.

Sicarius sat next to the gear, his back against the side of the bed, head ducked low to stay out of sight. Amaranthe faced forward, pulling her hood lower over her eyes.

As the enforcer vehicle drew even with them, she sat, shoulders hunched. Just an innocent traveler, beaten down by the rain. Out of the corner of her eye, the people in the cab came into view: two men and a woman. The latter looked their way.

Amaranthe twitched with surprise. Of course, she had not been the only female enforcer in the city, but they were so rare she knew most. She recovered and offered a nod toward the woman while searching her memory for the face. Nothing came to mind.

After a brief survey, the woman returned her attention to the road ahead. Nobody yelled at Maldynado to halt, and Amaranthe sighed with relief, glad she did not have to use her sketchy story.

The enforcer vehicle pulled ahead. A dark oilskin tarp protected the large lorry bed from the elements, but the rear flap was rolled up, allowing a view of the inside. At least thirty soldiers in army blacks crowded the benches, each man with a sword and rifle wedged between his knees.

Perhaps noticing her stare, one stood and untied the flap. It fell into place, hiding the interior.

"Since when do enforcer vehicles get used to transport the army?" Amaranthe asked.

"I have a more pertinent question," Books said. "Are they going where *we're* going, and, if so, should we revise our itinerary?"

Sicarius came forward, crouching behind Amaranthe.

"Thoughts?" she asked him.

"An enforcer vehicle traversing the countryside isn't uncommon," he said.

"Whereas a convoy of steam trampers and black army troop transports might cause the population alarm?" she asked. "Especially when there's hardly anyone to war with to the east?"

"How delightful," Books said. "Not only are they going someplace where a platoon of soldiers is required, but the situation is so dire people need to be kept in the dark."

"It's the empire," Amaranthe said lightly. "People are usually kept in the dark."

"How comforting," Books said.

"This road leads to several destinations," she said. "Let's not get concerned until we're sure we have something to worry about."

"So, we should go back to teasing Books about his lady friend?" Maldynado asked.

"Perhaps we could travel in silence for a while." Amaranthe gave Books a sympathetic smile.

The silence lasted almost a minute before the eye patch debate came up again. Amaranthe sighed and studied the craggy mountains ahead. Halfway up the green slopes, snow started, cold and forbidding. What else lay up there, waiting for them?

CHAPTER 10

A MARANTHE BENT TO PICK UP A BRANCH THAT AP-
peared somewhat less damp and muddy than the others.
When she stood, a rivulet of raindrops dripped off the top
of her hood and spattered her nose. Frogs croaked in the stagnant pond
stretching alongside the campsite, their enthusiasm undaunted by the
gloomy weather or the green film painting the water's surface.

Arms laden with damp wood, Amaranthe returned to the fire Basilard had coaxed to life. A canopy of evergreens over the camp provided
some protection from the rain. The flames bathed a rusty iron tripod,
which supported a pot where beans simmered. Basilard manned a skillet, turning sausages, beans, and onions into something that smelled far
more delectable than one would expect.

Maldynado and Books wrestled with poles and a tarp, fashioning a
tent beside the lorry. Inside the cab, Akstyr read his book in the fading
daylight. Sicarius had disappeared as soon as they arrived "to scout."

"Boss," Maldynado said, "how come some of us are working hard
and *some* of us are reading books?"

Amaranthe set down her load of logs and arranged them in a tidy
pile while she debated the merit of the complaint. Akstyr *did* have a
predilection for reading his books instead of helping out; in fact, those
tomes seemed to get especially interesting when physical labor needed
to be done. He was a tricky one to manage, whining and shirking duties
when assigned them. Since he bristled at receiving orders, she always
felt she had to find creative ways to coerce him. Maybe guilt today?

"Because," Amaranthe said, "some of you like me more than others
and go out of your way to make my day easier."

"Sicarius isn't helping," Akstyr said without looking up.

She opened her mouth to point out Sicarius did his share to make her day easier, but Books spoke first.

"Is he truly someone you want to emulate? Maybe it's time you grew up and shared group responsibilities without being asked."

Akstyr glared over his shoulder. "You think you're my father? I didn't ask for your advice."

Books blanched, and Amaranthe grimaced, sure the words made him think of the days when he *had* been a father and how all that was lost. She was going to have a hard time keeping him in the group if all the interactions with the men were unpleasant ones.

"Can you even understand any of the words in that book?" Maldynado asked. "Or do you just carry it around, pretending to be useful, so you can get out of chores?"

"I understand plenty. I'm learning about healing. Don't you think that could be useful out here?"

Maldynado staked down a tent corner. "You don't actually believe you'd be able to do anything in an emergency, do you? Learning magic from a book? Come now, let's be serious."

Akstyr scowled. "I can do things."

"We don't ever *see* you do things."

"Because it's the empire, Stupid. You get hanged for practicing the Science."

Amaranthe strode to the lorry and draped her arms across the side of the bed, trying to nonchalantly end the bickering before it escalated. "Looks like Basilard's preparing a nice dinner, gentlemen. The sooner we have the camp set up and the firewood gathered, the sooner we can eat."

Amidst grumbling, Books and Maldynado returned to work. Akstyr sighed dramatically and climbed out of the lorry, though he kept the book tucked under his arm.

"Anything interesting in there?" Amaranthe nodded toward the tome.

"What?" He stared at her, as if surprised she had asked. "Oh. Sure. There are some exercises I found. I need someone to practice on though."

"Someone injured?"

Akstyr nodded. "So I can try to heal them."

Basilard banged a wooden spoon against his pot, and the three men hustled over. Amaranthe perched on a stump near Basilard, and he handed her a bowl.

"Wasn't it Sicarius's turn to cook?" Amaranthe asked. "I thought you switched with him yesterday."

Basilard lifted a dismissive hand, even as Maldynado and Akstyr shook their heads vigorously.

"We've been meaning to talk to you about that," Books said. "We feel that Sicarius already takes on so much responsibility in regard to our training that it's not fair to force him to engage in meal-preparation duties. His own training is, of course, paramount to him as well, so we would not wish to burden him with this additional responsibility."

"I see." Amaranthe held back a smile. She wondered if Sicarius was close enough to hear. "Just to be clear, are you afraid to ask him to perform the duty when it's his turn, or do you just not want to eat what he prepares?"

"Afraid?" Maldynado scoffed.

Akstyr snorted. Basilard flicked his hand in dismissal.

Books lowered his voice and leaned toward Amaranthe. "The man doesn't believe in seasonings. Not even salt!"

With a morose head shake, Basilard stirred his beans and sausage and took a bite.

A howl echoed from the woods.

Amaranthe flinched, almost dropping her bowl. Answering yips and yowls stirred the hair on the back of her neck. The frogs fell silent. Basilard squinted into the gloom, head cocked.

"Just coyotes," Maldynado told Amaranthe. "You really haven't been out in the forest much, have you?"

"No," she admitted, chagrinned her concern was so transparent.

"Well, then, I reckon it's my job to educate you on what we'll likely encounter up here."

"Excuse me?" Books lifted a finger. "How much time have *you*, a dandy from the warrior caste, spent in the mountains? Weren't your formative years spent in salons with tutors instructing you in the ways of arrogance and pomposity?"

"Sure." Maldynado winked. "But we went hunting on family vacations."

"Go ahead," Amaranthe told Maldynado. "Keep in mind that I *have* read books, and I'm not going to be fooled if you try to convince me about made-up monsters that live up here."

Maldynado touched his chest, eyes wide. "I wouldn't consider such a thing."

"Uh huh."

While Maldynado explained the local fauna, everyone else ate. Akstyr balanced his book in his lap while he spooned food into his mouth. The old tome was hand-written in a painstakingly clean script. Amaranthe wondered how the scribe who had penned it would feel about someone slopping beans onto the pages.

"Are you listening?" Maldynado asked at one point, prodding Akstyr with his foot. "I'm divulging wisdom here."

"Huh?" Akstyr lifted his head.

"You think your magic is going to help when a bear or ignak lizard tries to eat you?"

"If I learn these healing techniques," Akstyr said, "I can help if something tries to eat *you*."

"As if the forest creatures would be so rude." Maldynado removed his hat, fluffed the peacock feather, swiped moisture off the brim, and replaced it at a rakish angle. "We're still waiting for a demonstration of this great magic you're learning."

"Science," Akstyr said.

"Either way, we haven't seen you do anything except that trick where you made a flame. And you probably just had a match secreted in your hand for that."

"Did not."

"Prove it. Heal my hangnail." Maldynado managed to display said nail while making a rude gesture.

Akstyr put aside his book and food and lunged to his feet, fists clenched.

"What's the matter?" Maldynado also stood. He prodded Akstyr in the chest with a finger. "Afraid we'll find out you're a fraud?"

Amaranthe set her meal down, not sure what Maldynado was trying to do or if she should stop it. Despite his size and his dueling skills, he was a laid-back sort, and she had never seen him pick a fight.

Akstyr slapped the finger away and glowered at Maldynado, a challenge in his eyes. Though slender by comparison and inches shorter, he did not back down.

When Maldynado lunged at him, Akstyr was ready. He jumped to the side, escaping a bear hug designed to force him to the ground. Maldynado reacted quickly, though, and hooked an arm around Akstyr's waist. Akstyr pulled back, but tripped over a root. He went down, landing on his rump with a cry of pain, or maybe rage. Maldynado scrambled on top of him. Though usually an agile man, he launched a sloppy punch at Akstyr. The bout of fisticuffs resembled a drunken barroom brawl more than a serious scrap, judging by Maldynado anyway. Akstyr appeared confused, hurt, and angry.

Books wore a bewildered are-their-brains-malfunctioning look. Basilard lifted his skillet, pointed at Maldynado, and raised his eyebrows.

"No, don't hit him on the head yet," Amaranthe said, though if the scuffle went on much longer, she might do it herself.

"Get off me, you—" Akstyr yelped.

"Problem?" Sicarius asked from behind Amaranthe's shoulder.

His silent appearance caught her by surprise, as usual, and she jumped.

"I think we're about to find out if Akstyr truly has magic skills," she said.

"Science practitioners require concentration, which is not a state easily achieved when—"

Akstyr cried out when a fist connected with his nose. Blood spattered his baggy shirt.

More coyote yips and howls echoed through the forest, loud enough to drown out the grunts and thumps of the men's fight. Maybe because she was an inexperienced city girl, the yowls sounded eerie to Amaranthe. It was spring. Shouldn't those coyotes be off finding alluring opposite-sex coyotes to mate with instead of serenading the trees with those agitated shrieks?

Maldynado rolled away and jumped to his feet, landing in a balanced ready stance. He held a hand out. "We're done."

On his knees, hands balled into fists and chest heaving, Akstyr snarled at him. "We're *done*? What addled ancestor jumped into your head and made you start that?" Blood streamed from his nose. He dashed it away with a sleeve.

"A capricious one." Maldynado grinned. Though mud smeared his fine clothing and smudged his jaw, he appeared unwounded. "I thought you'd appreciate the opportunity to practice healing."

Akstyr stared for a long moment before unclenching his fists. "You pummeled me into the ground because you wanted to *help* me?"

"Yup. You're a mess now," Maldynado said. "Can you practice on yourself? Magic, I mean." His lip quirked.

"It's easier on other people." Akstyr sniffed and dabbed at his nose.

"Oh." Maldynado pushed up a sleeve. "Well, I scraped my elbow on that stump. Want to help it?"

"Right now, I wouldn't help you if you staggered up to me with a spear sticking out of your chest. I'm going to study. Don't talk to me again tonight. Any of you." Akstyr snatched his book and his blanket and stalked to the lorry.

"How long before he realizes he won't get much studying done without a light?" Books murmured.

Amaranthe dug a lantern out of their gear, lit it, and took it to the lorry. Without a word, she set it down beside Akstyr, who was propped in the back, scowling at his book. She returned to the campfire.

After a moment of sullen silence, Akstyr said, "Thanks."

"Interesting tactics," Amaranthe told Maldynado.

"Yes, I'm creative. Like a brilliant general inspiring his army to acts of greatness."

"Or acts of mutiny," Books muttered.

"Hush, or I'll thump you up for Akstyr to practice on."

Sicarius crouched next to Amaranthe. "Something is off out there."

"What do you mean?"

He flicked his gaze toward the pond, where the frogs remained silent. Mist gathered amongst the ferns overreaching the filmy water.

Amaranthe strapped on her short sword and a pistol, then followed him to the water's edge to talk privately.

"What is it?" She turned her back to the pond, preferring the view of the fire—and their lorry full of weapons. The coyotes and the mists had her thinking of stories her father had told her as a girl: tales of dark nights when people were haunted by deranged ancestor spirits resentful of their living kin.

A twig snapped in the distance. Amaranthe's hand brushed her pistol before she caught herself. Just some nocturnal animal hunting for grub. Besides, Sicarius stood an arm's length away. He could probably kill anything in the forest barehanded. Though the way something in the woods arrested his attention stole some of the comfort his presence usually offered.

"Sicarius?" she prompted.

"I'm as much a city-dweller as you," he said, "but I had complete wilderness-lore training, and I've spent many nights in forests."

"I don't doubt it." She shifted her weight. It was not like him to verbally defend his skills—there was no need.

"The coyotes sound…off," he said. "Those aren't their usual cries."

"Off, how?"

"Fearful, distressed. I've been scouting, and many animals are displaying signs of agitation."

"Maybe our presence is disturbing them," Amaranthe said.

The coyotes picked up their cries again, closer now. This time, she did let her hand come to rest on the butt of the pistol.

"You stand first watch," Sicarius said. "Let me sleep for a couple hours, then I'll take the rest of the night."

"We do have six people here," Amaranthe said.

"Not that I trust to stay awake and alert."

He strode back into camp before she could respond. She understood doubting Akstyr or Maldynado, but she had faith Books and especially Basilard, who seemed more comfortable in the forest than any of them, would stand a responsible watch. She had more faith in them than herself. In the city, she knew what to expect. Out here, how did a novice tell the difference between the innocent activity of nocturnal creatures and more sinister sounds?

Amaranthe poked around, looking for a good spot to stand watch. Meanwhile, Sicarius unloaded her repeating crossbow and handed rifles to the men.

"Sleep with your boots on and your weapons close," he told them.

They accepted the rifles grimly. Sicarius applied poison to Amaranthe's crossbow quarrels and headed over to where she had found her

lookout position—a broad tree leaning over the pond. She could put her back against it and see in all directions except the water.

"One of my school friends said you can tell a man likes you when he starts doing you little favors," Amaranthe said. "I wonder if she would have counted the application of poison to one's weapons."

Sicarius handed her the crossbow and pointed at her pistol. "You have powder and balls?"

"Yes. No comment on favors, eh?"

Sicarius handed her a cloak, threw a second around himself, and headed into the darkness. He skimmed up a tree with low branches and settled into a crook ten feet up.

"You are an eccentric and unique individual, Sicarius," she said under her breath.

She tried to imagine him married and living in a house in the countryside with a passel of toddlers running around. The vision did not evolve far. If he ever married, it'd have to be to someone who would follow him into the woods and up a tree.

With dinner done, the men settled in. Maldynado talked Basilard into a Strat-Tiles game, proclaiming his interest in educating him in the ways of Turgonian military strategy. And perhaps he would like to wager a few coins as well? Basilard proceeded to beat Maldynado three times.

Once everyone was asleep, either in the tent or the back of the lorry, Amaranthe grew more aware of the night pressing in around her. The mist thickened, obscuring the surface of the pond, though occasional plops and splashes reminded her the water lay behind her. Now and then leaves rustled and branches rattled. Small creatures darting through the area, she assumed.

The forest seemed busy for night, but she did not have enough experience to know what was normal. The coyotes' agitated wails continued to assault her ears, but she found a calm detachment after a while. A distinct eeriness pervaded the area, but nothing had bothered them yet. No need to worry.

A soft crunch came from her left, then another. Not like the passing of the earlier creatures, more like the soft malevolent step of something stalking closer.

Now there was a reason to worry.

Her grip tightened on the crossbow. She could shoot five rounds before reloading, plenty to handle a predator. She hoped.

Amaranthe cocked an ear, listening for a repeat of the noise. Though her vision had adjusted to the darkness, deep shadows turned bushes into indistinct blobs and trees into barriers that could hide a coyote—or ten.

Two green glowing spots appeared. Her breath caught. Eyes?

She blinked, thinking her own straining eyes were playing tricks. The glowing points disappeared.

"My imagination," she breathed.

Heartbeats thumped past, and the lights did not reappear. She realized she had been gaping in the same direction for a long time and quickly scanned the rest of the area. Lastly, she craned her neck to peer around her tree backrest.

Across the pond, luminous green eyes stared at her.

Amaranthe forced her breathing to remain steady and calm, though sweat dampened her palms. This time, when the eyes disappeared, they tilted before winking out, like a head ducking sideways.

She fingered the trigger of her crossbow. Should she wake Sicarius? If this was some trick of her imagination, she would appear foolish in front of him. It shouldn't, but his favorable opinion mattered more than most. Perhaps because he offered it to so few.

She decided to find out what lurked out there before waking anyone. It was not as if she had no combat skills to call upon if the moment required it.

Amaranthe strode to the lorry. The fire burned low with only scattered flames guttering amongst the red and gray coals. While keeping an eye toward the surrounding forest, she dug a few fire-starters out of the footlocker. Akstyr snoozed, so she took his lantern. The soft light showed no sign of the cuts and bruises he should have sported after Maldynado's pummeling. Huh.

A low growl emanated from the underbrush on the other side of the road. Amaranthe hooked the lantern over her forearm, so she could hold the crossbow in one hand and a fire-starter in the other. She lit the incendiary ball and lobbed it onto the road. It burned heartily, illuminating the wet concrete for several feet around. Nothing waited within the light's influence.

Trusting the fire-starter to burn for a few minutes, Amaranthe headed back to her spot by the tree. Another growl rumbled through the night. Ahead of her, green eyes glowed.

She lit another fire-starter and lofted it. The eyes flashed away before her projectile hit the ground, but not before she glimpsed gray fur and four legs.

"A wolf?" she whispered, thinking it too large for a coyote. Though it did not remind her of the killer soul construct she had faced in the city, she did not relax as the tiny bundle of flames smoldered on the wet leaf litter. What kind of wolf had glowing eyes? It had to be something magical, or—

"What are you doing?" Sicarius's voice floated from his tree perch.

"The usual night-watch activities." She tried to keep her tone light. Neither the creepy forest nor the creepy wolves were going to make her nervous, thank you very much. "Staying awake, counting trees, throwing fire at wolves with glowing eyes."

"Glowing what?"

The ferns behind the smoking fire-starter shook. A wolf leaped across the burning ball and charged Amaranthe.

She fired the crossbow, scarcely taking time to aim.

The quarrel slammed into one of the beast's eyes.

Relieved by the accuracy of her reflexes, Amaranthe started to lower the weapon. But the wolf did not slow down. It sprinted at her, quarrel protruding from its eye.

She dropped the lantern to pull the lever and chamber another bolt, but the beast moved too quickly. It leaped, fanged maw stretching open.

Amaranthe hurled the crossbow at the wolf and dodged behind the tree. She tore her sword free.

The beast landed, whirled, and sprang at her again. She whipped her blade across, slashing into its jugular.

She ducked as the wolf's momentum carried it toward her. It clipped her shoulder, tumbled across her back, and crashed into the tree. She lunged away and whirled to face it again, blade raised.

Sicarius halted at her side, his black dagger poised, as if he had been about to jump into the fray. The wolf lay still, though, its legs akimbo. Amaranthe lowered her sword, pleased she had handled it without his

help. Though a simple forest predator should not have taken two killing blows to die.

Sicarius put his back to the tree and scanned the surrounding darkness. "Wolves don't have glowing eyes."

"Yes, I'm a tad new to mountain life, but I thought not." Amaranthe retrieved her crossbow. "I think there's more than one. I'm going to wake…"

Across the camp, near the back of the lorry, a pair of green eyes watched her. Three more sets appeared on the road, milling. Claws clacked softly on the concrete. A twig snapped on the other side of the pond.

"Go." A throwing knife appeared in Sicarius's hand. "Wake them."

He hurled the weapon toward the lorry. It landed with a fleshy thump. The glowing orbs slumped downward, then winked out.

"Wake up, gentlemen!" Amaranthe ran to camp, crossbow in her right hand, short sword in her left. "Mutant wolves are attacking."

Basilard lunged out of the tent, rifle in hand. Books stumbled out after.

"Build up the fire," Amaranthe told them as she ran by to wake the others.

Snores emanated from the back of the lorry where Maldynado had joined Akstyr. She raised her sword to thump on the metal side. A figure blurred out of the darkness, sailing toward the lorry bed.

"Look out!" Amaranthe fired the crossbow one-handed.

The quarrel took the wolf in the lung, but she dared not trust it to die promptly. She tossed the crossbow into the bed and scrambled after, sword still in hand.

"What the—" Maldynado leaped over the other side, hitting the ground in a roll.

The injured wolf landed an inch from Akstyr, claws screeching on metal. It spun toward Amaranthe. She stabbed at its eyes with the short sword, but it whipped its head to the side, and her blade only clipped its snout. The wolf leaped back, hurdling Akstyr.

He lay so still, she feared him under some spell—or worse.

The wolf wheezed and gurgled. That lung shot ought to have killed it. Its lips rippled as it snarled, and blood dripped from its fangs.

Before Amaranthe could decide if she wanted to attack over Akstyr, the wolf lunged for her. A paw landed on Akstyr's gut, and he sat up with a grunt. The motion distracted her, and snapping jaws almost clamped onto her arm.

She sidestepped and drove the short sword into the wolf's ribcage with all her strength. Bone crunched and gave. Her blade sunk so deep, the falling body pulled the weapon out of her hand.

Akstyr was scrambling to his feet, but the wolf slumped against him. He staggered back under its weight, then heaved the dying beast over the side.

"Akstyr," Amaranthe groaned.

"What?"

"My sword was in that body."

A rifle cracked nearby, drowning his reply and reminding her they still had work to do. Three wolves snapped at Books and Basilard, who stood back-to-back in the center of camp. No one had had a chance to build up the fire. Beside the lorry, Maldynado clubbed another wolf with the butt of a rifle. She did not see Sicarius. Shapes darted through the shadows all around the camp.

"Help Maldynado." Amaranthe picked up her crossbow.

She launched her remaining three quarrels at the wolves harrying Books and Basilard. Each thunked home. Again, the wolves seemed not to notice. She had to trust the poison on the tips would slow the beasts somewhat.

She started to repeat her order to Akstyr, who was still in the lorry, but he had his eyes closed, hands lifted. He clenched them, and the campfire roared to life. Orange light threw back shadows, improving the illumination all around.

"Thanks," Amaranthe said. She spotted Maldynado's sword lying next to his blanket and handed it to Akstyr after he dug his own blade out. "He'll need this."

Amaranthe hopped down, leaving her crossbow to retrieve her sword. She planted a foot on the dead wolf to yank the weapon free.

The improved lighting showed Sicarius battling with the three wolves on the road. Though he had a dagger for each hand, he was out of throwing knives. The wolves attacked together, trying to surround him and bring him down like a wounded elk. He moved as quickly as they did, darting and dodging to stay on the outside where he only had to fight one at a time. Dagger blurring, he eviscerated one wolf as it leaped for him. Two remained.

She hesitated, wondering if she should join him. With his style of fighting, she might get in his way. More wolves lurked on the outskirts of the camp, though, and she would rather have him at her back than risk being surrounded herself.

One wolf slipped around Sicarius. It and the other timed a strike, leaping at him simultaneously.

Amaranthe sprinted for the road, thinking he might need help after all. He angled past the one jumping at his throat and opened its jugular with a dagger. It crashed into the second wolf, midair. Sicarius sprang back, blade slashing again. The second creature fell.

She lurched to a stop at the edge of the road, her sword raised. He lifted his eyebrows.

"I thought you might need a footstool to throw at them," she said sheepishly, lowering her weapon.

He grunted and headed off to retrieve his throwing knives.

Dead wolves littered the road and the camp. None remained standing, nor were any slinking away. If all they had wanted was a meal, they never would have fought to the death; they would have fled as soon as the odds turned against them.

"Is everyone all right?" Amaranthe called. "Any wounds?" She peered up and down the road as she cleaned her blade, half-expecting some shamanic beast-master to be lurking along the wayside. If such a person existed, he was not considerate enough to show himself.

"Books jabbed me in the ribs with an elbow," Maldynado said.

"I thought you were a wolf," Books said.

"Then I guess I'm lucky you don't know the pointy thing is supposed to go into the enemy." Maldynado waved at Books's sword.

Akstyr laughed and Basilard grinned.

"They're all right." Amaranthe smiled to herself.

Sicarius returned to her side. She tucked loose strands of hair behind her ears and waited, expecting a chastisement for being so slow to wake everyone. Nobody should have been caught sleeping when the attack came. If she hadn't been worried about losing face…

"Good fighting," Sicarius said.

"Huh?" she blurted before something more intelligent could form in her thoughts.

"Your accuracy with the crossbow was pinpoint, your sword skills adequate."

"Oh. Thanks." From him, "adequate" was high praise, and she'd never heard him use the word pinpoint to describe any of her maneuvers. He must not have seen her get her sword stuck between that wolf's ribs.

He prodded the nearest corpse with a muddy boot. "These were more difficult to kill than wolves should be."

"Wolves don't generally attack people either." Maldynado strolled up. "Also, in case it wasn't mentioned, that glowing-eye effect was a mite odd."

"Magic?" Amaranthe assumed.

Akstyr knelt beside one of the wolves. "Not that I can tell."

"Er," Amaranthe said. "What else could it be?"

"I suppose it's possible something has been done to them," Akstyr said, "but the wolves *themselves* don't feel crafted by a Maker. Not like the soul construct from this winter."

"Bas?" Amaranthe asked. "Your people live up north in these mountains. Any ideas what we're dealing with?"

Basilard shook his head.

"They appear to be simple eastern timber wolves," Books said, "native to these mountains, but hunted nearly to extinction in the last century by farmers and shepherds concerned for their stock animals. Though carnivorous by nature, these creatures are a smaller, less aggressive offshoot of the giant frontier wolves. Attacks upon humans are rare. Most incidents have involved individuals, not groups, and the wolves were starved from a harsh winter."

Maldynado made a show of yawning. "It's bad enough I had to get up in the middle of the night; I didn't think lectures would be involved."

Books opened his mouth to respond.

"What could explain this behavior?" Amaranthe blurted, hoping to head off a verbal sparring match.

"Maybe the professor can dissect one and let us know," Maldynado said. "What do you think, Booksie?"

"I was a history professor, you simian twit. Not a biologist."

"So…no dissections?" Maldynado asked.

Amaranthe lifted a hand to end the discussion. "Let's…" She considered the carnage, crinkling her nose at the butcher-house scent. Even if they moved the bodies out of camp, the blood would attract scavengers that would keep her team up the rest of the night. "Pack and get back on the road."

"Who has to drive and stoke the firebox, and who gets to sleep?" Maldynado asked, eyes narrowed.

Books, Akstyr, and Basilard stepped back. That left Maldynado in the front.

"I believe you've been volunteered," Amaranthe said.

Maldynado groaned. "This trip is off to a horrible start. When I agreed to help you so I could become famous and have someone make a statue of me, I thought my tasks would involve bad-man thumping by day and soft beds by night."

Amaranthe patted him on the back. "Statues don't come easily, my friend."

"So long as it's a big one when it comes."

CHAPTER 11

BOOKS ADJUSTED HIS RUCKSACK AND SWORD AS the lorry drove away, gravel crunching beneath the wheels. Amaranthe, Basilard, Akstyr, and Sicarius were driving off to investigate the suspicious lot while Books headed in—unannounced—to the Spearcrest estate.

A hand thumped Books on the shoulder.

"Thanks for requesting me for this side trip, Booksie." Maldynado carried a rifle and ammunition in addition to his usual gear, all over-shadowed by his ridiculous hat. He pointed the weapon toward a stone-and-timber home at the end of the driveway. It and a carriage house overlooked the wide river as well as the main road through the pass. This early in the morning, the craggy valley walls cast shadows over the homestead.

"*Requesting* you?" Books asked.

"Sure, the boss told me how you thought my family connections could get us a friendly welcome and a warm bed." He tilted his head back and yawned. "And that sounds particularly fine after last night's interrupted snooze."

"Amaranthe told you that, did she?" She might be right, but Books wondered at her claiming the words had come from him. Did she think to ingratiate him to Maldynado? "I hope the fact that you're disowned doesn't get us turned away."

"Nah, these remote, rural Crests haven't an inkling of what goes on in the capital. Look over there. Do you see that?" Maldynado pointed at a tiny shack downhill from the house.

"An outhouse?" Books asked.

Maldynado shuddered. "This place is as antiquated as the pyramid in the city."

"Not quite."

A rustic home did not mean these people could not get news from the capital, but Books shrugged and followed as Maldynado headed up the driveway.

Snowy peaks scraped the sky behind the rocky valley. Giant boulders had fallen in eons past and lay in jumbled heaps along the river's banks. Upstream, a mill perched with an old waterwheel turning in the current, its wooden frame gray with age. A pretty landscape, though nothing suggested the sort of wealth one associated with the empire's aristocracy. A garden and greenhouse waited for the sun to peep over the crags, though they did not likely provide enough vegetables for more than a couple of people. Even timber was scarce on this side of the river; it must have been cleared in the previous generation.

On the way to the front porch, Books and Maldynado drew even with the carriage house. The doors stood open, revealing two steam vehicles. A couple of young men labored beside one, shoveling coal into the furnace.

Books halted. Not just "young men." Soldiers. And the red-and-silver vehicle was the one that had passed the team on the road.

A pair of dogs raced around from the back of the house. They bayed as they ran toward Books and Maldynado.

"Maybe we should have kept the others with us longer." Books tensed, hoping the hounds were simply announcing visitors. At least their eyes weren't glowing.

Maldynado squatted and spread his arms. "Hullo, puppies!"

"You're going to be missing a throat in a second," Books said.

"Nah."

The dogs sniffed around Maldynado. He ruffled one's ears. The other kept its distance, huffing and grumbling, but it did nothing more threatening. The friendlier one leaned against Maldynado's leg and cocked its head for the ear rub.

"Must be female." Books muttered.

He doubted the soldiers would be so easily won over. The two young men came out of the carriage house, brushing coal dust from their hands. Suspicious frowns darkened their faces.

"Howdy, lads," Maldynado said, still petting the dog. "Is the lord of the manor home?"

The front door opened. Thirty soldiers streamed out, rifles in their hands. Three enforcers, including the female, followed.

"We're in trouble," Books murmured.

A bald, bow-legged man stepped onto the porch. He was missing one arm. A white-haired woman stood in the doorway, fingers touching her lips. She emanated apprehension. Books probably did too. He held his hands away from his weapons, expecting the soldiers to arrest—or shoot—them, especially now that his face adorned wanted posters.

The soldiers marched past, scarcely glancing his way as they headed for the back of the lorry with their gear.

"Think they spent the night?" Books relaxed slightly as the last man passed him.

"Probably," Maldynado said. "If you're warrior caste, you're obligated to help the emperor's troops if they pass by your land."

Further tension ebbed from Books's muscles as the last soldiers climbed into the lorry. But he relaxed too soon. The enforcers were not so quick to pass, and the woman stopped before him.

The top of her head came to Books's nose—tall lady. Hair clipped close to her skull accented angular cheekbones and a strong, square jaw. Sergeant's pins glinted on her lapels, making her the highest ranking enforcer there. Her hard brown eyes shifted from Books to Maldynado and back again.

"Morning, ma'am." Maldynado offered a deep warrior-caste bow, arms stretched away from his weapons. "Is there trouble at the Spearcrests? I certainly hope not. We've—"

"I know who you are," she said. "Both of you."

"Erp?" Books managed.

Maldynado splayed a hand against his chest. "You do? You've heard about my roguish but charming personality? My daring escapades? I've always wanted to be famous."

Books kicked him in the ankle. Even if he and Maldynado could defend themselves against the female enforcer and her male cohorts, the soldiers were not far away. Also, the man and woman on the front porch were probably the lord and lady of the estate. Brawling with enforcers in front of them might make the cover story Books had planned less believable.

"I don't have time to arrest you two now," the sergeant said.

"Darn," Maldynado said.

Books kicked him again. "Where are you rushing off to with all those soldiers?" he asked.

The sergeant snorted and strode toward the carriage house. "If you're around when we're on our way back, we'll deal with you then."

"Looking forward to it." Maldynado lifted his foot to avoid the third kick directed at his ankles. "How many days will we be waiting exactly?"

She did not answer or look back at them.

"Think Amaranthe was that stuffy when she was an enforcer?" Maldynado asked.

"I think," Books said, "she's changed a lot since she started working with us."

"True, true. We're a good influence."

"*Some* of us perhaps," Books said.

The lorry rumbled into the driveway, belching smoke into the crisp, mountain air. Maldynado headed for the porch.

The man who was presumably Lord Spearcrest stood watching, his single arm propped on his hip. The sleeve of his other was pinned along the side and did not quite hide the outline of a stump that extended from his shoulder. He wore a glower darker than the inside of a smokestack. The woman relaxed against the door jamb as the lorry disappeared from view.

Books jogged to catch up to Maldynado. "Let me do the talking up there. Your charms have proven ineffective this morning."

"I don't think one enforcer is a large enough sample size to justify statements like that." Maldynado stepped aside, however, letting Books ascend the stairs first.

Lord Spearcrest's glower deepened, and Books wondered if he should have let Maldynado lead—and take the brunt of the man's displeasure—after all.

"Good morning, Lord and Lady Spearcrest." Books offered a semblance of a bow, though he clunked his elbow on his sword hilt—no chance of these people mistaking *him* for warrior caste. "I'm Professor Mugdildor, and this is my patron." He decided not to mention Maldynado's name in case news of his disownment had reached the estate. "I work at Bartok University, and I'm researching dialectal variations in

the Turgonian language across the satrapy. How much does distance from the capital, remoteness, and proximity to outlying communities affect our mother tongue?" Books ignored the fact that his "patron" was rolling his eyes. "I hope to take my studies empire-wide eventually. I was wondering if you'd—"

"Who's here now, Father?" a feminine voice asked. A *familiar* feminine voice.

Vonsha.

Books's mouth sagged open as she stepped into view behind her parents. A bandage wrapped her neck, and stitches laced a cut on her chin.

"Hello, Books," she said.

He groped for words, and she smiled. She was a handsome woman even with the cuts and bruises.

"Should have known someone who yapped like that was a friend of yours, Vonsha," the old man said. He stalked back into the house without a greeting, grabbing his wife with his arm. "Get rid of them. We don't need any more overnight guests."

"Sociable chap," Maldynado muttered.

"When you suggested cider," Vonsha told Books, "I thought you meant at a cafe in the city."

"Yes, of course," Books said. "I did. I didn't know you'd be here. I mean, I knew this was your family's estate because you were researching this land and you told me, and, er…" He rubbed his lips, rattled not just by her smile, but by the fact that his cover story was useless now. She would never believe coincidence had brought him here.

"He wanted to make sure you were well," Maldynado said.

Vonsha's eyes widened. "You followed me all the way up here just for that?" She leaned to peer past Books. "You didn't even bring a vehicle. How did you—"

"We got a ride," Maldynado said. "Booksie here felt guilt-stuffed after he had to run off, leaving you in enforcer hands. But he had to on account of a tiny problem with the law, you see. Entirely a misunderstanding, but it does make it needful for him to flee when those big steam carriages roll up. And Books was oozing blood out of all sorts of unsavory cuts, so he had to tend himself as well. He felt terribly disturbed by the turn of events that interrupted your research, and he

couldn't rest until he checked up on you. I came along to keep an eye on him." Maldynado slung an arm across Books's shoulders. "He's an academic, not a warrior, you know. He needs my assistance from time to time."

Vonsha gazed up at him, listening to Maldynado's every word.

Books's fingernails dug into the flesh of his palms. Though Maldynado was trying to help, Books hated the way his charisma—or pretty face—seemed to be charming Vonsha. *Books* was supposed to be charming her.

"I see," Vonsha said when Maldynado finished. "That was thoughtful of you to come with him. Are you two—" she eyed the arm slung over Books's shoulders, " —a couple?"

"What?" Books gaped. "No!" He shoved Maldynado's arm away.

"Really, Booksie," Maldynado drawled. "You needn't act so affronted. I'm quite a catch, you know."

Books planted a hand on Maldynado's chest and pushed him back. "He may be incorrect about that, but he's right that I felt badly about abandoning you. I wanted to make sure you weren't seriously injured, but also to talk to you about the explosion. And those men who started it. Do you know them? Is there a reason someone would be after you?"

Vonsha touched the bandage around her neck. "Don't take this as a slight, but I was hoping they were after you, not me."

Though that *was* a possibility, Books said, "I don't think anybody knew I was going to be at the real estate library then. Besides who would want to blow me up for…" Careful, he told himself, remembering his story. "Researching retirement properties?"

Maldynado snorted.

"Hm," Vonsha said.

She didn't believe he was telling the truth, of that he was certain. But he doubted she was telling the whole truth either. *Why* would her family be concerned about the boundaries of their property at that particular moment? Dare he risk telling her more of what Amaranthe's team had uncovered? Maybe he could make Vonsha an ally. Whoever had thrown that explosive had targeted both of them, after all.

"Why don't you come in?" Vonsha said. "We should talk."

* * * * *

Eyes gleaming, Akstyr grinned like a bully on the trail of a weakling as he maneuvered the lorry. The vehicle bounced and lurched, and Amaranthe had to grip the railing with both hands to keep from being hurled out. Basilard sat on the driver's bench with Akstyr, and he pointed at the road ahead of them, but Amaranthe could not tell if it was to suggest detours around the craters in the weed-infested dirt road or to encourage Akstyr to drive through them. The old, rusty lorry groaned and squealed at the maneuvers.

"I never thought I'd miss Maldynado's driving," Amaranthe said.

Sicarius stood near the firebox, alternately monitoring the steam levels and surveying the rocky terrain. The road followed the river, though the hisses and clanks of the vehicle drowned the sound of rushing water. If the bumpy ride bothered him, he gave no indication of it.

The road bent around a wide stump sprouting three saplings from its decaying top. A dilapidated wood-and-rope suspension bridge came into view. The property they had come to investigate started on the other side.

Basilard and Akstyr bent their heads low, pointing and discussing.

"…can make it," Akstyr said.

Even as Amaranthe shook her head and reached for Akstyr, Sicarius said, "No," in a flat, hard tone that cut across the clanking machinery.

Akstyr's shoulders slumped, but he angled the lorry off the road. Basilard offered a sheepish shrug.

"We're enrolling you two in structural engineering classes when we get back," Amaranthe said. "I'm not sure it's even safe to *walk* across that bridge."

Akstyr cut off the lorry. Amaranthe grabbed her rucksack and climbed out, taking a moment to appreciate the solid unmoving nature of the ground.

A pile of donkey dung adorned the entrance to the bridge, suggesting the usual mode of transportation in these parts. A rusty bicycle missing a tire leaned against a stump. Across the river, the road dwindled to a narrow, twisting path that climbed a steep hill, disappearing into new-growth forest.

"Looks like we continue on foot," Amaranthe said.

"I'll stay with the lorry." Akstyr hefted his book out of the back. "I have a lot of studying to do."

"Really," Amaranthe said.

"Sure, you want me to be able to heal you if wolves attack again, right?"

"Won't you find that hard to do if you're here, and I'm five miles up the trail, bleeding to death?" Though Amaranthe was giving him a hard time, she had already planned to leave someone behind. It would bc foolish to desert the vehicle since it held all their gear and Sicarius's gambling-house winnings. "All right, Akstyr. You stay. And Basilard, will you stay too?" She rubbed her fingers in a sign just for him: *Watch the money*.

He nodded.

Amaranthe strapped on a rucksack full of food, water, and spare clothing. "Sicarius, are you ready for a hike?" She faced him only to find he had armed himself—more so than usual. In addition to his daggers and throwing knives, he held two rifles, two pistols, two cargo belts laden with ammo pouches, and a bag of his smoke grenades. "Or a single-handed all-out assault on the forest?"

He gazed back without comment.

"Is any of that for me?" she asked.

Sicarius handed her a rifle, pistol, and ammo belt.

"I guess we're prepared if any badgers look at us the wrong way," she said.

Sicarius, of course, did not smile, but neither did Basilard or Akstyr. She was not sure if it was because they dared not laugh at Sicarius, or because they were concerned at seeing him load up with so many weapons. Maybe he knew somcthing they did not and believed they would face something truly inimical.

Feeling weighted down, Amaranthe decided to leave her crossbow. She followed Sicarius, letting him set the pace. A brisk one, of course.

Though the suspension bridge might not support the weight of the lorry, it proved sturdy enough for two hikers. It still swayed and creaked more than Amaranthe would have preferred.

She paused in the middle to gaze upriver, wondering if she might be observing the source of the tainted water. The craggy mountains rose in the background while spring wildflowers peeped out along the banks.

On a steep hillside, a mountain goat grazed between patches of snow. Everything appeared...normal.

She trotted to catch up with Sicarius, who apparently had no interest in pausing to admire the landscape.

"Basilard and Books pointed out this river would be large enough to feed the agricultural lands around the city as well as the aqueducts," Amaranthe said as they left the bridge and started up the trail. "But there'd be a dam up here somewhere if it *was* servicing Stumps, right? There'd be a need to control the influx nature gives us, don't you think?"

"It's a long river," Sicarius said.

"True, but this is one of the main passes to the east. It seems like it'd be hard to hide a dam anywhere around here." Amaranthe pictured Books's terrain map in her head. "Of course, the river and the road aren't always side by side, and this mountainous terrain could hide a lot. I suppose if we see any mutilated bodies washed up on the shore, we'll have a clue we're on the right waterway. If this is the *wrong* waterway, we won't find whatever killed those dead people in this valley." She probably should not admit to being disappointed. Another thought occurred, and she snapped her fingers. "Do you suppose the water problem is what the enforcers and the soldiers are up here to investigate? Could they have figured things out and gotten a team together as quickly as we did? Or maybe the enforcers realized the bodies in the aqueducts came from someplace upstream. They could even know about that Waterton Dam. Drat, I wish we could have followed them. Say, next time a lorry full of soldiers passes on the road, you should jump onto the other vehicle as it passes, spy on them, and then report back to me."

This earned her a long backward stare. She tried to decide if it signified amusement or annoyance.

"If you want me to stop talking so you can more efficiently monitor the wilderness, let me know," Amaranthe said.

Sicarius did not speak right away—maybe he was mulling over her offer—so his answer, when it came, surprised her: "Sometimes useful ideas come from your burbling."

Burbling? Hm. "Thanks, I think."

A moss-draped wooden sign by the side of the path read: TRES-PASSERS WILL BE SHOT. MANY TIMES.

They stopped and Amaranthe unfolded the plat map. "The owner of the property is Lord Hagcrest. Ever heard of him or his kin?"

"No."

"Whatever emperor gave him his land must not have liked him much," she said, perusing the map. "The only thing you could farm up here is rocks, and I doubt you could even get machinery in to log. It'd all have to be done by hand. Any special value in any of these trees, I wonder? Or ore on this mountainside? A gold or silver deposit could definitely spur interest in the land."

While she talked—or maybe it was burbling again—Sicarius examined the trail and the surrounding area. He stopped to dig something out of a dent in the wooden sign. A musket ball.

"Guess that warning isn't an exaggeration," Amaranthe said.

Sicarius scraped blood off the ball.

"Not an exaggeration at all," she murmured.

CHAPTER 12

BOOKS SHIFTED ON THE HARD LOG CHAIR IN THE
Spearcrest's great room. A cushion would have been nice,
but if the one-armed seventy-year-old lord of the manor did
not need cushions, Books supposed he could do without.

Though large, the inside of the Spearcrest home did not bespeak
wealth any more than the outside did. No dust plagued the mantel
ledge and little clutter perched on tables, but the house held numerous
signs of delayed repairs: water damage at the top of a window frame,
chipped bricks on the hearth where Maldynado lounged, and a broken
banister rail on stairs leading to a second floor. The upholstered sofa
next to Books was as threadbare as the rug that covered the dented and
scratched hardwood floor.

Vonsha entered the room carrying a tray, and the scent of steamed
cider wafted to Books's nose. She handed a cup to each of them.

"There are honey pear tarts left," she said. "May I get you one?"

Books started to say "No, thank you," and that they had eaten breakfast, but Maldynado lifted a finger. "Absolutely."

As soon as Vonsha left, Maldynado leaned forward. "Why don't
they have any servants? That's unheard of."

"Maybe they prefer a simple life that doesn't include ordering people
around like subhuman minions simply because they weren't fortunate
enough to be born into a landed family."

"Or maybe the Spearcrests are destitute," Maldynado said.

"This house hardly qualifies as an abode of the destitute."

Vonsha returned with a plate of pastries.

"Excellent." Maldynado plucked three tarts off for himself.

Books curled a lip at him. Maldynado could eat less of their food if
he was worried the family was destitute.

Books selected a small tart for himself. "Thank you, my lady."

"Vonsha, please. We're not formal out here." She set the plate down and sat on the sofa across from Books.

"She's feeding them?" Lord Spearcrest's voice drifted down the hall. Vonsha put a hand over her face.

"Why?" Spearcrest went on. "You only feed people if you want to encourage them to stay." A door thumped, cutting off the rest of the tirade.

"Please forgive my father." A flush of embarrassment colored Vonsha's cheeks.

Books liked the warm glow it gave her face. Besides, he had been the one flustered in all their conversations thus far. It was nice seeing her equanimity jostled.

"He was a general before his injury forced retirement," Vonsha went on. "He's spent his life yelling orders, even at his children."

"You have siblings?" Books asked.

"My brothers are off serving in the marines. Not that they're much help when they're around." Her lip curled.

"Not your favorite relatives?"

"They tormented me a lot when we were younger, and they've given me a hard time over...events in my adult life as well."

Events like being ostracized for failing the emperor, Books guessed. "Sorry to hear that."

Maldynado, who had already devoured two tarts, made a face. His eyes rolled and his brows twitched in a manner that either meant he was choking on his food, or he wanted Books to take this conversation somewhere more interesting.

"Alas, we all have these family members and people we're cursed with." Books gave Maldynado a pointed look. "Sometimes working with them requires us to go spelunking to new depths of patience."

Maldynado groaned. "Spelunking to new depths? *Don't* say things like that to women, Booksie. Not if you ever hope to get your sheets toasted by more than a fire-warmed brick."

Vonsha chuckled. Books forced his lips into a smile, though it was a slight one. She was supposed to chuckle at *him*, not his over-muscled sidekick.

Maldynado did not appear to notice her attention. His gaze had shifted to the doorway. Lord Spearcrest stood in the hallway, scowling. Vonsha noticed and waved for her father to leave. It was a call from his wife that bestirred him, not his daughter's gesture.

"What were those soldiers and enforcers doing here?" Maldynado picked a crumb off his shirt, tossed it in his mouth, and licked his fingers.

"They're on some mission in the mountains," Vonsha said. "They spoke little of it, just showed the emperor's seal and requested lodging for the night. Naturally, it's our privilege to put them up."

The emperor's seal. So, young Sespian knew there was trouble up here. Amaranthe would be excited to learn that. If the team helped with the problem, maybe it would lead to the recognition she wanted. Books wished he could be happy working toward that goal himself. What he wanted was something he could never have again: his son back. He missed being a part of a family, of knowing someone needed him—that he mattered. Surely it was too early to think of finding that with Vonsha, but his mind did linger on the idea.

"What could they be doing up here?" Maldynado frowned at Books, probably wondering why he was not asking the questions. "They didn't look like they were continuing across the pass. They drove off the other way, going higher up in the mountains."

Books straightened. He needed to pay attention.

"They didn't see fit to tell us their business," Vonsha said.

"Has anything unusual happened here that you or your parents have noticed?" Books asked.

"Well..." She studied him, perhaps wondering if she could trust him. "You know that Kendorians are sometimes spotted in imperial territory on the other side of the mountains, right? That's why Fort Dretsvar sits at the bottom of the pass over there. Soldiers usually come through every month, some heading to the fort for a new assignment and others rotating out. They usually stay the night here, but my parents said there haven't been any visitors for two months."

"You believe there's a problem at the fort?"

"If there is..." Vonsha frowned. "My parents live up here, in the path of potential trouble. They have few neighbors so, if something has happened to that fort, there'll be nobody around to help them defend the property."

"Vonsha," Lord Spearcrest said from the hallway.

Books flinched. He had not heard the old man slip up on them again.

"I will discuss matters with these men," Spearcrest said. "Privately."

"Father, they came to see me and—"

"Now." He rapped his knuckles on the doorframe. "Go help your mother in the kitchen."

Vonsha sighed. "No matter how old you are, you're still a child when you visit your parents' home. Pardon me, gentlemen."

As soon as she left, her father stalked in. He propped his lone arm on his hip and scowled down at them. An old service pistol that had not been there before hung from his belt.

Books stood. "My lord."

Maldynado continued to lounge on the floor. He scratched an armpit.

"Who are you boys?" Spearcrest demanded. "And what're you doing spying about up here?"

"We're simply friends of Vonsha." Books eyed the pistol, noting the cocked hammer. The old man stood far enough away that he would have time to draw and shoot before Books or Maldynado could cross the distance and tackle him. "I was in the accident with her at the real estate library," he said. "I wanted to check on her."

"That's not the story you started out giving me." Spearcrest's hand descended to rest on the pistol butt.

Books tried not to wince. That was right. He had changed stories when Vonsha came out. He suddenly found himself admiring Amaranthe's ability to think—prevaricate—on her feet. Oh, how he preferred the settled calm of a library.

"That is true," Maldynado said. "We weren't sure you'd see Books if you knew."

"Knew what?" Spearcrest asked.

"His real reason for coming," Maldynado said.

"Which is what?" Spearcrest spoke slowly, enunciating each annoyance-laden word.

Books raised his eyebrows at Maldynado, wondering where he was taking this.

"That Books came courting," Maldynado said. "Your daughter's not married, right?"

Books was not sure if his jaw dropped as far as Lord Spearcrest's or not. It felt like it.

The old man opened and closed his mouth several times before speaking. "No. She lost her husband in the Western Sea Conflict. She said… Well, it's been so long, me and Mother just figured she wouldn't remarry." He turned an appraising eye on Books.

He squirmed like a sixteen-year-old boy come to ask a girl's father for permission to take her to the stadium to watch the races.

"Some fathers are particular about who their daughters marry," Maldynado said. "We weren't sure, so Books figured on the story as a guise to get to know you."

"I'd have preferred honesty," Spearcrest said though his face softened a smidgeon.

"Yes, my lord," Books said. "It was cowardly of me to spin a fabrication."

"Vonsha's old enough to make up her own mind on such matters. That's truly your reason for being here?"

"What else would people come way up here for?" Maldynado asked.

"Nothing," Spearcrest said. "Not a thing."

He left abruptly.

Maldynado threw a smug smile at Books. "You're welcome."

"Welcome!" Books struggled to keep his voice down. "When he tells her—she's going to think I want to marry her. That's ludicrous. We've barely spent an hour together uninterrupted. I just want to…"

"Sheath your sword in her scabbard?"

"No!" Well, yes, but not *just* that. "I merely wish to get to her know better."

"Without clothes on." Maldynado winked.

"You're incorrigible."

"Yes. But I kept Spearcrest from shooting you, so you're indebted to me."

"He wasn't going to shoot me."

"He had a hand on his pistol," Maldynado said.

"Yes, but you were the one lounging on the rug like a spoiled hound. Not to mention how much of their food you've already eaten."

Maldynado said nothing, though his mouth formed a silent, "Oh."

Books sank back in the hard chair, wondering what he was going to tell Vonsha when her father shared the "news" with her.

* * * * *

Amaranthe and Sicarius hiked three or four miles with the trail growing narrower and rougher with each switchback up the slope. Dirty patches of snow hunkered in depressions. Trees rose anywhere there was soil—and sometimes even from rock faces and boulders. Despite the wildness of the land, someone had cut the low branches back from the path, and they even passed a rough-hewn bench in one spot.

Sicarius paused to examine something on the ground. Amaranthe readjusted her rucksack and wiped moisture from her eyes. Though all the training they did kept her breathing slow and her muscles from growing weary, the brisk pace and the steep incline had her sweating. Her shirt stuck to her back, and damp spots bunched beneath the rucksack straps. She would shoot herself with the rifle before complaining about Sicarius's pace though.

"Anything interesting?" she asked when he stood.

"Fresh prints."

"Lord Hagcrest, I presume."

"Perhaps."

He continued onward without expounding.

The trees thinned, and the trail led them into a clearing. A small, square log cabin rested on a flat stretch of moss and wildflowers. Though simple, the structure appeared in good repair, and the split-cedar shingle roof had yet to fade to gray. A smokehouse tacked with rabbit and raccoon hides shared the clearing, while an outhouse hunkered downhill.

"I guess we should be wary of that threat to shoot trespassers." Amaranthe pointed to a stuffed bear head mounted under the eaves above the front door. "It seems our homeowner is a decent shot."

Sicarius was already gliding about the clearing, eyeing tracks, touching trees, and sniffing the wind. Amaranthe headed for the front door. She figured the homeowner was unlikely to shoot a woman whereas a black-clad man roaming the perimeter might make a trigger finger twitchy. Besides, she earned more answers from talking to people than from poking around their properties.

She climbed three wooden steps to a limestone porch. "Hello, Lord Hagcrest? Are you home?"

Amaranthe lifted a hand to knock on the door, but stopped. It stood open a crack. Her nose caught a faint scent: blood.

Sicarius had disappeared. She chewed on her lip a moment, then set her rifle against the wall and drew the pistol. She stood to the side, closed her eyes, and listened. No sound came from the cabin. Pistol ready, she pushed the door open, then flattened herself against the outside wall, so she would not expose herself to anyone inside.

Nothing stirred within. Amaranthe stuck her head around the jamb for a quick peek. When nobody shot at her, she leaned in for a longer examination.

Shutters covered the cabin's sole window, so the only light slashed in through the doorway, leaving the interior dark. When her eyes adjusted to the gloom, she eased inside.

A bearskin rug stretched before a hearth adorned by a single battered pan hanging on a hook. A lone wooden chair sat before the fireplace, a threadbare cushion its only concession to comfort. In the shadows at the back of the room, a narrow bed rested against the wall.

"Guessing this fellow doesn't invite many house guests up," Amaranthe muttered.

Another rug lay on the floor before the bed. No, not a rug.

A body.

The white-haired old man wore a faded nightshirt afflicted with moth holes, and he appeared grouchy and sour even in death, just the sort of fellow who would put up that trespassing warning.

"I guess you *are* home, Lord Hagcrest," Amaranthe whispered.

No obvious wounds marked his body, though trails of dried blood rain from his nostrils and the corners of his eyes.

"Just like in the loading bay," she said.

After a deep breath to brace herself, she crouched and slid her fingers along the cold skin of Hagcrest's neck. She found what she sought near his hairline: a bump covered with scar tissue. As soon as she touched it, it slithered away without breaking the skin. She yanked her hand back and wiped her fingers on her trousers.

"All right," she murmured, "who's making the killer magic doodads that are smart enough to hide themselves at the promise of detection?"

A draft tickled the back of Amaranthe's neck.

She lunged to her feet, swatting at the skin there. Nothing. She did not lower her arm until she had probed her neck thoroughly. Who knew how these devices had found their way into these men?

"Imagination," she told herself. Probably just a bug or a breeze from the open door.

A rifle leaned against the wall an arm's length away, and a powder horn and knife belt hung from the bed post. Hagcrest had not had time to grab either. Perhaps he had never seen his attacker. Had he somehow been implanted with the device without his knowledge, and then it killed him through a remote command? If it was possible to create something like that with the Science, she was impressed. And concerned.

Papers scattered the bed next to an open drawer in a side table. She took them to the door to read in the afternoon light slanting inside. Army promotions and signed certificates for awards for Lord Major Hagcrest. He probably had a stack of medals somewhere. Amaranthe searched the cabin for more interesting paperwork, like the property title, but did not find it.

A shadow blotted out the daylight. Sicarius stepped inside and took in the body without a blink. "Is he the only one who lived here?"

"Looks like it." Amaranthe waved at the sparse room. "Remember the strange way the man at Farth Textiles died?"

"Yes."

"Hagcrest had a bump on his neck that moved when I touched it," she said. "Same killer, it seems."

"Possibly," Sicarius said. "Possibly not. An artifact crafted by one practitioner can be used by another. Some can even be used by those ignorant of the mental sciences."

"So one person could have made a bunch of these killer devices and distributed them to someone else—or to an *organization*—to be used at will?"

"Yes."

Amaranthe thought of the note Sicarius had stolen from the gambling house, the one thanking Ellaya for providing the name of an accomplished Maker. Was *this* an example of that Maker's work?

"Did you find anything outside?" Amaranthe asked.

"Four sets of fresh footprints."

"The same ones you noticed on the trail up?"

"There were only two sets of fresh ones on the path."

"How fresh is fresh?" The smell of death was turning her stomach, so Amaranthe walked out to the porch.

"Early this morning," Sicarius said. "Maybe late last night."

She inhaled, appreciating the clean smell of moss and damp leaves. "You can't tell me the exact hour?" She smiled. "I thought you were better than that."

Sicarius stepped onto the porch and gazed at her, the faintest crinkle to his brow.

"What?" she asked.

"People don't tease me."

"Ever?"

"No."

Because they were afraid of him. As Books had pointed out once, she was probably foolish not to be. That he tolerated more from her than the others was no proclamation of friendship. At times she wished she did not know that Sespian was his son and not the direct heir to the throne, a secret that would throw the empire into civil war if it came out. Sicarius killed those who threatened him, and even if she had sworn to keep the knowledge to herself, he had to see the simple fact of someone else knowing as a threat. Sometimes she wondered how much his sticking around had to do with a belief she could help him clear his name and become someone Sespian wanted to know…and how much he just wanted to keep an eye on her. Would he let her walk away from him with that knowledge in her head?

Amaranthe shook the dark thoughts away and forced her smile back. "No one's *ever* teased you? Truly? Not even as a child?"

"To tease is to mock or provoke in a playful way."

"Yes…" She arched her eyebrows.

"There was nothing playful about my childhood." Sicarius pointed north. "The tracks lead that way."

He strode off the porch, heading the indicated direction. Back to business.

"You know…" Amaranthe had to jog to catch up with him. "If you missed out on games and fun as a child, you could try playing now."

"What do you suggest?"

That he answered surprised her, and she was not sure how to respond.

Two deer browsing on the edge of the clearing started at their approach. They bounded into the trees and disappeared. A game trail led along the hillside, parallel to the river, and Sicarius headed down it. Pockets of mud held footprints.

"You could tease me," Amaranthe said. "Or, once in a while, do something for no logical reason. Be whimsical."

"Whimsical." He said it with all the warmth of a kid discussing spinach.

"Yes, it's the opposite of what you always are."

Gray clouds drifted down from the mountaintops. Depending on how long this trek took, they might not make it back to the lorry by dark. She hoped they would not have to spend the night huddled under branches with rain dripping down their collars. Somehow she could not see Sicarius cuddling to share body heat. He would probably suggest pushups to stay warm.

They padded along the trail in silence for a time. The trees grew less dense and the ground more rocky. Far below, the river wound through the valley.

Sicarius stopped beside one of the last trees before a landslide. A meager trail crossed the boulders and loose shale, but one would be in the open crossing the area.

"Think there's anybody watching the area?" Amaranthe asked.

Sicarius lifted a finger to his lips. He pointed, not across the landslide, but down it. Several hundred feet below, two men were poking around the rock field. One carried what might have been a clipboard.

"Prospectors?" she whispered.

She and Sicarius stayed behind cover and watched. The men continued their poking about for several minutes before heading north. They disappeared into a strip of forest on the far side of the landslide. The faint smoke of a campfire wafted from another open area beyond the trees. Amaranthe bounced on her toes, hoping the men's presence meant she was close to answers.

Sicarius raised an eyebrow.

"There's something out here that's interesting someone." She winced, realizing how vague and unhelpful that sounded.

"I'll investigate," Sicarius said. "Stay here."

"Wait. Wouldn't you prefer to have something distracting them while you're sneaking about, remaining unseen?"

"I don't need a distraction to remain unseen."

True.

"But I presume you have some scheme," he added.

"I brought along some of your earnings, so I could feign interest in purchasing this property. I'll head in and have a friendly palaver with them, see what I can learn."

"Palaver."

"Chat. Discuss. That thing you never do at length."

"Why put yourself at risk? I can grab someone and we can interrogate him."

Amaranthe rubbed her face. How was she going to convince good-hearted Sespian to pardon someone whose answer for everything was a dagger to someone's throat? "That didn't work in the loading bay, remember? And if more people up here have been injected with those devices... Well, it's inconvenient to have the person you're questioning pitch over dead."

Sicarius grunted a concession.

"Here's the plan: I'll go in and palaver while you surround them."

"Surround them," he said. "By myself."

"Just be ready to shoot a warning shot or two when I signal."

Amaranthe lifted her hand to her forehead to demonstrate, then handed him her rifle and sword belt. She would likely get further if she did not appear threatening. She kept her knife and pistol, adjusting the jacket to hide them. Sicarius watched, face stony. No doubt, he thought walking into the enemy camp was stupid. He was probably right.

"We'll try your way if my way doesn't work," she said.

"If *your* way doesn't work, you may be dead."

"That is a possibility."

CHAPTER 13

WHEN VONSHA RETURNED, HOLDING A NOTEPAD, she said nothing of the marriage discussion. Indeed, she glanced around the room, as if to ensure her father was gone.

"We convinced your old man to leave," Maldynado said.

Her eyes widened. "You're the first then."

She drew a chair close to Books and sat, her knee almost touching his. That faint perfume she wore teased his nostrils, a hint of honey and a bouquet of wildflowers.

An annoying smirk rode Maldynado's lips.

"Why don't you go explore the grounds?" Books told him. "Play with the dogs, perhaps."

"Nah, I'm comfortable here."

Books glared. Maldynado's smirk broadened.

Vonsha laid the papers so they rested across her and Books's knees. Her fingers brushed his thigh, and he gulped, unable to focus on the words on the page. He told himself he was forty-five and far too old to be nervous and flustered around a woman or to need to worry about shifting his jacket to hide—

"What's this?" He draped his arm across his lap and pointed to the page.

Maldynado snickered under his breath.

"Some notes I took the last time I was home," Vonsha said. "The reason I was double-checking the lot lines is that Lord Hagcrest, the neighbor across the river, has been up to something. He made an offer on my parents' land. He lives on the parcel *you* were looking up." Her eyes searched Books's face.

She must wonder if she could trust him or if he was involved somehow.

"I heard it might be for sale," Books said. Almost the truth.

"People have been snooping around over there, at least one fair-skinned and light-eyed. I'm concerned Hagcrest is working with foreigners, perhaps to allow a toehold into Turgonian territory. These mountains are treacherous, and the only pass for two hundred miles lies through this valley."

Books thought of the dead woman in the aqueducts whom they believed had been an appraiser. Was it possible this neighbor had called her up to calculate the value of the land, then killed her to keep her from telling anyone? If so, where had the horribly gashed dead men come from? The bodies must have originated in roughly the same area since they had been bumping up against the same grate in the subterranean channel. But if Hagcrest had ordered an appraisal, prior to making an offer, it should have been on the Spearcrest's land, not his own. Unless he was thinking of selling both lots to foreigners at a profit? Was that permitted? He would have to ask Amaranthe about real estate laws.

"Lord Hagcrest wouldn't tell me anything when I went to see him," Vonsha said. "He's an old grump, worse than my father. I'd actually been thinking of heading east myself after I recovered from the explosion." She touched the bandage at her neck. "To see what's going on at the fort. I have a feeling the presence of foreigners in this valley means something vile has happened over there. Perhaps..." She leaned closer and laid a hand on Books's arm. "If you don't mind my asking, how are you involved in all this? I'd like to trust you, but I don't know who you truly are. You're...wanted by the law?"

Books licked his lips. How much should he volunteer? His reason for coming here had been to acquire information, not give it away. He looked to Maldynado for an opinion, but a house cat had strolled in, and he was busy coaxing it onto his lap.

"Our leader calls us The Emperor's Edge...." Books spent the next few minutes explaining Amaranthe's group and their intent to earn Sespian's recognition, though he left out names. Sicarius, at the least, would not appreciate being mentioned.

"You roam around the city looking for good deeds to carry out?" Vonsha asked when he finished.

"Uhm." That sounded more charitable than they truly were, but maybe Vonsha would approve of noble deeds? "Basically."

"Sometimes we roam outside the city too." Maldynado petted the cat that purred in his lap, its tail swishing in time with the strokes.

Vonsha considered Books for a long moment, and he feared she would burst into laughter.

Instead she nodded. "You're what I need then. *You* should go out to the fort. I'm certain more answers await there, but my father is reluctant to let me go on my own. I've no knack with weapons, I fear, and if there *are* foreign militants about...."

"We'd have to check with the rest of the group," Books said. "They're going to see your neighbor."

"They are?" Vonsha frowned.

Er, maybe he shouldn't have given out that information. "Is that a problem?"

"No, no." Vonsha patted his arm. "They'll just find out for themselves how stubborn and difficult the man is. When they return, perhaps you can convince them of the need to check the fort."

"What about the enforcers?" Maldynado asked.

"What?" Vonsha asked.

"When the enforcers and soldiers drove away this morning, they went that way." He pointed toward the mountaintop. "You'd think if something fishy were going on at the other end of the pass, they'd have headed through."

"I don't know their assignment," Vonsha said. "It's possible their mission is unrelated to the business with Hagcrest's lot. There are numerous families and towns up in these mountains, as well as mining camps."

"Maybe the enforcers are investigating the phosphorescent-eyed wildlife," Books said.

"The what?" Vonsha asked, even as Maldynado nodded and said, "Ahhhh, right."

Books explained the wolf attack.

"That's troublesome," Vonsha said.

"Nothing like that has bothered you here?" Books asked.

She hesitated. "No."

"You're sure?"

"Yes."

Books let it drop, though he noted it for later consideration. He might not have Amaranthe's enforcer instincts, but even he could tell the family had a secret or two.

"If the mountains have grown that dangerous," Vonsha said, "I'm doubly sure this is a job for an outfit like yours. My father is too old to traipse about, hunting for infiltrators, and my mother and I are the only other ones in the household right now. Perhaps I could pay you a small fee."

Books waved away the offer. "No need for that, my lady. We aim to help the empire whether there's monetary compensation or not." He caught Maldynado rolling his eyes. The spiel *did* sound self-aggrandizing.

"Will your comrades return today?" Vonsha asked. "Can you ask them if they'll take on the trip?"

"Tomorrow would be my guess," Books said. Though spring had arrived, the days were still not long, especially up here in the mountains.

"Ah." Vonsha glanced toward the hallway. "You must stay here tonight then. I'll handle my father. Don't worry."

"Thank you." In a spasm of courage, Books put his hand on Vonsha's arm. "We'll do what we can. Maybe when all this is resolved, and your family is safe, we can have that cider at a nice cafe in the city."

Tension ebbed from her, and she gave him a genuine smile. "I'd like that." Vonsha stood. "Please relax here. I'll tend to rooms."

"Looks like you'll get your bed tonight," Books told Maldynado after she left. He also appreciated the idea of warm blankets, and a private room sounded fabulous after the previous night's adventures.

"Looks like," Maldynado said. "Funny, though, don't you think?"

"What is?"

"How much she wants us to take a trip across the pass."

"She explained her reasons."

Maldynado plucked at a thread on the faded rug. "I guess so."

His words made Books realize how little Vonsha had shown him of her notes. If he had not been distracted, he would have taken them to study. Maybe he could investigate the house that night, see if he could learn a little more. He nodded to himself. Yes, a little nocturnal exploring was in order.

* * * * *

Amaranthe picked her way past ferns and around boulders, following boot prints in a muddy trail. The scent of the campfire wafted through the air.

The forest gave way to a rocky landscape again, and the men she had seen earlier came into view. They sat around their fire, heating cans of carp for a late lunch or perhaps early dinner. Noon had long since passed, and the high peaks would bring twilight early. Clouds closing in further darkened the skies and promised rain.

The two men were the only people in view, though beyond them a canyon mouth parted a fifty-foot-high cliff running parallel to the river far below. From her angle, she could not see into the gap, but, judging by the breadth of the entrance, the ravine could hold an army. Faint clanks and rumbles emanated from within.

Amaranthe left the trees and strolled toward the campfire. As soon as the men noticed her, she spread her arms, palms open. Theirs faces screwed up in suspicion, but they did not reach for the bows propped nearby. One glanced toward the canyon. Was their boss inside? Amaranthe shifted the angle of her approach to ensure no one could come out without her noticing.

"Afternoon, gentlemen," she said. "I'm looking to speak with the, ah, *new* owner of this property."

"Is that so?" The speaker, a snaggletoothed fellow with tufts of bristly hair sticking out from beneath a wool cap, gave her a long leer.

Given the unimaginative bun confining her hair and the distinctively unsexy trousers and jacket she wore, she figured he had been up on the mountain without female company for a while. The second man eyed her more professionally and his hand went to a bow.

"What are you doing out here?" he asked.

"The same thing as you are," she said.

Snaggletooth's brow furrowed. "Quarrying rock?"

She managed to keep the surprise off her face. Rock? Surely a rock quarry could not justify all the interest in this land. The entire mountain range was made from limestone. It could be quarried from anywhere.

"Looking to acquire this property for my own purposes." Amaranthe waved in the direction of Hagcrest's cabin. "I came to see the owner, but it seems he's passed on recently."

"No kidding?" Snaggletooth smirked.

"I run a few businesses down in the capital," she said. "I have funds available for acquisitions. Perhaps I could make an offer to the new owner. I'm guessing Lord Hagcrest had no next-of-kin, and whoever holds the title now holds the land?" In the city, it would not be that simple, but out here it probably was.

"You have money?" Snaggletooth leaned forward, eyes bright. "With you?"

"Of course not. Who would go hiking with a rucksack full of ranmyas? My armed men are watching it somewhere safe and defensible."

The speculation did not leave Snaggletooth's eyes.

"Why," the bowman asked, stroking his chin, "would someone from the capital be interested in land all the way up here?"

"I could use the timber and limestone for my construction business. Since this lot is located on the river, it'd be easy to ship the raw materials out of the mountains." There. That sounded plausible. Right?

"Shipping stuff down that river won't be easy for long." Snaggletooth snickered.

His comrade glared at him.

"Oh?" Amaranthe considered the rocky hillside below. The river flowed past, its view impeded by only a few boulders and scrappy trees sprouting from the cracks. "Changes afoot?"

"Nothing we can talk about," the bowman said.

"Of course." Perhaps if she took things in a more roundabout direction.... "How'd you fellows get stuck working up here, anyway? It's kind of a forsaken plot, isn't it?"

"Got that right," Snaggletooth said. "Ain't a woman for miles, unless you count old Lady Spearcrest, but she's about a hundred and not worth raiding the property for."

The bowman leaned over to dig an elbow into his comrade's side. "Shut up," he whispered. "You're yapping too much."

"Slag off," Snaggletooth said back, not bothering to lower his voice. "We ain't had no womens to talk to in ages."

Amaranthe waited, happy to let them argue, hoping they would divulge more.

Someone walked out of the canyon. Braids of pale brown hair swayed around his sleeveless buckskin vest. His bare arms lacked the tattoos she associated with Kendorian shamans, but he otherwise had the look. Or perhaps he was another Mangdorian?

Well over six feet, the man towered over Amaranthe as he approached. If he was a Mangdorian, he was a tall one.

"Greetings." Amaranthe lifted a hand and hoped she kept the concern off her face. "Are you the new owner of this property? I'm interested in making an offer on it."

The man's green eyes lacked the sinister chill of some megalomaniacal villain intent on overthrowing the empire, but he did not appear pleased to see her. His face had a frazzled cast to it.

He waved for the two other men to grab their weapons and scoot out of earshot, though not out of bow range. His eyes shifted to Amaranthe, but they grew unfocused for a moment. A tingle grazed the back of her neck. Her imagination? Or perhaps he was a shaman, inspecting her through some otherworldly skill.

"You want me to believe you are businesswoman?" he asked, voice heavily accented.

Amaranthe had to concentrate to understand him. "Yes. I'm prepared to offer you a respectable sum, considering this is a remote, forsaken piece of land."

"Not enough forsaken. Too many people are showing up here. Who tells you this land good? Spearcrests?"

Amaranthe kept her face blank, but inside her gut twisted. If the Spearcrests were involved with what was going on over here, which, at the least included their neighbor's murder, then sending Books and Maldynado to visit may have been a mistake.

"Are you able to discuss selling the land?" Amaranthe asked. "Or are you merely someone's henchman, here to stand guard?"

"I no henchman." He jerked his chin up and thumped his chest with a fist, causing his braids to sway about his torso. "I valued partner."

"I see. And would you and your partners be piqued by an offer of fifty thousand ranmyas?" It was a few thousand below the appraisal amount on the waterlogged note the men had retrieved from the woman's body. A good starting point to negotiations.

The shaman snarled and slipped a primitive bone-blade knife from a sheath.

Maybe not a good starting point after all.

"That's not my final offer," Amaranthe said.

Knife in one hand, the shaman reached for her with the other. She hopped back, evading the grasp. If he *was* a Mangdorian, he was doing a horrible job following his pacifist religion.

"I see you're a foreigner and perhaps not educated in Turgonian business practices," Amaranthe said, "but trying to kill the other party is not an acceptable negotiation tactic."

"I no here for money, and land is no for sale."

"Why *are* you here?" She did not expect him to answer truthfully, but one never knew. Maybe he would feel the urge to confess.

He swiped at her with the knife.

Or not. Amaranthe evaded him again. He had reach with those long arms, but his size stole some of his speed, and she read the attacks easily. He lacked the practiced moves of an experienced fighter, so she decided not to reach for her pistol or signal Sicarius. Not yet. The bowmen were watching, but neither had an arrow nocked.

"To keep people like you from nose about," he answered.

"Nosing," Amaranthe said.

The shaman grumbled under his breath in a different language. He stopped advancing and lifted a hand toward the bowmen.

"Are you sure I can't interest you in coin?" Amaranthe said, meeting the bowmen's eyes. They seemed more likely to be persuaded by money. "Five thousand ranmyas if you simply tell me what it is you men are doing up here. Offer open to anyone."

Snaggletooth grew thoughtful.

"Enough," the shaman said. "Shoot her."

"Wait." Amaranthe lifted a palm toward each bowman. "You'll be dead if you try it. Do you think I'd come out here alone?"

The shaman snorted and waved for his men to carry out his order.

Amaranthe touched her forehead.

A rifle shot rang out from a high ledge overlooking the canyon and the campfire. Snaggletooth flew backward, landing spread-eagle, a bloody hole in the center of his forehead.

"Cursed ancestors," Amaranthe breathed. She had told Sicarius to fire a *warning* shot.

The dead man had a salutary effect on the remaining two. The second guard lunged behind a boulder. The shaman's knife drooped, and he gaped about, searching for the source of the shot. Rock and scrub brush dotted the top of the ledge and provided copious hiding spots. Amaranthe saw no sign of Sicarius.

"As I was saying, I did *not* come out here alone," she said.

The shaman muttered something under his breath. His eyes grew glazed.

Afraid he meant to hurl some magic at Sicarius, Amaranthe stepped forward, hand slipping inside her jacket for her pistol. The shaman snapped out of it and stopped her with a glare.

"*One* man," he said. "Only one man."

"Only one, yes, but he's very good. He can pick your people off one at a time from up there."

"Not if I kill him." The shaman turned his gaze toward the ledge again, focused, then sucked in a startled breath. "The assassin! Sicarius!"

Uh oh. How could he know that? Sicarius was under cover.

"He's here," the shaman breathed. "I didn't think... I mean, they say at the end, they would show us where he was. That if we cooperate we could—" He snapped his mouth shut and glared at Amaranthe.

Though she had not yet removed the pistol, her hand gripped the butt, and her finger found the trigger.

"You work with this monster?" Accusation—almost a look of betrayal—hung in the shaman's green eyes.

"If your people are responsible for Lord Hagcrest's death, then you're no better than he. What killed the old man anyway? Did you make that device under his skin?"

His stare did not waver. "Fifteen years ago, you know news? You know what happens in our country?"

"Kendor?" Amaranthe still did not know where the man was from.

"Mangdoria! Chief Yull unite tribes, make plans to negotiate for lands back from your empire. Your people think him a threat. Chief

Yull was peaceful! Your assassin—that *monster*—kills royal family. All family. Mother and children also. He cuts off their heads to deliver to your emperor." The shaman pointed a finger at Amaranthe's chest. "For much time we no know who responsible. He enter and leave without nobody see. Like ancestor spirit. But we know truth now. Partners tell us, promise help us get his head. Even if we fail, now all Mangdorians will know this monster, what he do."

The loathing in the shaman's eyes stole any rebuttal Amaranthe might have made. If she could come up with one. She knew what Sicarius had been and what, in many ways, he still was. Just because he was nominally *her* monster now did not make him less of one to the rest of the world.

"Your *partners* told you?" she asked. "Partners who wanted you for some ends of their own? Like to kill Hagcrest and claim this land with your magic? How can you rely on their word? They could simply be using you."

"That man is monster. You work with him, you must die."

"I thought Mangdorians were pacifists." Amaranthe slid the pistol out of its holster a couple of inches.

"Chief Yull was pacifist, and it get him killed. Old religion no good when empire for neighbor. You help Sicarius? Slay our chief? His family?"

"First off, it doesn't sound like you have any proof that he did it. Second, I was a child then, so, no, I couldn't have helped. Either way, this is history and has nothing to do with what's going on here." She hoped. "Unless you're here as part of some revenge attempt on the Turgonian government."

She watched the shaman's face, but he did not seem to hear. His gaze had returned to the cliff top.

"Did they tell you to kill Hagcrest?" she asked, trying to draw his attention back to her. If he could detect Sicarius with his power, he might be able to attack him with it too. "To get his land? You must know you'll be hunted for that. The emperor doesn't appreciate foreigners coming in and killing warrior caste veterans."

"They handle your emperor. They say—" The shaman snapped his mouth shut, eyes narrowing. "You a nose woman."

"Nosey," Amaranthe said. "I'm nosey, not a nose."

"My people never want to fight. Only to find way to get land back. Hard life in mountains. Seasons too short for farming. Long winters. People hungry. Always hungry." The shaman clasped his hands behind his back as he spoke, oddly unconcerned over his dead man or the weapon Sicarius likely had trained on him. Perhaps he could deflect a rifle ball, as the Nurian wizard Arbitan Losk had deflected crossbow quarrels and daggers. "Our people never want fight, but they are fools. Many have mastered the Science. Many could kill with a thought."

"Or with a tiny device that burrows beneath a man's skin?" Amaranthe asked.

"We will avenge the royal family's death." He said it calmly. His rage and his desire to kill her seemed to have vanished.

Amaranthe kept an eye on the canyon entrance and the second man, who still hunkered behind the boulder. She glanced over her shoulder, wondering if the shaman might be stalling while someone crept up on her. Had he signaled to his workers when she had not noticed? Nothing moved behind her.

But she was not the main threat. It was Sicarius the shaman needed to worry about.

Her heart lurched. Did he have some magical attack planned for Sicarius?

Amaranthe stepped forward. "Perhaps Sicarius is not responsible for what you think. Why don't we discuss things in your camp?"

"Yes." The shaman lifted a finger. "You *will* come my camp."

A boom thundered through the valley and echoed from the mountaintops. The earth rocked beneath Amaranthe's feet. A cloud of dust mushroomed into the air on the plateau where Sicarius waited.

"No," she whispered.

The ledge crumbled. Earth and rock sloughed down the cliff side, throwing more dust into the air at the bottom. Debris hurtled from the explosion, clacking to the stones around Amaranthe. A shard of rock struck her cheek. Blood trickled down her face, but she barely noticed. All she could do was stare at the cliff top, waiting—hoping—for some movement when the dust cloud dissipated. If her idiotic plan had gotten Sicarius killed...

The shaman lunged, reaching for her.

Acting on instinct, Amaranthe jumped back. She yanked the pistol free and fired. The ball thudded into his shoulder.

She whirled and sprinted toward the trees. Scree shifted and flew beneath her boots. She zigzagged and ducked around boulders, fearing an arrow would land between her shoulder blades any second. The bowman would not be worried about snipers on the ledge any more.

Something snagged Amaranthe's legs, constricting them like a rope wrapping around her ankles. She pitched forward. She tried to turn the fall into a roll, but something rooted her feet. The ground came hard and fast. She barely managed to keep from smashing her nose against a rock.

Amaranthe shoved herself upright and scrabbled at her ankles. Nothing visible or tangible bound them.

The shaman strode toward her, pain and fury contorting his face. He gripped his shoulder with his free hand, and blood ran through his fingers.

The bowman followed. He stopped a few paces away, nocked an arrow, and pointed it her direction. Amaranthe gave one last yank to her legs, but they remained rooted.

"We talk now." The shaman grabbed her wrist and yanked her to her feet.

The pressure wrapping her ankles disappeared, but it was too late to do anything. The shaman had an iron grip, and the bowman appeared competent.

Amaranthe gazed up at the cliff top to the destruction left by the shaman's magic. If Sicarius had survived the explosion, it seemed he had no means to help her at the moment. If he had not survived…it was her fault.

CHAPTER 14

THE FIRST DROPS OF RAIN SPATTERED, LEAVING wet stains on the rocks. Wind whistled through the canyon, tugging at Amaranthe's clothing and battering the tents surrounding her. The moist air smelled of burning coal and a coming storm. The approaching clouds were almost as dark as the black plumes wafting from a pair of steam shovels working on either side of the camp.

Amaranthe sat on her knees before an unlit fire pit. Ropes bound her ankles to her wrists, which were pulled behind her back, making her shoulders ache. The shaman had marched her past piles of limestone on the way in, but she still had no idea what the men sought. Surely not the rock itself.

The shaman strode out of a tent with a slight wiry man at his heels. The attendant clutched scissors in one hand, tweezers in the other, and a bloody rag dangled over his arm.

"Please, wait, sir. I'm not finished."

The shaman snarled a chain of words in his tongue. The attendant, who had the darker skin and hair of a Turgonian, lifted his arms in bewilderment. "If you would just sit down for a moment..."

The shaman stopped before Amaranthe. From her knees, she had to crane her neck back to find his eyes.

His bone-blade knife came out, and he rested it at her throat. "Before you die, you will speak to me all you know of Sicarius. All weaknesses, all everything."

She sat straighter. "Does that mean you didn't find his body? That he's still alive?"

The shaman had dispatched a team of men to check, but they had not returned yet.

He scowled. "Much rubble. Probably he dead and buried. You tell me his weaknesses anyway."

"If he has any, I don't know them." She shrugged, deciding on a casual response rather than open defiance. She would tell him nothing, but it would be foolish to declare that and imply there was no point in keeping her alive. "Though he is a poor conversationalist. I don't know, can you use that?"

The shaman glowered. "You are no funny."

"No, I suppose not."

"Sir," the attendant said. "You're bleeding all over camp. Shall I get that pistol ball out first?"

The shaman returned his knife to his sheath. "Yes. Mundane weapons no always best way to get answers, and I must have concentration for other ways. No pain."

They strode into a nearby tent together, leaving Amaranthe wondering what non-mundane interrogation methods he might subject her to. Best to escape and not find out.

The camp lay deep within the canyon. To escape she would have to run past several pickaxe-wielding workers as well as the ambulatory machinery. One step at a time, she told herself. Hands first.

The bowman sat on a boulder, oiling the limbs of his weapon, glancing at her from time to time. She shifted slightly to keep her hands hidden behind her back while she worked at the ropes, trying to dig a thumbnail into a knot. Inside the tent, the shaman spoke to someone in a language she could not understand. He wasn't conversing with the Turgonian surgeon. So, who was he talking to?

She had encountered a communication device before, in Larocka's basement, and wondered if the shaman had one inside. Though he had not asked Amaranthe her name, someone, maybe a lot of someones, would soon know Sicarius was up here. If he wasn't dead.

Amaranthe did not want to consider that possibility. He was too aware; he would have seen or sensed the attack coming. Even if it was magical. He would have run off the ledge before it collapsed. But, if he *was* alive, wouldn't he be doing something to help her escape the camp? And to get rid of the shaman before he could report Sicarius's whereabouts?

Maybe he was injured and needed her help.

Amaranthe doubled her efforts on her bonds, scraping skin raw, but loosening them infinitesimally. She eyed the camp as she worked. If she managed to free her hands, she would need a distraction, a big one considering the shaman could immobilize her from a distance.

Wind battered the tents framing the fire pit, though not enough to blow open flaps so she could see inside. A crate sitting beside one caught her eye. A faded stamp read, *Blasting sticks*. That, not magic, must be what someone had thrown at Sicarius. She grimaced. It made little difference.

Pained curses came from the shaman's tent. His assistant must be pulling the pistol ball out. Little time left.

A young man Akstyr's age jogged into the camp. He paused to eye her curiously before angling toward a tent. Dirt smudged his cheeks, and stubble fuzzed his chin, but neither hid the handsomeness of his face.

"Afternoon," Amaranthe said as the youth passed her.

He twitched in surprise and glanced behind him, as if checking to be sure she was addressing him.

"I'm Amaranthe," she told him. "What's your name?"

"Er, Dobb."

Her guard kept sliding a rag along his bow, but his eyes lifted, tracking the exchange.

"What're you doing working up here?" she asked the youth.

Dobb shrugged. "Need the money."

"Looks like hard work. Hope it pays well."

"Not really."

The rain grew heavier, pattering on the tent roofs. Amaranthe hoped it kept the shaman from hearing her chitchat. She continued to pry at her bonds as she talked.

"Then why work way out here?" she asked.

"I don't know. It seemed like a smart thing to do when they offered the job. I didn't have any work in Stumps."

"Dobb, quit your yammering and get back to work," the bowman said.

The knot Amaranthe was working on loosened. Careful to keep her shoulders from moving too much, she untied it.

"Gonna be a big storm," Dobb said. "Pit boss said to get the lanterns lit and bring tarps to cover the machinery."

"Then you best do that," the bowman said.

Amaranthe sat up straighter at the words "lanterns lit." Dobb slipped into the tent, revealing crates and food sacks before the flap fell shut. When he came out, he carried a large folded tarp. A box of matches stuck out of his pocket.

"With your looks, you could be working as a female companion," Amaranthe told him.

The tarp slipped from Dobb's arms. "A what?"

"An escort for well-to-do women seeking handsome men to attend social events with them." Amaranthe unwound the rope from her wrists.

Dobb stared at her. "You can get paid for that?"

The bowman stood. "Get back to work, Dobb."

"Paid well," Amaranthe said, eyes locked with the youth's. "One of my comrades used to be in that business. Maybe I could have him arrange an introduction for you."

"An introduction? Like to vouch for me?"

The bowman stalked over and grabbed Dobb's arm. "I said, get to work."

Dobb yanked his arm free. "You're not the boss here."

The bowman took him by the collar. "I'm in charge of the prisoner, stupid. Don't let her talk you into—"

With her hands free, Amaranthe lunged to her feet. She yanked the match box from Dobb's pocket, then sprinted around the bowman, kicking him in the back of the knee as she passed. He crumpled, grasping his leg. Dobb jumped backward to avoid him and fell through a tent wall.

Amaranthe threw open the lid to the crate and grabbed two blasting sticks.

"Get her!" the bowman yelled.

She tore open the box of matches, spilling them everywhere. She snatched one, swiped it against the crate, and lit the fuse.

"Idiot, don't let her—"

Amaranthe tossed the stick into the center of camp as the shaman stepped out of his tent.

"What—" he started.

"Run!" The bowman crashed into him in his race to escape the camp.

Amaranthe snatched a handful of spilled matches and ran toward the mouth of the canyon. Ahead of her, dozens of men chiseled at the stone walls with pickaxes, and two ambulatory steam shovels belched smoke.

The explosion rocked the earth, its thunderous boom echoing from the walls.

The workers dropped their pickaxes and gaped in her direction. She veered toward one of the rock walls, hoping she could follow it to the mouth of the canyon before someone shot her.

"Get woman, or nobody get paid!" the shaman roared, voice muffled.

Amaranthe hoped a tent had fallen on him.

Despite his ultimatum, most of the workers scurried out of her way when she waved the remaining blasting stick. The closest steam shovel operator did not. He rotated his machine toward her, and it rolled forward on its huge treads.

She kept going, hoping she could outrun the steam shovel. She lifted the blasting stick in one hand and a match in the other so the operator could not miss her threat. Amaranthe did not want to blow anyone up, but she was not going to let him crush her beneath those treads either.

As she ran, rain blew sideways, stinging her eyes. More orders to stop her came from the remains of the camp.

The operator continued toward her, narrowing the gap between the machine and the wall. He must think the metal cab enclosing him would make him invincible to the blasting stick. Not likely, she thought grimly.

Amaranthe slowed down to swipe the match. She tried to light the fuse without stopping completely, but running made it difficult.

An arrow clattered on the rocks a half foot from her. No, she dared not stop. The match flame brushed the fuse. It smoldered but did not light. Too wet.

The steam shovel bore down on her. Another arrow skimmed past, stirring her hair. Her match went out.

"Cursed ancestors." She gave up on lighting the fuse and pumped her legs faster.

Amaranthe hurled the unlit stick toward the smoke stack, thinking she might get lucky and it would drop inside and ignite. It bounced off the roof of the cab. The driver swung the long, extendable shovel at her. It scraped along the wall, sheering off rock as it veered toward her head.

She ducked low but did not slow down. Shards of rock thudded onto her shoulders and head, and warm blood trickled down the back of her neck, but she pressed on. The shovel was not agile enough to outmaneuver her. She escaped its reach and sprinted for the end of the canyon. Ten meters and she could run around a corner and disappear in the forest. She hoped.

A dark figure stepped from around that corner, rifle raised.

At first, she saw only that weapon trained her direction. It fired, billowing smoke into the soggy air. Sicarius.

A cry sounded behind her. The driver tumbled from the cab, a pistol flying from his fingers. It fired when it hit the ground.

Relief washed over Amaranthe, both at seeing Sicarius alive and at his action. That weapon had surely been aimed at her back.

The driverless steam shovel crashed into the wall.

Amaranthe sprinted around the corner, slapping Sicarius on the shoulder. She wanted to wrap him in a great hug, but there was no time. They needed to put distance between themselves and the shaman.

She ran several steps before realizing Sicarius was not following. Thinking he had paused to reload, she whirled to tell him to do it later. He was not there.

One of the rifles, the one he had fired already, leaned against the rock face where he had been standing. Amaranthe backtracked and peeked around the corner.

Sicarius stood, the second rifle raised, using the crashed vehicle for cover.

Before she could decide whether to join him or yell at him to get out of there, he fired. The steam shovel blocked her view, and she did not see what—who—he hit, but she could guess.

"The shaman?"

"Yes." Sicarius jogged past her without slowing. "They're gathering weapons."

Amaranthe grabbed her rifle and chased after him.

"He knew you were out here," she said when they reached the trees.

He slowed so she could run beside him.

"He knew your name and your history with Mangdoria," Amaranthe went on. "I think he told someone. Someone who speaks Mangdorian. If

it's Ellaya, well, she's already irked with me for destroying her gizmo-making machine. She'll want us extra dead now. Me anyway."

"I'll kill her when we get back."

Amaranthe missed a step. His cold, blunt efficiency should not surprise her by now, but sometimes, when he was acting more...human than others, she could forget about it. "She didn't actually seem to loathe you, not the way this man did. Maybe I can talk with her, convince her she doesn't want to be our enemy."

"Doubtful."

"You're in a dour mood. Is it because I almost got you blown up?" She eyed him as they jogged between the trees, mud splattering with each footfall. With his black attire, it was hard to spot blood, but he appeared unharmed. "I am sorry about that, but..." She started to make an excuse, to explain that it was the shaman sensing him that had caused trouble, but it had been her scheme to go down and talk to him in the first place. "I'm sorry. How did you escape?"

"They weren't as stealthy as they thought. I'd moved before they threw the blasting stick."

"Good. I'd feel—" utterly and irrevocably devastated, she thought, "—a little upset if I got you killed."

He slanted her a flat look. "You should."

Thunder boomed through the valley, and the rain picked up.

"I found out some new information at least." More about him than the mystery, but her mind did not want to process that yet. Safer to think about the land and the water plot. The pieces of that puzzle floated on the periphery of her mind, and she felt close to drawing them together into a cohesive picture.

Her comment only made Sicarius's expression harder, and she wished she had said nothing about his history with Mangdoria.

* * * * *

Books fought back a yawn. He shifted in his hard chair and turned his gaze from the crackling fireplace toward the log bed—and its soft, inviting quilts. He had the room to himself and the opportunity to enjoy a serene night of sleep. Too bad that was not the plan.

A thump occasionally sounded downstairs, audible over the rain pelting the roof. Someone in the household remained awake. In another hour, he might be able to leave his room to investigate. Amaranthe would call it snooping.

He wanted to accept Vonsha's explanations as truth, but Maldynado was right: she had shown them no evidence to justify a trek through the pass.

His chin drooped. He dozed until his own snores woke him.

The fire burned lower. Books listened but heard no footsteps, no bumping about, only wind buffeting the walls.

He stood and removed his boots, not trusting his ability to walk stealthily in the clunky footwear. He padded to the door in his socks. A floorboard creaked like a howling coyote.

"Oh, yes, this will work," he grumbled.

Books slipped into the hallway. And stopped. Where should he go to snoop? Rambling through the sprawling house, hoping to find some sign of nefarious plots, seemed unlikely to deliver results. Would Vonsha have her notes in her room? He shied away from the idea of sneaking into her bed chamber. He remembered passing a study on the bottom floor. Maybe Lord Spearcrest kept information about the property there. That might be a place to start.

No sooner had he started down the hallway when a door ahead opened.

Books halted, not sure whether he should flee back to his room or concoct some excuse for wandering.

Vonsha stepped out, a lacy nightgown swirling about her calves. Her hair tumbled about her shoulders in brown waves, almost hiding the bandage on her neck. The thoughts spinning through Books's head ground to a halt, and he could only stare.

"Books?" she asked. "Were you going somewhere?"

"I…wanted to talk to you." Not exactly, but maybe he could obtain his information from her. He would have to take charge of the question-asking though. No sitting close and smelling her perfume and definitely no gazing at the bare flesh revealed by that sleeveless, low-cut nightgown.

"Talk?" Vonsha asked. "I don't usually 'talk' to men in my bedroom while I'm at my parents' house, but I guess I'm too old for them to chastise about such things now."

"I—uhm." Books swallowed.

She took his hand and led him into the room. The only thing he noticed inside was the bed and how its sheets were already turned down.

Vonsha stepped close, her chest brushing his torso. "Are you always shy and awkward, or do I make you nervous?"

"Oh, I'm *always* awkward, but yes to the latter." Of course, some of that nervousness was due to the fact that he was supposed to be investigating. If he didn't feel obligated to research the place, he would—

She stood on her tiptoes, and the floral scent of her perfume teased his nostrils. Her lips brushed his, warm and inviting.

He slid his arms around her waist and forgot about research, and about being shy as well.

* * * * *

Rain hammered the top of Amaranthe's head, while wind whipped branches into her eyes. Daylight had vanished from the valley. She stumbled along behind Sicarius, stretching out a hand every few moments to make sure he still walked in front of her. Soaked clothing stuck to her body, chafing and rubbing skin raw. A tree snapped and crashed to the ground behind them.

"Where are we going?" Amaranthe yelled to be heard over the wind.

"The cabin," Sicarius said.

"We need to get back to the lorry and over to the Spearcrests. The shaman knew about the family, so I think it might have been a mistake sending Books and Maldynado there."

"Not tonight."

Lightning flashed. For a moment, trees and branches stood out, stark and cold in the white brilliance. Seconds later, thunder rumbled, a great peal that rang in Amaranthe's ears. Up here, surrounded by mountains, the storm seemed louder, rawer, and more dangerous than any she remembered from the city.

"You don't understand," she said. "I may have sent them into a trap. We have to warn them."

Sicarius spun about even as lightning flashed again, highlighting his wet blond hair and the hard angles of his face. "It's foolish to stay out in this. Going—"

Thunder drowned out the rest of his words, but she got the gist. Going down that trail in the dark would be treacherous. She knew it in her head; her heart was what objected.

Amaranthe was about to nod and wave Sicarius onward, when the hair on her arms stood on end. Her skin tingled, as if ants crawled all over her.

"Down!" Sicarius dropped, pulling her with him.

She tucked her head under her hands, burying her face in the ground. The sharp earthy scent of mud flooded her nostrils.

Lightning struck, and a boom hammered her ears.

The air stank of charred wood. A tree groaned, then cracked like rifle fire. Branches snapped. She wasn't sure whether to look up or keep her head buried.

Something—Sicarius's arm?—snaked around her waist, tearing her from her huddle.

Mud and trees blurred before her eyes as she was yanked several feet. She landed hard on her rump, her back thudding into Sicarius.

The trunk of a massive tree smashed to the ground where she had lain. Eyes wide, chest heaving for breath, she gaped for several long seconds. Sicarius held her, arm wrapped around her waist.

"Are you injured?" he asked.

Amaranthe waved her hand in dismissal, not trusting her voice.

He released her and helped her to her feet. She wiped rain out of her eyes with a shaking hand. Despite the downpour, flames leaped where lightning had struck the tree. Their orange glow helped her find her rifle.

"The cabin, you say?" she asked.

"Yes," Sicarius said dryly.

She followed him back to the clearing without further suggestions of getting off the mountain that night. The wind continued to rail, flinging branches into their path, and flashes of lightning illuminated the mountains. The rain turned to hail and pounded their heads and shoulders.

The cabin came into view, and Amaranthe broke into a run. Even knowing a dead man waited on the floor inside could not dim her relief at the prospect of sanctuary—though she almost hugged Sicarius when

he dragged the body outside by himself. She decided a comment about it being good of him to help with the house cleaning would be in poor taste.

While he tended to that grisly task, Amaranthe laid a fire. Water dripped from her clothing and pooled on the cold hearth stones beneath her knees. The hurried trek across the hillside had kept her from noticing the chilly air that had ridden in with the storm, but it made her shiver now. Though the long wooden matches had heads the size of coins, it took her shaking hands several tries to strike a flame. Fortunately, Hagcrest had kept the cabin well-stocked, and enough wood for the night was stacked in a bin near the hearth.

Sicarius returned as her fire started crackling. He did not say what he had done with the body, and she did not ask. She doubted any scavengers would be out in the downpour to bother it. They could build a funeral pyre in the morning.

"Venison." He laid strips of dried meat on the table and headed for his rucksack.

She added a final log to the fire. "You purloined food from a dead man's smokehouse?"

"He doesn't need it." Sicarius removed a set of neatly rolled dry clothes and tugged off his shirt, revealing the hard, lean muscles of his back.

Amaranthe caught herself staring. She grabbed the fireplace poker and turned away from him, cheeks heating. Too many hard angles, she told herself. It would be like sleeping with a rock. Who would want that?

Me, some insidious thought whispered.

That worried her. Even if there were not already enough reasons to keep the relationship purely business, the shaman's revelations alone should have horrified her enough to keep the notion from entering her mind. What would her father think of her, daydreaming about an assassin? A man who had killed, not just soldiers in a combat situation but innocents as well.

The empire had always considered it cowardly and dishonorable to attack someone who could not fight back, so Hollowcrest and Emperor Raumesys had gone against seven hundred years of imperial mores by raising and employing an assassin. Perhaps they had sensed a future

when brute force would no longer be enough to keep the conquered subjugated, or they had realized the rest of the world would catch up with the empire's engineering and metallurgy advancements, and that their edge would eventually slip away. To understand their reasoning and condone it were different matters, and here she sat with the one who had done the dirty work for them.

"Did you do it?" Amaranthe prodded a log with the poker. "Kill the Mangdorian chief and...his family?" Including the children, she added to herself.

"Yes."

She closed her eyes. It did not surprise her. She knew what he was by now and had heard enough from others to guess at much of what he had done. Sometimes she forgot, though, because she had never known him when he was purely Hollowcrest and Raumesys's assassin. It was jarring to be reminded that his reputation was entirely founded.

"Was it... Do you regret it?" she asked.

No note of remorse had colored his "yes," but he was so good at hiding his thoughts and emotions, one would never know if he actually felt something.

Sicarius set his boots by the fire and held her rucksack out to her. "Do you want me to go outside?"

"What?"

"While you change."

"Oh." She had forgotten the water dripping from her hair and clothing. "No need. I'll go over there."

Thanks to the disease Hollowcrest's crazy dungeon scientist had infected her with, Sicarius had seen her naked before. Or maybe not. She was not sure if he had bothered looking. Despite everything he was, and knowing what she should and should not want, that disappointed her.

She grabbed her rucksack and walked to the bed, wet boots squeaking with each step. She turned her back to the fireplace and dug out dry fatigues. Alas, she did not catch him peeping while she changed.

They shared the purloined food, then Sicarius settled on the bearskin rug, one leg stretched out and the other bent, arm resting on his knee. His shirt was untucked, and he was barefoot. Amaranthe did not bother him outside of missions and training time, so she had never seen him

in even that bit of undress. He almost looked…relaxed. She had never seen that either.

It did not seem right, considering the day's revelations, but it was old news to him even if it was not to her.

Amaranthe sat on the rug, close enough to enjoy the fire's warmth and talk to him—should he deign to converse—but she was careful not to intrude on his space. Strange that she could joke with him, however one-sidedly, while working, yet words eluded her now. Must be the bare feet. Most of the time, she felt comfortable around him. Indeed, over the last few months, when she dared not visit her old friends or enforcer comrades, he had become the person she confided in most. She trusted him to have her back in a fight—or a lightning storm. She wished she knew if his willingness to protect her represented fondness or if he was only interested in keeping her alive because she might be his best bet to one day establish a relationship with Sespian.

"Sicarius…" Amaranthe pulled her knees to her chest and wrapped her arms around them, eyes toward the fire instead of him. "You were watching the camp there at the end, I assume. If I hadn't… If that shaman had started to interrogate me…" She licked her lips, not sure she should ask a question she might not want to hear the answer to; he never prevaricated, so she expected a blunt and honest response. "I'm guessing you had your rifle in hand, ready to fire, before I threw the blasting stick and escaped. If I hadn't done that… Given what I know about you and…Sespian…and given what happened when I originally learned what I learned… Well, I wonder sometimes if you wouldn't feel your secrets were more secure if I weren't around."

Wood snapped, and sparks disappeared up the chimney. Amaranthe waited, then finally looked his way. He returned her gaze but said nothing.

"Well?" she asked.

"Well, what?"

"You're not going to answer?"

"You didn't ask a question."

"I did too."

"A question is denoted by a higher pitched tone at the end of the sentence. Your voice never did that." Curse him, his eyes glinted with amusement.

"*Sicarius!* This isn't the time for you to practice being whimsical."

He turned his dark eyes toward the fire. "It wasn't in my mind to shoot you."

Not exactly a proclamation that he would never under any circumstances consider harming her, but she had not expected that. Hoped for, but not expected.

"Good," Amaranthe said. "My ego likes to think I'm not expendable."

Sicarius leaned back on his hands. Amaranthe added a couple more logs, relishing the heat that warmed her face. Rain hammered the roof, and wind beat at the shutters of the single window, but inside it had grown comfortable.

"Sespian was there," Sicarius said.

"What?" Amaranthe blinked.

"When I returned from the mission to Mangdoria. With the heads. The emperor and Hollowcrest always wanted proof of a task completed. Sespian was there."

"Oh." She feared she did not want to hear the next part, but she gave him an encouraging nod anyway. She could not remember many times when he started a conversation or volunteered personal information. "How old was he?"

"Five. He was on the floor next to Raumesys's desk, playing with wood blocks. Building something creative." Sicarius continued to stare into the fire as he spoke, lost in the memory perhaps. "I asked Raumesys if the boy should leave. He said no. Sespian needed to be tough if he was to rule one day." His jaw tightened.

"So he was sitting there when you dumped a pile of heads on the floor." Amaranthe rubbed her face. A five-year-old boy confronted with that....

"Yes. I should have refused to do it with him in the room. I was..."

"Indoctrinated to obey the emperor," Amaranthe said.

His gaze shifted to meet hers.

"I know. Even as an enforcer, I had a lot of that drilled into me," she said. "Obey your chain of command without question, and the emperor's law is immutable. If we want you to have an opinion, we'll give it to you." For the first time, she wondered what kind of person she would be if she had gone to a city school. Her father had sacrificed much to send her to Mildawn to study business, where she had received a far more

liberal education than typical in the empire. By the time she entered the Enforcer Academy, she had been old enough to know her own mind and her obeisance had often been outward only.

"Yes," Sicarius said.

A question she had wondered more than once trickled into the stream of her thoughts. With him more open than usual tonight, maybe he would answer it. It was on her tongue, but she hesitated. He had been the one to bring up Sespian, but he might not appreciate her prying.

Curiosity overruled wisdom.

"How did you come to be Sespian's father?" Amaranthe asked. "Did you love his mother?"

He did not react with surprise to her questions—he never did. Just that schooled mask that revealed so little.

"Sorry," she said. "I retract my question. It's none of my business."

He snorted softly. Yes, he knew she wasn't retracting anything; she wanted to know.

Amaranthe shrugged. "At least I pitched my voice higher at the end of the question."

She wondered if a man who could kill without remorse or self-doubt possessed the ability to love. Sespian's fate mattered to him, but did he love his son? Or was his protectiveness born from a sense of duty? That imperative ran deep amongst Turgonian men. Duty to the emperor, duty to one's family. That wasn't the same as love.

"No," Sicarius said.

It took a moment for her to realize which question he was answering. The love one.

"Oh." She was not sure what answer she had hoped for. "No" could mean he had never loved anyone, and he never would. If he had said "yes," it would have warmed her to know he had the capacity to love someone, but then she might be jealous of some long-dead woman.

"All right, no love," Amaranthe said. "Then how... I mean, I know *how*, but why did she want you?" Oops, that sounded insulting. "I mean, of course I know *why* she'd want you because you're smart and athletic, and I'm sure you'd make wonderful children, and, uhm..." She cleared her throat and avoided his eyes. "What I mean is how did things come to happen?"

Fortunately, her stumbling tongue did not seem to offend him.

"You know Princess Marathi was Raumesys's second wife," Sicarius said.

Amaranthe nodded. "His first wife, Alta, died of influenza." She had been a toddler then, but it was well-known history.

"The first was killed because she didn't produce an heir."

"Ah? That's not what the record books say." An uneasy thought occurred to her. "Did you do it?"

"Raumesys did it himself. He married Marathi a week later. A year passed and she had not conceived either."

"I'm guessing it was Old Raumesys's rifle that wasn't fully loaded. Poor Alta. Murdered because her husband was impotent. So, Marathi made some assumptions and figured Raumesys was the problem. To avoid Alta's fate, she decided to get herself impregnated by someone else and let Raumesys think it was his doing."

"Yes."

"And she picked you." Amaranthe nodded. While his training no doubt accounted for much of his martial prowess, a great deal of that skill had to be natural aptitude, something that ought to be passed along to children. Thinking of the way he had flawlessly drawn copies of ranmyas for her counterfeiting scheme, she had little doubt he would be good at any endeavor that relied on speed, dexterity, or coordination, all traits admired in the empire. Strange that Sespian's interests did not lie along martial lines. Or perhaps not. Maybe Marathi had worked hard to make sure she did not raise a killer. "She had iron guts. Risking death if Raumesys found out. And approaching *you*. I can't imagine…" Amaranthe couldn't even tell Sicarius she had feelings for him. She certainly could not see herself brave enough to show up at his door to seduce him. "Or were you more cuddly and approachable as a teenager?"

His eyebrow twitched at the word cuddly. "No."

"That was gutsy of you too. Sleeping with the emperor's wife—that had to be a death sentence if you were caught. And you admitted you were inculcated to obey Raumesys. You certainly seem to have killed everyone he and Hollowcrest asked you to." She winced. That had come out more accusing than she intended.

"Fifteen-year-old boys don't do much thinking when pretty women show up at their doors."

Fifteen? He *had* been young.

Sicarius stood and retrieved a canteen. "Also, I was recovering from punishment that nearly killed me. I wasn't kindly inclined toward Raumesys at the time." He took a swig of water, and she wondered if the conversation was making him wish he had something stronger. Not that she had ever seen him drink anything alcoholic.

"Punishment for what?" she asked.

"Failure." His clipped tone did not invite further inquiry.

"At least it was an opportunity for you to…know something you might not have otherwise. Did you get to spend any time with him as a boy?"

"That would have been suspicious." He screwed the cap back on the canteen.

"Surely, with your ability to be stealthy, you could have sneaked in for a moment here or there."

Sicarius turned his back to her and set the canteen on the table. "Marathi did not want me around. And my presence scared Sespian."

Of course. After seeing Sicarius deliver a pile of severed heads, Sespian must have been terrified of him. A son, yes, but one he could only watch from afar. And one who grew up fearing and hating him.

"Go to sleep," Sicarius said. "I'll take first watch tonight."

The wind still howled outside, and thunder rumbled from time to time. She doubted anyone would intrude on them that night, but he was a stickler for running a watch, and she did not want to argue with him. She padded over to the bed.

"Sicarius?"

"Yes?" His eyes were hooded, wary.

Amaranthe wanted to tell him she was sorry his life had been chosen for him from his first day and that he never seemed to have known happiness. She wanted to tell him *she* never would have told him to stay away from his son. And she wanted to tell him she loved him.

"Good night," she said.

Coward.

CHAPTER 15

GOING DOWN THE MOUNTAIN SHOULD HAVE BEEN easier than climbing up it, but Sicarius set a pace that would have tired a steam tramper. At least the storm had passed. Overhead, budding branches created a latticework framing a blue sky.

While admiring that sky, Amaranthe slipped on a wet, mossy stone. The barrel of her rifle caught on a tree and the butt jabbed her in the ribs. She winced at her klutziness. "Any reason we're in such a hurry?"

"You find this pace taxing?" There was a hint of something in his tone—like maybe he intended to practice that teasing she had offered to receive.

"No." Teasing aside, she suspected he would read any admission of weakness as a request for extra training. "It's just that a more leisurely pace would let me think about everything. I meant to cogitate more last night, but I fell asleep as soon as my head touched that stiff, straw-stuffed object Hagcrest placed in the pillow position." It was probably good she had fallen asleep before she could dwell overmuch on the fact she was sleeping in a dead man's bed.

"We left Akstyr and Basilard alone with our lorry and more money than they've likely seen in their lives," Sicarius said.

"You think they'd steal everything? And strand us?"

"Many would."

"They're better men than that."

Sicarius gave her a long look over his shoulder. Most people would have tripped over a root if they lifted their eyes from the trail that long, but no mischievous tree protuberances dared tangle his toes.

"You trust too easily," he said.

"Even if they *aren't* better men than that, they'd be afraid to cross you. Fear motivates people into good behavior." Though it was not a tactic she preferred to use, she understood its effectiveness.

"We'll see."

The rush of the river grew audible. Amaranthe's stomach grumbled in anticipation of boiling water for tea and having a meal. Sicarius had pushed her to leave before eating.

"I hope Basilard has breakfast waiting." She sniffed the air, hoping to catch a whiff of eggs cooking. "It's amazing what he finds in the forest when he goes foraging. I wouldn't have a clue about what's edible and what's not. He's a good man. I have faith in him."

Sicarius glanced back. She expected a comment about how hard it was to monitor their surroundings with her prattling, or perhaps a suggestion that she should be trying to figure out the greater puzzle they were involved with. Instead, he said, "I can forage."

She almost laughed. Maybe her praise for Basilard had made him envious? "Oh? I've not seen you do it."

"It's not the right season. Summer and fall."

"What about those tuberous things Basilard found by the side of the road the other night? And mixed with the sausages? They were good. Nice crunch."

The next glance Sicarius leveled her direction was more of a glare. She decided not to push his humor with further teasing.

The frothing river water grew visible through the trees. The suspension bridge came into sight, and, on the far side, the lorry waited where they left it. Amaranthe resisted the urge to throw a triumphant, "I told you so," at Sicarius. Team leaders were probably supposed to be more mature than that.

No camp fire burned, and no eggs waited. As Amaranthe and Sicarius crossed the bridge, she expected the men to come out and greet them—or berate her for leaving them to the elements—but nothing moved. Basilard and Akstyr must have been miserable during the storm and found shelter elsewhere.

A furry lump came into sight near the base of the bridge: a dead raccoon. She rolled it over with the tip of her rifle. A hole the size of a pistol ball ran through its skull.

"I'll scout," Sicarius said.

"Akstyr?" Amaranthe called. "Basilard?"

A bird tweeted a querulous response. While Sicarius circumnavigated the area, Amaranthe checked the lorry. She passed two dead squirrels, a fire lizard, and a mangy opossum.

She lifted the tarp in the back of the vehicle. "The gear's still here. Soggy but here."

"The money?" Sicarius asked.

Amaranthe climbed into the cab and checked under the driver's bench where she had secured the strongbox. It was gone. She winced.

"No."

"Come." Sicarius stood by a pine tree growing out over the shallows. He pointed downstream. "They went this way."

More small animal corpses littered the trail.

"Any theory on the dead raccoons?" she asked.

Sicarius lifted a hand for silence. He tilted his head for a moment, then slipped into the undergrowth, barely rustling the ferns. Before Amaranthe could decide if she should follow, the foliage swallowed him from view.

"What's that?" she muttered. "You want to explore on your own? Very well. I agree." Amaranthe snorted. He might leave the scheming up to her, but she would be delusional if she thought herself the absolute boss over these men—especially him.

Not sure whether Sicarius had detected some enemy, she refrained from calling Akstyr and Basilard's names as she continued forward. But a familiar voice soon reached her ears.

"…gotta be safe to get down by now," Akstyr was saying. A moment passed, and he spoke again. "Dead? What dead? I don't know that sign."

Amaranthe stepped around a cluster of trees and the two men came into view. They perched in the crotch of an ancient aspen, rifles clutched in their hands. Their damp clothes hugged their bodies, and Akstyr's hair appeared more bedraggled than usual. His foot pressed into Basilard's chest while Basilard's head lolled off to one side, neck crooked awkwardly. If they had spent the night in the uncomfortable spot, they had her sympathy. She had seen lovers less entwined.

"Good morning," Amaranthe said.

Akstyr fell out of the tree.

"Sorry." She jogged over to help him up. "I didn't intend to startle you."

The toe of her boot clunked against something hard. She brushed aside leaves and found the strongbox. They must have removed it from the lorry to guard it as they ran away from…what?

"Did you spend the night up there?" Amaranthe asked. "And, if so, why?"

Basilard climbed down.

Akstyr pointed at him. "Say nothing."

Basilard swatted the finger away and signed to Amaranthe: *Attacked. Flee here. Make defense.*

"What attacked you?" Her gaze drifted to a dead squirrel in a puddle.

Basilard lifted his hands to sign again.

"Bears," Akstyr blurted. "*Big* bears. And…grimbals!"

"I believe grimbals only live on the northern frontier," Amaranthe said dryly.

Sighing, Basilard pointed at the squirrel. *After storm, small creatures come. Rabid. Eyes shine. Bite and claw us.*

Akstyr pushed back a baggy sleeve to display a long gash.

"A squirrel did that?" Amaranthe wrestled with her lips to keep them from smiling. No doubt it had been a crazy night for these two.

"A raccoon," Akstyr growled. "A giant raccoon."

Basilard winked and held his hands less than a foot apart to illustrate the not-so-giant size of the raccoon.

"It was bigger than that," Akstyr said.

Basilard moved his hands closer.

"Oh, why don't you eat the dung on every street in the slums?" Akstyr kicked a pine cone. "It was hectic and dangerous, all right?"

"I understand," Amaranthe said. "Thank you for protecting the money. The, ah, giant raccoons didn't try to take it, did they?"

"No." Akstyr glowered suspiciously, probably thinking he was being mocked. "We just didn't want to leave it."

"Good thinking." Amaranthe hoped the compliment would appease him. "Something suspicious is definitely going on out here."

Sicarius glided out of the trees, carrying a pile of leaves. They glowed faintly.

"What'd you find?" Amaranthe asked.

A grassy, decaying odor tainted the air, and she crinkled her nose. Sicarius laid the leaves on the ground, revealing a regurgitated mess on top of them. A *glowing* regurgitated mess.

"Disgusting," Akstyr said.

"Is that…?" Amaranthe pointed at the heap.

"Vomit," Sicarius said.

"When I implied I'd like to see your foraging skills, this isn't what I had in mind," she said.

Akstyr snickered. "*That's* why we don't want him to have a turn making meals."

Sicarius turned his cold stare on Akstyr.

"Sorry." Akstyr skittered back several feet. "Just a joke. A bad joke."

Basilard pointed at the radiant pile. *Color eyes.*

"Same hue as the eyes?" Amaranthe thought of the wolves. "You're right. So maybe it's something they're eating that's making the animals crazy. And, er, luminous." She blinked. "Or something they're *drinking*."

Sicarius's eyes locked onto hers. "Possibly."

"I wish I had a copy of this morning's paper," she said, "so we could see if there's any more news about people getting sick in the city." In particular, she wondered if anyone's eyes were glowing. Could that and the aggression be a symptom of continuing ingestion of the contaminated water supply? "Akstyr, would it be possible for a magic-user to poison a population's drinking water?"

He stuffed his hands in his pockets and studied the ground thoughtfully. "You could put something into water to poison it or a really smart practitioner could alter the basic structure of water at its tiniest level to be something just a little different that makes it poison to humans and animals. But to do it for the whole city, I don't know. The *quantity* of water you'd have to alter would be huge, and it's not like it's just pouring out of some steady source, right? There'd be new snow melting into a river or lake or whatever, so you'd have to keep applying your power to keep the water flowing downriver poisoned. I can't imagine the energy required."

It always amazed her when Akstyr spoke more than a sentence. He could be halfway eloquent when discussing magic.

"So, if we're dealing with a practitioner," Amaranthe said, "it's a very powerful one."

"*Very,*" Akstyr said.

She looked at Sicarius. "Probably not the shaman you shot then."

"He could not even stop a rifle ball to his chest," Sicarius said.

"Yes. A true wimp." She did not mention how he had captured her easily enough. "Basilard, can you tell us anything about your people's abilities with the Science?"

Basilard's eyebrows rose, and he touched his chest. *My people?*

"The woman who ran the gambling house and had that contraption in the basement was Mangdorian, and so was the shaman we just dealt with. He may have killed Lord Hagcrest."

Basilard signed: *My people not killers.*

"I know," Amaranthe said, "but sometimes things happen and people stray from their values." That was vague, but she certainly was not going to tell him what sort of revenge had been motivating that shaman.

Basilard nodded, eyes downcast, and Amaranthe winced at her clumsy tongue. She had not meant to remind him of his bloody past.

"Suppose something crazy happened," she said, "and a couple of your people chose to go against their religion and get revenge on...the empire. Is there anyone you've heard of who could do the sort of magic that might poison the water or kill people through devices embedded under the skin?"

Basilard hesitated, then shook his head.

Sicarius watched him, eyes hard. Amaranthe had a feeling he would interrogate Basilard without qualm at that moment. Now that Sicarius knew the Mangdorians had him targeted, he would want to find out everything he could.

Amaranthe gazed across the river in the direction of the canyon they had visited. Foliage and distance hid it from view. She wondered if she had let the storm drive her away too quickly. Perhaps she and Sicarius should have tried to capture and question one of the workers.

"Someone's coming," Sicarius said.

"They heard we have raccoon vomit for breakfast," Akstyr muttered.

"Amaranthe?" Maldynado's voice floated through the trees. "You around? I've got news."

Relief washed over Amaranthe when he and Books ambled into view. They must not have found trouble at the Spearcrest estate after all. But maybe they had answers for her.

"What are you all doing back here in the trees?" Maldynado glanced downward. "And why are there dead squirrels everywhere?"

"Don't tell him about our night," Akstyr pleaded.

Yes, Maldynado would tease Akstyr for days over this.

"Just more quirky incidents with the wildlife," Amaranthe said. "It's not important now. What matters is—"

"That vomit is glowing." Maldynado stared.

"Well, yes, but I'm more interested in what you two learned," Amaranthe said.

Books eyed the vomit, but dismissed it with a shrug. He wore a relaxed smile that twitched into a grin now and then.

"Books?" she asked. "You have news?"

"The news is that old Booksie got his snake greased last night," Maldynado said.

Books gaped at him. "That statement is crude, boorish, and…"

Maldynado's eyebrows rose.

"…undeniably accurate," Books finished, standing straighter.

"*That's* the news you ran out here to tell us?" Amaranthe asked.

"News?" Maldynado said. "More like a once-in-a-decade miracle."

"It hasn't been *that* long," Books said.

"I'll bet my finest sword that Raumesys was still on the throne."

Amaranthe rubbed her face. Akstyr and Basilard covered smirks. Sicarius watched the forest, head cocked to listen, eyes always scanning. At least one member of her team preferred business to antics.

"Gentlemen," Amaranthe said. "While I'm delighted to revel in your conquests with you, I'd like any information you might have found related to our mission."

Books's smile faded to an embarrassed foot shuffling.

"No information?" Amaranthe asked.

"Vonsha doesn't know who bombed us," he said, "but she claims the neighbor tried to buy her family's land. She suspects him of colluding with the Kendorians, possibly to give them a foothold in our pass."

"*Kendorians?*" Amaranthe asked. "We haven't seen a Kendorian since this started."

"She was adamant the neighbor is up to something," Books said.

"The neighbor is dead," Amaranthe said.

"Oh," Books said.

All the men's eyes swiveled toward Sicarius.

"*We* didn't do it." Amaranthe relayed the previous day's events. "Akstyr, do you know of any artifacts that could burrow beneath someone's skin and kill when the wizard or whomever isn't around?"

Akstyr shrugged. "If you're good enough, you can Make just about anything. Sounds intricate though."

"Could this be the work of the person also responsible for the big device in the gambling house vault?"

"I guess."

Well, that was not particularly helpful.

"Any other information?" Amaranthe asked Books and Maldynado. She rushed to add, "Of the useful-to-our-goals kind?"

Maldynado snapped his fingers. "Forgot to tell you: we saw that female enforcer sergeant and the soldiers leaving the Spearcrests' place."

"Sergeant?" Amaranthe asked. "She's a sergeant?"

Her first reaction was surprise, and then...bitterness. After all the years she had spent trying to get promoted to sergeant. All that hard work. As far as she knew there were no female enforcer sergeants. Until now, apparently.

"Yup, believe so," Maldynado said. "And, er, she recognized us. Said she'd be back for us later."

"Whatever they're on assignment for must have priority over capturing outlaws," Amaranthe said, "but we figured that. Where'd they go?"

"Back to the road heading up the mountain, not toward the other side of the pass."

Amaranthe started pacing and thinking aloud. "There's a lot of interest right now in the properties on either side of this river, but it doesn't seem to be the source of the water to Stumps, so *it's* probably not the problem. Somewhere up in these mountains, there's a water supply that's being tampered with, making animals crazy and effecting people all the way down in the city. What if the whole reason the water is being fiddled with is so people here, in this valley, can profit?"

"Profit from what?" Akstyr asked.

"If the city's current water supply is suddenly unusable," Amaranthe said, "then they'd have to look for another source. Quickly. Coincidentally, there's a beautiful river here and a valley that could be turned into a lake if a dam was built. Of course, Sespian isn't the kind of emperor who'd kick a couple of warrior caste families off their land. He'd compensate them. Richly perhaps, at least in comparison to what these people are eking out on this unyielding land."

"Building a new dam and altering the underground infrastructure that delivers city water would be a huge undertaking," Books said.

"More efficient to kill the person fouling the water," Sicarius said.

Amaranthe tapped her chin. "Good point. Maybe that's what the enforcers and soldiers are on their way to do." More than ever, she wished she had told Sicarius to hop onto their lorry and follow them up the mountain.

"Although," Books said, "if the water *was* somehow made permanently undrinkable, your limestone quarry might also provide a means for profits."

"Raw materials for the dam?" Amaranthe guessed.

"The imperial mixture for underwater concrete used for such structures requires a great deal of limestone," Books said.

"You can harden concrete underwater?" Akstyr asked.

"Yes, it's quite fascinating," Books said. "The original engineers who stumbled upon the formula were working near a volcano and found that a mixture of volcanic ash, sand, finely crushed rock…"

A minute or two into Books's explanation, Maldynado slapped Akstyr on the back of the head.

"What was that for?" Akstyr blurted, interrupting Books.

"Asking a question that could result in a lecture."

Books's eyes narrowed.

"You realize what you're saying," Amaranthe said, hurrying to speak before an altercation got underway. "If both of these property owners stood to profit, one or both of them may be responsible for the whole scheme."

Books pointed across the river. "Hagcrest is the one with the quarry."

"But Hagcrest is dead."

"He wasn't when the plot was conceived," Books said.

"He lived in a sparse, one-room cabin. He doesn't seem like the type of man who would have been plotting for profits." Amaranthe understood Books did not want his lady friend to have been one of the guilty parties, but the woman *had* been down in the real estate library, checking lot lines.

"Vonsha is warrior caste," Books said. "To suggest she would plot against the entire city for financial gain is preposterous. It's not as if they'd stand to earn a fortune from selling the family land. The emperor would give them fair market value perhaps but not a vast sum."

"Hm." Amaranthe thought of the bottled water sellers in the city. It didn't seem like anyone stood with enough to gain to mastermind something that threatened the entire capital.

"Besides," Books said, "if the Spearcrests are involved in a scheme, I'm sure it's the father who thought things up. Not Vonsha."

"The old man was a crotchety badger," Maldynado said.

"We could go talk to them," Amaranthe said, "or try to find the enforcers and soldiers and maybe the source of the bad water."

"I don't think the Spearcrests would take kindly to questions." Books glanced at Sicarius. He probably wanted to save Vonsha from unpleasant interrogation methods, if possible.

Amaranthe could not blame him. She wanted to hurry after the soldiers anyway. They could always question the Spearcrests later, but her insides clenched at the idea of coming all the way up here and having some other team vanquish the villain and claim the honors. It was selfish—surely the good of the city was what mattered—but it was there in her heart nonetheless.

"Let's get back to the vehicle," Amaranthe said. "It's time to find the source of our tainted water."

Maldynado fell into step beside her. "Sorry you had to hole up with Sicarius overnight." Sicarius walked a few paces ahead, so Maldynado kept his voice low. "That must have been torturous."

She watched him out of the corner of her eye, wondering if he was angling for something. "I'm surprised you didn't think there'd been snake greasing going on."

"With Sicarius and *you*?" He roared with laughter but caught himself when Sicarius glared back at them. He lowered his voice again. "Not only would that be disturbing to imagine, but I know you can do *much* better. You need a nice, good-hearted man. Someone noble. Like you."

She missed a step. "Dear ancestors, you've got someone in mind, don't you?"

"I'm glad you asked. Why, yes, I do. In fact, we had this whole birthday shindig planned, and I was going to introduce you to Lord

Deret Mancrest. His father owns *The Gazette*. He'd be perfect for you. And maybe you could exude your charms and get him to write nice things about our team. Especially me. And how statue-worthy I am."

Amaranthe had her hand up through most of his speech, intending to reject him instantly, but the mention of *The Gazette* made her pause. She had no interest in dating this man, but it might be beneficial to know someone with a link to the newspaper business.

"We'll see," she said.

"Excellent!"

Sicarius leveled another dark glare over his shoulder at them.

CHAPTER 16

TOWERING PINES ROSE, THEIR BRANCHES BLOCK-ing the sky and turning the road into a twilight tunnel. The lorry shuddered and wobbled as it groaned up the steep incline.

Amaranthe sat cross-legged in the back, reading a newspaper they had picked up in the last of the tiny towns on the mountain. Across from her, Sicarius sat in an identical pose with his knives, a pistol, and a disassembled rifle lying on a towel before him. The rest of the men rode up front, taking turns driving and tending the firebox.

"This is interesting." Amaranthe tapped a middle page of the paper. She had already read the news on the "epidemic" and promises that the water was fine. No need for alarm. The empire was taking care of everything, thank you very much. Nothing she had not expected. But this small story in the back.... "Remember Farth Textiles? The Kendorian owner was taken into custody by the enforcers on suspicion of magic, and her business is being sold at an auction."

Sicarius ran a bore brush through the barrel and blew out flecks of carbon.

"Why do I have a feeling she was set up?" Amaranthe said. "First Klume wanted you to assassinate the woman, and then we stumble across those thugs doing...we never did figure out what. I thought they might be stealing something, but if they're linked to everything else— and they must be if they had the same death-causing bumps under their skin, right?—then they had to be up to more than petty theft. Maybe they were scouting the place in anticipation of a return trip, one where they would plant false evidence of magic. But why would the same people responsible for a Kendorian textiles plant folding want to foul the city water? Is Books's theory right, and they want to build a dam on that other river, then sell the land to the empire all prettied up and ready to become the city's new water source? Is all of this about profits?"

Sicarius ran an oiled rag along the outside of his barrel.

"It's your turn to speak," Amaranthe said.

"Have you attended to your weapons? If you intend to continue with the rifle instead of the crossbow, you need to clean it frequently to minimize malfunctions."

She slumped against a pack. "Is that your way of telling me my theories are ludicrous and I should retire from the speculation game? Or were you just ignoring me?"

"No." He handed her a cleaning kit.

Amaranthe chuckled and fished out her firearms to work on. He was probably right. Thinking and figuring things out were good, but getting killed because of a weapons malfunction would make all her thoughts meaningless. She kept the pistol loaded in case they ran into trouble, but disassembled the rifle to work on.

"Perhaps they intend it to be a privately owned dam," Sicarius said.

Amaranthe grinned. "I knew you were listening."

"A private dam that the city was forced to use would put a lot of power into the hands of the owners."

She tapped her bore brush against the rifle barrel thoughtfully. "But would someone be allowed to keep a private dam if the capital city relied upon it? The law says the emperor can go in and *take* land if he wants to."

"If he has the power to act freely." Sicarius laid down his work and leaned forward, elbows on his knees. After a glance toward the cab, where the men chatted, he spoke in a low voice, "With Hollowcrest and Raumesys dead, the only record of my mission in Mangdoria would be in the Imperial Intelligence Office in a locked filing cabinet. That this information is just coming out now is telling."

"You think Forge or whoever we're dealing with has a man inside? Someone working at odds with Sespian's interests? Someone who might be a threat to him if he doesn't comply?"

Sicarius bent his head and snapped the parts of his rifle back together with more vigor than the task required.

"You'd like to be in there with him, wouldn't you?" Amaranthe said. "Standing at his side? Glaring at, or killing, anyone who gives him trouble."

"That was the plan," he said quietly.

Plan? How long ago had he first imagined that, she wondered. She turned her head to scratch an itch and caught Basilard gazing out the back of the cab at them. He looked away as soon as she met his eyes. She lowered her hand slowly. He could not have heard their conversation, not over the chugging of the engine. But he seemed more interested than usual. Because Mangdorians were involved?

"Yo, boss!" Maldynado called. "This fine mountain road is particularly well-maintained, don't you think? Especially since it goes nowhere."

"I've noticed that," Amaranthe called back. "I looked over the map earlier, and there's a recreational area and a small trapping community at the top. There's some logging on the next mountain over, but it's still original growth forest here. That in itself is odd considering our proximity to the capital."

Despite the truck's struggle with the incline, the road remained smooth with no potholes or gouges marring the concrete. Though branches grew overhead, lower ones had been cut back to ensure they did not impede a vehicle's progress.

"We just going to keep driving until we reach the end?" Maldynado asked.

Something tan flashed from the trees behind Sicarius.

"Down," Amaranthe barked, lifting the pistol and firing.

The ball took the cougar in the chest, but its momentum carried it into the lorry. Sicarius had rolled away before she voiced her warning, but she lost sight of him as the mass of fur filled her vision. She grabbed for a sword. Paws hit the floor of the bed, scattering the weapons and sending them out of reach.

Glowing eyes skewered her.

Claws flashed at her face. Amaranthe scrambled backward, and her shoulders rammed against the side.

Sicarius leaped in and plunged his black dagger downward. The sturdy blade crunched through the cougar's skull, sinking to the hilt. The huge cat shuddered and dropped.

Amaranthe willed her heart out of her throat and pointed at the blade. "Clean that one extra well. It deserves the imperial treatment."

She tried to push herself to her feet, but her palm slipped in blood. She thumped down, slamming her elbow on unyielding metal.

Sicarius gripped her other arm and pulled her up.

"Good shot," he said.

"Thank you."

She doubted the cougar would have landed on him before he sensed the attack and rolled away, but his simple praise warmed her. Though she had needed help to vanquish the darned cat, she was glad no accusation of acting like a footstool came from Sicarius's lips this time. Indeed, he held her eyes for a long moment, and she thought a hint of appreciation lingered there.

"Amaranthe, are you all right?" Books scrambled out of the cab and looked her up and down.

The lorry had stopped, and the men piled into the back.

Maldynado put a hand on her shoulder. "Did you get gouged?"

As they surrounded her, Sicarius backed away. He retrieved his dagger with a yank.

"I'm fine." She lifted her hands. "It jumped at Sicarius, not me. It came out of nowhere. Well, actually it came out of those trees over there."

Even as she pointed that direction, Sicarius hopped to the ground and headed into the forest.

"More crazy glowy-eyed creatures?" Maldynado nudged the dead cougar. "Guess that means we're heading the right direction."

Amaranthe picked up the towel and wiped the blood off her hands. "So you're saying this attack is good news, eh?"

"Maybe?"

"Let's get this critter out of here," she said. "Then you boys can fight over who gets to help me clean."

They groaned in unison, all except Akstyr, who held up his book. "Not me, I'm on an extra important section. Need to keep studying."

"I'm going to start learning magic so *I* can get out of work all the time," Maldynado said.

"When do you do work as it is?" Books asked.

Amidst more sniping, the men rolled the cougar over the side and off into a ditch. Amaranthe risked Maldynado's ire by using a bottle of his "safe water" for washing away blood. She paused. Blood stained the corner of the towel Sicarius had been using for weapons cleaning, and it held a faint glow.

At this point, she was not surprised, but she wondered again at the effects on people in the city, people who might still be drinking the water. Were these creatures worse off because they were closer to the source where the concentration might be denser? Or did these strange symptoms represent prolonged exposure?

Sicarius reappeared. "There's nothing else in the forest, but there's a road up ahead that isn't on the map."

They climbed back into the lorry and drove a quarter of a mile to a gravel lane veering to the right. A chain dangled between mossy posts on either side, and a rusty metal sign read: LOGGING CAMP.

"Could be nothing," Amaranthe said.

"Could be a logging camp," Akstyr said.

"A vehicle passed this way recently." Sicarius, who had remained on foot, pointed to a muddy divot in the ground.

"Might as well check it out," Amaranthe said.

Sicarius picked the lock on the chain, and the lorry turned onto the gravel road.

Overgrown branches slapped the cab and clawed at the sides. Amaranthe, sitting in the back, ducked frequently to keep pine-needle brushes from combing her hair. Sicarius did not return to the lorry. The bumpy road forced a slow pace, and he trotted ahead, sometimes in sight, sometimes not.

Miles rolled past. Amaranthe finished scrubbing the blood off the floor of the bed, tidied the gear, and loaded her weapons. As she worked, she tried to keep a watch on the woods as well, not sure what creature might leap out at them next.

Sicarius sprinted back to the lorry, arm raised for them to stop. The steam brakes squealed. Amaranthe grabbed the side to keep from being hurled on top of the gear.

"What's wrong?" She jumped to the ground.

"There's a lake ahead, and your soldiers are camped alongside it."
Sicarius's gaze shifted to the black plumes of smoke rising from the
lorry's stack.

Amaranthe winced. The smoke probably wafted above the tree
canopy. "Think they've spotted us?"

"If their man on watch is conscious," Sicarius said.

"So there's hope they haven't?"

"Depends on whether the enforcers are in charge or the soldiers."

She propped her hands on her hips. "Was that a slur against
enforcers?"

The men had joined them on the ground, and Maldynado leaned an
elbow on her shoulder. "Motley lot. Good thing you're not one of them
any more."

Sicarius glared at him. Maldynado removed his elbow.

"Park over there and cut off the engine," Amaranthe said. "Everyone, grab your gear. We'll take a roundabout route through the forest to
get to the lake. Sicarius, lead please. Basilard, can you cover our trail?"

Basilard rubbed his head dubiously. *Maldynado, Books, and Akstyr
leave trail like marching army.*

"Do your best," she said, delighted he had not lumped her in with
them.

The swiftness with which her team prepared and departed made her
proud. Though they chatted—bickered—a lot, they were developing an
efficient, professional streak.

Maldynado paused to pee on a fern, not bothering to turn his back or
give himself any privacy.

"There's a lady here, you crude troglodyte," Books said.

"I know. That's why I'm displaying my wares." Maldynado winked
at Amaranthe.

She sighed and amended her earlier thought. Her team might be
efficient, but the term "professional" was a stretch.

Walking through the forest without the benefit of a trail proved more
difficult than her city-raised mind had thought. Verdant underbrush and
brambles clogged the ground between the trees. Branches protruded
in every direction, snagging at her weapons and rucksack. Invisible
strands of something—spider webs?—stretched across every other gap
and stuck to her face.

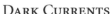

A squirrel reared on an overhead branch and chattered at them.

Basilard thumped Akstyr on the chest, pointed at it, and signed: *Watch out.*

Akstyr scowled. "Not funny."

Basilard grinned.

"What's your sign for shut up?" Akstyr asked.

"Quiet," Sicarius said.

He lifted a hand and stopped. Everyone hunkered down. Voices grew audible on the road behind them. They belonged to men, but distance muddled the words.

Though it would have been better not to have their vehicle discovered, Amaranthe was almost happy to hear the soldiers. Their presence validated her choice to take this arduous route.

The conversation continued for a while. They must have reached the lorry and were deciding what to do. Amaranthe's thighs started to burn from crouching down. Sicarius could have continued on without making a noise, and perhaps Basilard as well, but she figured the group should remain still until the men left.

"Well, someone's here," one voice said, loudly and distinctly.

The other answered in a hushed tone.

As Amaranthe listened to the men, she wondered where the enforcer woman was and if she was in charge. She had enough rank to be the leader of the enforcer mission, but surely the soldiers would not obey her. They never would have obeyed Amaranthe anyway. She rolled her eyes at her thoughts. She should wait until she actually met the woman before growing jealous of her.

The voices faded. After a few moments, Sicarius waved for her team to continue.

Thanks to the absence of trails, it took an hour to push through to the lake where the trees gave way to reeds and marsh. A blue heron standing on one leg turned a malevolent glowing eye upon them. Amaranthe touched the hilt of her sword, but the creature did not attack.

"Guess this is the right place." Maldynado nodded toward the leggy bird.

Beyond the wetlands, a blue lake gleamed beneath the afternoon sun. Steep, valley slopes marked the northern and eastern boundaries while, to the south, a massive gray concrete wall stretched. A watch

tower rose on either end. If men observed from within, Amaranthe could not see them. The roar of water drifted from beyond the wall.

"Waterton Dam?" she guessed.

"This is *not* on the map." Books sounded affronted, as if he could not believe some cartographer had betrayed his integrity to misrepresent the mountain.

"The camp is over there." Sicarius pointed toward a tree-filled peninsula between them and the dam. If the road they had been following had continued on straight, it would have come out there.

"Not a logging camp?" she asked dryly.

"No," Sicarius said. "Tents and the enforcer vehicle."

"Many people there?"

"Not immediately visible, but I came back to find you before scouting."

The heron ruffled its wings and turned to face them squarely. Amaranthe wondered if a shaman could spy on people through an animal's eyes.

"I sense something." Akstyr stood, eyes closed, hands spread.

"Indigestion?" Maldynado asked. "You didn't eat any of that glowing vomit, did you?"

Akstyr opened one eye and issued a cold glare Sicarius could not have topped. "It's a presence, an...emanation. Yes, that's the word. Like you feel handling that key fob from the gambling house."

Amaranthe had felt nothing except warmth when she handled the fob, but she nodded for him to explain further.

"Much, much stronger though." Akstyr closed his eyes again. "Like the difference in light between a star and the sun."

"It's a device?" Amaranthe asked. "Not a person?"

"A Made artifact, yes."

"Is it what's causing the problem with the water?" she asked.

"I can't tell what it is or does, just that it's here."

Amaranthe turned to Sicarius and Books. "Thoughts?"

"Nothing natural is causing the peculiarities with the wildlife," Sicarius said.

"Agreed," Books said. "I don't know much about magical devices—"

"*Made* artifacts," Akstyr said.

"Right," Books said. "I don't know much about them, but it seems likely this is the source of our problems."

"Where is this artifact?" Maldynado was lounging against a tree, exchanging glowers with the heron. The bird seemed transfixed by the feathered plume jutting from his hat—angry that some fellow bird had died for fashion? "We'll send Amaranthe in with her pistol to shoot it like she did the other one."

She sighed. She should not have shared the details of her brief incarceration in the gambling house.

"I think," Akstyr said, "it's at the bottom of the lake."

"That sounds...problematic," Amaranthe said. The steep walls of the valley, carved from glaciers long ago, probably extended below the water's surface. She doubted this reservoir had many shallow spots.

Maldynado stroked his chin. "How long can you hold your breath, boss?"

"Even if it was a long time," she said, "black powder doesn't light underwater."

"What's the plan?" Sicarius asked.

Yes, time for action. "You, Basilard, and I will check the camp. Books, Akstyr, and Maldynado, I'm putting you on artifact-investigation duty."

"Investigating something at the bottom of a lake will be difficult," Books said.

"I agree," she said. "That's why I want your brain cogitating on how to do it."

Books lifted his chin. "I understand."

Maldynado snorted. "Books's brain will probably tell him to give it a lecture."

Books sneered at him.

"Books, you're in charge of those two," Amaranthe said. "Use them as you see fit."

His irritated expression turned speculative, and a faint smile crept onto his lips. "In charge, you say?"

"Wait a minute." Maldynado pushed away from his tree. "Books is in charge of me?"

Amaranthe waved his objection away. "Akstyr, get them as close as you can to the artifact. Books will figure out a way to take a look at it.

It'll be dark in a couple of hours, so you better get moving. I probably needn't say it, but stay out of sight. The soldiers are here to investigate the same thing we are, and they may have patrols around the lake. Patrols that would be happy to shoot outlaws foolish enough to cross their path."

The heron ruffled its wings, then flapped them and took off.

CHAPTER 17

A SURPRISING AMOUNT OF SMOKE THICKENED THE air, hanging low amongst the ferns and evergreens. The soldiers were certainly not being discreet. The smoke stung Amaranthe's eyes and tickled her nostrils. She blinked away the irritation and hung back, letting Sicarius and Basilard lead the way toward the camp. After her admonition to the others to be careful, *she* did not want to be the one to step on a twig and alert everyone to their approach. The last time she had been forced to fight enforcers with Sicarius at her side, it had gone poorly...for the enforcers. A victory against those she wanted as allies was no victory.

Sicarius had offered to scout the camp on his own, but she wanted to see what the enforcers and soldiers were up to. Assuming they had the same goal she did, they had a day's head start. What had they done with it?

Ahead of her, Basilard and Sicarius stopped.

Much smoke, Basilard signed.

No cook fire, Sicarius signed back.

Amaranthe had not realized he had learned Basilard's hand code, nor had she seen him use it, but he did so now flawlessly. She crept up and joined them. They found a spur of high ground where they could gaze down upon the camp with copious trees in between for cover. On the pebbly shore, a huge bonfire burned, easily eight feet long. The two male enforcers tended it, tossing on more wood.

Not a bonfire, Amaranthe realized. A funeral pyre.

"Looks like they had an eventful night," she murmured, wondering if it had been wise to split her group.

The female enforcer sergeant paced into view.

"We should be in there with them." The woman clenched her fists as she stalked about the pyre.

"You've got to stay here, Sarge," one man said. "Those monsters like women."

Basilard's head jerked up.

"They seemed to like the men fine too." The sergeant jabbed her hand toward the funeral pyre.

Amaranthe leaned forward, resting her hand on the papery bark of a birch. She wanted more information, but the woman paced back into a tent. The men at the fire said nothing. If there were others in the camp, they were in the tents or otherwise hidden from view.

Sicarius signed, *Go?*

Amaranthe exhaled slowly, tempted to watch longer or even approach. If there were only three people in there...

She pointed at the camp and signed, *Number?*

Sicarius's eyes narrowed slightly. He probably sensed her scheming something.

She smiled innocently.

He flicked a finger for Basilard to go one way while he went the other. Amaranthe stayed by her tree and nibbled on a fingernail while she watched the enforcer men pile more wood onto the fire. The longer she watched, the more sure she became that she wanted to question the sergeant.

Sicarius returned first. *Three sleep in tents.*

Amaranthe had not seen him get close enough to check inside the tents. Actually, she had not seen him at all between the time he left and the time he returned. She held up six fingers, not sure if he had counted the woman.

He nodded. *Basilard checks...* "lorry," he mouthed. No signs in Basilard's hunting code for steam machinery.

A moment later, Basilard returned and informed them no one was on the road or in the vehicle.

Amaranthe backed away from the camp so they could talk more freely. Irritated birds jabbered at each other in the trees. One dove at another for no reason—neither was carnivorous. The weaker shrieked and flew off, while the larger assumed a surly pose on a branch.

"I want to talk to her," Amaranthe said. "If there's something dangerous in the dam, it'd be useful to know what before we walk in." She recalled the three dead men, men she believed came from this very dam, and the huge gashes on their bodies. Monsters, the enforcer had said. More soul constructs crafted by a wizard or shaman? Or natural creatures twisted by the water's power?

"Is the dam a priority?" Sicarius asked.

She caught her lip in her teeth. He had a good point. Destroying or nullifying that artifact in the lake had to be their main goal if it was responsible for fouling the water.

"If something's killing soldiers and city workers, I'm sure the emperor would appreciate us taking care of it," she said.

He sent men to hunt, Basilard signed. *Yes?*

"Yes, but they may lack our unique skills," Amaranthe said.

Basilard looked at her skeptically. Sicarius simply looked at her.

"Fine, fine," she said. "The artifact is the priority. I still want to talk to the woman and find out what's going on. Basilard, you recognized something when they were talking of monsters."

He hesitated, started to shake his head, but turned it into a shrug. He slashed two fingers in a claw-like motion. Amaranthe did not recognize the sign.

She spread her hands. "I don't—"

"Makarovi," Sicarius said.

The word sounded familiar. "Isn't that some mythological creature of old?"

Basilard shrugged again, an embarrassed flush reddening his cheeks.

"They're real," Sicarius said.

Basilard flicked him a surprised glance.

"Real but rare," Sicarius said. "Their habitat is in the drier eastern half of the mountains, especially up north where the Mangdorian tribes were pushed. Centuries ago, they were hunted relentlessly in the empire, and they've been absent here since."

"So, someone from Mangdoria brought them here?" Amaranthe asked.

Basilard slashed his hand in a "no" sign and added: *Too dangerous. Nobody could harness them.*

"A powerful practitioner could," Sicarius said.

That drew another "no" from Basilard. *Not for a long trek. Shaman must sleep.*

"Let's just worry about the fact that they're here for now," Amaranthe said. "And that they're apparently so awful they were hunted close to extinction. What did they do exactly?"

"When our ancestors first pushed east and encountered them, the creatures killed many of our people," Sicarius said. "Women in particular were targeted. After numerous gruesome deaths, Emperor Skatovar placed a bounty on them."

"Why did they target women?"

"Unknown." Sicarius looked to Basilard.

He grimaced, face apologetic as he signed. *Favorite prey. They eat female organs.*

"Great," Amaranthe said. "I've always wanted to be some horrible creature's culinary delicacy."

A branch snapped nearby. Sicarius disappeared. Basilard darted behind a shrub. Amaranthe ducked behind a knot of roots protruding a couple of feet above the ground. The earthy scent of moss filled her nostrils as she peeked over top.

A soldier came into view, weaving between the trees. Performing a routine patrol or searching for the owners of the abandoned steam lorry? The scouts on the road must have reported back by now.

He drew closer, head rotating from side to side. His hands gripped the rifle tightly. Yes, he anticipated trouble.

Something brushed Amaranthe's arm, surprising her. Sicarius had joined her behind the roots.

He pointed to the soldier, whose back was to them as he moved past their position. Sicarius said nothing but she guessed his meaning: should he grab the man for questioning?

"I want to talk to the woman," Amaranthe breathed.

Sicarius stared her in the eye, his gaze hard and unwavering.

A dozen justifications floated through her mind, though she knew any one would sound like an excuse. They could probably get the same information from the soldier. It was curiosity that motivated her choice, nothing wiser. She lifted her chin in what she hoped was a regal commanding expression that proclaimed she had made her decision and would not rescind it.

"If we question her and let her go," Sicarius said, "she'll report our presence to the soldiers. They'll know exactly who is here."

She grimaced, realizing that meant he had not planned to let this soldier go after questioning. She doubted that meant tying the man up to release later.

"The soldiers knowing we're here is acceptable," Amaranthe said. "In fact, it's good. If nobody knows we're here, nobody will know we're the ones who save the city. I know you prefer stealth and secrecy for your work, but if we're to..." She glanced at Basilard, mindful not to hint too much of Sicarius's interests in front of anyone. "If we're to earn exoneration from the emperor, it's not enough to help the empire. We need Sespian to *know* we're helping the empire, so the more people who know of our work, the better."

"Very well." Sicarius did not appear happy, but then he never did.

"How shall we arrange this?" Amaranthe rubbed her hands. "I can go in there, and you can cover me while I palaver, and—"

"No."

She lifted her hands. "What are the odds of another team having blasting sticks to hurl at you?"

"Wait by the water," Sicarius said, apparently uninterested in estimating odds. "I'll bring her to you."

"No violence," she said.

He snorted.

"No permanent, scar-producing violence that will leave her disinclined to listen to me," Amaranthe amended.

Sicarius stalked away, ignoring Basilard who was signing to ask if he could help. Basilard lifted his eyebrows in her direction.

"Do I ask for too much?" she asked.

He pointed the direction Sicarius had gone and rocked his hand back and forth. Just too much for Sicarius then. Well, everyone thought that.

"We better do as he says and wait by the water." Amaranthe took a few steps that direction before noticing Basilard was not following. "Coming?"

He signed: *I stay. Help if he needs it.*

For a few heartbeats, Amaranthe watched him, noticing how he avoided her eyes. He didn't want to be alone with her. Did he fear she

would question him, and he would reveal things he did not want to share?

"Basilard, if there's something you know that might help us," she said, "I hope you'll consider telling me. If one of your people is working for whomever is behind all this...he's already abandoned your tenets, right? By killing or creating devices that do the killing for him?"

Basilard studied a particularly interesting fern at his feet.

Amaranthe left him and made her way around the spur to the marshy zone that stretched along the lake. The sun had dropped behind the mountains, casting shade across the valley.

She propped a foot on a bird-poop-stained rock at the water's edge. Ducks stared at her as they paddled past, eyes glowing. Amaranthe had to admit, she could think of places she would rather spend time alone. She wondered if not drinking the water would be enough to keep them safe, or if the artifact's powers permeated the land and the air about the lake too. The thought of waking up for watch and stumbling upon an aggressive Sicarius, eyes glowing, was the stuff of nightmares.

She shook the idea from her mind and windmilled her arms to loosen tense muscles. She redid her bun, smoothed her fatigues, and brushed mud from her boots. The sergeant's opinion should not matter, but Amaranthe did not want to appear like some vagrant booted from the force due to sloth and dishevelment.

Reeds rustled behind her.

Amaranthe whirled and pulled her short sword free.

A three-foot-long lizard hurtled toward her. Green eyes burned brightly in its dark, scaled face. Its maw gaped open as it ran, rows of needle sharp fangs glistening.

Amaranthe lunged to the side and thrust her blade downward. Steel pierced leathery hide and pinned the lizard at the neck. It thrashed with surprising power. Leaving her sword, she skittered back to avoid its whipping razor-edged tail.

She evaded it, but her heel sunk into mud. Thick muck snared her boot, and she lost her balance. She went down with an ungraceful splash. Muddy water washed over her clothing and splattered her cheeks.

The lizard flailed one last time and lay still. Amaranthe glared at it.

Three figures walked out of the trees. Basilard, Sicarius, and the enforcer woman. Though Sicarius's knives were sheathed, a long thin

cut at the woman's throat dripped blood. Her cold dark eyes could have
been carved from obsidian. Sicarius gripped her arm, and she remained
quiet, but the tendons standing out along her neck suggested she would
be happy to lunge at Amaranthe and complete the task the lizard had
failed at.

Struggling to maintain dignity, Amaranthe shambled out of the mud
and onto solid ground. Caked in grime, with clumps of wet hair hanging in her eyes, she doubted her appearance impressed the woman. For
once, she was relieved Sicarius let nothing of his thoughts show on his
face. Oh, well. Carry on.

"Good afternoon," Amaranthe said, her tone light and—she hoped—
non-threatening. "How are you, Sergeant? Good? Good." She pried her
sword free from the dead lizard. "I was just catching a spot of dinner.
Say, Basilard, are these lizards good eating? Wait, scratch that. It's probably not healthy to ingest magically altered animals."

The enforcer woman's nostrils flared at the mention of magic. Or
maybe they were flaring at the entire situation.

"What do you want?" she demanded. The name tag sewn on her
uniform jacket read: YARA.

"To help," Amaranthe said.

"I *know* who you are."

"And does that preclude a belief that we could be helpful?"

"Yes!" the woman roared.

"Ah. That'll make this conversation difficult then."

"You're criminals," Yara growled, shoulders hunched. "You tried
to assassinate the emperor, and this—" she whipped her head toward
Sicarius, "—beast has killed dozens—*hundreds!*—of soldiers and enforcers. How can you stand here with him? What payment could he give
you to betray the empire and your co-workers?"

The words surprised Amaranthe to silence, not because the woman
loathed Sicarius—that was expected—but because Yara knew her by
sight, knew about the emperor's kidnapping, and apparently knew Amaranthe's history as an enforcer. The kidnapping had been in the newspapers, but Amaranthe's previous employment had not been mentioned.
No doubt, it would besmirch the reputation of the force.

"I may work in the farmlands," Yara said, "but we hear what happens in the city. I know what you did to Corporal Wholt and his men."

Amaranthe winced. The weeks that had passed since that incident had done little to dull her guilt. Even if Yara believed Amaranthe and the others were up here to help, which was doubtful given the fury emanating from her, she would not forgive Amaranthe for that night. Not with Sicarius standing behind her.

"Why don't you tell me about the beasts you're dealing with?" Amaranthe asked. Best to change the subject and get the woman's mind on work. "Are they what killed your men? Are they the makarovi?"

Yara's nostrils flared again. "They're in the dam. Go see for yourself."

"Is that what you came to investigate? The dam? Or are you here about that artifact in the lake?"

Yara's lips flattened. Sicarius drew his black dagger with a slow, deliberate rasp.

"I'm not intimidated by your master," Yara said, "and I won't answer questions that will help you destroy the city. Kill me if you wish."

Master? Not likely. "As I said before," Amaranthe said, "we wish to help."

"You're probably responsible for all this," Yara said. "How could you go rogue? I used to look up to you. People always said good things about you. We all thought you'd plant the tree for the rest of the women on the force to climb."

Amaranthe rocked back on her heels. "You'd heard of me? Before, er, when I was still an enforcer?"

"Of course! There was only a handful of women across all the precincts. Your record was flawless. We all figured you would be the first to make sergeant, maybe more."

For a moment, Amaranthe forgot her questions and her reasons for pulling Yara out. Why hadn't any of those women talked to her? Sent her a message? But then, shc had never sought them out either, since they worked in other districts in the city.

"It looks like you made sergeant first," Amaranthe said.

"Last month," Yara said. "Me and another woman. They were special promotions from the emperor." An awed tone crept into her voice. "I didn't know he knew I existed."

Amaranthe closed her eyes. It seemed Sespian had found another enforcer to admire. Or perhaps his disappointment in what he believed Amaranthe had become had led him to reward others. Either way, it

stung. If she had never attracted Hollowcrest's attention, maybe she would have had her promotion by now. Maybe—

"How could you betray him?" The fury snapped back into Yara's voice. She shifted her weight, as if to pull away from Sicarius, but he did not let her move an inch. "How could you join forces with a dung-kissing *assassin* to kidnap the emperor?"

Basilard, who stood back where he could keep an eye toward the camp, signaled: *Time.*

"It's a long tale," Amaranthe said, "one you wouldn't believe right now." Perhaps ever. "But I give you my word we're here to help. Both of us. Do you know how the artifact got in the lake? Do you know who made it?"

"Of course, I know. My partner and I were the ones to come across his lair. How do you think enforcers got involved in all this?"

"What lair? Where is it? Who's responsible?'"

But Yara seemed to have decided she had said enough. Her lips flattened, and she lifted her chin.

"Please," Amaranthe said. "Tell us what we can do."

Yara snorted. "You want to help? Get that thing out of the lake and those monsters out of the dam."

"We will," Amaranthe said, drawing another snort of disbelief from the woman. "Tell us more about the person who did this. Is it a single man? A magic user? Is it a Mangdorian?"

"Find your own answers, rogue."

"Sergeant Yara," a man called from the camp. "Where'd you go?"

"Let her go," Amaranthe told Sicarius.

She expected an argument, but he released her without comment. Yara sprinted toward the camp.

"Time for us to disappear," Amaranthe said.

Sicarius led the way into the woods. Amaranthe hustled after and left Basilard to cover their trail. She did not know if Yara believed anything or not. Either way her duty would demand she try to capture—or kill—Sicarius and Amaranthe.

Thrashing sounds behind them verified her guess. Sicarius pressed deeper into the woods. Twilight descended, casting darkness across the forest floor. Basilard had fallen behind, so Amaranthe called a halt. Fog curled in from the lake. She no longer heard their pursuit.

Sicarius crouched with his back to a tree to wait. Amaranthe sank down beside him.

"Did you learn anything?" he asked.

She puzzled over the question. Since he had been there and heard everything she had heard, she feared it might be sarcastic, though that was not an attitude she associated with him. He was dry on occasion but rarely sarcastic, unless he was irked at her.

"Are you saying that was a waste of time?" she asked.

"No."

"Oh."

Frogs croaked out in the marsh. The bird chatter had fallen silent, but mosquitoes whined.

Sicarius gave her a sidelong look, his face cloaked with shadows. "Do I ever not say what I mean to say?"

"Well. You never say what I wish you'd say, and you frequently say nothing at all when it's clear you *should* say something, so it's not entirely fantastical that you'd say a certain thing when you mean something else entirely."

He opened his mouth, shut it, and considered the ground briefly before responding. "I remember studying Fleet Admiral Starcrest's Mathematical Probabilities Applied to Military Strategies as a young boy and finding that less confusing than what you just said."

Now it was her turn for a stunned pause before answering. "Sicarius?" She laid a tentative hand on his shoulder. "Was that a joke?"

"A statement of fact."

"Hm. It tickled me, so I'm calling it a joke. Stick with me, and I'll help you develop your sense of humor."

He sighed.

She withdrew her hand but not her smile. "I didn't understand your first question. You were there, so you know what I learned."

"You learn things others don't when you speak to people."

"If that were true," she said, "I'd get a lot more from you."

"You get more from me than most."

Though it sounded like another "statement of fact," the words warmed her. "Maybe you give me more than you give most."

Basilard caught up before Sicarius could deny her comment. Amaranthe had to squint to make out his signs in the dim light.

Injured soldier comes from dam. Tells enforcers go to fort, bring reinforcements. They leave search, leave camp.

Amaranthe thought about taking her team into the dam and helping those soldiers, but Sicarius was right: the artifact in the lake was more important. The creatures had likely been put in the dam as a distraction or to keep the workers from reporting to the city.

An agitated howl echoed through the darkening forest.

Basilard gripped Amaranthe's arm and pointed toward the water. She let him lead them through the trees to a nearby beach.

Out in the center of the lake, a subtle green glow emanated from the water.

* * * * *

Books shifted from foot to foot as Maldynado stroked back to shore. He was an adept swimmer, and he had been underwater a long time. Long enough to get a good look at the submerged device?

With night's fall, the location was unmistakable, but its distance from shore suggested depths one could not reach by swimming. Unless, instead of lying on the bottom, it hung suspended somewhere beneath the surface. The fact that the light was visible gave him hope. He had already run the calculations, figuring the brightness an object had to possess to be visible through twenty, fifty, and one hundred feet of water.

Across the lake, the large fire at the soldiers' camp was burning down. Books paced about the beach, nominally on watch, while Akstyr read his healing tome. The eyes of youth apparently had no trouble picking out sentences in the deepening gloom.

Naked and shivering, Maldynado splashed out of the shallows. Books handed him dry clothes.

"Did you see it?" Books asked. "What did it look like? Fragile? Destructible?"

"Mind if I dress first?" Maldynado's teeth chattered. "Nobody wants to be interrogated in his brothel suit."

Books paced. He had let Amaranthe down by sleeping with Vonsha instead of investigating the house, and he felt the need to redeem himself. She was too nice to do more than raise an eyebrow at his bedroom exploits, but he knew. He had failed. He wanted to succeed here.

"It was too deep for me to see," Maldynado finally said. "The glow got brighter as I went down, but that's it."

"Emperor's eternal warts." Books clenched his fist. "We can't stop it if we can't get close to it."

"I reckon they've had the same problem." Maldynado waved toward the camp across the lake.

"If we could fish it up somehow," Akstyr said, "and I could look at it, maybe I could figure out a way to destroy it."

"Not happening," Maldynado said. "It's got to be one- or two-hundred feet down."

"We do have that much rope back in the lorry," Books mused. "And I imagine we could fashion a hook. It'd take a lot of luck to find it down there, but the light would be something of a beacon. I wonder if it's magnetic."

"It's big," Akstyr said. "Probably too big to lift. I can sense that much."

"Someone lifted it to chuck it in the lake in the first place," Maldynado said.

"Telekinetics," Akstyr said in Kendorian, a word Books knew only because he had been teaching the young man enough of the language to read those magic texts. Turgonian had no terms to describe the different mental sciences. It was all "magic" in the empire, and none of it existed supposedly.

"Huh?" Maldynado asked.

"He said we either need to hire a gifted shaman," Books said, "or we need to physically get down to the bottom of the lake to examine this artifact up close."

"He said all that in one word?" Maldynado asked.

Books heaved a sigh. "Go stand watch, you uneducated lout."

"You're enjoying ordering me around far too much. I can't believe I dove into a frigid glacier-fed lake for you. Next time I'm making sure Amaranthe puts me in charge." Maldynado adjusted his belt and swaggered toward the head of the beach, though he paused to question Akstyr on the way by. "You didn't really say all that, did you?"

"Naw," Akstyr said.

Books turned his back on them and rested his chin on a fist. "What we need," he muttered to himself, "is a diving bell."

Perhaps he could make one, something they could lower down by rope that would be big enough for Akstyr and perhaps one other to fit inside. It would have to be spacious enough to cup plenty of air beneath its concave form. That would allow Akstyr to take short trips out to investigate the artifact. Unfortunately, the forest would not provide anything suitable for the purpose.

"I wonder what kind of tools and equipment are in the dam," Books said.

An owl hooted, a cranky sound rather than the usual inquisitive one. Twilight lay thick amongst the trees, and more eyes than the owl's glowed from the shadows. The effect was...eerie.

"Should we light a fire?" Maldynado asked.

"It'd be visible from the soldier camp," Books said.

A mosquito nipped at Books's neck, and he slapped it with more urgency than normal. What if being bitten by something that drank the water could pass along the strange symptoms?

"Do we care?" Maldynado asked. "Maybe they've got some hard cider or brandy over there. When the forest is full of creepiness, humans should band together."

Something that sounded like a dog whining came from behind them. Books turned his back to the lake. He could no longer make out Maldynado and Akstyr's faces.

Leaves rustled. A thunk came from Maldynado's direction, the sound of a hammer being cocked. Books tensed.

"It's us," Amaranthe called.

Three figures appeared out of the darkness.

"Find anything, Books?" Amaranthe asked.

"Not yet, but I have an idea." He explained his diving-bell concept.

"That would provide enough air to stay down long enough to study the device?"

She sounded more impressed than disbelieving, and Books allowed himself to feel a touch of pride. Had she not heard of such a thing? Perhaps all the trivia nestled in his brain had a use for this group after all. He went on to detail the historical precedent, citing instances where diving bells had been used within lakes as well as the sea. Maldynado groaned several times during the spiel, but Amaranthe listened patiently.

"You think you can make such a thing?" she asked when he finished.

"I should not wish to oversell my manual abilities, but—"

A hand clamped over Books's mouth.

"Yes," Maldynado said. "Yes, he can make it."

Books shoved his hand away. "I need supplies. I'm hoping I can find them in the dam."

"And *I'm* hoping we don't have to spend the night out here amongst the plagued and eerie," Maldynado said.

Silence fell after their words. Amaranthe faced Sicarius for a long moment. He said nothing, as usual. Books wondered what she got from exchanges with him.

"Something wrong?" he asked when the silence continued.

A retching sound came from the woods. A snarl followed, then a snapping of jaws and a squeal of pain.

"Wronger," Maldynado said.

Sicarius spun and fired into the dark. Books jumped. Something dropped to the ground. Wordlessly, Sicarius reloaded.

"The dam may not be safer than the forest," Amaranthe said, "but if your supplies are there, we will go."

Books's earlier pride faded as he wondered what trouble his idea would land them in.

CHAPTER 18

THE IRON DOOR OPENED SOUNDLESSLY ON OILED hinges, uncovering a narrow tunnel. Though night had fallen over the lake, a denser darkness waited within.

Amaranthe adjusted her rucksack and steeled herself. "Who's got the lamps?"

Metal clanked as Maldynado and Basilard withdrew lanterns from their packs. Amaranthe checked her rifle, missing the familiar heft of her crossbow, but she feared these creatures would be even less affected by her quarrels than the forest animals. Best to take firearms. Or maybe cannons.

"Ready." Maldynado held his lantern aloft.

"Let's get in, find Books's supplies, and get out as quickly as possible," Amaranthe said. "We'll let the soldiers handle the creatures."

"If they can," Akstyr muttered.

The tight passage would force them to walk in a single line. While Amaranthe was debating whether it would be pusillanimous to suggest she and her tasty female organs should let someone else lead, Sicarius headed in first. She thanked him silently and followed.

Inside the tunnel, the scent of mildew permeated the air. Maldynado's broad shoulders brushed against the gray concrete walls. Rifles and rucksacks scraped and bumped in the confining space.

The passage sloped downward as they traveled deeper. Moisture beaded on the ceiling and rolled down the wall. In spots it dripped with such enthusiasm Amaranthe feared for their lanterns' flames.

"Should this place be leaking this much?" Maldynado asked.

"This dam would have been constructed one segment at a time," Books said, "leaving enough room between the joints to allow for the expansion and contraction of the materials in cold and warm weather.

Some seepage is to be expected. See that drain in the floor? The design would have—"

"Yes," Maldynado said, voice raised to cut Books off. "The answer to my question is yes."

"Forgive me," Books said. "I thought you might wish to educate yourself on something besides womanizing and drinking."

"Not at this particular moment."

Sicarius lifted a hand and stopped. Amaranthe thought he might tell the men to shut their mouths, but he tilted his head, listening.

Gunfire. The concrete and the omnipresent roar of water muffled it, but the sound was distinct. Multiple weapons firing.

"At least we know the soldiers are still alive," she said.

"That'd be more reassuring if we didn't have bounties on our heads," Books muttered.

A deep, guttural bellow sounded in the distance.

"I don't think that was a soldier," Maldynado said.

Amaranthe tried to see Basilard, who walked at the end of the line, but the men blocked her sight. Did he recognize the bellow? Was it one of the creatures?

Sicarius was the one to answer her unspoken questions. "Makarovi." He met Amaranthe's eyes. "Continue?"

She waved him forward. "We have to find Books's tools."

Less than a minute later, the tunnel ended in a large chamber, perhaps a cavernous one. The weak flames of their lanterns did little to pierce the darkness more than a few meters away. The walls and ceiling disappeared in blackness. Only the roar of water flowing over their heads proved barriers existed.

Rows of unfamiliar machines stretched ahead of them. Amaranthe could identify some of the parts—flywheels, pistons, and rotating shafts—but boilers and fireboxes were missing, so they were not steam-powered. Whatever purpose they served, they were not serving it now; they simply loomed, giant metal skeletons. Mazes of pipes ran along the floor between the machines, and some rose vertically, disappearing into the dark depths above.

"What are these machines, Books?" Amaranthe asked.

The men had eased from the tunnel and fanned out, weapons ready.

"I'm uncertain," Books said.

"Two words I never thought I'd hear him string together," Maldynado said to Akstyr, who muttered something back and snickered.

"Perhaps they're powered by the water," Books said. "Some experimental technology?"

Another bellow echoed from the depths ahead, or perhaps to the side. The walls and tunnels distorted sound. Amaranthe had the sense of a vast subterranean complex within this massive concrete tomb. She frowned, not liking that her mind had chosen that last word.

Sicarius strode toward a dark shape on the floor ahead of them. Amaranthe followed with a lantern. A faint odor of blood mingled with the pervasive mildew smell.

"Dead soldier," Sicarius said before she drew close enough to identify the shape.

The flickering lantern light revealed parallel gashes across the man's shoulder and neck, so deep they had nearly torn the head off.

Sicarius crouched for a closer look.

"Why do I always end up stumbling over decapitated bodies when I'm with you?" Amaranthe asked him.

Engrossed in his examination, he did not answer.

"He's probably responsible for most of them," Books muttered.

"Have you seen anything in here you can use to get us under the water?" she asked him.

"I'll look." Books took a couple of steps but paused when nobody followed him.

Maldynado, Akstyr, and Basilard were watching Sicarius, who was poking at one of the wounds with his knife. Amaranthe's belly squirmed.

"Company would be appreciated," Books said.

Maldynado ambled over and threw an arm around his shoulders. "Booksie, you're not afraid to go off alone in the dark, are you?"

Books shucked the arm. "Of course not. Anything suitable to be used as a diving bell will be heavy. I'll need someone large, musclebound, and brutish to lift it."

"Maldynado's your man," Akstyr said.

"Akstyr is mocking me?" Maldynado pressed a hand to his chest. "That shouldn't be allowed. He's barely old enough to show a lady a good time."

"Go." Amaranthe shooed Books and Maldynado. "Take Basilard too. Akstyr, you're with Sicarius and me. I want to know if there's any magic about. We won't go far."

The three men took a lantern and shuffled away. Sicarius had finished his examination of the body.

"Makarovi?" Amaranthe asked.

"Yes."

"It looks like this fellow was running toward the exit when it caught him," Amaranthe said. "Shall we take a walk and see where he came from?"

Sicarius's look reminded her they were supposed to be here for Books's tools, not a monster hunt, but he led onward. He paused to pick up an army-issue rifle, the hammer uncocked. A bloody knife lay a few meters away.

"Looks like he got a couple of blows in before..." She waved toward the dead man.

"Yes, there are blood drops about," Sicarius said. "Makarovi are difficult to kill."

"Good thing we have Akstyr." Amaranthe noticed the young man's face had grown pale beneath his unshaven stubble. "Perhaps our fledgling wizard will have a few tricks for them."

"You should have given me a book on monster slaying if you wanted that," he said.

More bellows and gunfire sounded in the distance. Sicarius led them through the rows of machinery. Their lanterns reflected off the metal parts, creating tiny eyes in the darkness. Amaranthe found herself wishing for a window, even if it only gazed out upon a night-darkened river or forest.

"Ought to be gaslights in here somewhere..." She trailed off as a new stench came to her nose. Rotting flesh.

"Ungh," Akstyr grunted.

As they continued forward, the odor grew stronger. Breathing through her mouth did not help as much as Amaranthe wished it would.

Sicarius paused and faced a snarl of pipes and machinery.

"Light," he said.

Amaranthe handed him the lantern.

He raised it and stepped closer. The light revealed...too much.

A woman in the shredded remains of a city worker's uniform hung over a horizontal pipe, her back bent in an impossible arch. Her torso was split open, her insides ravaged. No, Amaranthe corrected, feasted upon.

Bile rose in her throat. She ripped her gaze away, turned her back, and bent over her knees. She gasped for air, not wanting to vomit. The sight she could block out, but the stench surrounded her. The air was too close, too confining.

Nearby, somebody retched. Akstyr. She clasped a hand over her own mouth, fighting the reflex to do the same.

Sicarius rested his hand on her shoulder. Amaranthe closed her eyes, and forced calmness into her breaths. Like him.

After a moment she found, if not detachment, control.

She nodded to Sicarius. "I'm all right."

He went for a closer look at the corpse. Akstyr wiped a sleeve across his mouth. If he had been pale before, he was white now. Though apparently too shaky to make an excuse, he avoided her eyes. She was glad for his presence. While she appreciated Sicarius, especially his support, his unflappability sometimes made her feel too human. Too weak.

"This happened more than a week ago," Sicarius said when he returned to her side.

"When things were just getting started." Amaranthe gestured for him to continue onward. She did not want to linger where the stench hung so thickly.

They soon reached another narrow tunnel identical to the one that had brought them into the large chamber. Sicarius paused before the last machine and plucked a tuft of fur off a protruding lever. He sniffed it, then handed it to Amaranthe.

Though smelling fur could do little enlighten her, she obliged him by inhaling. Earthy, musky, and distinct. Her recently riled stomach churned anew at the hint of blood.

"That's their smell?" she asked.

"Yes," Sicarius said.

"It sounds like you've encountered them before. Personally."

"Once."

"On your—" she glanced at Akstyr and lowered her voice, "—mission to Mangdoria?"

"Yes," Sicarius said.

"Did it attack you? And you killed it?"

He turned his back to Akstyr. "It chased me out of the mountain pass. I sunk several of my throwing knives into its face and torso, but it kept coming. I eventually climbed a cliff where it could not follow to escape it."

"Oh."

They need not have worried about Akstyr overhearing. He wore a distant expression and faced away from them, toward some corner or object hidden by darkness.

"How did our ancestors kill them?" Amaranthe asked.

"Battles of attrition," Sicarius said. "If you drive enough holes into them, they'll eventually die, but even head shots are not certain to kill. They have blubber and skulls thick enough to withstand firearms and bows. There are stories of cannons being used. A couple of drownings. Their density makes them poor swimmers."

Amaranthe perked up. "Poor swimmers? We're surrounded by water. Maybe we could convince them to jump in."

Sicarius grunted dubiously.

A rifle fired. Here, at the tunnel entrance, the noise was louder than it had been earlier. She eyed the stygian passage, debating whether to go deeper.

"If they catch your scent," Sicarius said, "you won't be able to escape them, and we lack the firepower to stop them."

"Right," Amaranthe said. "Let's check the rest of this chamber and see if there's anything of interest." Such as giant vats of water they could use to drown monsters.

"This way," Akstyr said, surprising her.

Before she could ask why, he strode to the left, following the wall away from the tunnel. His head was up, almost like a hound following a scent.

Shrugging, Amaranthe trailed after him. His senses led him past a broken machine, its flywheel torn off and bolts scattering the floor. They came to a corner, and she thought Akstyr would turn to follow the new wall, but he stopped and pressed his palms against the concrete.

Amaranthe shifted from foot to foot while Sicarius stood guard. A distant flame glowed, visible between a pair of thick vertical pipes. She assumed the lantern belonged to Books and the others. If they were standing still, perhaps they had found something useful.

"Something Made behind here," Akstyr said, dropping his hands.

"You're not sensing the thing at the bottom of the lake, are you?" Amaranthe asked. "We've descended below the surface of the water."

"Wrong side," Sicarius said.

Amaranthe retraced their route in her mind. He was right. This wall stood between them and the waterfall side of the dam, not the lake side.

"It's a similar feel, but smaller," Akstyr said. "Less energy and... there are more devices."

"*More* magical devices?"

"Intricate ones, yeah."

"Somebody's got an active hobby shop going." Amaranthe touched the wall. It thrummed with the power of thousands of gallons of water flowing overhead, but she could sense nothing else.

"A master Maker," Akstyr said, his tone reverent. "I can tell from the sophistication of the work. I can't wait to get a look at the artifact in the lake. I bet it's brilliant."

"So..." Amaranthe said. "You think our opponent is some genius craftsman who's probably a lot smarter than any of us."

"Daunted?" Sicarius asked quietly.

"Of course not. You know I like a challenge." She wondered if her confident smile was at all convincing.

They explored the chamber further and found more machinery and more dead bodies: some fresh—soldiers—and some not—dam employees. They came upon the rest of the team in an alcove on the lake-side of the chamber. Basilard, Maldynado, and Books bent over crates, their backs to the entrance. Piles of tubing, tools, and smashed wooden casks scattered the floor, as well as boots and a heap of leather material or perhaps clothing.

Amaranthe cleared her throat.

The men jumped. A large, brass helmet clanked to the floor.

"Watch," Sicarius said.

Nobody misinterpreted the single word. Basilard grabbed his rifle, jogged to the corner, and put his back against the wall to stand guard.

"Sorry. We got distracted." Books waved to encompass the alcove. Pegboards full of tools hung from the walls and equipment cluttered workbenches. "This place is *perfect*."

Amaranthe shrugged. "You're the ones who'll get eaten if a makarovi sneaks up on you."

"But, we'll look extra fine when they come." Maldynado plucked the helmet off the floor and deposited it over his curls. It engulfed his head and neck, and a stiff, leather bib extended a couple of inches down his chest and upper back. A glass faceplate in the center allowed a view of his broad grin. Hinges, bolts, and flat cylinders sticking out at the ears made him look like something that had crawled out of a scrap pile at a smelter. "What do you think?" he asked, voice muffled. "Fetching, eh?"

"You look like a discarded toy built by a drunken automata maker," Books said.

"Huh?" Maldynado ticked a fingernail against an ear cylinder. "Hard to hear in here."

"You look great," Amaranthe said. "The ladies at the Pirates' Plunder will be sure to give you special rates."

"Special *high* rates," Akstyr said.

Maldynado tugged the helmet off. "The right person could make brass fashionable."

"What is all this?" Amaranthe asked.

Books took the helmet from Maldynado, tossing in a shoulder shove to butt him out of the way. "Diving gear. Helmets, body suits, and even gloves. I wasn't hoping for anything this ideal, but it makes sense that workers would have to be able to go out and inspect the dam from time to time."

"You mean we can put those on and go down to the bottom of the lake?" Dare she hope it would be that easy?

"Well, there's a problem."

Ah, she knew it.

Books nudged one of the shattered casks. "The suits are more advanced than what I've read about, and I'm not positive how everything works, but I believe these are—*were*—for supplying air. They've all been destroyed."

"Whoever stuck that device on the lake bottom probably didn't want people visiting it," Amaranthe said.

"I imagine not." Books scratched his jaw. "But there's a lot of tubing in that crate over there. Naval diving is done with surface supplied air. Perhaps with time I could rig something up. Enough for two suits anyway."

"Take whatever and whomever you need to help," Amaranthe said.

"Akstyr definitely needs to go down," Books said.

"And see the artifact up close?" Akstyr grinned and plucked a helmet out of a crate. "Nice."

"And probably me as well." Books sighed.

"Not me?" Maldynado reached for the helmet in Books's hands.

"No." Books wrapped his arms more tightly about it. "Akstyr knows about magic, so he must go. And I know...everything else."

Maldynado snorted. "Fine, then I can stay up top and watch. I want to see these things working."

"I require a serious and trustworthy assistant up above, watching over things."

"You insult me, Books," Maldynado said. "More than usual."

"Take Basilard instead," Amaranthe said. "As for the rest of us, shall we go back outside and help Books or go find..." The soldiers? The makarovi? The new magical doodads Akstyr sensed?

"Trouble?" Sicarius suggested.

"That's...probably a word that encompasses everything I'm thinking of," she admitted.

"Was not the plan to leave the makarovi for the soldiers?" he said.

"That was before we knew about the additional magic. And if they've sent for reinforcements, they may really need our help."

"Amaranthe," Sicarius said, voice low. The others had turned back to the equipment, all save Basilard who remained on watch, attention outward. Sicarius drew her to the side. "If there are many makarovi, we'll not be able to defeat them."

"We'll think of something. Besides, wouldn't it be great if we could do something heroic right in front of the soldiers?"

"Heroics get people killed," Sicarius said.

Clanks sounded as Akstyr and Maldynado rummaged in a new crate.

"They get people noticed too." Amaranthe held his gaze but did not sense any give behind his eyes. "We'll be fine. We have a well-trained group of men with unique talents and skills."

"Ouch, ouch, get it off!" Maldynado hollered.

He was hopping about with a hand clamp hanging from...ah, that was a nipple. Amaranthe dropped her face into her hands.

"Oops," Akstyr said.

Amaranthe avoided Sicarius's gaze as she helped Maldynado unfasten himself. "Need anything else, Books? How long will it take you to set up?"

He lifted a hand. "I should not wish to make promises about time or even success. If that artifact is as deep as Maldynado believes, we may have trouble with water pressure. Bones and muscle can hold up, but air-filled spaces in our bodies, such as the ears and lungs—"

"*Books*," Maldynado groaned.

"If we *do* go in, we should walk in from the shore and gradually let our bodies acclimate. Likewise, it could be hazardous to come up quickly."

"All right," Amaranthe said. "Go get set up. You can wait for us to return to go into the water. I don't want you somewhere vulnerable without lots of help up above to ensure you're kept safe."

Books blew out a relieved breath. "Good."

"Of course, if we all get eaten, you'll have to do it on your own," she said.

Books's relieved expression turned to a worried frown. Even Sicarius gave her a dark stare.

Amaranthe patted Books on the arm. "We'll be careful."

She headed for the main chamber, but Maldynado paused and pointed at Books.

"Watch out for the giant man-sized catfish while you're down on the lake bottom. I hear they're carnivorous."

Books scoffed. "Those are stories told by uneducated rural mountain folk, nothing more."

"Sure, Booksie. You believe what you want to believe. Just make sure to take a sword down there. Can't fire a rifle underwater, you know."

"You're a bastard at times," Amaranthe told Maldynado when he fell in beside her. Sicarius was already leading the way toward the tunnel.

"Yup, but he deserved it. I wouldn't have done anything unsafe when he was underwater."

"Perhaps it's your insouciant manner that leads others to believe you shouldn't be placed in positions of responsibility."

"Yes," Maldynado said, "but I thought Books bright enough to see past a man's painstakingly cultivated levels of insouciance." He wriggled his eyebrows.

"Are you saying you have hidden depths?"

Maldynado scratched an armpit. "Naturally."

"Hm," was all she said.

The new tunnel, too, dripped copious amounts of water and stank of mildew. It continued to slope downward and soon came to a T-section. A faint draft of fresh air whispered from the right. Maybe that passage led to the top of the dam where those towers perched.

"Left," Amaranthe said when Sicarius paused. "Akstyr's magic is that direction, right?"

Wordlessly, Sicarius headed left. They reached a doorway in the side of the tunnel. Inside lay a small room with a panel on a wall, hanging diagrams, a desk and chair, and a series of levers.

Amaranthe unclasped a bolt and pushed on the panel. It slid sideways, opening a window of sorts. The roar of water intensified, and cool misty air gusted inside, spraying dampness onto her face. A panoply of stars gleamed in a clear, black sky, while a quarter moon shone silver on three streams of water pouring from flood gates open beneath them. A half a dozen more closed flood gates marked the dam wall.

Maldynado joined her. "Looks like we found the control room."

"I wonder how they open and close those heavy gates." Amaranthe leaned out and twisted her neck to peer upward, but whatever mechanism did the work was hidden in the walls.

"Here." Sicarius stood behind them, an eye toward the exit, but he pointed at one in a series of diagrams on the wall.

Amaranthe studied it. "Ah, I see. Those things on the top of the dam aren't watchtowers after all. Or at least they're not *just* watchtowers."

The diagram showed cranes housed in each structure with cables that could pull up the heavy gates. The next display riveted her attention for longer. It displayed vertical and horizontal lines—pipelines—and the topography of the surrounding area, all the way down to Stumps and the lake.

She ran her finger along the diagram. "This pipe routes water to the aqueducts that lead into the city. These go to fields. The river itself flows south and empties into Little Sister Lake over one hundred miles from the capital. Whichever emperor was in charge when this was built sure didn't mind making a lot of extra work for people."

"Isn't that every emperor that's ever existed?" Maldynado asked. "Making work, that's their job, isn't it?"

"Are warrior-caste men allowed to make snide remarks about our rulers?" Amaranthe poked into the desk drawers, hoping for something illuminating.

"They are if they're disowned with bounties on their heads."

She spotted a crumpled piece of paper on the floor behind a desk leg and grabbed it. "Hm."

"Is that a page from the dastardly villain's diary?" Maldynado asked. "One carelessly dropped that conveniently reveals the secret to destroying these vile artifacts?"

"It's an invoice."

"Villains get bills?"

"It's the invoice for the appraisal on Hagcrest's land," Amaranthe said. "The woman must have brought it up here to meet with her client, expecting to get paid..."

"And she got a knife across the throat. Who would have thought being an appraiser could be a deadly line of work?"

Amaranthe tucked the paper into her pocket, though it held nothing so helpful as a name and address for the person who ordered the appraisal.

Rifle shots cracked, clear and close.

"Guess the dam tour is over," Maldynado said. "Too bad. I liked this room. Fresh air, a good view..."

"No corpses," Amaranthe said.

"That did improve the general ambiance."

Sicarius was already heading back into the tunnels.

"Time to see what they're firing at," she murmured.

They did not walk far before the darkness ahead changed from black to a greenish gray. Amaranthe frowned at the unnatural hue. No lantern could be responsible for that.

Moist, guttural snorts and snarls filled the air. A stench wafted from ahead: blood again, along with the musky, earthy odor of that fur. Amaranthe's grip tightened on her rifle. It was not too late to back out, to leave the soldiers to their fate. If her team destroyed the artifact, that would be enough, wouldn't it?

Agitated voices murmured, barely audible over the animalistic sounds.

"Hurry up," someone said.

Sicarius paused. Amaranthe stood on tiptoes to peer over his shoulder. A few paces ahead, the tunnel changed from an enclosed passage to a metal walkway, open on one side.

"Let me by," she whispered.

Sicarius did not, though he moved forward. He stopped again as soon as they stepped onto the metal grating of the walkway.

To their left, the wall continued, but to the right, a dim chamber opened up with a floor twenty-five or thirty feet below them. A massive pipe, perhaps twenty feet in diameter ran through the chamber parallel to the walkway. Ten soldiers stood or crouched atop it. They were busy reloading their rifles and watching huge, bulky creatures that milled on the floor. Lanterns perched between the soldiers, but the source of the sickly green light was a small, flat glowing device attached to the top of the pipe. Men knelt on either side, tools out, trying to disarm it or perhaps pry it loose.

Amaranthe pictured the schematic from the control room. "That's the pipe leading to the city."

"Figures." Maldynado had come up behind them. He was tall enough to observe over her head. "Those the makarovi down there?"

"Yes," Sicarius said.

The shadows made it hard to count, and the great pipe hid the back half of the chamber, but Amaranthe guessed at least six beasts prowled, each one more than ten feet tall.

Without warning, one leaped. It made it to the top, but could not gain purchase on the smooth, sloping side of the pipe. It hung, claws squealing as it tried to dig in.

A soldier fired a rifle at its face. The creature dropped. It landed on its feet, shook itself like a dog recovering from a smack on the nose, then began stalking about again.

"I guess it *does* take a cannon to drop one," Amaranthe whispered.

"I knew we were forgetting something," Maldynado said.

"Though...if they can be drowned, we might not need a cannon." She nibbled on a fingernail, thinking of Sicarius's earlier words and the diagrams in the control room.

"Whatever scheme you're concocting," Sicarius said, "remember there are several down there. Several who will go after you first and be impossible to deter once they get your scent."

"Funny they haven't noticed her yet," Maldynado said.

"Yes," Sicarius said. "It must be the collars."

Collars? Amaranthe squinted into the gloom.

A second makarovi leaped, hurling itself toward the soldiers tinkering with the glowing box. One man jerked back and almost fell off the opposite side of the pipe. Only a reflexive grab from his comrade saved him.

Three rifles fired, and the creature dropped out of sight again, but not before Amaranthe, watching for it this time, glimpsed the collar. Partially hidden by the shaggy black fur, the silver chain wrapped the makarovi's neck like a choker.

"Now there's a sexy look for the homeliest beast in the mountains," Maldynado muttered.

"The collars are magical?" she asked, figuring they had found the multiple devices Akstyr sensed.

"Yes," Sicarius said.

"Who's there?" a soldier called. He faced the walkway, rifle gripped in both hands. The wan green light illuminated crossed muskets embroidered on his sleeve, the rank of a sergeant.

"Is it the enforcers?" another asked while Amaranthe debated how to answer.

"Did you get the rest of the garrison to come up here?"

"Ssh," the sergeant said, his gaze never turning from Amaranthe and her men. "It's too soon to be them."

He lifted his rifle, not yet aiming it at her, but the barrel pointed at the walkway below her feet.

Sicarius tried to draw her back into the tunnel where the walls would protect them from fire, but she braced herself with a hand on the corner.

"We're from the city," she called. "Can we help?"

The snarls intensified below, and the makarovi shuffled closer to the walkway below her. Something seemed to stop them, though, some invisible pull. It drew them back to the pipe below the glowing box.

"Who are you?" the sergeant asked again, brow furrowed. "Random people from the city don't know about this dam." His finger flexed on the trigger.

"Maybe she's the one behind all this," another said. "Some witch who made these slagging contraptions."

"No," Amaranthe said. "We're just typical imperial citizens, but we can help. We have weapons."

"*We* have weapons too," one of the men fiddling with the box said. "They're not doing much."

"We *are* running low on ammo," someone muttered, so quietly Amaranthe almost missed it.

"We talked to Sergeant Yara," she said, hoping the soldiers would prove more amenable if she implied she knew their ally. "She said you needed help."

"She told you to come in here?" The sergeant stared, mouth slack. "You know what these things do to women?"

"We saw," Amaranthe said. Even as they spoke two beasts broke away from the pipe again and drew closer to her. Moist snuffles and smacking lips assaulted her ears. The creatures' stench floated up, stronger than ever. "We have a man who may be able to disarm that device." Maybe if they hurried back to the machine room, she could catch Akstyr before he went outside with Books and Basilard.

"Help disarm a magical device?" The sergeant scowled. "That's an unlikely skill for 'typical imperial citizens.' Who *are* you?"

She hesitated. They might believe Sicarius ecumenical enough to help, but they would never let him. He was watching her, and he shook his head once when she met his eyes. All right, she would simply tell them her name. She could bring Akstyr out, and Sicarius could stay in the shadows.

"My name is—"

Sicarius gripped her arm. "Do not—"

One of the creatures below jumped and hit the bottom of the walkway. The floor heaved, and Amaranthe stumbled back. Claws slipped through the grating. One bear-like paw gripped the edge of the walk-

way. Sicarius stomped on it, then stepped back, joining her in the tunnel mouth.

His boot had no effect on the makarovi, and it continued to cling to the bottom of the walkway. Its lower half thrashed as it tried to pull itself up. Another creature jumped, banging its head. The walkway trembled and shuddered.

Maldynado brushed past Amaranthe. He lowered his rifle so the barrel poked through the grate, and he fired into the makarovi's eye. The orb exploded, splattering liquid. The creature dropped. For a moment, the scent of black powder overpowered the animal stink.

Amaranthe expected—hoped for—the thing to die, but it rose again after it hit the ground.

"You better get out of here, woman," the sergeant said. "These things aren't fierce bright, but you might excite them enough to figure out the way from the lower level to the upper. And we don't want them where they can jump across and get to us. We've got to..." He waved at the device.

While Maldynado reloaded his rifle, Amaranthe mulled. She could retrieve Akstyr to work on the device, but only if the soldiers allowed them onto the pipe. However Akstyr's knowledge of magic would make him suspect in their eyes and perhaps earn him a quick death. She had to win the sergeant over somehow. If—

Sicarius bent over the rail, distracting her from her thoughts. He sighted down his rifle and shot a makarovi. The creature's collar snapped, and the broken band clanked to the floor.

The soldiers murmured. Sicarius withdrew into the tunnel to reload.

"How'd he manage that shot in the dark? Who is that over there?"

Amaranthe was too busy watching the creature to answer. As soon as it was free of the collar, it bolted to her corner of the chamber. It jumped, claws scraping at the metal grating. Saliva flung from its jowls, spattering the wall. As soon as it fell, it leaped again. It snorted and whined in frustration, unable to reach its target—her. For the moment. If there was another way up...

For the first time, true fear clutched Amaranthe's heart, and she had to fight to stay there instead of fleeing back outside. "Any particular reason you did that?" She meant her tone to sound casual, not terrified, but the last word cracked.

"To see if it was possible," Sicarius said. "Without the collars, they'll return to the wilds eventually."

"*Eventually.*"

"Look." The sergeant pointed at the makarovi trying so hard to reach her. "It's stopped being a guard dog for this ancestors-cursed contraption. It's acting more like a normal hungry predator now. An agitated hungry predator denied its favorite food."

"Lovely way to put it," Amaranthe said.

"Sergeant." One of the soldiers leaned close to his leader and whispered in his ear.

"We should try to get the rest of those collars off," a corporal said. "It'll be easier to figure out that device without those bastards leapfrogging over each other, trying to get to us."

"Wait!" Amaranthe said, a plan solidifying in her head, a plan that would be much easier to implement if they only had to face one makarovi at a time. "I have an idea how to kill them. If you leave the collars in place for just a half an hour, I can—"

"Are you sure?" the sergeant asked, responding to his soldier's whispered comments. He squinted into the gloom on the walkway, eyes toward the tunnel and Sicarius.

"Uh oh," she muttered. "I think they figured out who—"

Sicarius brushed past her and stepped onto the walkway again. He ignored the leaping makarovi below him and, in one swift motion, brought his rifle up and shot the device.

The ball clanged off without damaging it or diminishing the glow. The soldiers near it fell to their bellies in surprise.

Amaranthe jumped, almost as startled.

"You lunatic!" the sergeant yelled. "You could have shot one of us."

"Unlikely," Sicarius said.

"It *is* Sicarius," one said.

"Fire!" the sergeant yelled.

Atop the pipe, all the soldiers lifted their rifles, sights seeking Sicarius. This time, Amaranthe went with him when he pulled her back into the tunnel. A rifle cracked and the ball slammed against the wall above the walkway.

"Give us a half an hour," Amaranthe called into the chamber without poking her head around the corner. "Don't shoot off any more collars!"

Nobody answered. She hoped the soldiers listened to her, though that seemed unlikely now.

"You need to stop taking Cold and Flinty here with you when you're trying to talk people onto our side," Maldynado told Amaranthe.

"We've talked enough." Sicarius strode back the way they had come, reloading the rifle as he went.

"He's such a warm fellow," Maldynado said. "Can't see why people try to kill him so often."

Amaranthe trotted after Sicarius—why was she always running after that man?—and caught up with him in the machine room. Books and the others had cleared out of the alcove. She would have to get Akstyr to look at the device later.

"Where are you going?" Amaranthe had to jog to keep up. "I have a plan."

Sicarius did not slow down. "Telling a room full of armed soldiers our names should not be part of it."

Ah, so that was why he was miffed. "I wasn't going to give them your name, just mine. And they figured it out on their own anyway. It doesn't matter. They have to know who we are if the emperor is to find out about our work."

"Leave them a note afterwards."

He entered the narrow tunnel and she could no longer walk beside him. She stopped. Her plan did not involve leaving yet.

Maldynado caught up and patted her on the shoulder. "Problem, boss?"

"I don't think he appreciates my strategy of obtaining information and making friends by talking to people."

"Probably because it doesn't work on him."

Her first inclination was to argue that it did work on him, somewhat, but the splinters of information she teased from Sicarius would not impress any interrogators. And whether or not he would call her a friend was no sure bet either.

"Coming?" Sicarius asked from the shadows.

She had not realized he was still there. "We've work to do here."

"The soldiers can shoot the rest of the collars off," Sicarius said. "You don't want to be nearby when they've completed that. We should assist with destroying the lake artifact. It may be unnecessary to remove the other if the first is nullified."

"That still leaves a pack of makarovi alive and roaming the dam. How will the soldiers get off that pipe? They're running out of ammunition, and what they have isn't effective anyway. I want to get rid of the makarovi."

"How?"

"Yes, how?" Maldynado asked.

"Lure them up top one at a time, use those cranes that open the floodgates to hook the creatures, and dump them over the side of the dam. If they truly have trouble swimming, they'll drown. Even if they don't, they'll probably travel miles downriver before they escape the water. That'll leave them far from the dam in unpopulated wilderness."

"That's...a crazy plan, boss," Maldynado said.

"Too dangerous," Sicarius said.

Amaranthe gave them her best smile. "We can do it. Look who I have with me: the deadliest assassin in the empire and the best duelist in the city."

Maldynado lifted a finger. "Which of those professions was supposed to prepare us for hooking giant man-eating monsters with cranes?" He turned to Sicarius. "Did you learn that in little assassins school? Because I don't remember that lesson from the fencing academy."

"You're both agile and smart," Amaranthe said. "That'll be enough. Besides, we'll just lure one up at a time, snare it from the safety of the tower, and then go back for the next."

"Lure," Sicarius said, tone flat.

"How?" Maldynado asked.

Amaranthe swallowed. "Since I'm the most appealing bait, I figure that will be my job."

"That's a bad idea, boss," Maldynado said. "We won't be able to get them off you. Our rifle balls are bugging them less than mosquito bites."

Though Sicarius said nothing, the way he crossed his arms over his chest and glared let her know his opinion.

"Maldynado, give us a moment, please," Amaranthe said.

"Oh, sure, I'll just go hang out with one of the corpses."

"We won't be able to draw them into reach without bait," she said after Maldynado moved away.

"I'll do it," Sicarius said.

She supposed it was cowardly, but she was tempted to agree. She was a decent athlete, but she could envision all too many scenarios in which she could trip at the wrong time and be overcome by a snarling beast. But, no. She could do it. "Unless you've been keeping even more secrets from me than I thought, I'm the more logical choice to attract them."

"No."

"It makes sense."

"You're not—"

"Fast enough? Strong enough? Agile enough?" She did not necessarily disagree, but she wanted him to have faith she could do this.

"Expendable," Sicarius said.

"Oh." She blinked. "Because you care and would miss me or because nobody else would be around to come up with these crazy schemes if I weren't here?"

"It would be..." The lantern light kept his angular features in shadow, but they seemed to soften an iota. "Inconvenient."

"We better set this up so there's no chance of me dying then. Coming to help?" She pointed back toward the T-section where she guessed the unexplored tunnel led to the higher levels. Maldynado yawned and scuffed his feet a few meters away.

"One more concern," Sicarius said.

Amaranthe met his eyes. "Yes?"

"Removing the collars. It's likely the person who placed them there will sense their dormancy."

"And come to check on his guard dogs?"

"Yes."

"We'd best hurry then." Her smile was grim.

CHAPTER 19

FOG BLANKETED THE SHORELINE, HIDING THE diving suits and curling about the air pumps. Books found himself cussing and hunting for things. The fire Basilard had started did little to help.

Akstyr belted out a yawn noisy enough to drown out the coyotes yapping in the distance. "We aren't going down there tonight are we?"

"Given the proximity of animals wishing to slay us, it would behoove us to finish as promptly as possible." Books counted to himself as he measured arm lengths of hose. "As soon as the others return, we'll go down."

Basilard leaned against a tree, a rifle cradled in his arms. The glowing-eyed forest creatures were still about, though Books felt safer out here than in the dam. He worried for Amaranthe and wished she had let Maldynado and Sicarius handle further explorations. He should have told her he needed her help out here.

"How're we going to see what we're doing at night?" Akstyr asked.

"If it's truly thirty meters or more below the surface, then it'd be dark down there even if it was noon. The deeper you go, the more sunlight is absorbed, thus diminishing visible light. Though this water appears relatively clear, I'd estimate the artifact well below the euphoric depth. Fortunately the light from the device itself—"

"Crap," Akstyr said.

Books glanced up from his work, thinking the youth had seen something.

Akstyr was shaking his head at Basilard. "Maldynado isn't here to slap him and shut him up when he goes off like that."

Books felt his jaw tightening and forced it to relax. He went back to measuring hose and simply said, "Perhaps it isn't wise to irritate the man arranging the air flow to your diving suit."

"You need me down there. I'm not worried," Akstyr said.

"Until the device is destroyed," Books said. "After that, the mission would be unaffected if you were eaten by Maldynado's giant catfish."

The fire did not provide enough illumination to drive the shadows from Basilard's face, but white teeth flashed in a quick smile.

Akstyr had no response. Actually, he appeared not to have heard. He was staring across the lake.

Afraid the enforcers had returned, Books followed his gaze. The camp was dark and silent, but an orb of white light glowed on the hillside above it. His heartbeat quickened. That light did not burn with the natural yellow of a torch or a lantern. The darkness hid terrain features, but he guessed it to be moving along the road leading to the enforcer camp—and the dam.

"We better put out the fire," Books said, though he feared if he could see the orb, its owner had already seen them.

* * * * *

Amaranthe did not want any extra weight slowing her down, so she carried nothing but a lantern. Sicarius strode before her, a rifle in each hand, pistols stuck in his belt, and his half dozen knives, as always, within reach. Grimmer than death, he said nothing as they traveled deeper into the concrete passageways.

On top of the dam, Maldynado waited in one of the guard towers, ready to hurl a great hook on a chain to snag the makarovi and swing each one out over the falls for release. It had sounded good when she laid out the plan, but the men's skeptical expressions—a wide-eyed mouth-sagging-open one from Maldynado and a slight eyebrow twitch from Sicarius—had assured her they did not believe it would be so simple. Amaranthe hoped the soldiers had listened and not shot the other collars off.

The route to the control room felt longer than she remembered. The farther they had to travel to find the creatures, the farther she had to run before reaching the dubious safety of the tower. She had no doubt the ten-foot beasts could cover ground more rapidly than she.

They turned the final corner. Amaranthe strained her ears, expecting to hear more than the drip-splat of tunnel seepage. Nothing. Had the soldiers run out of powder in the half hour she, Sicarius, and Maldynado had spent preparing the tower?

They drew close to the walkway and the pipe chamber. Still no voices or rifle fire stirred the air.

Perhaps the soldiers had shot those collars off and the makarovi, with nothing left to bind them to the place, had left the dam altogether. But if that had happened, where were the men?

Then she heard it: the moist sucking and tearing sounds of someone—some*thing*—eating.

Dear ancestors. One of the soldiers must have fallen off the pipe.

Sicarius stopped and gave her a long look over his shoulder, a look that asked: *Do you want to go on?*

Amaranthe nodded once.

The sounds increased as they crept forward. Sweat slithered down her ribcage. She shifted the lantern from one hand to the other, so she could wipe damp palms on her trousers. Her instincts clamored for her to flee. Those instincts knew what her mind refused to contemplate.

Her breathing sounded hoarse and uneven in her ears. She struggled to steady it with deep, calm inhalations, but the stench—musk and blood—kept her nerves jangling.

The sickly, green glow grew visible over Sicarius's shoulder. He and Amaranthe edged closer. The licks and tears continued—louder.

Sicarius stepped onto the walkway. His shoulders stiffened. Dread curdled in Amaranthe's belly, but she squeezed out of the tunnel beside him to look. Or try to. His arm came up to block her, an immovable iron bar.

It did not keep her from seeing what had happened.

Four makarovi had found a way onto the pipe. They were gorging on dead soldiers, including the sergeant who had spoken to her. Other creatures remained on the lower level, also eating. Half the men had fallen—or been knocked—below. No one was left alive.

Even if she and her men drove the makarovi out of the dam, there would be nobody left to acknowledge the good deed. Amaranthe winced, hating herself for the shallow thought. She glowered at the device on the pipe, transferring her self-disgust to its maker, the person responsible for bringing these monsters here. It glowed, undamaged.

One of the makarovi on the pipe lifted its shaggy head. Nostrils flared. It wore no collar. None of them did.

"Go," Sicarius whispered.

The beast spun toward Amaranthe and reared on its hind legs. Dark eyes glittered with hunger.

Amaranthe stepped back as Sicarius spun her and shoved.

"Go!"

She sprinted back into the tunnel, but not before she glimpsed the makarovi bunching its thighs to spring. She did not see it land, but she heard it. Like a wrecking ball crashing into a building, it slammed onto the walkway.

A rifle fired behind her, then a second.

"Run!" she yelled as she raced down the tunnel. She almost spun back to see if he needed help, but she knew he would not want that, and she had no weapon regardless.

Sicarius had better not risk his life to buy her time. Frustration lent strength to her limbs, and she ran faster. She careened around the corner by the control room, pushing off the wall to keep from crashing. Her lantern scraped against the concrete, and the flame wavered.

More wrecking ball sounds signaled more makarovi landing on the walkway. She sprinted for the T-section and the stairs beyond it.

She risked a glance back. Darkness engulfed the passage. If Sicarius was behind her, he was too far back to see.

Tears blurred her vision. Curse him. Why couldn't he just run?

Amaranthe pushed her burning thighs to pump faster. Scuffles and grunts broke the silence behind her. Close. The makarovi were close. She had no idea how many.

Sweat streamed from her brow and stung her eyes. She turned the last corner and a cold draft whispered down the stairwell, licking her damp skin. Stars gleamed beyond the open door at the top.

She lunged up the steps three at a time. A thump sounded below her, a creature hitting the wall. Pistols fired, the echoes deafening in the stairwell. Sicarius. Still with her.

A few steps to go. With a great push from her legs, she leaped the last couple of stairs and raced outside. Water roared in her ears.

Twenty meters ahead, lanterns burned in the windows of the closest tower. A large dark shape inside waved—Maldynado.

Amaranthe could not respond, not now. She focused on the ladder until she saw nothing else. She ran, ignoring the gusting wind as it tore hair from her bun and whipped it into her eyes.

Heavy, rasping breaths sounded behind her. That was not Sicarius.

Less than ten feet behind, a shaggy form towered, black against the night sky. No sign of Sicarius.

Urging her trembling legs to greater effort, she leaped for the ladder. She caught it several rungs up and climbed, fearing she would be too slow. With a single jump, the makarovi could tear her from the ladder.

Amaranthe tried to climb too quickly, and a sweat-slick palm slipped off a metal rung. She lurched and missed a foothold. She almost dropped, but thrust her arm through a hole. Her armpit caught a rung, but she dangled helplessly.

Hot breath stinking of blood blew into her face. Only a foot below, dark, hungry eyes stared up at her. She scrambled to find the rungs with her boots, but she knew it was too late. The fang-filled maw leered open, and the makarovi lifted a paw to tear into her.

She kicked it in the snout. The creature grunted, and its head lurched to the side.

A shadow leaped onto the creature's back. Sicarius ran up the makarovi as if he were climbing stairs. His black dagger snaked around the shaggy head and plunged into an eye.

The makarovi reared and staggered. Sicarius leaped over its head and onto the ladder. Amaranthe glimpsed five more creatures charging across the dam before his body blocked her view.

"You should be climbing," he said, already skimming past her. He did not so much as bump her with a knee.

Amaranthe righted herself and sailed up the last few rungs. Sicarius and Maldynado pulled her through the trapdoor.

"Sorry," she panted.

Maldynado slammed the door shut and threw a bolt that appeared far too flimsy to deter the makarovi.

"Was...admiring your...nicely timed...intervention," she finished.

Sicarius and Maldynado shoved a desk on top of the trapdoor as something smashed into it from below. Amaranthe doubted the creatures could use the ladder, but it might not matter if they could jump as high as the tower.

"At least they shouldn't fit through the door." Amaranthe forced her weary legs to stand.

"Their claws will," Maldynado said. "And there's no way to close these windows."

He waved at the large openings on each wall. Lacking glass or shutters, they had been designed to provide a panoramic view of the lake, dam, and river, not keep monsters out.

"Ready that chain," Amaranthe said. "Time to hook these fish and fling them into the sea."

"On it," Maldynado said. Thumps against the floor almost buried his words.

During their preparation, Sicarius and Maldynado had unhooked the crane from the floodgate it was designed to lift, and Maldynado had had time to familiarize himself with the controls, but he did not appear certain as he manipulated a pair of levers. "These critters don't have belts or anything. What or where am I supposed to grab?"

"Between the legs," Sicarius said.

"You want me to stick a hook in something's balls? That's terrible."

Sicarius advanced, lifting a hand as if he meant to take over the controls.

"Let him do it," Amaranthe told him. "I want you guarding." She put a hand on Maldynado's back. "You can handle this."

"Ball hooking. Got it." Maldynado pushed a lever and something ground and clanked beneath the floor.

She had been too busy climbing to admire the crane built into the base of the tower, but they had deduced earlier that the water of the dam powered the contraption. They *thought* the crane was maneuverable enough to do more than its original purpose.

"Just keep those things from bashing through the door," Maldynado said.

The sturdy concrete tower did not shake or shudder as the makarovi jumped against it from below, but the wood of the trapdoor was a weak-

ness. Even with the heavy desk on top, it splintered and groaned under the onslaught. Claws scraped and gouged.

Amaranthe grabbed her rifle from the corner where she had dropped her gear. She hooked her short sword and a pistol onto her weapons belt as well, fearing she would need them. And more.

The trapdoor shuddered and the desk jumped. Sicarius pushed it back into place with his foot.

She leaned out a window and shot the first makarovi she saw. The rifle ball disappeared into the unkempt fur without doing apparent damage. Sicarius merely waited, his own weapons ready.

As Amaranthe reloaded, Maldynado let out a war whoop.

"I got One-Eye!" he yelled over the clamor coming from below.

Amaranthe rushed to his side. He had snagged the makarovi Sicarius knifed. The creature yowled and thrashed, and she feared it would tear free, but its gyrations only drove the hook deeper. Maldynado chomped down on his lip, his brow creased with concentration as he maneuvered the makarovi over the side of the dam.

Amaranthe clenched her fist. "You're doing it. It's working."

"Don't get too happy yet, boss. I don't know how to release it into the water."

"Can you, uhm, jiggle it?"

The creature was still thrashing, unaware of the fall waiting, should it elude the hook. Maldynado manipulated the crane arm back and forth, trying to turn the makarovi into a pendulum. Between one eye blink and the next the beast fell, plunging out of view.

"Good," Maldynado said. "One down and—"

A rifle fired. Sicarius stood before the back window. Despite his shot, a makarovi hung there, its arm hooked over the concrete sill. Amaranthe lunged past the desk, pulling her pistol out on the way. Sicarius lifted his rifle and hammered the clinging arm with the butt. She leaned out and fired into the creature's fang-filled mouth.

It roared in pain, but clung to the sill. She fired her rifle as well, landing a shot in its right eye.

This time it let go. Before it dropped out of view, another jumped up, claws slashing. Sicarius dragged Amaranthe back as he leaped forward, his black knife leading. It sliced into the makarovi's snout. The

wound distracted the beast, and it fell before it could hook an arm over the ledge.

"That knife works better than the firearms," Amaranthe said, backing toward the center of the tower to reload her weapons. "Are you ever going to tell me the story of where it's from and how you got it?"

While keeping his eyes toward the windows, Sicarius poured powder down the barrel of his rifle and rammed a ball home. "You never asked."

"I didn't? Are you sure? I don't usually miss an opportunity to pry."

"I've noticed."

The trapdoor lurched, heaving the desk into Amaranthe's stomach. She grunted and shoved it back into place. Two makarovi caught opposite window sills at the same time.

"Might want to hurry it up, Mal," she yelled, fumbling to finish loading her firearms.

Sicarius handed her his rifle and attacked the closet makarovi with his knife before it could pull itself inside. She raised the weapon and advanced on the second. It too clawed at the window, trying to pull itself inside.

Its meaty arms flexed, and the bear-like head appeared over the lip. She fired. Her ball bounced off the creature's skull and ricocheted into the night.

"Unbelievable." Amaranthe dropped the rifle, yanked her short sword out, and stabbed at the creature's eye. It jerked its head, and her tip glanced off its cheek. She tried again. One way or another, she had to keep it from scrambling inside.

"Two down!" Maldynado called. "Going in for a third."

Good, but her makarovi would not let go. She jabbed at vital targets on its face, yet it inched farther and farther inside. Blood matted its fur and ran down the inside wall below the window. Its efforts did not abate.

Growling, Amaranthe aimed for the eye again. It saw the blade coming and swiped a paw at her. She dodged and was ready to stab again, but the attack unbalanced the creature. It slipped and fell.

"Another one going for a ride," Maldynado announced.

It was working. Chaos surrounded them, but her plan was working.

Amaranthe almost laughed, but it was too early for cockiness. Reload. She had to reload her weapons.

"Look out!" Sicarius fired past her shoulder.

She spun as a dark shaggy body barreled through her window.

Amaranthe stumbled back, lifting the rifle to shoot, but she had not had time to load it properly, and it misfired. The makarovi launched itself at her.

She dropped and rolled under the desk. "Need help!"

But Sicarius was busy fighting his own makarovi. He glanced her direction and missed a third beast rolling through the window. Its paw hammered the back of his head, and he hit the floor, rolling into the desk.

Blood stained his blond hair and streamed down his face. He appeared dazed and did not move.

Then she lost sight of him. Makarovi filled the room. She could not see Maldynado either. A lantern hit the floor and went out, halving the light.

The desk—her shelter—was hurled across the room. Wood smashed against her shoulder, jarring her with pain. A makarovi loomed over her. She rolled to the side and came up with her sword ready.

Claws raked across her back. Streaks of pain seared her, and she gasped, instinctively pulling away, but that put her closer to the makarovi in front of her. She tried to hurl herself sideways, but the upturned desk blocked her. Surrounded, she could not escape. She slipped in a puddle of water and crashed to the floor.

Not water. Blood. Her blood.

Sword still clenched, she tried to crawl for the desk while slashing at the dark shapes hovering above. Maybe if she could get under it...

But she could not move fast enough. A heavy weight slammed down, smothering her.

"Maldynado!" Sicarius's yell, oddly far away, was the last thing she heard.

CHAPTER 20

"JUST KEEP THE HOSE FROM GETTING TANGLED," Books told Basilard after showing him how to operate the air pumps.

With the fire snuffed and the fog shrouding the lake, Books could not see Basilard for signs, but he sensed the man's concern. Or maybe that was a reflection of his own concern.

"And watch out for glowing-eyed animals," Books added, all too aware that Basilard would be the only one up there while he and Akstyr descended. "And the man with the white orb."

The newcomer—the shaman responsible for all this, Akstyr said—had gone into the dam. Books wished he knew a way to pass him and warn the others, but the artifact had to take priority. It was fortuitous the shaman had gone inside instead of investigating around the lake. That's what he told himself anyway.

"A lot for one man to watch out for." Akstyr fiddled with his diving suit. The large helmet lay in the fog at his feet. "Didn't Amaranthe say to wait for her?"

"That was before our shaman showed up." Books placed the helmet over his head and fiddled with the clasps that fastened it to the suit for a watertight fit. Though the clear spring sky brought cold air, the heavy gear was stifling. In addition to the suit, he wore lead weights to counteract the buoyancy of the rest of the outfit. It would probably feel good to immerse himself in the water.

A branch snapped, and footsteps pounded toward them. Books unfastened the helmet and searched for his rifle. Basilard faced the sounds, his own weapon poised.

"Akstyr?" Maldynado called, then added in a lower voice, "Cursed fog. Where's the slagging beach?"

"We're here, by the lake." Books grabbed a couple of lanterns and turned them up. He shoved the logs back together in the fire ring.

A few flames burst to life in time to show Maldynado racing into camp. Sicarius came on his heels and...

The helmet dropped from Books's fingers. Amaranthe, soaked in blood and bandaged all about her torso, hung limp in Sicarius's arms. She was not moving. Books was not sure she was even breathing.

Sicarius's face was as hard and cold as a marble statue. "Akstyr," he barked.

Akstyr gaped, eyes shifting from Sicarius to Amaranthe and back.

Maldynado ran for the gear pile, yanked out a bedroll, and spread the blanket by the fire. Sicarius laid Amaranthe on it. Books stepped forward, then stopped. He wanted to help but did not know how.

"Akstyr," Sicarius said again. "Get over here."

Mouth drooping open, Akstyr shook his head.

Books wrenched his gaze from Amaranthe. "You have to try, Akstyr."

"I can't—is she even..."

"She won't be for long if you can't do anything for her," Maldynado said.

"I don't know how to... I've just done cuts and I've barely started learning to—"

In an eye blink, Sicarius lunged around the fire, grabbed Akstyr by the collar of his diving suit, and yanked him close. Though Sicarius's hard eyes were not directed at him, Books found himself stepping back.

"Heal her." Sicarius forced Akstyr to his knees at Amaranthe's side. Sicarius did not say "or else." He did not have to. The threat hung in the air, as dense as the fog.

Akstyr did not speak again. He knelt, rested his hands on Amaranthe's bandages, and closed his eyes.

"Do you think," Maldynado murmured, uncertain eyes turned toward Sicarius, "he knows enough to..."

Sicarius shook his head once, slowly.

A lump swelled in Books's throat. Without Amaranthe, there'd be nobody to hold the team together, nobody to give them purpose, nobody to care about them. About him.

Sicarius lifted a hand to his face, clenched it into a first, then dropped it and stalked to the edge of camp. He put his back against a

tree, putatively on watch, but his eyes remained focused on Akstyr and Amaranthe.

A realization came to Books in that moment, one that shook his beliefs even more than when he had learned magic existed: Sicarius cared.

Books was not sure what deal kept Sicarius working with the team when he so obviously did not need their help to accomplish missions or evade bounty hunters, but he had never doubted there was a practical motivation. It had never occurred to him the man might be sticking around, at least in part, out of loyalty—or more.

"It was awful, Books," Maldynado muttered, stirring him from his musings. None of that mattered now anyway. "I was hooking them and throwing 'em, just like our plan. Got rid of the first three, but the other three got inside and...they got past Sicarius and went for her, tore her up. He got over to her and stood above her with that knife of his. I've never seen someone move that fast. Just a blur, you know? He cut 'em up, hurt them more with that knife than we could with our rifles, and he kept 'em off. While they were distracted, I pulled the chain inside and got the hook around their necks and yanked 'em out one at a time. They didn't even notice. They were so fixed on..." He scrubbed his hands through his hair, then turned them over and stared, seemingly surprised to find them stained with blood. "I wish there was something we could do."

"There is." Books lifted his chin. "We can finish the mission." He picked up his helmet. "That's what she would want us to do. We have to destroy that thing at the bottom of the lake."

"You're going *now*?" Maldynado asked. "Don't you need..." He pointed to Akstyr.

"He's busy."

The idea of walking down a hundred feet beneath the surface already intimidated him. Doing it alone sounded more daunting, but if he could not take Akstyr, then who?

Basilard, though he cast concerned glances Amaranthe's direction, remained at his guard post. He would still be a good man to have up top, monitoring the air supply and the hose—and the woods. If Books took Maldynado down, it would be based on needing strength. It might be better to have someone with knowledge of magic. Sicarius knew as much, if not more, about the mental sciences as Akstyr. That made him the logical choice. Unfortunately, he appeared unapproachable at the moment.

Books cleared his throat. "Ah, Sicarius? Will you take the other suit and go down with me?"

"No." He did not lift his head, did not even consider it.

"We don't have much time," Books said. "The shaman is in the dam. He'll soon figure out we're over here."

Sicarius's gaze ratcheted onto Books. "The shaman is here?"

"Akstyr said it was our man. He had a magic globe for a light source."

Sicarius stepped away from the tree. "I'll find him."

"Er, but we don't want to find him, do we? We want to disable his device before he figures out that's our intent."

Sicarius was not listening to him. He pointed at Maldynado. "You watch her." Though unspoken, the threat was there again.

He disappeared into the woods before Books could protest further. Maybe Sicarius thought the shaman capable of healing Amaranthe. Capable and coercible were different matters, though, and Books wondered if even Sicarius could force the person powerful enough to make these devices into helping.

Though...the shaman might prove less obstinate if his goods were destroyed and his plans thwarted.

Yes, Books *had* to do this. He nodded and grabbed a tool pouch. After a moment of debate, he strapped his sword belt around his waist. A foolish choice perhaps—with his luck, he could cut his own air hose—but he was not positive nothing inimical lurked in the depths.

"Maldynado, want to help me down there?" Books asked.

"I'm not going against *his* orders." Maldynado jerked a thumb in the direction Sicarius had gone.

"Akstyr is with Amaranthe, and Basilard can keep an eye on everything else."

"He said watch her, I'm watching her."

Books huffed an annoyed breath. "The mission—"

"I don't disagree," Maldynado said. "But I'm not defying him. I'm young. I want to live."

"Fine." Books jammed his helmet on. He struggled to clasp the fasteners on his shoulder blades.

A hand patted him on the back. The helmet's faceplate limited his vision, so he had to turn around to see who it belonged to. Basilard twirled a finger, telling Books to face front again, and he finished the clasps. A moment later, he pressed thumb and middle finger together in his "ready" sign.

Books breathed deeply, ensuring he could, then put a pair of rubbery gloves on and walked toward the water. The outfit did not have boots in the traditional sense, though the heavy foot coverings provided some protection. He felt the rocks beneath his soles and the sensation of water when he stepped into the shallows. The sword bumping against his legs and the weights dangling from the suit made his gait awkward. He continued onward.

Water lapped about his calves, then his thighs and hips. He sensed the coldness of the lake, but it did not chill him the way it would against bare skin.

When the water reached his neck, he turned to check his support. The hose snaked back toward the beach where Maldynado stood, helping Basilard reel it out while maintaining the air pump. Basilard lifted an encouraging arm.

No excuse not to go down.

Books took several more steps. When his head slipped below the water, again he paused to check everything. Air flowed through the hose, and he could breathe fine. No water crept under the helmet. He released a relieved sigh. It was working.

Slimy pebbles shifted beneath his feet as he delved deeper. He stepped carefully, not wanting to test the suit by pitching over sideways.

Pressure built in his ears and sinuses. He took his time, trying to let his body acclimate. Crisp and clear, the water allowed for good visibility, though night provided little to look at, especially to the sides where curtains of blackness shrouded the lake's mysteries. Ahead, the glow of the artifact brightened as he drew closer.

Fish flitted across his path. Though none were larger than his arm, he brushed his fingers against the sword hilt for reassurance.

The light intensified, and he squinted as he descended the last twenty meters. Near the end, he lifted his arm to shield his eyes and kept his gaze toward the algae-coated pebbles beneath his feet.

Something brushed his calf, and he started. A foot-long water lizard with fish-like gills. It did not bother him, but green glowing eyes winked in its head as it swam away. The creatures living in the lake were likely as addled from the device's influence as those on land.

Books reached the base of the artifact. The light emanated from a twenty-foot wide bowl facing the surface. It stood on a thick bronze pillar thrust into the slimy rocks. The entire contraption reminded him of a mushroom with an upside down cap.

Not sure if some sort of magical barrier might protect it, Books eased toward the base, one hand stretched outward. Nothing stopped him or zapped his fingers, and he was able to touch the smooth metal. The surface trembled faintly, as if machinery operated inside.

Beneath the bowl's shadow, the light level was more tolerable. Nothing so helpful as an on/off switch revealed itself, but the thick glass faceplate hindered his sight. Books slid his hands along the bronze, probing the mushroom "stem" for controls.

Something sharp clamped onto his arm.

Books yelped and jerked away. Whatever it was hung on.

He pulled his arm before his faceplate. A three-foot-long fish had latched onto him, dozens of tiny sharp teeth puncturing the diving suit—and his flesh. Its jaw tightened, and its body whipped from side to side, as if it was trying to tear a chunk of his arm off to eat. Green glowing eyes burned in its scaled skull.

Cursing, Books yanked his sword free left-handed.

Another fish rammed into his side. The hilt slipped from his grasp. New pain stabbed his arm as his original iron-jawed assailant sank its teeth deeper.

Books punched the fish between the eyes. It gnashed down harder.

Something knocked him in the back, and he stumbled forward, almost smacking into the artifact. An eel curled past his shoulder and thumped its head into his faceplate. Books whipped his free arm up, grabbed it, and smashed it against the bronze stem.

He panted, fear tensing his muscles. How many ancestors-forsaken fish were down there? It was as if they were working together against him.

Calm, he told himself, glaring at the fish still latched to his arm. He had to stay calm.

Gritting his teeth against the pain, Books crouched and groped on the slick bottom for his sword. Rock, rock, stupid fish—there. His fingers curled around the hilt.

He stood, feeling light-headed. He was breathing too quickly, too deeply for the amount of air flowing through the tube. There was no way to tell Basilard he needed more.

"Calm," Books ordered himself again.

The heft of the sword in his hand reassured him. He kept from taking a wild swing—if he cut that hose, he would truly be in trouble. Instead he waited as the fish flexed from side to side. He timed the gyrations and stabbed upward.

Steel sliced into scales and flesh. At last, the sharp jaws abandoned his arm.

Blood clouded the water, more the fish's than his, Books hoped. Cold water leaked into his suit where those teeth had cut into it. He had best not stay down here too long.

A second giant fish angled toward him, but he was ready this time. Though the water slowed the speed of his sword strike, he cut into the gills deeply enough to deter his scaled foe.

The sight of him with a weapon—or perhaps it was the blood in the water—kept the remaining fish in the shadows. Books returned to examining the artifact, though he wished he had someone down here to watch his back. Then again, Maldynado would be mocking him for having an epic battle with a fish. Perhaps solitary exploration had its perks.

Books sheathed his sword so he could swim and pushed off the bottom, veering toward the lip of the bowl. His gear dragged at him, but his momentum carried him far enough.

When he clasped the rim, a fresh wave of pain radiated from his wound. More than that, it tingled, as if ants were crawling around beneath his flesh. Pain from the bite was understandable, but the other sensations?

The water, he realized. His skin—his *blood*—was exposed.

If drinking a small sample downriver could make a person sick or turn an animal rabid, what power might it have this close?

"Nothing to be done," he muttered, trying to push the new fear to the back of his mind.

Books focused on the bowl. Wishing the faceplate was tinted, he pulled himself up to peer over the lip. This close, the brilliant glow had the intensity of the sun. The light seared his eyes, and he could not make out anything. He squinted them shut and pulled himself over the lip. He crawled toward the center, exploring by feel rather than sight.

The smooth metal beneath his knees and gloved hands exuded warmth. His fingers brushed against a protrusion. A small cylindrical bump. The gloves interfered with his tactile senses, and it took him a moment to identify it as a simple nut. He found another, then a crease. The edge of a thin plate fastened to the surface, perhaps? After his knee found another nut—painfully—he reached a head-sized orb in the center. He slid his fingers over it, but, with the gloves on, could sense little.

Books removed the glove on his right hand. He was already exposed to the toxin in the water. At this point, it probably did not matter if more of it reached his skin.

A disturbing thought, that. Had he already condemned himself to a dour ending down there? All because he had insisted on going down? He had never wanted to be a hero. It had been guilt over his failure at Vonsha's home that had driven him to want to redeem himself, to do something useful for Amaranthe and the group. Though he surely did not want people in the city to die, he would not have chosen the role of savior—of martyr—for himself. He had just wanted a family, to matter to a small group of people. If he was truly dying, he would never have that again.

Tears formed behind his closed eyelids. Without thinking, he lifted a hand to swipe them away, but his knuckles rapped against the helmet's unyielding faceplate.

"Idiot," he grumbled.

The bump brought him back to the situation. Enough self-pity. He needed to finish the mission. Besides, Akstyr might know how to heal him. Yes. He held onto that thought.

He touched the orb with fingers quickly growing numb. The warmth emanating from the surface contrasted with the icy water. A perfect sphere, it felt smooth all over, like spun glass. It attached to the bowl via a metal stem four inches thick, which must line up with the pillar below.

If the orb *was* made from glass, maybe he could break it.

Books slid his sword free and tapped the device warily. It clinked like glass. He drew himself to his knees and gripped the hilt with both hands. The water drag would diminish the power of his blow, but he would do his best.

Careful not to place his air hose in the blade's path, he lifted the sword over his shoulders and hammered down with all his strength. He expected a blast of energy to slam into him when the orb broke.

But it did not break. The sword clanged off, jarring his arms so badly he dropped it.

Books cursed, throwing in a few Mangdorian ones so the artifact would understand him. He slid his fingers over the orb. There was no doubt he had hit it, but not a crack or even a scratch marred its surface.

"New plan," he told himself. He just had to figure out what it was.

The tingles ran up his arm all the way to his neck and spine now. More than ever, he sensed time running out.

Books shifted, and his knee bumped one of the nuts. He froze. He *had* a wrench along. If he could not destroy the orb, maybe he could disassemble it.

His deadened fingers fumbled at the clasp of the tool pouch. Annoyed, he switched to his left hand again. Even that side seemed less dexterous than it should be. He dropped the wrench three times while adjusting it. That stuff was going to reach his heart soon and....

He focused on the first nut. Eyes still shut against the light, he worked by feel. The nut thunked to the bottom of the bowl. He worked his way around the orb, awkwardly unfastening the rest.

Three quick, questioning tugs at the air hose interrupted him. Basilard wondering where he was probably. How long had he been down?

He tugged back, wishing he had taken the time to arrange signals, and returned to work. The last nut dropped. Books found the edge of the plate and levered his sword into the crease. Though heavy, the plate lifted on one side. He pushed it over with a grunt.

The light reddening the backs of his lids softened, and he opened an eye.

The orb still glowed like a sun, but it lay on its side, and the panel shielded Books. Tangled cords attached to the bottom led into a hole, the hollow core of the pillar. Gears rotated within, and he could only guess

what the complex machinery in the shadows below did. But he did not need to learn how it worked.

He dragged the sword close and pressed it against one of the cords. He sliced through it, and a shocking buzz ran up his arm and clenched his chest. His muscles tensed involuntarily, and he dropped the sword. The orb flickered.

Scared but encouraged, he picked up his sword. He left the cords and jammed the blade between the teeth of the closest set of rotating gears. A displeased grinding issued from the core. He waited, hoping he would not have to cut more of the cords. The artifact started quaking.

He mulled over his sabotage. Maybe having his sword stuck in there would break the engine, maybe not.

Numbness plagued the entire right side of his body. He might as well ensure his efforts were irreversible. He slashed the sword through the remaining cords.

Power surged, hurling him backwards. He spun a somersault, hit his helmet on the lip of the bowl, and tumbled over the edge. He landed on his back in the pebbles. Light flashed several times, then disappeared. Blackness swallowed the bottom of the lake.

He lay, stunned. A drop of water splashed onto his nose.

With his mind dazed and befuddled, it took him a second to realize his helmet was leaking. He must have cracked the faceplate. He had to get up and climb out of the lake, but he could not move his limbs. He could scarcely breathe.

A white light appeared at the edge of Books's vision.

"Now what?" he groaned.

He struggled to rise, and, when that failed, to roll over. His body would not cooperate. Water ran down his cheeks and pooled beneath his head.

The light drew closer, illuminating the artifact, which stood dark and skeletal. Though he feared death was approaching, Books drew satisfaction from the pathetic way the stem listed to one side.

A figure floated into his field of vision. The shaman. It had to be.

Protected by an iridescent bubble, the man hovered above the lake floor, his fists clenched, his pale face contorted with rage. Angry green eyes bored into Books. Then they shifted, focusing on something above his head.

The air hose. With a wave of his hand, the shaman could finish what the fish had started.

Did Basilard and the others know the man was down here? Surely not or they would be trying to help somehow. Books feared he was on his own.

He coughed, spitting water. It was dribbling in faster now and filled the helmet to his ears.

"Where is the assassin?" the shaman asked in Turgonian.

Books stared. He could have understood an accusation about the artifact or being a warmongering Turgonian, but a question about Sicarius?

The shaman floated over and grabbed the air hose. Again Books struggled to rise so he could die on his feet. His limbs would not move. He could not even feel them. Water reached the corners of his lips.

The shaman tied a knot in the hose and pulled it down, holding it before Books's eyes.

"*Where* is the assassin?"

Anger simmered within Books, and he hated that he had no power to lash out. He did not love Sicarius enough to die defending him, but he was dead either way.

"Hunting you," he said, water leaking into his mouth.

The shaman sneered, and lifted a hand. As if someone cut off a switch, blackness swept over Books and awareness vanished.

CHAPTER 21

PAIN BROUGHT TEARS TO AMARANTHE'S EYES before she opened them. Her breath snagged, and she reached for her abdomen. Her fingers scraped against rough bandages, an act that brought more pain. She yanked her hand away. She tried to draw in a deep inhalation to calm herself, but that hurt too. As she opened her eyes and struggled to focus them, she settled for short, shallow breaths.

She lay on her back. Bare branches stretched below a gray sky promising rain. Daylight had come, though she could not guess whether it was morning or afternoon.

Something touched her cheek. She turned her head slowly since her neck, too, had complaints.

Sicarius sat cross-legged beside her. Relief flooded her at seeing him alive—and at being alive herself.

He lifted his hand, seemed not to know where to put it, and settled for resting it on her shoulder. Though the pain dampened her humor, she managed a smile. "I must look really bad...if you're deigning to touch me." It hurt to speak, and her voice rasped like sandpaper on wood.

His eyebrows rose infinitesimally.

"You usually only do that in combat practice." She kept her voice soft so she need not take big inhalations. "Or to pull me out of the way... because I've gotten myself in trouble."

His jaw flexed, and Amaranthe regretted the last sentence. He might feel he should have been faster and pulled her out of the way this time.

"Sorry," she whispered. Her ancestors knew it was not his fault she had nearly died. *He* had tried to stop her from the ludicrous plan.

"For what?" He spoke quietly. His gaze flicked toward the lake.

The susurrus of men's voices came from that direction. A conversation, not casual but argumentative. There was still trouble. Amaranthe would ask what it was soon, maybe even attempt something ambitious, like sitting up, but she wanted another quiet moment before the need to plan overwhelmed her. Besides, there was a hint of downward pressure from Sicarius's hand, as if he knew about, and did not approve of, her thoughts to sit up and get involved.

"I'm sorry," she said, "for risking all our lives on something that we could have left for others to handle, for getting mauled, and for being a burden. I should have listened to you. Next time I will. I'll...acquiesce to your wisdom."

His eyes crinkled. "You will not."

"No, I will. I've learned my lesson."

"Doubtful." Was that a smile on his lips? Ever so slight? If so, it faded quickly.

"Akstyr did his best to close your wounds," Sicarius said, "but he detected the beginnings of an infection."

"Those makarovi claws *did* look dirty." She smiled, though Sicarius's tone, even grimmer than usual, warned her worse news was coming.

"The knowledge of how to heal it is beyond him. He did better than I expected, but he lacks experience."

"Well, I'm tough. I bet my blood schemes just as much as my brain, and it'll figure a way to destroy any pesky infections."

Sicarius said nothing. He *always* said nothing, but this time he avoided her eyes, and she had no trouble reading his silence: he thought she was dying.

"She's awake!" Maldynado blurted. "She's *alive*!"

Footsteps pounded her way. Maldynado, Basilard, and Akstyr knelt around her. Sicarius stood and backed away.

"Boss, are you all right?" Maldynado asked. "How do you feel?

Amaranthe blushed, feeling foolish to have gotten herself in so much trouble that she needed this much attention. But emotion welled inside her too. It meant much that they cared enough to provide that attention.

"I'm alive," she croaked around the lump her in throat.

Basilard pushed Maldynado to the side, lifted a canteen, and raised his eyebrows.

"Oh, right," Maldynado said. "You need to drink."

He slid a hand under her shoulders and elevated her head gently. He waved for the canteen. As much as Amaranthe appreciated his solicitude, she would not have minded being taken care of by Sicarius. Just the two of them. Alone. Maybe in her weakened state, he would pity her enough to let slip a few more tidbits about his past. That would almost be worth the price of...being wounded. Yes, being *wounded*. A temporary state. No way was she going to let some stupid animal claw bring about her death.

She inhaled a touch too deeply, and a pang in her abdomen made her gasp. Water spilled and ran down her chin.

"Oops," Maldynado said.

Basilard smacked him on the shoulder.

Amaranthe sipped from the canteen more carefully. Sicarius had retreated to the trees to stand guard, though he glanced her way now and then. She sighed and fiddled with one of the bandages wrapping her torso.

"Akstyr fixed you up real good," Maldynado said. "I'm sure you'll pull through. Because we need you. We've been squabbling. Without you here to keep us glued to—what are you doing?"

Amaranthe froze in the middle of loosening a bandage. "Er, nothing?"

"You're not trying to take them off, are you?" Maldynado said, stern as a schoolteacher reprimanding a wayward pupil. "Akstyr helped, but you're all sorts of messed up under there. Better not remove them."

"No, I was just..." She cleared her throat. "They were crooked. Akstyr," she said before her admission could draw comments, "thank you."

He stuffed his hands in his pockets. "Sorry I couldn't...you know. All the way."

"I'll just have to talk the shaman into doing it."

All four men stared at her.

"Not even conscious five minutes, and she's already concocting crazy plans," Maldynado said.

"I'm sure it's been closer to ten," Amaranthe said.

Maldynado was still propping her up, giving her a decent view of the beach and the diving equipment.

"Where's Books?"

The men's faces darkened.

"The shaman got him," Maldynado said. "Books broke the thing in the lake, but somehow... We didn't see the shaman go in the water. If we had, we would have thumped him."

"Got him?" Amaranthe swallowed. "Is he..."

"We think he's alive, otherwise why would that blond bastard have taken him, right?" Maldynado looked to Basilard and Akstyr for confirmation, but they only shrugged. "But we don't know where they went. He flew out of the water in this bubble wrapped around himself and Books, and then they poofed away."

"Teleported," Akstyr said.

"Either way, we have no idea where they are now. In slagging Mangdoria probably." Maldynado kicked one of the air pumps across the camp.

Amaranthe closed her eyes. A few raindrops pattered on her cheeks. "I wonder what his reason was for taking Books with him."

"Torture," Sicarius said. "Revenge for thwarting his plans."

"Or perhaps he assumed we'd come after Books," she said.

"Why would he think that?" Maldynado asked. "Books is a tedious, lecturing know-it-all, something the shaman will figure out after about two seconds of talking with him. Why assume we'd risk our butts to get him back?"

"Because that's what friends do for each other." Amaranthe rotated her head to find Basilard, wondering if he would continue to keep things from her with Books's life at stake. "Will you have a problem battling a countryman to get Books back?"

Basilard gazed at the dam, but not for long before shaking his head. *I wouldn't help someone who harnesses makarovi. Who kills.*

Amaranthe pointedly did not mention Basilard's own record of kills, but his lips twisted wryly, as if he guessed her thoughts.

The wryness shifted to sadness. *I wouldn't help me either.*

"Sorry," she said.

Maldynado lifted a finger. "I'm confused." He paused, glancing around, almost as if he was waiting for Books to insult him. "Why would the shaman want us to start with? Unless he's after bounties, but if he can make something like that—" he waved toward the defunct artifact in the lake, "—he could earn a million ranmyas legitimately. Well, legitimately outside the empire."

"There are other reasons to want someone," Amaranthe said.

"But he could have had us when you were unconscious and I was concentrating on healing on you," Akstyr said. "He had Books helpless and just would have had to go through Maldynado and Basilard."

Maldynado propped his fists on his hips. "*Just*? Basilard and I are burly and formidable."

"What were you able to do against that wizard, Arbitan?" Akstyr asked.

Amaranthe watched Sicarius while the men argued with each other. Where had *he* been during Books's kidnapping?

"I don't recall," Maldynado told Akstyr. "My face was busy being scrubbed by his carpet."

"May I have a moment alone with Sicarius?" Amaranthe asked.

Maldynado arched his eyebrows. "Shouldn't you surround yourself with pleasant things when you're healing?"

As Sicarius stepped to Amaranthe's side, he fixed a glare on Maldynado, who threw his hands up and backed away. Akstyr shrugged and went down to the water. Basilard—the one she most wanted out of earshot—picked up a spyglass and joined Akstyr.

"Where were you during all this?" Amaranthe asked when Sicarius crouched beside her.

"In the dam, looking for the shaman." His dark glare returned to Maldynado. "I was told he was in there."

"I agree with Maldynado that it's strange this fellow would take Books as bait for one of us, but these Mangdorians have made it clear they want you."

"This whole plot would not have been conceived to get at me."

She checked on Basilard. Too far away to listen in on their conversation, he was scanning the opposite shoreline with the spyglass. Maldynado sat on a stump, ears turned toward Amaranthe and Sicarius. Though she was not sure he was close enough to hear, she caught his eye and waved for him to move farther away.

"Maybe the shaman isn't worrying about his partners or the water scheme at this point," Amaranthe said. "Maybe, with you in his sights, he's changed focus. He could have taken Books, hoping you'd come for him or that Books would provide information on you." When Sicarius

LINDSAY BUROKER

did not respond, she lifted a hand, palm up. "Either way, we have to find the shaman and get Books back."

"He could be anywhere," Sicarius said.

"Not if he wants you to find him."

"I can't track teleportation," Sicarius said.

"He has a hideout."

A beat passed, but Sicarius remembered without prompting. "The enforcer sergeant did not tell you where."

"No, but she's on her way back with reinforcements, right?"

Maldynado ambled over. "You two done being private and secretive yet?"

"No," Sicarius said as Amaranthe said, "Yes."

Maldynado took that as an invitation to sit down.

"She's on her way back with reinforcements," Sicarius said. "Probably a company or two from the garrison. She'll be surrounded."

"I just need a few minutes with her."

"You need to rest," Sicarius said.

"I agree with him," Maldynado said. "Did you see yourself when you were unconscious? You looked dead."

"We need to talk to her," Amaranthe said.

"I will question the woman," Sicarius said.

"No!" Amaranthe tried to sit up, but agony ripped through her belly, and she flopped back with a hiss. "No. Sicarius, you're, uhm, I appreciate your willingness to help, but diplomacy isn't your biggest strength."

"I wasn't going to be diplomatic."

"I know, and therein lies the problem. When they get back, I need to go. We'll take it slow, wait for nightfall. Sneak in, chat, then leave. No problem."

"Five minutes," Sicarius said.

"What?"

"How long you lasted *acquiescing* to my wisdom."

"Oh." She gave him a sheepish smile. "Are you sure it wasn't closer to ten?"

* * * * *

Raindrops pattered on the forest floor. Cold water dripped from the branches and splashed onto Amaranthe's neck, dribbling under her collar. The stink of burning coal hung over the lake and irritated her eyes and nose. The soldiers had brought a caravan of steam vehicles this time.

Though she leaned against Sicarius for support, her abdomen and back stung with each slow, carefully placed step. Sweat bathed her face, and she breathed through gritted teeth. Under other circumstances, she might have appreciated the heat of Sicarius's body and the corded muscle beneath his sleeve, but she was busy distracting herself from her discomfort by mulling over what she planned to say to Sergeant Yara. Should she explain the whole story? Everything that had happened since last they talked? No, best to keep it succinct. It was unlikely Amaranthe would get more than a few minutes with Yara, if that. Let the woman research on her own and form her own conclusions.

Sicarius steered her away from a route that would have ended with her crashing into a tree. "We're close," he said in a tone that implied paying attention would be good.

"We sure this is a good time to infiltrate their camp?" Maldynado asked softly. He, Akstyr, and Basilard gathered close.

All around the lake, lanterns glowed as soldiers searched the area in pairs. Campfires burned ahead, and Amaranthe could make out the outline of tents through the trees. Many more tents than had been there previously.

"Must be nice to get paid to show up after all the work's done," Akstyr said.

"Not *all* the work," Maldynado said. "We've got to get Booksie back."

Amaranthe smiled. For all that those two sniped at each other, Maldynado actually seemed to consider Books a friend. She was not sure Books reciprocated that feeling, but perhaps he would one day.

"Yes," she said. "It's a shame the soldiers are too late for the fun. I wonder..."

"What." Sicarius's tone did not make it sound like a question.

"Nothing. Let's find Sergeant Yara."

"Back to my original question," Maldynado said. "Shouldn't we wait until everyone is sleeping? These people are..." He lowered his

voice as a pair of soldiers trod past twenty meters ahead. "These people are looking for trouble."

"Yes, but most of them are outside of the camp," Amaranthe said. "If they're still worried about the makarovi, Sergeant Yara will likely be inside." Unless the soldiers left the enforcers behind when they decided to return en masse. She frowned at the thought. As aloof as Yara had been, she already knew about Amaranthe. It would be harder to stalk in and convince a stranger of her team's deeds.

"Still plenty in the camp," Sicarius said.

True. Several men stood guard at points around the perimeter, while others dug latrines, shoveled coal for the steam vehicles, and performed other tasks they had probably not anticipated when they enlisted. A couple of soldiers stood outside the tent Sergeant Yara had occupied the last time Sicarius dragged her out to talk. A flag proclaimed it had been turned into headquarters.

"We'll have to create a distraction." Amaranthe considered Maldynado.

"I'm always happy to be distracting," he said, "though it's usually the ladies who are likely to stop and ogle. What if we get in a tussle with these boys? How do you want us to defend ourselves?"

"We can't kill anybody," Amaranthe said. "All the work we've done out here will mean nothing if we kill a single soldier. They won't believe anything we say."

"Don't we have that problem anyway?" Akstyr asked. "Nobody is left alive who saw us in the dam."

"That's right," Maldynado said. "As far as the soldiers know, they can credit this to some anonymous good-deed-doer."

"That licks donkey crotch," Akstyr said.

"Relax, gentlemen," Amaranthe said. "I intend to make sure we get credit *and* find out where Books is located."

She waited, anticipating more of an argument. Surely, they would realize she had nothing with which to back up her promise. Sicarius, especially, would know she had not won over Sergeant Yara. Even if Amaranthe could convince her their story was true, having a rural, female enforcer on their side was hardly the fast route to a pardon. Yara would have little power or sway outside her precinct and perhaps not much more inside.

"All right, boss," Maldynado said. "We trust you. What's this distraction you want?"

Amaranthe smiled bleakly. Skepticism would have been easier to deal with. Instead the mantel of expectation weighed upon her shoulders.

"We could grab a couple men," Maldynado said when she did not answer right away. "Knock 'em out, steal their clothes, and walk in, pretending we're soldiers."

"They have a challenge and password system to prevent that," Sicarius said.

Akstyr snorted. "Even gangs aren't moronic enough that they wouldn't recognize their own people."

"Well, it's dark," Maldynado said.

Amaranthe was only half-listening to them. To one side of the camp, partially visible through the trees, the trampers and lorries idled. A soldier opened a furnace door and shoveled coal inside. Someone must fear the company would need a quick escape.

"Couldn't we thump the password out of someone when we're stealing his clothes?" Maldynado said.

"Depends how much damage you want done," Sicarius said. "Soldiers are trained to resist torture."

"Maldynado really wants to take someone's clothes off," Akstyr said. "Maybe he prefers men."

Maldynado sniffed. "If I do, your homeliness will save you from ever knowing."

"Whatever."

"Let's go with my idea," Amaranthe said, watching the soldier close the grate and move onto the next vehicle in the line. "Maldynado, Basilard, and Akstyr, it's been a while since you stole someone's vehicle. Are you interested in reacquainting yourselves with that hobby?" She leaned, trying to find Basilard in the shadows. His inability to talk made it difficult to communicate with him in the dark. He touched her shoulder. She hoped that was an affirmative.

"You want us to march into this camp full of well-armed men," Maldynado said, "jump into their vehicles, race off chaotically, and lead a posse of soldiers on a crazy chase?"

"Yes," she said. "Problem?" It seemed like the type of ludicrous sport someone who had ridden a printing press down an icy hill would appreciate.

"Nope," he said, a grin in his voice. "Just wanted to make sure I got the order right."

"Keep them busy, and meet us up the road, where we left our lorry, when you're done. If it's guarded, stay hidden. We'll find you."

"Got it, boss."

"And don't get caught this time, please," Amaranthe said. "I don't know where the closest jail is."

Maldynado thumped Akstyr on the back as the three men slipped away. "This'll be fun."

Amaranthe hoped they were careful. Soldiers would be harder to rattle than enforcers.

She shook away the worry. She needed to focus on her part of the mission.

"Think the sergeant has been good enough to locate herself in the same tent?" she asked Sicarius. "It had a lovely water view."

"A primary tactical consideration."

"Let's get closer."

Before they had gone far, two lights appeared behind them—soldiers approaching. Amaranthe stepped around a tree, hoping it would be enough to hide her. She dared not dive for cover, not when her wounds might make her cry out. Sicarius eased in front of her, guarding her. By night, his black clothing helped him blend in.

The soldiers drew even with the tree. One glanced toward Amaranthe and Sicarius, and she held her breath.

"Halt." A man stepped from behind a tree several paces ahead. A rifle, the barrel wet from the rain, gleamed in his hands. His appearance drew the other two soldiers' attention. "The coyote cries."

"By night's full moon," one of the soldiers responded. "Archton and Bedloe. Dog Platoon."

"Pass."

After the soldiers went into camp, Sicarius whispered, "Stay here. I'll nullify the sentries. They'll be less alert now than when the commotion starts."

Amaranthe kept herself from reminding him to choose a non-lethal nullification method. He knew what she wanted by now, and he was probably tired of her nagging.

After he disappeared, she slumped against the tree, a hand to her belly. Her scabs had flexed and torn as they walked, and she knew she was bleeding beneath the bandages. She shivered, too, and it was not that cold. She touched her forehead and tried to decide if it felt feverish. Sicarius never should have said anything about the infection. It would prey on her mind now. Either way, she feared she would be useless in a physical encounter and might prove a liability for the men. If not for Books, and her growing fear that she needed magical aid, she would be inclined to leave the shaman for someone else to confront. Though maybe that was still a possibility. She scratched her jaw. Those soldiers might be disappointed if they came all the way up the mountain for nothing.

"Look out!" someone shouted on the other side of the camp. Surprised curses followed. "They're taking the lorry!"

"Stop them!"

"Go get—" Steam brakes squealed. "Look out!"

Amaranthe allowed herself a small grin. A tent went down amongst snapping poles and shouts of fury. If Maldynado had a skill beyond charming women, it had to be crafting mayhem.

Sicarius appeared a few feet in front of Amaranthe, limned by torch-light. He strode toward her and offered an arm.

"That's not your usual entrance." She shifted her weight from the tree to him. "You usually sneak up so softly I don't know you're there until you startle me into jumping."

"I didn't want you to aggravate your injuries." He guided her toward the back of the command tent.

"That's considerate."

"Yes."

She almost laughed. It was as if he wanted her to know he was going out of his way to be thoughtful.

They stepped around a pair of gagged and unconscious men tied to a tree. Two officers and a woman—Sergeant Yara—were standing in front of the tent, gesturing expansively. The noise from the vehicles and the shouts about camp made it impossible to hear the discussion.

Another tent went down. Someone fired at the cab of a second stolen lorry, and metal clanged like a bell.

Maldynado, or maybe Akstyr was driving that one, veered out of camp and up the road, though not before flattening several crates of supplies.

"Are you sure killing them wouldn't have annoyed them less?" Sicarius asked.

"Not entirely, no."

Sergeant Yara took a step toward the chaos, as if she meant to lead the pursuit herself.

One of the officers stopped her with an outstretched hand. "I'll take care of it. You stay here."

"That's one of our vehicles," Yara said. "I can help."

"It's too dangerous for a woman."

"I doubt the makarovi are the ones stealing our vehicles."

"You shouldn't even be up here," the officer said. "Stay with Lieutenant Berkvar. Sergeant Betlor's team should report in soon. Keep updating the map." He jogged away.

Amaranthe squeezed Sicarius's arm. This was probably the closest they would get to finding the sergeant alone. He left her to slip around the tent. Amaranthe moved around the opposite side, carefully choosing her steps through the churned mud.

"Too dangerous for a woman," Yara grumbled. "I'm tired of hearing that. Do I look frail and incapable, LT?"

Sicarius chose that moment to grab the lieutenant in a headlock, his arm snaking around the man's throat, cutting off air. He dragged the officer behind the tent.

Yara ripped a sword free, but Amaranthe closed in and poked her in the back with stiff fingers to mimic a pistol. Since her men were trashing the camp, she decided pulling an actual weapon would not help matters.

Yara glanced over her shoulder. "You!" Disgust curled her lip. Sicarius returned to the front of the tent, and she added, "And you!"

"Us," Amaranthe agreed. "Inside, please."

Not sure if others awaited within, she nudged Yara, encouraging her to lead the way. Fortunately, only cots and a map-strewn table occupied the tent.

"Sit, please." Amaranthe pointed to a cot. "I need to talk, and it'd be appreciated if you'd listen."

"What polite outlaws." Yara pulled away from Amaranthe and spun, hand hovering near her sword.

Sicarius appeared at the sergeant's side. He did not draw a weapon, but his presence convinced Yara to lower her hands. She did not sit down.

Amaranthe nodded for Sicarius to guard the entrance, then met Yara's eyes and launched into her spiel. "We weren't fast enough to save the soldiers, but we got the makarovi out of the dam and over the falls. You may be able to verify that if some of the corpses get washed up on the shore downriver with, er, interestingly placed puncture wounds, as if from a giant hook."

Skepticism twisted Yara's face, but Amaranthe hurried on before she could interrupt. "Also, my man, Books—Marl Mugdildor—single-handedly deactivated the contraption tainting the water. He's a good person who doesn't deserve a bounty on his head. I doubt the device left inside the dam on the pipe will be trouble without the main artifact, but, with the makarovi gone, it should be easier to destroy now. Books saved the city a lot of trouble. He deserves a pardon. And, if you're later able to gather evidence that corroborates our story, we would appreciate it if you would inform any of your superiors or co-workers who might listen. Since the emperor is aware of you, a note sent to his office would also be appreciated."

"Oh, really?" Yara jammed her fists against her hips. "Perhaps I could arrange a parade for you as well. Or commission a statue that we could put on display at the entrance to the pass? No, better, a giant carving of your team's faces in the side of the mountain. How would that be?"

Amaranthe almost quipped that Maldynado would love Yara forever if she could arrange the mountain carving, but she suspected they did not have much time before someone returned to the tent.

"We need to know where the shaman's hideout is," she said. "He has Books."

Her lack of response to the sarcastic tirade deflated the sergeant. Yara's hands lowered, though she still glowered.

"Please," Amaranthe said. "If you hate me and you hate Sicarius, fine, but Books has done nothing to harm the enforcers or the empire. The only one with reason to hate him is the one holding him prisoner, doing ancestors only know what to him. Books risked his life to destroy that artifact. To help the city and make your job easier."

Yara sighed. "The northern-most of the abandoned Kaker Mines. Base of the mountains."

"Thank you." Amaranthe nodded. Time to play her last tile. "The shaman's artifact is destroyed, but he's not done attacking the city. He believes the empire responsible for the slaying of the Mangdorian royal family years ago, and he'll not stop until he's exacted revenge." She could not yet know how much of that was true, but she had to worry the soldiers if she wanted them to help.

"We didn't have anything to do with that." Yara frowned at Amaranthe, then considered Sicarius, and her frown deepened. "Did we?"

Amaranthe had not meant to implicate Sicarius, and she had to smother a wince at the quickness with which Yara put together the pieces. She imagined his eyes boring into the back of her head. Oh, well. It was not as if he could have stuffed this secret back into the Imperial Intelligence files to lock it away; too many people already knew.

"It's what the Mangdorians believe," Amaranthe said. "That's all that matters. If I were you, I'd make sure these soldiers get to those mines before it's too late."

"If you were me," Yara said, "you never would have betrayed the city and killed your co-workers."

Amaranthe gritted her teeth. She wanted to issue a biting retort, but if there was any hope whatsoever of Yara acting on these words, Amaranthe dared not irritate her more. "Don't make the mistakes I did then. Warn the soldiers. Protect the city."

She strode out, trusting Sicarius to guard her back.

CHAPTER 22

B OOKS WOKE WITH A GASP, ESCAPING SOME NIGHT-
mare where he was falling—and suffocating. He lay on his
back with cold darkness enveloping him. He blinked, trying
to make out shapes, but his eyes failed to penetrate the blackness.

Memories hiccupped into his thoughts: the lake, the shaman, the
artifact. He was alive, but was he truly in the dark or had he gone blind?
Fear chilled him further. Maybe he had worked in the artifact's blaze for
too long.

"Easy," he told himself. No panicking. Especially considering the
numbness that had taken over his body in the lake was gone. "Definitely
a positive development," he muttered.

Either the shaman had healed him or the effects had worn off. The
details did not matter. Figuring out where he was and getting back to the
others—that mattered.

Cold seeped into his back from a rough, uneven floor. Stone. He
rolled to his knees and landed in a puddle. A quick pat-down informed
him the helmet and his tools were gone, though he still wore the diving
suit.

He explored further. On three sides, dirt and rock walls rose to meet
a low dirt and rock ceiling. Faint reverberations coursed through the
stone, as if machinery labored somewhere in his underground prison.
A different texture comprised the fourth wall of what he realized was
his cell. Smooth and hard, it sent a buzz up his arm when he touched it.
When he pressed harder, a stronger buzz coursed through him, making
his hair stand on end. It reminded him of the power he had felt when he
broke the artifact, and he decided not to risk hurling himself at it.

Books swept his foot along the floor, hoping to find something that
could suffice as a latrine. No luck. A rusty bolt clattered across the

ground. He found a few more scraps, but nothing larger than a hand-length scrap of twisted iron. It had a sharp edge, and he might have used it to file his way free if his captor had been considerate enough to put him in a cell with an iron gate instead of a magical barrier. He kept it on the chance the shaman might be foolish enough to come inside.

He pulled the top half of the diving suit down and was surprised when his movements did not bring pain. He pushed a sleeve up to check his wound. No fish tooth marks violated the flesh of his arm. The shaman had healed him. To what ends?

Books pushed the suit lower so he could relieve himself. At that moment, footsteps sounded to his left. A familiar white globe of light floated into view, illuminating a rough-hewn tunnel running past his cell. A rusty ore cart rail bisected the center of the passage.

He started to clamp things off, but a defiant thought curled his lip. Let the bastard find Books peeing on the floor of his hideout.

"What do you want me to do?" a female voice asked. Books's eyes bulged. A *familiar* female voice.

"Just identify him."

Two figures strode into sight behind the light globe. Books fumbled, hurrying to button himself in, though he feared she had already seen him in action. Heat flamed his cheeks. Why did these things happen to him? No villain would presume to walk in on *Sicarius* while he was peeing.

Vonsha and the shaman stopped before Books's cell. She wore a dagger at her belt and carried a lantern. Her stance said "not a prisoner," though it stung him to admit it. She did seem surprised to see him, so maybe she was not in on the larger scheme.

Something skittered along the floor behind them, a silver spider-shaped creature the size of a fist. A coin-sized circle on its front glowed red. As the spider passed below the shaman's light, Books realized it was not a creature at all. The tiny "legs" moved mechanically, and metal, not skin, comprised the carapace. It disappeared into the darkness, heading deeper into the tunnel. Neither person facing Books reacted to it.

"You recognize him?" the shaman asked. His green eyes were calm instead of raging today. Lines creased the corners of those eyes, making him older than Books had first guessed. Fifty or sixty perhaps. Old enough to have mastered his craft.

Vonsha hesitated before answering. "He's one of the party that came through the pass."

She knew more than that. Was she protecting him? Maybe she truly liked him. But the fact that she was here with an enemy of the empire....

"I know *that*," the shaman said. "Is he close to the assassin? Is he a murderer too?"

"I haven't murdered anyone," Books said, figuring he better speak for himself before he was condemned for more than wrecking the artifact. "I just came to thwart the threat to the city's water supply."

"Yes, we know about *that*," the shaman said.

A tendon flexed along Vonsha's neck, as if Books's statement annoyed her equally. But she defended him. "He's not a killer; he's a history professor."

"He's working with that gutless butcher, Sicarius."

"I know, Tarok," Vonsha said. "But I don't think Books would—"

Something clanked in the distance, and the shaman glanced the way the spider construct had gone.

"What are you *doing* with him?" Books mouthed to Vonsha.

She had time for nothing more than an apologetic shrug before the shaman's attention returned to them.

"What are you to the assassin?" he asked Books. "Will he come for you?"

Of his own accord? Not likely. Amaranthe would, but Books did not know if she was alive. He dared not volunteer either piece of information. "I don't know."

"He's the one who killed Yereft, too, isn't he?"

"I don't know who that is." Books guessed it was the other shaman Amaranthe mentioned.

"Who is the Mangdorian who travels with you?"

"Nobody who'd be friends with someone like you. Why are you doing this? Attacking the empire?" Yes, there. Books ought to be asking questions. Amaranthe would have had this fellow's story by now.

"Chief Yull was a friend," the shaman said. "I've sought his killer for a long time, and now that I know who it is, he won't escape me."

Chief Yull? Books had a feeling Amaranthe had forgotten to tell him something crucial, but he could puzzle things together.

"You need to kill innocent people and make the whole city sick to get at one person?" Though Books was responding to the shaman, he watched Vonsha. She lifted her chin and stared back. Did she have a reason to want revenge on Sicarius too?

"I'm no killer," the shaman—Tarok she had called him—said. "I simply make the artifacts. That's the deal." He hitched a shoulder. "They can be used for a number of purposes."

"You knew what that device would do when you put it in the lake. Doesn't your religion forbid you from hurting people?"

"*I've* not harmed anyone," Tarok said.

"Your artifacts have."

"Many people make devices that can be used for good or evil. You cannot blame the blacksmith when the swords he crafts are used to kill."

"And can you also not blame the person who leads a pack of monsters into a dam to kill all the employees?" Books asked.

Tarok looked away, as if that particular part of the plot might not sit well with him. Books wished he knew how to use that information.

"Your people have killed thousands, maybe hundreds of thousands of mine," Tarok said. "You pushed us out of fertile valleys and into these inhospitable mountains. And that assassin..." The shaman's calmness faded, and he gritted his teeth, glaring. "Do you know what manner of demon you travel with?"

Books did not answer. How could he? Sicarius was one person he could never defend, not on a question of morality.

"Tell me," Books said instead.

While Tarok launched into a diatribe, Books nonchalantly leaned against the wall near the cell entrance. He checked up and down the tunnel, trying to see whatever device maintained his prison. Nothing on the far wall. He leaned his cheek closer to the barrier. The air crackled with energy. There. Less than a foot from the barrier, a small white box protruded from the wall on his side of the tunnel. Though it lacked the telltale glow of the device in the lake, it did not appear like something Turgonian miners would have left behind.

"Enough about the assassin." Vonsha touched the shaman's arm. There was a familiarity in that gesture that turned Books's stomach. "Can you fix your artifact?" she asked. "If the city water returns to normal... all this was time wasted, and your employers won't be pleased."

The shaman shook her hand away. "Yes, of course. But not now. I want that man dead first. I should have grabbed the woman." He thrust a finger toward Books. "You'd better hope the assassin comes for you."

He stalked back up the tunnel, taking his light globe with him. Shadows threatened, until Vonsha turned up her lantern.

"He leaves me in the dark a lot," she said, "in all senses of the saying."

Books pressed his hands against the invisible barrier, ignoring the jolt. "What are you doing with him? Vonsha, I thought..." What? That they could find happiness together? Form a family? Dear ancestors, surely he was too old to be that naive. To fall for a woman he barely knew, one whose placement and actions had been suspicious from the beginning.

"Books, I *tried* to get you out of the way." She slumped against the stone wall opposite him. "Why couldn't you go off to the other side of the mountains, like I suggested?"

"Because you were lying."

"Yes, but you weren't supposed to figure that out." She smiled sadly.

"What's in this for you? Why are you working with him?"

"I'm protecting my parents. They wanted my family's land, and they were offering a fraction of its value. My father refused—where would my parents go with so little money?—and those people would have killed him if I hadn't intervened. I nosed around, ran into Tarok, and through him met the leader of this scheme. I found out why they wanted the land."

"To build a dam and take over control of the city water supply?" Books said. "That's what they're doing on the other side of the river, isn't it? Quarrying rock for the new dam."

"I wasn't dumb enough to try and blackmail the woman in charge," Vonsha said, ignoring his questions, "but I arranged a better deal. My family will keep their land, and when the dam is built they'll receive a share of the profits."

"That's blood money, Vonsha."

"People would have been killed whether I did anything or not. And this way I know my parents are taken care of. It's not ideal, and I know it, but it's better than the alternative. You have to understand, I'm the reason my parents had to leave the capital, to move up here in the first place. My failure during the war was more than an embarrassment for the family. It was..." She folded her arms across her belly and gazed at the floor. "It doesn't matter now. I have to make sure things are right for them."

"But dealing with Forge? That's foolish isn't it? Aren't they the ones who tried to blow us up in the library? What makes you think they'll honor a deal with you?"

Until that moment, he had only known Amaranthe suspected the Forge organization—he did not think they had any proof—but Vonsha did not deny it.

"I wasn't the target that night," she said. "I'm told you triggered a magical alarm that had been placed on the map file in case the enforcers caught a whiff of the plan and investigated prematurely. Forge wasn't anticipating you or your assassin friend, or they would have sent more qualified personnel. Those thugs probably didn't even know who they were working for much less who I was."

"Fine," Books said, "they didn't attack you, but these people are not to be trusted. Do you know they were the ones responsible for the emperor's kidnapping a couple of months ago? They tried to kill him."

"I've little reason to care for our emperors."

"Sespian is different. You're warrior caste. That entitles you to an audience, doesn't it? If you'd gone to him with information about—"

Something moved at the edge of Books's vision: the spider, or another one, skittering up the tunnel this time. It stopped before the cell and rotated, first facing Books, then Vonsha, then continuing along its route.

"What are they?" he asked after it disappeared into the darkness.

"His security constructs. They monitor the tunnels. He'll know, through them, if your friends come."

Not sure if he had "friends" coming, Books chose to focus on his more immediate concern. "What's the name of the woman you dealt with? Do you know who's in charge of this whole scheme?"

"I know enough to keep my mouth shut," Vonsha said. "They're powerful. They want the emperor's law revoked and foreigner-owned businesses out of the city, so there'll be no competition. Owning the new dam will simply be a side perk for them."

"So...foreigners are being framed?" Books thought of Amaranthe's newspaper article, of the successful Kendorian turned in for supposed magic use. "If citizens think outsiders are using magic to get ahead, they might believe foreigners are responsible for the water problems?"

"You haven't seen the latest papers. People *are* assuming that. With enough pressure from the populace, Sespian will be forced to rescind his policy."

"So innocent people will be blamed instead of Forge and the Mangdorian allies they've won by outing Sicarius," Books said. "I can't say I'm sorry I broke that artifact."

Vonsha pushed away from the wall. "It won't matter. Tarok will fix it, and he'll put it deeper in the lake this time. Your friends won't be able to do anything."

She strode up the tunnel.

"Wait," Books called. "Can't you at least turn that thing off?" He nodded to the device on the wall. "Let me out of here?"

"I haven't that knowledge," she said over her shoulder. "And even if I did, I like you enough that I wouldn't let you out. Tarok has deadly constructs guarding these tunnels. If we're able to get things working again, I'll see about getting you released."

She continued on, leaving Books in darkness again.

* * * * *

Inside the dilapidated Kaker Mines office, Amaranthe opened a dented metal cabinet. A rat scurried out. She was too tired to do more than yawn in response. Her wounds throbbed, and with each movement her clothing abraded her fevered skin. She kept her hands and her mind busy, trying to ignore the fact she was getting worse.

Beams of morning sunlight slanted through holes in the ceiling, highlighting the cracked concrete floor. She and the men had driven all night along roads made treacherous by the dark. Their stolen enforcer lorry waited out front. Thanks to an overly efficient squad of soldiers, their own vehicle had been too well guarded to recover. Necessary though it may have been, the theft made Amaranthe all too aware that their quest to win favor with the authorities was not going as well as she had hoped.

"Stop cleaning, boss," Maldynado said from across the room. "You're injured."

Amaranthe caught herself wiping the dusty shelves with a rag. "I'm merely removing a layer of dirt in case a map is cowering beneath it."

While Basilard searched rusty filing cabinets, Maldynado inspected the drawers of a desk so old and water damaged it wobbled every time someone walked past it.

"And is that also why you scraped that fungus off those shelves in the corner?" Maldynado asked.

"No, that was a health issue. Inhaling those spores can't be wholesome."

"There's nothing wholesome about anything here. There's nothing in this desk either. Your enforcer buddy told us which mine the shaman is in, right? Why do we need a map?" Maldynado thumped the lower drawer shut. Wood cracked, and it dropped onto the floor. The desk trembled, then collapsed in a heap. "Oops."

"You've a knack for destruction." Amaranthe pulled out a book on the chance it contained information about the mines. Only numbers greeted her, an accounting of the ore pulled from the mountain.

"What if we don't find anything here, and this was a waste of time? You look horrible, and Books is probably being tortured."

"We didn't all need to check the mine entrance." Amaranthe leaned the side of her head against the cool metal of the cabinet door. "If the shaman has indeed returned to his hideout, Sicarius and Akstyr can let us know. If we find a map, maybe it'll have a backdoor into the tunnels, one the shaman isn't guarding. And it's worth waiting a few hours to see if the seed I planted sprouts. If the soldiers come, they'll be the ideal distraction at the front door."

"*If* they come," Maldynado said.

"If they don't, I'll think of something else." In truth, she already had a distraction in mind. She needed to talk the shaman into healing her anyway, so she could keep him busy while the men sneaked in to rescue Books.

Maldynado pushed his hands through his hair. "I just don't want Books getting killed because some crusty, magic-slinging Mangdorian wants revenge on Sicarius."

Amaranthe froze. Maldynado *had* been close enough to hear her conversation with Sicarius.

Basilard halted his search and signed, *What?*

"That's just a theory." Amaranthe did not glare at Maldynado, not with Basilard watching, but she wanted to. "We don't know why the shaman took Books. Keep looking for maps, please."

She returned the accounting book to the cabinet and made a show of searching, hoping Basilard would not request clarification on Maldynado's comment. But he joined her, face questioning.

Sicarius? His sign for Sicarius was a knife being drawn across his throat. Too apropos for the moment.

"The other shaman in the canyon recognized him." Amaranthe spoke slowly to buy time to think. She did not want to lie to Basilard, especially not when she might be caught in that lie later, but to tell him the truth could irrevocably alienate him from Sicarius—or worse. Basilard would have been young when the Mangdorian royal family was slain, but not that young. Twenty, perhaps. He would remember the crime. "There was...loathing involved in that recognition," she said.

Basilard nodded once, as if to say that was expected. Who didn't feel that way about Sicarius?

"If this other shaman hates Sicarius for the same reason, maybe he wants him dead too."

What Sicarius do? Basilard signed.

Amaranthe twitched a shoulder and forced herself to meet his eyes. "He's irritated a lot of people in his career. He doesn't tell me the details." True, though she had a knack for finding those details out on her own.

Basilard watched her, and she tried not to squirm.

Before I see dead in dam, Basilard signed, *I think...stay quiet...not speak of...Mangdorians.* He grimaced, and Amaranthe could tell he was annoyed with the limited signs of his hand code. He held up a hand, found a paper and pencil stub, and returned. He wrote out the rest and handed it to her.

I wasn't sure I wanted to betray my countrymen. I didn't know what plot they were a part of, but my loyalty has never been to the empire. I have a lot of reason to hate the empire and Turgonians.

As if he knew exactly where she was on the page, Basilard touched the scar tissue at his throat. Amaranthe nodded and finished reading.

You give me hope though. That we can eventually influence Emperor Sespian and I can communicate with him to find a better solution for my people. I have come to trust you.

"Thank you, Basilard," she said, though his honesty only made her feel guiltier for withholding the truth from him. "I don't know all of Sicarius's secrets, and it's not my place to share the ones I do know. I—"

"Found something," Maldynado said.

"What?" Amaranthe rushed to join him for reasons beyond curiosity.

He rotated a cobweb-cloaked chalkboard standing on wheels in the corner. A giant diagram was tacked on the backside. Several warrens of horizontal, vertical, and diagonal lines crisscrossed the paper.

"The mines." She tapped a circle that represented the northernmost one.

"You're welcome." Maldynado puffed out his chest.

Amaranthe traced the line leading from the circle. "Different levels, twists, and forks. This is a maze." She squinted at words scrawled in the faded ink. "Not to scale. Not representative of all tunnels. See Document Four A dash Six for complete map. Uhm, anyone seen that?"

Maldynado deflated. "Er, no."

Basilard shook his head.

Amaranthe eyed the broken desk and surrounding furniture.

"We've searched everything," Maldynado said. "If there were other maps here, I figure that fungal mass ate them."

"I told you it wasn't wholesome." She ticked her fingernail against the chalkboard. "It doesn't look like the adjoining mine connects to the shaman's. The only other way into his is..."

Maldynado pointed to a long, vertical line that connected with the mine of interest. "Looks like a backdoor to me."

"Looks like a long drop down a hundreds-of-feet-deep shaft to me," Amaranthe said.

"Enh, we've got rope. And Sicarius has trained us all to be expert climbers. Of course, I was already an expert."

Basilard's eyebrows flew up. *Last month, you fell.*

"That wasn't a fall. It was a premature release, due to that beautiful lady ranger who was strolling along the base of the cliff. She had the biggest—"

"Problem," Amaranthe said.

"Hm?" Maldynado asked.

"I suspect this shaft only exists for water removal purposes. There'll be a steam engine on top that was designed to power a pump far below."

"Well, it won't be working, right? Unless the shaman is doing a little hobby mining on the side. Maybe the shaft is big enough that we can climb down it around the equipment."

Basilard shook his head slowly, catching on before Maldynado.

"If they needed a pump during the mine's heyday," Amaranthe said, "it was because the lower levels filled with water. If the pump hasn't been operating...."

"Oh," Maldynado said. "Guess we should have brought the diving suits along."

Amaranthe tapped the vertical line. "I'll have you, Basilard, and Akstyr check it anyway. If it's flooded, you come back and go in the front. With luck, I'll get the shaman out of his warren by then and give you time to search for Books."

Maldynado shared a bewildered expression with Basilard. "How're you going to do that?" he asked. "And what will Sicarius be doing?"

"Nothing he'll be happy about," Amaranthe said.

CHAPTER 23

BOOKS SCRAPED AND POKED AT THE DIRT AROUND the rocks in the wall nearest the white box using the broken piece of iron he had found earlier. He kept running into slabs of rock too large to dig around. His fingers bled, he could not see what he was doing, and more hours than he could guess at had passed. His cracked lips craved water. His stomach growled so ferociously it was drowning out his side of the conversation he had been having with it. He had stopped worrying whether or not it was healthy to talk to himself.

At least the pile of dirt and stones gathering on the floor beneath the wall was growing. If he could reach the back of that box, perhaps....

Soft clacks sounded in the tunnel.

Books pulled his makeshift chisel out of the hole and sat, leaning against the wall. He brushed the rubble beneath his legs as a tiny red light marched into sight. One of the spiders.

In the darkness, Books could make out none of its features, but he had no trouble picturing the thing. The red light turned toward him, a thumbnail-sized dot against a black backdrop.

"How about asking your master to send dinner down?" Books asked.

The red light shifted from side to side, giving the impression that the spider thought him suspicious. He propped an elbow on a knee, hoping to appear the perfect image of a bored and unambitious prisoner. A bead of sweat streaked down the side of his cheek, perhaps belying the facade.

What kind of mental capacity did the shaman's inventions possess?

The light continued to beam at him. The reverberations from the distant machinery pulsed against Books's back. Water dripped and spattered into a pool somewhere in the depths.

Finally, the light winked out as the spider turned to skitter up the tunnel, out of sight. Up, the direction Vonsha and the shaman had gone.

Books returned to his hole and doubled his efforts. If the mechanical creature was off to tattle on him, he might not have much time. Sweat soon bathed his brow and dampened his shirt. His bones ached from scraping and pounding at the earth, but his efforts were rewarded. His makeshift file thunked against a new material.

He wriggled his fingers about until he touched flat metal: the back-side of the box. He tapped it a few times, fearing some magical punishment for his brazenness, but nothing happened. Books dug around it carefully. Minutes trickled past, but eventually it came loose in his hand.

Not sure whether to pull it back through the hole or try to hurl it down the tunnel, he stuck his free hand out to test the barrier. It remained in place.

Books tried to drag the box through the hole so he could examine it in the cell. It bumped the edge and fell to the ground.

"Dead deranged ancestors," he growled.

All that time spent, and he dropped the thing. He twisted his arm, trying to reach through the hole and to the floor outside. His fingers swiped only air.

He yanked his arm back into the cell, scraping his shoulder in the process. Fists clenched, he lunged to his feet and kicked the barrier.

His foot met no resistance, and he almost pitched over backward.

Books's anger evaporated. He probed the front of his cell, but the barrier was indeed gone. He stepped outside.

He could see nothing in the black tunnel. Arm stretched forward, he took a couple of tentative steps up the passage...and smashed into the barrier. Lovely. It must simply stretch across any opening parallel with the box. He found he could kick the device and push the barrier farther up the passage. He knelt, figuring he could angle it so he could pass, but he paused.

Presumably, the exit lay somewhere up the tunnel, but the shaman waited there too. And Vonsha had mentioned constructs.

Books left the barrier as it was and headed the opposite direction, deeper into the mine. Somewhere below him, machinery worked. Maybe he could sabotage something important, draw the shaman down to check on it, and slip past him to escape.

"Sounds easy," he muttered, sure it would be anything but.

Groping his way through the darkness, he kept the ore cart track to one side and followed the wall with his hand on the other. Regularly placed wood timbers supported the ceiling and donated slivers as he brushed past them. The sound of dripping water grew louder, and he formed a hunch about the purpose of the distant machinery.

When he rounded a bend, the darkness receded. Another bend took him into a natural cavern with small globes of light mounted on the wall like torches. A serene pool occupied half of the space with the water lapping over the tracks in spots. Several pieces of machinery hunkered on the other side of the cavern. Steam-powered excavating equipment, most of it rusted beyond use.

Books stopped to admire a tunnel-boring machine in better condition than the rest. A pile of firewood lay nearby. Maybe the shaman had used the borer to excavate extra rooms for his lair. Books rubbed his lips. The idea of tunneling his way out of the place created a nice image, but he doubted the device could grind through more than a couple of feet of rock an hour.

He checked a few wooden crates and found they held tools, bags of nuts, bolts, screws, nails, and other appurtenances he could not guess at. Raw materials for making evil shamanic contraptions, perhaps.

Beyond the pool and the machinery, the tunnel continued. Books followed it, glad that lighting illuminated this section. Water from the pool spilled into the downward-sloping passage, and he squished through a steady flow. The rumble of machinery grew louder, but the water also deepened. When it reached his knees, he thought about stopping, but the noise promised he was close to the source.

He entered a second, smaller chamber, this one carved by man and filled with machinery. The pumps.

A current sucked at his legs as he splashed through the water to peer up a hole in the ceiling. Pipes and machinery disappeared into darkness a few feet up. If daylight and escape lay that way, it would be a long climb up damp walls—with a short and deadly drop if he fell.

"You can do this," Books told himself. He was not the same ungainly awkward man he had been a few months ago. He was in good shape now. Prime health.

His stomach whined. Either it was mocking him, or it wanted him to hurry up.

He grabbed the side of the pump casing and climbed toward the hole in the ceiling, but churning thoughts slowed his progress. If the shaman came down and found him, a gout of fire hurled up the chute could end his escape quickly. Also, if he left now, when Tarok seemed capable of repairing the artifact in the lake, that might put the team in no better a position than when they had started the mission.

Books was here, in the villain's lair. Shouldn't he sabotage something?

"Bet that bastard would have a hard time fixing anything with all his tools underwater," he murmured.

Nodding to himself, he dropped down and jogged back up the tunnel toward the cavern.

* * * * *

Wind gusted through the foothills, railing against the stump Amaranthe crouched behind. Rain slanted sideways, battering her flushed cheeks. Despite her fever, shivers coursed through her as she watched the mine entrance through a spyglass. Darkness hugged the hillside, but she could make out a pair of constructs guarding the tunnel.

Their heads, similar to the clunky diving helmet Books had worn, did not shift or twist, though crimson eyes burned behind glass plates. With barrel-chests and column-like legs, they had a humanoid shape. She doubted they were pretty when they walked, but they did not need to be, not with the four scaled-down harpoon launchers adorning each arm.

"Those things are fantastic," Maldynado whispered.

He and Basilard knelt near Amaranthe.

"Wouldn't it be great if we could get one to guard our hideout?" Maldynado added.

Amaranthe said nothing. She was too tired for chitchat. She was surprised Sicarius and Akstyr had not found them by now.

No sooner had she had the thought than a touch on her shoulder startled her.

"Leave us," Sicarius told the others and crouched beside her.

"More secrecy," Maldynado moaned, but he slouched off a few paces.

Basilard frowned suspiciously at Sicarius before joining Maldynado. Something else to worry about, but not that night, Amaranthe hoped. Akstyr came up the trail out of the darkness and joined the two men.

Amaranthe sank down, her back against the stump. "Report?"

"You're worse," Sicarius said.

"Yes, I've been told." Her voice cracked. "Have you confirmed the shaman is inside? Are the soldiers coming?"

"Yes and no."

"No sign of them? You're sure?"

"Yes," Sicarius said. "We must act alone. And soon. You may be dead by morning."

"Have I mentioned how endearing your bluntness is?"

"I believe we can destroy these constructs with mundane means," Sicarius said, "but doing so will alert the shaman of our presence."

"Don't worry. You're not going that way. I am."

"Explain."

Amaranthe told him about the vertical shaft they had identified on the map.

"You want us to retrieve Books while you're being taken prisoner?" Sicarius said.

"No, I want *them* to retrieve Books. I have to talk the shaman into healing me, and you're the only bargaining chip I can think of to tease him with." She smiled, hoping he would not be offended. It would not be the first time she used him or his reputation as a tool.

"Explain," he said again, his tone cooler this time.

"I'd like you to wait up on the hillside—there's a canyon called Crest Crevasse. I'll go in and tell the shaman I'll take him to you, but that I need him to heal me so I can make the climb. My life in exchange for his revenge. Of course, you'll have time to pick a place, set up traps, and do whatever other assassinly preparation is required. I assume you'd prefer to face him on territory of your choosing rather than of his."

Amaranthe waited for a response. It was not a brilliant plan or even a creative-enough-to-possibly-unsettle-the-opponent plan, but she had come up with nothing better. And, like he said, she feared they had to go in tonight, while she retained the ability to walk and think.

"I would *prefer* not to face him at all," Sicarius said.

"Me too, but I *have* to face him. I need someone to heal me, and he's the only candidate."

"You would not need his services if you hadn't insisted on confronting the makarovi."

The accusation surprised her. Not because it was untrue, but because Sicarius, whatever his opinions of her intelligence might be, did not usually voice them. Hearing his disapproval stung.

"Probably true," she said, "but I did and now I do."

"Your recklessness has nearly gotten you killed more times than I can count, and your plans continue to put my life in danger."

"I'm sorry," Amaranthe said, "but I thought you... Don't you believe one must take great risks in order to achieve great rewards?"

"The only reward I want requires me to live to appreciate it."

Amaranthe closed her eyes. She already felt like a hot ingot on a blacksmith's anvil. Why did he have to choose this moment to snipe at her?

"Look," she said, "if you have another plan—"

"I *plan* to rethink this arrangement. You would put a master shaman on my trail, and for what? This will not help me earn my 'reward.'"

"Sicarius...."

"I will wait in your canyon." He stood. "Until dawn. After that, I'm leaving."

"What do you mean you're leaving? Leaving the group? Permanently?"

"If he doesn't like your plan, and he decides to kill you, there's no point in me staying." He gazed down at her, eyes as cold and distant as when they first met. "Books is nothing to me, and I'm not coming in after you."

Amaranthe swallowed around a lump in her throat. "I didn't ask you to."

Sicarius strode into the darkness. She scowled after him. Just the day before he had risked his life to keep the makarovi off her. Emperor's balls, that was *heroic*. How could one decide something like that had been a mistake?

Because, her mind said with a sneer, he realized how close he came to dying because of your stupid plan.

And then there was the blasting stick that had been launched at him the last time she went in to talk to a shaman. Maybe Sicarius was right to be tired of her shenanigans. That knowledge did not keep tears from stinging her eyes.

CHAPTER 24

FLINT RASPED AGAINST STEEL, SPRAYING SPARKS onto the thin undershirt Books had been wearing beneath the diving suit. Now it was serving duty as a fire starter since the shaman had not been considerate enough to leave matches and tinder along with the wood. The shirt worked, and he soon had flames crackling in the tunnel borer's firebox. A cool draft stirred gooseflesh on his bare arms, but a garment was worth giving up if it meant flooding the lair and perhaps destroying the rest of the shaman's cursed projects.

With his back to the cavern, and the open furnace door blocking his view, he was in a poor position to monitor the exits. An uneasy feeling whispered across the back of his neck. He turned his head, expecting to find the shaman watching.

He did have a visitor, but not a human one. One of the tiny spiders observed from the tunnel leading to the higher levels. As soon as he spotted it, the creature scurried off.

Books clenched a fist. He might have fooled it before, but it would not fail to report his escape this time.

He sprinted across the cavern. With legs much longer than the spider's, he had little trouble catching up. Before wiser thoughts could stop him, he jumped and stomped on the device.

Shards of metal tinkled against the rock walls. Books lifted his boot. In his enthusiasm—or perhaps desperation was the better word—he had smashed the thing to bits. Good.

He ran back to the cavern. It would take time for the water in the boiler to heat enough to produce steam to power the vehicle.

Books tried to work calmly and efficiently as he stoked the fire, but he could not keep from glancing at the tunnel entrance every few seconds. His expectations were answered.

A heavy *clank, clank, clank* echoed from the passage.

Books ticked the gauge on the boiler. It was close but not ready. No choice. He threw more wood on the fire and climbed over the borer's treads and into the cab. The number of levers daunted him, especially considering how little time he had to figure out how to drive the vehicle.

Something metallic glinted in the mouth of the tunnel.

Books threw a lever. In front of the cab, a great rotating cylinder started to spin.

"Forward," he muttered. "How do we move this thing forward?"

A massive cast iron creature clomped out of the passage, scraping rock and dirt off the sides with its broad body. Though reminiscent of the small spider Books had squished, this mechanical beast had more features. Such as fangs.

Black, iron teeth as long as his forearm gnashed together in a protruding jaw shaped like a dog's snout. Not two but six eyes glowed above that snout. Each of the eight legs below its bulky carapace had the heft of a pillar. Twin arms stuck out of the front, and crab-like pincers snapped. Steel razors gleamed, reflecting the light from the wall orbs. Without hesitation, the great spider clanked toward Books.

He tried another lever.

The tunnel borer lurched forward. Surprised, Books tipped backward, ramming his naked shoulder blades against unforgiving metal.

On the gauge, the needle wobbled beneath the ready mark, but Books had no choice. He set himself and pushed the lever to maximum. The borer picked up speed.

He chose one of two paired levers, figuring they must be for steering. His first try angled the machine into the wall. He lurched, nearly thrown back again. Pulverized stone flew, pelting the cab, and the noisy grinding drowned out the spider's approach.

Books pulled the other lever, and the borer veered away from the wall. He steadied the machine and drove it toward the spider. He curled his lips in a grimace of anticipation, anticipation that this might be messy. For him. The drills could handle rock, but what about cast iron? Cast iron possibly enhanced with magic?

Maybe he should wheel the borer around and try to outrun the spider to the pump room. If he could destroy the machinery before—

No time. The spider snapped its jaws and increased its speed, lunging like a wolf.

At the last second, Books hurled himself from the cab.

Metal screeched and squealed. He rolled away, arms sheltering his head. Shrapnel hammered the rock all around him and splashed into the pool. A fist-sized chunk slammed into his naked shoulder. Warm blood flowed down his arm.

Grinding noises and the smell of scorched metal filled the cavern. Books lifted his head and opened an eye.

The borer had crunched into the carapace of the spider, leaving a massive concave dent. The snout and pincers were missing, fallen to mingle with wreckage from the vehicle: shards of metal and broken drill bits. The construct was not dead yet though. It wobbled to the side as the borer, despite a snapped tread, continued to advance.

Books jumped to his feet and sprinted back to his vehicle. He ducked his head to avoid the newly warped frame of the cab and grabbed the levers, turning the machine to angle for the spider again. Even damaged it might be able to hobble back up to deliver a message to the shaman.

He braced himself and rammed the construct again. The collision jolted him, but he hung on. He pushed the spider before him, steering it toward the pool.

Even headless and eyeless, the creature seemed to sense its trouble for it tried to shamble sideways. Books kept it pinned and pushed it ruthlessly over the tracks and into the water. Once it was immersed to its carapace, he backed up and rammed it again. After three heavy jolts, it finally stopped moving. It slumped, smoke pouring from cracks in its seams.

Books backed the borer away. A cloud of black smoke swallowed the cab and made him cough. His own exhaust. Operating a steam vehicle in closed confines was probably not wise, but he did not plan to linger.

He veered toward the lower tunnel. The borer limped and lurched, and metal rattled with each chug of the pistons. He held his breath, not positive it would fit into the passage without having to drill, a task it was no longer fit for.

The borer knocked a few stones loose, but it squeezed into the tunnel. It smashed light orbs on the walls, causing blinding flashes that made Books's head ache. When he made it to the smaller cavern, he aimed for the pumping machinery with single-minded intent. He enticed every bit of speed he could get from the borer as it plowed into the deeper water.

Again, Books jumped free before the crash. This time he expected the screech of metal and the flying parts, but something heavy fell on him from above.

He staggered and lost his balance. He tried to catch himself, but the weight drove him down, forcing his face into the water. Not metal but a hand pressed on his back.

Shocked, Books spun onto his back and kicked out with his legs. His boots collided with flesh. He struggled to lift his head out of the water, but a solid grip held him. Water flooded his nose, burning his nostrils. He grabbed his assailant.

A shout sounded, distorted by the water. The hands let go.

Books came up sputtering—and swinging. His fist smashed into someone's abdomen. Water streamed into his eyes, but he glimpsed his opponent grunting and bending over. From his knees, Books drew his arm back for another blow.

"Books!" a familiar voice cried.

Books froze. He dashed water out of his eyes and gaped at the array of men before him. Basilard, Akstyr, and—

"Emperor's balls, Booksie, haven't we told you not to wander around with your shirt off?" Maldynado asked, a hand to his stomach. "Nobody wants to look at that hairy rug of yours."

Books groaned and climbed to his feet. "Good to see you too, you fodder-for-brains ignoramus." He peered about, confused as to where they had come from, then gazed up at the shaft. A rope dangled from the shadows. "You climbed down here?"

"We're here to rescue you," Akstyr said.

It was an obvious statement, but Books found himself surprised by it—by their presence here. That they actually cared enough to climb down that long shaft, risking a drop to their deaths, to get him....

"Though it looks like you started without us." Maldynado pointed at the smoking borer and the smashed pumps. "I'm impressed. I didn't know you had a knack for destroying things."

"You should see the spider," Books muttered. "Where's Amaranthe? Is she...doing all right?"

"Uhm." Maldynado traded uncertain looks with Basilard and Akstyr.

"She's not..." Books swallowed.

"Dead?" Maldynado asked. "No, no. At least, she wasn't when we parted ways, but she..."

"Has an infection I couldn't cure," Akstyr said. "So she's going to ask the shaman to heal her."

"*Ask* the shaman?" Books stared at them. "You *did* tell her he's the villain, right?"

"She has a plan," Maldynado said.

"Her plan is walking in with Sicarius and asking the shaman for help? That's not up to her usual creativity level."

"Actually, Sicarius isn't with her."

Books spent more time staring, then said, "Tell me what's going on."

They plodded out of the water while Maldynado shared the past day and a half's events and detailed as much of the overall plan as he grasped. Books had a feeling he was missing some insight into Amaranthe's thoughts, but, either way, the scheme did not sound promising.

"Let's go help her," Books said. "Anyone bring me a weapon?"

"We figured you could just run in bare-chested," Maldynado said, "and the shaman would think you were some sort of deranged furry predator and flee the other way."

Akstyr snickered. Basilard lifted his hands and mimicked a roaring bear.

"I'll take that for a no," Books said. Had he actually been feeling grateful that these louts came to rescue him? It had been far more peaceful with the malevolent machines. "This way. Follow me."

"You got it, Booksie."

* * * * *

An hour after the men left, Amaranthe headed up the hill toward the mine. A damp breeze tugged at her clothing, and the hem of her jacket flapped against her thighs. The noise did not matter, she reminded herself. She was not trying to sneak in.

The mechanical sentries waited, unmoving, on either side of the tunnel entrance. Their red eyes stared outward, burning into the night. Moisture gleamed on their metal shoulders. She supposed it was too optimistic to hope the rain had rusted the constructs' innards, and they would fall over when they tried to stop her.

Amaranthe approached slowly with her arms away from her sides. She had a knife tucked into her boot, but otherwise carried no weapons.

When she closed to within ten steps, the constructs stepped forward as one to block her route into the mine. Each lifted a right arm, and gleaming harpoon heads pointed at her chest.

"I need to see your..." Boss? Creator? The Mad Shaman who had crafted them? She was not sure what title they might understand. She settled on, "Maker."

They stared at her, inhuman eyes searing holes into her chest. At least the constructs were not shooting. Cold inhuman stares she could deal with. Thanks to Sicarius, she had all sorts of practice. She pushed him out of her thoughts.

"I have information your master will be interested in." Or so she hoped.

One construct returned to its place beside the entrance while the other rotated and strode into the mine.

"Uhm?" Amaranthe pointed at its back. "Am I supposed to follow?"

The remaining construct did not move. She shrugged and eased past it. It did not halt her.

"Guess I'm invited in."

Small, white globes hanging on support posts lighted the way. An ore cart track ran down the center of a rough-hewn tunnel high enough for the ten-foot-tall construct to walk without hunching. If it could hunch. Its broad, barrel chest did scrape the walls from time to time, causing a trickle of dirt to crumble free.

Other dark passages veered away at points, but her guide continued down the main, lighted tunnel. It sloped downward, and Amaranthe soon lost sight of the entrance. Eventually they turned into a side tunnel that dead-ended at a shiny copper door. It reflected the construct's crimson eyes.

When several heartbeats passed with nothing happening, Amaranthe edged closer. Maybe she was expected to knock.

She lifted a hand. Before she touched the copper, the door swung open silently. Amaranthe followed the construct into a long rectangular space that resembled a room more than a cave. A room filled with work-benches and machines.

A row of sleek, metallic creatures stretched along one long wall. Some were bipedal, some animal-shaped, and some vehicular, though none had the size or mass of a steam carriage or lorry. They must have been built to navigate these tunnels. Tables, shelves, and desks lined the opposite wall. They housed a variety of smaller devices, some with glowing orbs. How many of those contraptions were weapons? Was this some stockpile that could be used against the empire?

Busy gaping at the devices, Amaranthe almost missed the blond man leaning against a desk near the far end of the room. He wore factory-weave wool garments and practical boots typical of the style sold in Stumps. If not for his long blond hair and fair skin, he might have passed for an imperial citizen.

"Have you come to bargain for your man's life?" the shaman asked.

"Actually, I came to bargain for medical attention," Amaranthe said. "Your monsters tried to lunch on my insides, and it appears they didn't wash their paws before dining."

His eye twitched when she called them *his* monsters.

"Though I'm pleased to know Books is alive," Amaranthe said. "Thank you for that."

He snorted. "I didn't spare him for you. Where is the assassin? Mounting a rescue while you distract me?"

"Rescue? Sicarius? He's not that sort. Get yourself captured, and he'll be the first to let you know you were an idiot for not paying atten-tion. He'll leave it in your hands to escape—or not. Good training or the last lesson you'll ever learn." She wished she was lying, but after Sicarius's words outside, the statements were easy to make.

"Where is he? I want him." The shaman walked to the wall and placed a hand on a black metal machine that seemed inspired by spiked maces and flails.

Amaranthe leaned against the closest workbench. Usually she en-joyed talking to people, even the dastardly types who teamed up with the other side, but weariness dragged at her muscles. She would love to lie down somewhere.

"Listen, Mister...?"

"Tarok."

"All right, Mister Tarok. I'm told I'm going to die if someone with magic fingers doesn't tend me. I'm willing to do...quite a lot to ensure I wake up tomorrow. Sicarius has been a useful member of my team when he's bothered to do what we want him to, but life is life. I can tell you where he is if you help me."

"Perhaps—" Tarok strolled her direction, hands clasped behind his back, "—if I take you prisoner, he'll come to visit me. You're much prettier than the man."

Amaranthe rubbed her face. "As you said, he's an assassin. This is not the sort of person to develop attachments to others. He doesn't care about people beyond their ability to be useful to him. He's *not* going to rescue Books, me, or anyone else."

Tarok stopped and studied her, a crinkle to his brow. She was surprised he was having trouble believing this. Most people who had met Sicarius, or heard about him in passing, assumed this to be the case.

"I can tell you where he is," Amaranthe repeated. "I'll even take you to him, but I'll need some magicky medical attention to be fit for the climb."

"Magicky."

"We don't have a lot of words to describe magic in Turgonian."

He grunted. "On *that* you don't lie. You're ignorant barbarians. I pity you."

"Do you pity me enough to heal me?"

"Heal you? You've been a wart on my toe since you stumbled onto their plot. Your man nearly destroyed the *amaskort* beyond repair."

She did not like that he said "nearly." If there was hope to fix that thing....

"You can't blame me for that," Amaranthe said. "You're harming imperial citizens, and my group works for the emperor."

Tarok's blond eyebrows arched.

"Sort of," she amended. "The emperor doesn't actually know we work for him, but.... It's a long story. You're Mangdorian, right? Doesn't your religion posit the virtues of love for one's fellow man? And, er, woman? Even if I wasn't prepared to help you find Sicarius—which I am, remember—wouldn't you find it a noble choice to heal me?"

She watched his face, trying to determine if he was buying any of her spiel. His lip curled in a sneer. Guess not.

"Have you forsaken your people and your religion then?" Amaranthe asked. "You must have if you're willing to build devices that can murder people from a distance. And collars to capture horrible creatures that'll do the same up close."

His sneer faded. "You are right about our religion, and I would not have chosen to create devices that kill of my own volition. But sometimes...a great good, a victory for a nation, outweighs lesser evils."

"And you believe that victory is killing Sicarius?" Amaranthe asked.

Tarok lifted his chin. "I will bring his head to my people just as he took the heads of our beloved rulers. That will inspire them, show them that we do have the power to take back what was once ours."

"If what you want is Sicarius's head, why the plot against the city?"

"My cooperation in this matter was the price for information about Sicarius. All the information I would need to thwart him."

Amaranthe wondered what else those spies had pulled out of the files in Imperial Intelligence. "Well, I was kind enough to bring him to your mountain, so there's no need for you to continue working with Forge."

Since she did not know for certain Forge was the group behind everything, she watched him to see if he would deny association with the organization. He did not.

"As far as thwarting Sicarius goes..." Amaranthe nodded at the constructs along the wall. "You appear to be set for a battle."

"You're trying too hard to get me to go after him," he said. "You're attempting to lure me into a trap."

She offered her best who-me expression, then said, "No, I'm trying to live. Nobody else around here is qualified to help me."

"Unfortunate for you." He resumed his stroll toward her. "Do you know what your assassin did to my people?"

When she had said "your monsters," it had bothered him, and his word choice now bothered her. She did feel responsible for Sicarius, since she had chosen to employ him. "I was a child myself then," was all she could say. "He answered to another."

"Your emperor, I know."

"Who told you? Forge?"

"It doesn't matter."

"It does," Amaranthe said. "Their motivations aren't pure. They would've only given you that information because they wanted something." She nodded toward the machines.

"It doesn't matter. They had something I wanted in return."

He stopped two paces away from her, and she considered going for her knife.

"And you have something I want," he said. "The assassin's location."

The intensity of his gaze had increased, and Amaranthe took a step back. "I already told you I'd trade you that information for my health."

"Yes, but I can find out where he is without healing you. And, unlike what your lips are telling me, I'm sure what's in your mind will be truth."

"In my...mind?"

He lifted a hand toward her temple.

Amaranthe jumped back, gritting her teeth against a stab of pain from her wounds, and yanked her boot knife free. The shaman waved a hand. Heat flared from the handle, searing her palm.

Cursing, she dropped the knife and backed farther—or tried to. Her shoulders rammed against unyielding metal. Something vise-like clamped down on her shoulder.

Amaranthe twisted and tried to lunge away, but the grip held her fast. She craned her neck to see her captor. One of the humanoid constructs had left the wall and rolled behind her on wheels. She cursed herself for not hearing or sensing its approach.

Tarok grabbed her wrist with one hand and reached for her forehead with the other. She kicked him in the groin.

He staggered back and hunched over. Again Amaranthe tried to yank away. Scabs tore beneath her bandages, and agony seared her torso. She gasped, nearly pitching to her knees. In the end, her efforts were for naught: the construct merely tightened its grip.

Teeth bared, the shaman glowered at her. "Down."

The machine forced her to her knees, and she had no answer for its power. Tarok's hand came in again, and Amaranthe could not dodge or kick from her position.

At first, she noticed the cool, dry presence of his palm against her hot skin. Then all she was aware of was the fact that she was not alone in her head any more. Memories came unbidden to her mind. The battle on top of the dam, Sicarius's shooting of the shaman in the canyon, his last conversation with her outside the mine.

As the shaman dug deeper, Amaranthe tried to fight him. She drove her thoughts in directions she hoped would be useless. Old homework assignments, the enforcer training manual, the—

Pain ripped through her mind, and she gasped, back arched. Tarok squashed her attempts at distraction and barreled back to Sicarius with dogged tenacity. He drew everything up from the last few days, and Amaranthe struggled to keep tears of defeat from burning her eyes. Not only would he not heal her, but she would lay Sicarius's secrets at his feet.

For a moment, the shaman's presence faded, and she hoped he had enough, that he would not keep going, but his hand did not leave her forehead. He merely turned toward a machine she had not noticed approach. It was the barrel-chested construct that had guided her into the tunnels.

"Deal with them," Tarok told it, "and return to me. Take those ten."

With her mind a jumble, Amaranthe could barely think. Only when several constructs ambled past and into the tunnel did she realize: her team had been discovered.

"It seems you *are* the distraction while your men break in," the shaman said. "It won't matter."

Amaranthe wanted to voice a cocky retort, but her mind was working too slowly. Her stomach churned. Maybe if she smothered his boots with vomit that would annoy him as much as a cocky retort. It did not sound nearly as brave.

His touch grew firmer against her forehead, and he entered her mind again. He ripped into her thoughts, stealing everything.

CHAPTER 25

A SHEEN OF WATER COVERED THE WALLS AND rivulets trickled down the sloping tunnel floor. The ore cart tracks glistened. With the pump broken, it would not take long for the lower levels to flood, but Books did not think it would happen quickly enough to help them that night.

He, Basilard, Maldynado, and Akstyr walked in silence, listening for noise from above. Since Books had now destroyed two of the shaman's security devices, not to mention the pump, Tarok ought to be down here investigating. The fact that he was not suggested Amaranthe was up there playing the part of the distraction. That thought did not comfort Books.

The team entered a cavern with a ledge running along one side. Though the chamber appeared natural, wooden posts and beams supported the ceiling, and the far wall had seen miners' picks.

Books diverted to the ledge, jumped, and peered over it. Though he doubted any of the side passages held backdoors out of the mine, he would not mind being proven wrong—it might be easier to grab Amaranthe and escape deeper into the tunnels rather than out the front. The broad shelf, littered with trash and broken lanterns, ran back about eight feet, but simply ended at a wall.

"No sightseeing," Maldynado said.

Books caught up as the men continued out of the cavern and into the tunnel, following the cart tracks again.

"The boss is waiting," Maldynado added.

"Waiting...or captured," Books muttered.

Basilard stopped, lifting a hand. A thump emanated from the passage ahead, then a scrape.

"Uh oh," Maldynado said. "If that's him, then it means Amaranthe might be...no longer in a position to distract him."

"Let's go back," Books whispered. "You boys can hide on that ledge, and I'll face him. Maybe he won't know you're there, and you can get a few shots off while he's cursing at me for destroying his pump."

"You sure you want to be the bait?" Maldynado asked as they jogged back to the cavern.

"No," Books said. "Do you have a better idea?"

"No."

"Then there's no more to discuss, is there?" They entered the cavern again, and Books chose a spot in the middle.

"I don't know," Maldynado said as Akstyr and Basilard veered toward the ledge. "We could discuss strategy. Maybe you should try to look extra enticing so you keep his attention riveted."

"How do you propose I do that?"

"Show some leg?" Akstyr caught the ledge and pulled himself on top.

Maldynado snickered. "Nah, this is Books. He's more likely to entice someone by keeping his body fully covered."

"Have I mentioned how grateful I am you lads came to rescue me?" Books asked.

"No."

"Excellent." Books shoved Maldynado toward the ledge.

The first bulky, hard-edged shadow appeared in the tunnel ahead. Others followed. Books did not see the shaman or anything human-sized.

Ker-thunk.

Metal glinted as it flew toward him. Books lunged to the side. A harpoon clattered down inches from his feet. Sparks flew as it skidded, snagged, then flipped end over end.

Books raced for the shelf. He jumped, caught the lip, and cleared the edge without so much as scraping a shin against the rock. He rolled and hit the back wall before coming to a stop.

"Problem?" Maldynado asked, tone bland, though he lay on his belly, rifle butt nestled into the hollow of his shoulder, ready for action.

"The shaman isn't with them," Books said. "I don't think I can entice machines. No matter how much clothing I take off. Or leave on."

The first construct clanked out of the tunnel, continued several paces, then pivoted and faced Books. Glowing crimson eyes bored into him.

"Oh, I think they're downright enticed by you," Maldynado said.

Other constructs walked or rolled out, displaying a variety of means of ambulation. Each carried a barrage of weapons ranging from harpoon launchers to rotating saws to small cannons.

Akstyr whistled. "I want to learn to create artifacts that could power machines like that. So impressive."

"I'd admire them more if they weren't trapping us." On his belly, Books scooted up to peer over the edge between Maldynado and Akstyr.

"Look at the detailed etching on that cannon arm," Maldynado said. "Only a very bored or very obsessed man could have made all these machines." He tapped the frame of his rifle. "Or a man with an overbearing wife he's avoiding."

The mention of a wife made Books think of Vonsha. He hoped she was somewhere safe, preferably not the same somewhere as the shaman. "Either way," Books said, "it doesn't look like he's coming." He did not know whether to feel relieved or concerned. How did one negotiate with machines?

The constructs formed a line in the center of the chamber, facing Books and the others. The eight-foot-high ledge offered a modicum of protection, but not enough. Not against that firepower.

Basilard, on his belly beside Books, rifle readied, turned questioning eyes his way.

"I don't know," Books said. "I had all my brilliant ideas before you boys showed up."

"I can only think of one brilliant thing to do alone in a cell," Maldynado said, "and I don't want your details describing it."

"I meant escaping and destroying the pump, you nit."

Ker-thunk!

A harpoon hammered the wall a foot below the ledge. The construct's arm whirred, and another projectile rotated into place.

"Whose idea was it to climb up here and get ourselves trapped?" Akstyr asked.

Basilard pressed his cheek against the stock of his rifle, sighted, and squeezed the trigger. The ball smashed into the crimson eye of a bipedal construct with spinning saw blades for hands. The cylindrical head twitched, but the saws continued to whir, sharp steel teeth a blur.

The construct next to it in line slung a harpoon toward Books. He flattened, pressing an ear to the damp stone. The projectile stirred his hair on its way by. It cracked against the rock wall behind him, and the broken shaft landed on his leg.

"Why's it targeting me?" Books asked. "*I* didn't shoot one."

"You're the escaped prisoner," Maldynado said.

Something similar to a blunderbuss fired, and a burst of pellets hammered the ledge.

"Lucky me," Books said. "Given the enhanced attention I'm getting, it would have been even more thoughtful of you to bring me a weapon."

His comrades fired and reloaded. The rifle shots had little impact on the metal constructs, but nobody offered better suggestions. Akstyr closed his eyes at one point, as if trying to work some magic, but he shook his head and opened them again soon. The shaman's devices must be beyond his ability to tamper with. Books would have to come up with a plan.

He scooted back, careful not to lift his head—or anything else the machines might target. He grabbed one of the rusty lanterns abandoned on the ledge. A faint sheen of lamp oil residue smeared the inside of the cache. He hoped it was enough. He swiped the wick through it and made himself a couple of fuses.

Shots and curses peppered the air while he worked. A harpoon skimmed over Basilard's head and cracked against the wall behind Books.

He dropped onto his belly and slithered back up between the men. He fiddled with the clasps on Maldynado's ammo pouch.

"What are you doing at my belt?" Maldynado fired a shot, then rolled over to reload.

"I'm going to help." Books removed a flask of black powder.

"You're not taking off my pants, are you?"

"No." Books slid one of his fuses into the mouth of the flask. "Does anybody have a match?"

"No," Maldynado said, "and why are you taking *my* powder for this *help* you're planning? I'm going to need that."

One of the machines on treads rumbled forward, a human-sized shield extended. It rammed into the base of the ledge. The earth quaked beneath Books's belly, and pebbles trickled down from the ceiling. An overhead support beam creaked.

Maldynado fired his rifle and a pistol at the ramming construct, but his shots ricocheted off its metal hide, leaving only small dents.

"Let me borrow that." Books tugged the pistol from Maldynado's hands without waiting to see if he would object.

"Oh, that's why you wanted the powder?" Maldynado asked. "To reload for us? Good idea. You're not doing anything else useful."

Books ignored the jab. He tilted the pistol, cocked the hammer, and pulled the trigger, trying to direct the sparks onto his fuse instead of into the pan.

"You have to load the gun before you fire it," Maldynado said as he rammed a ball into his rifle.

"Thanks for the tip."

The construct with the shield slammed into the ledge. Rock crumbled and gave way. The support beam groaned again.

This time when Books pulled the trigger, sparks landed on his fuse. He blew them to life and tossed his makeshift explosive. It clinked onto the head of the construct ramming the ledge.

Maldynado grabbed his arm. "What are you—"

"Down!" Books barked.

The men imitated turtles.

The explosion rocked the ledge. A portion of it crumbled beneath Akstyr. He squawked in surprise, scrambling about, trying to catch the deteriorating lip. Books lunged over Basilard and caught Akstyr's arm. He braced himself, but the weight almost pulled him over too. Gritting his teeth from the effort, he dragged Akstyr back atop the shelf. A harpoon slammed into the rock at the base of the ledge, where Akstyr *would* have been without the help.

Books released the younger man and slumped back against the wall. If Akstyr had been hit, it would have been his fault.

He inhaled deeply. Dust and black powder smoke filled the air, bringing tears to Books's eyes and stinging his nostrils. Another round of pellets flung toward them. He flattened himself again and Akstyr

shuffled to the side, taking a second to glower at Books through the hazy air.

"I lost my rifle," Akstyr said.

"I'll trade you a pistol for your powder flask." Maldynado coughed and wiped at tears streaming down his cheek. "Some dumb lizard blew mine up."

"Someone had to do *something*," Books said.

Basilard thumped Maldynado on the chest and pointed over the edge. The thinning smoke revealed the closest construct, toppled and unmoving, its head missing, its torso warped and charred into scrap.

"And I *did* do something," Books said. "That one's not bothering us again."

Basilard nodded and gripped Books's arm.

"That *one*," Maldynado said. "And you used a third of our powder to destroy it. There are ten more over there."

"It's something at least," Books said. "The rifles are completely ineffective. You're just irked I used your powder instead of someone else's."

"You should have at least asked—"

A cannonball pounded into the ledge below Maldynado. Rock crumbled, and he disappeared over the side in a haze of dust and falling rock.

"Blast it!" Books lunged, lowering an arm again. He could not see through the dust. "Maldynado?"

A groan floated up, a groan muffled by layers of rock. A metal body on treads advanced through the haze.

Akstyr cursed. "He's crow food, isn't he?"

Books glared at him. "Mal, hurry up! Grab my arm."

Rubble stirred. Maldynado's dust-coated curls pushed through, and he shoved rocks aside.

The advancing construct rumbled closer, lifting an arm cannon. An orange spark shone through the haze.

"Move!" Books shouted.

Maldynado jumped up, sloughing rubble. The cannon fired. Books yanked his arm back and rolled away from the edge. The earth quaked again. Dirt and rock plummeted from the ceiling. A stone thudded onto Books's head.

Stunned, he flopped onto his back. Shrapnel rained down about him, pieces gouging through his clothing and into his skin. Black dots swam through his vision, and blood trickled into his eyes. Maldynado might have been right: creating the explosion had been a bad idea. It had only incensed the constructs to increase the intensity of their attack.

* * * * *

Amaranthe woke in less pain than she expected. Voices—the sha-man's and a woman's—murmured nearby, so she kept her eyes shut. She lay on her side on the floor, but the rough texture of a wool blanket pressed against her cheek. Strange courtesy from the man who had torn her thoughts out of her head.

"Take it," Tarok said. "For your family. I've spent most of what they gave me on tools and materials, but if the plan fails perhaps this will help."

"I don't want your money," the woman said. "I want you to give up this foolishness with the assassin. Revenge isn't worth dying for."

"You wouldn't understand, Vonsha. Your people have been con-querors for centuries; you don't know what it's like to be bullied and oppressed, shunted into inhospitable lands."

Vonsha? Books's Vonsha? Amaranthe opened her eyes. The woman stood near the door, facing the shaman, clasping his hands.

"Is it truly worth risking your life combating a man who kills for a living?" Vonsha asked, her grip tightening on Tarok's hands. "It won't bring your dead rulers back."

Tarok's head drooped, and his long blond hair covered his face. Amaranthe had to strain to hear his next words.

"No, but it will empower and unite my people. They've been frag-mented and squabbling since the royal line was extinguished. They don't always...understand my work, but they'll understand this. I'll finally find honor amongst the elders."

"Tarok..."

"I've made up my mind. One way or another, I'll make sure that man dies." Coins clinked as he pressed a bag into her hands. "Go, please. You should never have been a part of this madness. I want you safely out of here."

"Be careful." Vonsha walked out, shoulders slumped.

Not Books's Vonsha after all, Amaranthe decided, upset on his behalf.

The shaman turned to a task he had apparently started before she woke: packing a bag. Several small devices went inside, and he surveyed upper shelves, seeking some assassin-slaying ultra weapon, no doubt.

The constructs he had sent out earlier were still gone. Her stomach lurched. Had they found Books, Maldynado, and the others? Were they even now attacking her men? Maybe she could slip away and help them when he left. Or she could trail the shaman and assist Sicarius. If she was capable.

Since he did not seem to be paying attention to Amaranthe, she inspected her wounds. Her gut still ached, but fever no longer burned her skin. The other injuries did not hurt as severely as before either.

"Yes," Tarok said. "I drove out the infection. I didn't want to tax myself healing you completely, since I have a confrontation to attend shortly, but you'll live if you don't do anything foolish for the next couple of days."

"Why?" Amaranthe asked. "I mean, thank you, but, er...*why*? Do you think..." If he had been in her head, he could not believe she would help him against Sicarius.

"No, your loyalty, no matter how misplaced, is clear. His disinterest in returning that loyalty is unsurprising. You're a naive doll for thinking well of that animal at all, but otherwise you seem a good-hearted person. I thought you deserved a chance to straighten out your life. Perhaps one day you'll thank me for my next task. It may make yours easier."

Amaranthe sat up. She had to stop him, or at least warn Sicarius the shaman knew...far more than she had planned for him to know.

"You'll forgive me, I trust, if I summon a guard."

She groaned. That would make slipping out hard.

Sooner than she expected, a construct entered, the one that had first led her into the mine. The one that had led the other machines into the tunnels to hunt down her men. Blood smeared its barrel chest. Her fingers curled into a fist. Maybe she was too late to help anybody.

"They are defeated?" the shaman asked without looking up. He fastened the flap on his pack.

The construct clanked into the room, its gait more awkward than Amaranthe remembered. Someone must have damaged it. Hope stirred. Maybe Books had come up with something clever, and the men had defeated all the machines except this one, which had escaped to report back.

She eased to her feet.

The construct stopped a pace away from the shaman and raised an arm.

"Well?" Tarok faced his machine. "Are you impaired? Why—"

One of the harpoons fired into his chest. Amaranthe gaped, as shocked as the shaman. Two more harpoons slammed through his ribs, and the construct jerked its arm across, slashing the last blade across his throat. Tarok staggered back and collapsed.

Not sure what to expect next, Amaranthe snatched the closest tool off a nearby bench. Pliers. She brandished them like a knife.

The construct's arms came up, not to aim harpoons at her, but to grab its head. Amaranthe stared. It wiggled its head back and forth, then removed it, revealing...Sicarius's face. Blood matted his blond hair on one side, but he appeared otherwise hale. He tossed the hollow head-turned-helmet onto the desk, and Amaranthe glimpsed a few wires and broken innards inside it. Much more must have been torn out. Sicarius shucked the rest of the hollowed body parts and checked the shaman.

A half of an hour earlier, Amaranthe might have gotten in line to stab the man, but that was before he healed her and called her a good person. Of course, he had also called her naive and misguided for associating with...

"Pliers?" Sicarius asked.

"Er." Amaranthe loosened her death grip on the tool. "I've found them effective for snatching and twisting people's...important parts."

His eyebrows rose.

"Of course, I don't employ such methods on friends and colleagues." Amaranthe tossed the pliers on the bench. She stepped around the shaman and wrapped her arms around Sicarius. "I thought you weren't willing to come after me."

Sicarius did not return the hug, but he did pat her on the shoulder and endure the embrace without acting as if it was torture to do so. "Yes, you had to think that."

She leaned back, though she did not release him fully. "You knew? That he could swim around in my head, collecting coins from the bottom of the pool?"

"Telepathy is one of the mental sciences. The Nurians and Kyattese train in it far more frequently than the Kendorians and Mangdorians, but I suspected someone as accomplished as he might have developed the skill."

Amaranthe released him, wondering if he had come to kill the shaman to help her or just because he wanted to make sure his secrets did not find their way into someone else's head through her. She shook her head. It did not matter. He was there. Besides, he had saved her life in the tower when there was no time for premeditated thought, when it was simply about instincts. That meant...a lot.

"Next time," she said, "you might mention things like mind-reading foes before I stroll in to talk to one. It might alter my preparations."

"I'll consider it." Sicarius eyed her. "He healed you?"

"The infection, yes."

"How did you convince him?"

Amaranthe thought about answering honestly, that she had done nothing, but decided it might help her down the line if he believed she wooed the shaman with her tongue. Sicarius might have saved her life—twice in as many days—but she still believed he was sticking around because he thought she'd eventually be in a position to talk to Sespian on his behalf.

"You have your secrets," she said with a smile, "and I have mine."

A bang sounded somewhere in the depths of the tunnels. A rifle shot?

"The others," Amaranthe said. "Have you seen them? Are they still fighting?" She jogged to the workstation to search for a weapon. Twinges in her abdomen reminded her she was not yet healed fully. One more hour, she thought. She would rest if she could abuse her body for one more hour.

"I don't know," Sicarius said. "I saw several machines leave this workshop and head deeper into the mine. I drew this one away so I could attack it alone."

"How hard was it to destroy?"

"Hard." Sicarius drew his black dagger. "I was able to climb on the back of it, cut a seam at the base of its neck, and slice the control wires leading from the power source."

She peered in a toolbox but found nothing more lethal than the pliers. "Could you have done the job with a normal knife?"

"Slice the wires, yes. Cut through the seam, no."

Another gunshot rang out.

"They sound like they need help." She eyed the glowing orbs.

"It was difficult to destroy *one* construct. There are a dozen down there."

At least he did not say the men were not worth saving. A couple of months ago, he would have.

"I understand that," Amaranthe said, "but there must be something here that can help. What do the orbs do?"

"They're the power sources. The shaman creates them, then uses mundane technology to build the machines."

She thought of the one she had destroyed in the gambling house's vault. At the time, it had been good that it had caused no great explosion, but now she wished they could be used as tiny bombs.

Amaranthe grabbed the bag the shaman had packed. "Maybe Akstyr can do something if we can get this stuff to him."

"If he's alive," Sicarius said.

"Are there any optimistic assassins in the world?" She jogged for the door, relieved Sicarius followed her.

"That aren't dead?"

"Er, yes."

"No."

"Ah."

CHAPTER 26

SOMEONE SHOOK BOOKS. HE PUSHED AWAY THE FOG hazing his mind and focused on the face above him. Basilard. A rifle fired nearby. Akstyr.

"Mal?" Books rasped. A film of fine dirt caked his tongue.

Basilard pointed into the chamber.

"Is he...?" Books started.

A commotion interrupted him.

"Hah, missed me, you badger-kissing slag pile!" came Maldynado's voice from the far side of the chamber.

Books rolled onto his belly. Pain pulsed through his head, but he squinted through it and found Maldynado. He harried the constructs with his rapier, though the thin blade did little against their metal hides.

"Making friends, is he?" Books knelt and crawled to the edge of their dwindling perch. Another shot or two from that cannon, and the ledge would be dust.

But the constructs had changed their focus to Maldynado. He jumped and waved, evading their projectiles.

"Idiot," Books said. "What's he doing? If he can do that, he can make it back up here."

"He said he'd distract them so you could come up with something bright," Akstyr said.

"Oh. That'd be noble if it wasn't...stupid."

"You calling Maldynado nobly stupid?" Akstyr asked. "Or stupidly noble?"

"I can hear you!" Maldynado jumped out of the path of two bipeds trying to corner him.

Come up with something bright, Books thought. Yes, that was supposed to be his job. "Akstyr, Basilard, give me your powder."

They poured out a few rounds worth, then complied. Books found the other fuses and crafted two more explosives. How could he take out all of the constructs with so little? He had to get them all in one place somehow.

Maldynado yelped in pain. "Metal-headed dogs!"

Books did not look up in time to see the attack, but Maldynado clutched his arm. Blood flowed through his fingers. Still cursing, he dodged another harpoon, but all of the constructs were targeting him, pressing him back against the wall.

"Get out of there, fool!" Books called.

Basilard shot, but his ball ricocheted off without deterring the target. Books still had the unloaded pistol, and he could light one of the fuses, but Maldynado was in the middle of the mess.

"I'm trying!" Maldynado faked a step one direction, then angled for a gap between two of the constructs, but, through some intelligence no machine should have, they anticipated him and narrowed the opening.

A serrated blade spun out, veering toward his head. Maldynado scrambled backward, but his heel caught on the uneven ground. He went down.

Basilard jumped off the ledge and sprinted in to help. Books snapped the hammer on the flintlock, trying to light the fuse. Maybe if he threw the powder toward the backside of the constructs....

Before a spark landed on his fuse, he spotted movement at the tunnel entrance.

"Now what?" he groaned, fearing the shaman had decided to come help his creations.

But Sicarius burst out of the tunnel, and Amaranthe hustled after, an arm clutching her belly.

Taking the situation in with a glance, Sicarius flowed across the chamber and leaped onto the back of the construct with the saw. His black knife appeared in his hand, and he slipped it into creases between sheets of metal covering the machine's innards.

Amaranthe hobbled toward the ledge and tossed a satchel to Akstyr. "See if there's anything you can use in there."

Akstyr dug into it. Across the chamber, Basilard pulled Maldynado out of immediate danger, though little had changed. The constructs had three targets instead of one. Amaranthe stood, poised, her face thoughtful, as if she was considering jumping into the mess. She did not even have a weapon.

Books lay on his stomach and extended his arm. "Smart people up here. We have to figure out the solution."

"While it's flattering that you're including me in your group, I haven't done anything smart lately."

Books wriggled his fingers. "They like to shoot things this direction. Come up here to discuss it."

Amaranthe waved the hand away. "We have to get out of here. The shaman is dead. I doubt these will follow us past the mine entrance. How fast are they? Can we outrun them?"

"Oh!" Books perked. If all they had to do was outrun the constructs.... He hefted one of the powder flasks. "Maybe we can use these to—"

A crack and a screech of metal sounded, followed by a war whoop from Maldynado. A construct tottered, a cannonball hole in its torso. Metal parts rained from the gap like petals shaken from a flower. The construct toppled.

"Though," Amaranthe mused, "if we destroy them, we don't need to worry about some aspiring megalomaniac getting them and using them against the city later."

"I've arranged a nice flood, so I think that part is covered."

"Got something," Akstyr said. His eyes were bright as he sat back, a plain black box in his hands. "It feels like a controller. There's writing on it. I can't read the Mangdorian, but—"

Books slid it from his hands. "Attack, guard, and...hibernate."

"The last one sounds good," Amaranthe said without taking her gaze from the mad scrambling of the men.

"Agreed." Books rotated the box. "I don't see a switch or trigger though."

Akstyr snatched the device back. "That's because you're uneducated in the Science."

Books sniffed. "Really."

Akstyr, head already bent over the device, did not seem to hear. His tongue stuck out of his mouth, and his face scrunched in concentration.

"Look out!" Maldynado shouted.

At first, Books thought it a warning for Sicarius or Basilard, but the entire cadre of constructs had turned their attention away from Maldynado and the others. En masse, they advanced toward the ledge. No, toward Akstyr. And Amaranthe was in the way.

"Uhm, Akstyr?" Amaranthe crouched, ready to spring one direction or the other.

A cannonball flew over Books's head and cracked into the wall behind him. Shards of wood from the support beam flew.

"It's possible there's an anti-tampering device," Akstyr said, voice strained.

Books reached down, intending to grab Amaranthe, but he still clutched the pistol and one of the black powder bombs in his hands. He hesitated a half a heartbeat, then struck sparks to light the fuse.

"Out of the way, Amaranthe." He hurled the flask into the path of the advancing constructs.

In the second before the explosion, Books glanced toward the other men. Maldynado's eyes bulged, and Books feared he had made a mistake. A huge mistake. Sicarius lifted a hand toward Amaranthe, though his gaze was locked past Books's shoulder. A boom sounded. Wood snapped behind Books even as the explosion roared below.

The wall behind him collapsed. Rubble hammered him, throwing him into a landslide.

Rocks battered him from all sides. He clawed at them, trying to stay on top, but the moving pile dragged him off the ledge. He struck ground, and rocks pounded him into the earth. They smothered him, stealing light, and driving pain into his body from all sides.

He gasped, or tried to—it was as if a giant vise had clasped about his ribcage. What air he managed to suck in was hot, thick, and filled with dust. Fine powder coated his mouth, nostrils, and the back of his throat. It even seemed to paint the backs of his eyes. His body tried to cough, but agony ripped through him, and it came out as a whimper.

Had the others avoided the landslide? Or were they buried too? Were the constructs still harrying them?

Books tried to push up, but not a single rock budged. He might not even be pushing the right direction. What if he faced up or sideways instead of down?

He struggled to fight off panic, thoughts that he could die here. Buried alive.

Scratches sounded, echoing strangely inside his rock prison. They grew louder, and hope stirred in his breast. Another sound trickled through the rubble to him: voices. Books strained his ears.

"Books?" Amaranthe called.

Rocks shifted. A pinprick of light slanted into his black cocoon.

"Here," he gasped.

More rocks moved away, and fingers brushed his face. Grateful tears slid down his cheeks.

"We've got you," Amaranthe said.

"Is good?" he whispered. He wanted to ask a more intelligent question—or at least a grammatically correct one—but it hurt too much to talk.

"We're fine," Amaranthe said.

"*Fine?*" came Maldynado's voice. "I'm so covered with dirt and blood, I'd probably have to *pay* to get into a woman's bed right now."

"Maldynado is especially fine," Amaranthe said. "As are the others. That last cannonball took out the support. I saw Sicarius's expression and got out of the way. Akstyr was far enough from you to miss most of the rock fall. You, ah, chose an inopportune time to cause an explosion."

"Oops," Books whispered. He may have been premature in telling Amaranthe that "smart people" were on top of the ledge. Between Akstyr's fiddling and his own work, they had caused most of the trouble.

"You *did* destroy all the constructs," Amaranthe said.

"Good."

"Though...." Amaranthe lifted the last of several rocks off his back. "While we appreciate your efforts, I think you might want to retire from heroic deeds. Bad things seem to happen to you as a result."

"Library work is more my forte," he agreed.

Thanks to their efforts, Books managed to crawl out and stagger to his feet. Or tried. Pain burst from his knee, and he gasped and reached out for support. He caught the nearest shoulder, realizing afterward it belonged to Sicarius. Fine dust coated his black clothes and smudged his jaw, and blood stained his blond hair.

"Sorry," Books muttered, anticipating a glare—and the need to find a walking stick or someone else to lean on.

Sicarius looked at Basilard and jerked his chin toward Books. The two men draped Books's arms over their shoulders. Amaranthe smiled and pointed to the tunnel exit.

Maldynado offered her an arm though Books was not sure if it was so he could support her or she could support him. Both perhaps. The group definitely needed a rest.

Maldynado pointed at the destroyed constructs, half of them buried by rubble. "Nice work, Booksie. Though you owe me powder and a new rifle."

"You didn't lose your rifle," Akstyr said, taking up the rear.

"I know," Maldynado said, "but it's all bunged up, and that's Books's fault."

"It's still functional," Amaranthe said.

"But scratched and dented. You don't expect someone like me to run around with a weapon like that do you? I had it custom made. The inlay alone took a master engraver three days."

"Maldynado?" Books said. "You're an ass."

"But sort of a lovable ass, right?"

"Like the odd dreadful in-law one gets when one marries," Books said.

"So...you think of Maldynado as family?" Amaranthe smiled over her shoulder at him.

Books stumbled. Dear ancestors, *did* he?

Maldynado threw Books a wink.

Books eyed his and Amaranthe's backs then glanced from side to side at his escorts. Basilard's lips curved upward, and, while nothing would move Sicarius to smile, one of his eyebrows did arch slightly.

"Well, I..." Books thought of his long-dead father, a man he had barely known, a man who had always seemed to prefer spending time with his soldier friends to his nagging wife and a boy who loved words not swords. For the first time, Books thought he might, if not condone those choices, understand them. "My father used to say some families are made by shared blood and some families are made by spilled blood. I used to dismiss it as some pugilistic glorification of a combat unit, but I can see where spending enough time with the same folks, facing dangerous situations day in and day out, would tend to make one feel a familial kinship toward those comrades, even when they are people one wouldn't normally choose to spend time with in casual, everyday life."

"What did he say?" Maldynado whispered to Amaranthe. "I forgot to listen halfway through."

Books sighed.

"He said he loves you all like brothers," Amaranthe said, "and thanks for coming after him down here."

"Oh," Maldynado said. "Good."

Books's first thought was to dispute the preciseness of Amaranthe's translation, but the approving nods of the other men made him pause. Maybe it was good to have a woman in the "family."

A hollow, grinding noise came from the tunnel ahead.

"Please, not more fighting," Books muttered.

Sicarius left Books for Basilard to support and stepped in front of Amaranthe, a throwing knife at the ready.

A rusty metal ore cart rolled around a bend, its iron wheels following the track down the center of the tunnel. If not for the fact it was moving, it would have appeared normal. No weapons or advanced features protruded from it.

The cart rolled to a stop a few paces in front of Sicarius.

"Maybe it's here to give us a ride out," Maldynado said.

"I wish," Amaranthe said. "Let's—"

"It feels like it's been touched by..." Akstyr jogged past Sicarius to peer inside.

Amaranthe lifted a hand, as if to issue a warning, but Akstyr was already plucking something out.

"Just a piece of paper." He pulled a single page out and checked both sides. "I can't read this."

Basilard stood straighter, as if he might also leave Books to take a look.

Not wanting to lose his support, Books waved a hand. "Bring it here. Maybe it's in Mangdorian."

Akstyr shrugged and headed their way. "If it's secret Science stuff, you have to translate it for—"

Sicarius slipped the paper out of his hand as he passed. Books would not have noticed except Akstyr threw him a startled glance. Sicarius skimmed the note, crumpled it up, and pocketed it.

Basilard stiffened.

"A message?" Amaranthe asked.

A message? Who was down here except the dead shaman and what remained of his contraptions? Unless she thought Tarok had arranged for the note to be delivered before his death.

"It's nothing," Sicarius told Amaranthe.

Amaranthe lifted a shoulder. Too tired to argue, perhaps.

Sicarius turned a cool, assessing gaze toward Basilard, who did not quite keep the suspicion off his face as he returned it.

"We all ready to go back to the city?" Amaranthe asked, her words breaking the staring contest.

"Extremely so." Books closed his eyes. "Extremely so."

* * * * *

Late morning sun pried through the clouds, illuminating the countryside as the sloping foothills gentled to flatter lands dotted with farmsteads. The stolen lorry chugged along with all the men except Sicarius crammed in the cab. Amaranthe lay in the troop bed, propped on a rucksack leaning against a bench. If she did not move anything, she did not hurt. An improvement. Despite his injuries, Books sat with the others, chatting and even laughing. She still felt bad about the bounty on his head, but it seemed he had come to peace with being a part of a band of mercenaries.

Sicarius leaned against the back wall of the cab, his arms across his chest, his gaze roving the countryside and the road behind them. The soldiers had been pulling up to the mine entrance as her team slipped away. She wondered what they would make of the mechanical carnage left inside. More, she wondered if anything else would come of her words to Yara. The soldiers might have been too late to help, but their arrival *might* mean Amaranthe's trip into their camp had not been a waste of time. If the enforcer sergeant had relayed Amaranthe's ideas, and the soldiers had been acting on them.... Perhaps her team had succeeded in earning recognition or at least planting a seed in someone's mind that they might not be villains. She eyed Sicarius. Mostly not villains anyway.

Sicarius noticed her watching him and came to sit on the bench beside her. "You are well?"

"Well enough. Thank you for asking." Amaranthe tried to remember if he ever had. "And thank you for...everything up there."

Sicarius grunted. It was not a particularly inviting grunt, but she decided to say more.

"I know my plans aren't always the epitome of precaution and wisdom, but I appreciate your willingness to trust me enough to give them a try. And I appreciate you risking your life to protect mine, no matter how stupid I might be to put mine—and yours—in danger to start with. I would have died in that tower, if not for you." Amaranthe pictured him taking her hands and saying it would devastate him if he lost her.

Instead he said, "Likely," and returned to surveying the farms drifting past.

She sighed. Of course, she had not told him how much it would mean to her to lose him after she had nearly gotten him blown up above the canyon. Sicarius had been trained to be hard to read, to keep his thoughts to himself. What was her excuse? She might have died in these mountains, and she would have left the world without letting him know what he meant to her. Though it might hurt to love him and not be loved in return, wouldn't it be worse to never find the courage to let him know how she felt? Until it was too late?

"Sicarius," Amaranthe said quietly.

He bent low, eyes toward her face.

With the men laughing and talking up front, and the lorry clacking and chugging as the stack billowed black smoke into the air, this was scarcely a romantic spot. But maybe it did not matter. His response would not likely be to wrap her in his arms and kiss her. Whatever response he gave—if he gave one at all—she anticipated it would sting.

"I...uhm..." Amaranthe forced herself to meet his gaze. "I love you."

A long moment passed. She did not remember breathing.

Sicarius nodded infinitesimally. "I know."

Amaranthe looked away and cleared her throat. "Of course. I figured you did. I just wanted to make sure. That's all."

As the lorry rumbled on, she tried to tell herself she had not been an idiot for saying something. He knew. Of *course* he knew. Nobody had ever claimed *she* was hard to read.

Sicarius dropped from the bench to sit shoulder-to-shoulder, though not touching. "You are my employer."

Emperor's eyeteeth, he was going to explain to her why her feelings were foolish. She groaned inwardly and told herself to drop it, to say nothing else. But saying nothing was not her strongpoint. "That was your choice. I wanted to work with you, not order you around."

"Teams need leaders. Given the goals of this team, you're the appropriate leader. We've discussed this."

"Yes."

Sicarius spread a hand toward the others. "That this works, a woman leading five men, is a marvel. I suspect it would work less if you were sleeping with one of us."

Amaranthe stared at goats grazing beside the road and regretted sharing her feelings. That he was probably right made it worse. There would be resentment if someone, or two someones, got to have relations out in the woods while the rest had to pretend not to notice, but it was not what she wanted to hear.

"And there's Sespian," Sicarius said so softly she almost thought she imagined it.

She found his eyes again, sure her own were incredulously wide. "He barely knows me. Whatever he felt—he was drugged at the time. I'm sure he's over that initial interest."

"Perhaps," Sicarius said. "But there's already too much separating us. I would not wish to add that. Also—"

"All right." Amaranthe threw up a hand. *Now* he chose to be a garrulous person? "I don't need a list. I was just expressing a feeling. If you don't share that feeling, that's fine." She sank lower against the rucksack and avoided looking at him. She sounded huffy, and she knew it. She thought of the handful of coworkers she had rebuffed during her years as an enforcer; she had wanted so much to show her supervisors that she was serious about her job, that she would never consider something as unprofessional as a patrol romance. Now, she was in the shoes of the spurned. Fitting, she supposed. "Sorry," she said. "I wouldn't want to be a further wedge between you two either."

Sicarius's shoulder came to rest against hers. He laid his hand on top of hers.

Amaranthe grew still. He had *never* held her hand. She kept her head facing forward, half afraid eye contact would make him leave, like some timid forest creature.

"Just to be clear," she said, "you *don't* share my feelings. Right?"

He did not answer.

"Sicarius? That *was* a question. I made sure my tone went up at the end."

He snorted softly. "I care, Amaranthe. More than I thought myself capable."

"Oh," she mouthed.

Maldynado clambered out of the cab, munching on a fistful of dried pears. Sicarius released her hand.

"You two mind if I join you? Books is talking about his plans to invest Sicarius's gambling house earnings. Invest! What kinds of mercenaries invest? Team money should be for carousing and buying weapons." He rapped his knuckles on the roof of the cab. "Maybe acquiring transport that doesn't have enforcer logos on the side. Or rust."

"I thought you were just in this for your statue," Amaranthe said.

"I am." Maldynado snapped his fingers. "Say, do you think that enforcer gal is going to put in a good word for us? You won her over, right?" He ambled over, rounding Sicarius's feet with much room to spare, then plopped down on the other side of Amaranthe. "You don't mind me joining you, do you?" His eyes widened as he seemed to consider some possibility, but then he snickered dismissively. "You two weren't having some private rendezvous back here, were you?"

Sicarius said nothing, though there was more ice in his gaze than usual.

Amaranthe merely sighed. "No rendezvous, no."

"Good," Maldynado said. "Let's talk about your birthday celebration. This whole fiasco has crimped my plans terribly. The city is going to be a mess when we get back, and I'm not sure how we'll find a decent..."

As Maldynado burbled on, Amaranthe exchanged looks with Sicarius. Would there ever be a someday when they *could* have a private rendezvous?

EPILOGUE

In the boiler room of the pumping house, Amaranthe swept the last pile of dirt, hair, and walnut shells into a dust pan. Her weapons and packed rucksack leaned against the wall by the door.

Footsteps in the hall heralded Maldynado's appearance. He swaggered in wearing his peacock-feather hat. "What's the holdup, boss? Your party starts in an hour."

Amaranthe dropped the dust pan. "My what?"

"Your birthday party. We're having it at The Pirates' Plunder. Their establishment wasn't affected by the riots, and the Madame is willing to lend us the attic for the shindig. It'll be private—no chance of running into pesky soldiers or enforcers. Basilard is working with a caterer. We're going to make it the event of the season!"

"Just so I'm clear...you thought a brothel would be a suitable place to host a birthday party for a woman?"

"Books said almost that exact same thing, but I know you're not the uppity type. And this is a great place. If you want a pretty man, I can arrange that. They service all types. It'll be grand, you'll see."

"The fact that the pumping house was searched while we were out means we need to find a new hideout. Don't you think that should take priority?"

"Over birthday parties?" Maldynado asked. "Absolutely not. You have five minutes to finish up, or I'm going to pick you up and—"

Sicarius strode in, an envelope in his hand.

"Ah, me and the boys will meet you up top when you're ready." Maldynado hustled out.

Sicarius did not acknowledge him. He handed Amaranthe the envelope. "A youth delivered this."

"I'm getting mail again? Another sure sign it's time to leave this hideout."

"Agreed."

While she unfastened the seal, she asked, "Speaking of mail...what was on that paper in the ore cart?"

Sicarius closed the door. "The note was addressed to Basilard—to the Mangdorian in the assassin's party specifically. It contained a request to let Ellaya know the shaman died, so she could send word to his family."

"Huh. They must have been close. I wonder if he ever resented her for giving his name to Forge and getting him involved in all this. I know Tarok wanted you, but I don't think he wanted all those deaths on his hands." Amaranthe shook her head. It mattered little now. "Perhaps we should go to the gambling house and deliver that message to Ellaya. I'm curious if she had more to do with all this than matchmaking. After all, one of those dead dam workers was a customer of hers."

"She's gone," Sicarius said.

"What? You didn't, ah…"

"I went to ensure she would not be a further threat to us," he said. "The gambling house was closed, and no one knew where she'd gone."

So much for that idea. "What else was on the note?"

Sicarius gazed steadily at her.

"You glared at Basilard, so I know there was more."

"It also contained my name and a plea to Basilard to avenge the Mangdorian people."

"I see," Amaranthe said. "Let's hope it won't be a problem, since he didn't see the note."

"If it becomes a problem, I'll deal with it."

She grimaced, knowing exactly what he meant. She hoped it was not something she would have to worry about for a while. For now...

Amaranthe pulled two sheets of paper out of the envelope. The first surprised her with calligraphy, an artistic border, and an official stamp from Enforcer Headquarters. "It's a pardon for Books."

The second paper held a letter.

Lokdon:

We found makarovi bodies downstream, as you described. I do not trust you or your intentions, but it does seem your people assisted in this matter. I've arranged the pardon for your man. The emperor's seal is on your bounty, so no enforcer can lift that one.

Captain Branchok and I were called into a meeting with Emperor Sespian and his advisors. When questioned, Branchok said his men handled everything. It would have been wise of me to agree, but it's not in my nature to suffer lies in silence. I explained your presence and the possibility your men destroyed the device in the lake and killed the foreigner responsible. Captain Branchok called me a liar. The emperor would not believe Sicarius caused anything but trouble, but he did seem to think you might have honorable intentions.

I'm not certain what repercussions my statements will have on my career. I made an enemy of Captain Branchok. You'll forgive me if I hope I never see you again.

~Yara

Amaranthe showed the note to Sicarius, hoping he would not be disappointed in Sespian's response. When he lifted his eyes, she said, "You can't expect him to change his opinion of you overnight, but it's a start, right? He's aware you were there and that the plot was thwarted." Though it did not seem anyone knew Forge had ultimately been involved. Nor did Amaranthe know the person in that organization responsible—research for another day.

"A start, yes." Sicarius returned the note. "The others are right: you'd have an easier time clearing your name if I wasn't around."

Erp, when had he heard them say that? She did not like the sound of his comment either: less like one of his statements of fact and more like an offer to disappear. Emperor's warts, he did not need to develop a selfless streak now.

"I'd be dead a dozen times over if you weren't around," Amaranthe said, "so don't even think of leaving. One day, we're going to walk into Sespian's office to have tea with him. Together."

Sicarius studied her for a while, then inclined his head once.

"In the meantime," she said, "I don't suppose you'd like to go to The Pirates' Plunder and loom threateningly by my shoulder to ward off... whatever entertainment Maldynado has planned for me?"

"I thought I'd stand back and see what you do with the eye patch he bought you."

Amaranthe blinked. "I... I'm never sure if I'm reading you right."

His eyes glinted. "Good."

THE END

CONNECT WITH THE AUTHOR

Have a comment? Question? Just want to say hi? Find me online at:

http://www.lindsayburoker.com

http://www.facebook.com/LindsayBuroker

http://twitter.com/GoblinWriter

Thanks for reading!